Roper ca\
She jerked do\
bag of corn chips as she disappeared behind a pyramid of cereal boxes. He moved cautiously, keeping twenty-five feet back.

She looked smaller today, thinner, not gaunt, but with the kind of muscle tone he associated with honed athletes. A sliver of something stirred in his groin. He threw a quick roadblock around his mind. What the hell business did he have feeling attracted to her? Or even curious? Getting the job done depended on keeping his perspective.

A few stragglers wandered down dreary aisles, the worn wood floor a product of busier times. But the world offered too many choices these days, and a dingy little grocery store in Benton, Nevada could not compete.

Roper waited two beats before circling past the Rice Krispies. He stopped short. She stood at the other end of the aisle, staring at dog food bags as if the choice was the decision of a lifetime. As she bent down, her Navaho jacket rode up, revealing the backs of strong thighs.

Dog food. Aside from her German shepherd, she lived alone. There was the neighbor, Charlie Lemon, who ran a small ranch a mile and a half up the road from her. A full-blooded Paiute, the man clearly was on the down side of sixty. Charlie was her only visitor in the past three months of surveillance. The Bureau had dismissed a sexual relationship between them.

Craning her head, she took Roper in with a quick glance but continued studying dog chow. From a distance, she looked tough, like any woman resilient enough to survive alone in high-country desert. Bundled up against early September cold weather, she seemed indifferent to her own appearance.

Awards

2nd Winner of
Indiana's Golden Opportunity Award 2005

~~~~~

Comments

If you want a romantic suspense you can sink your teeth into, I heartily recommend LONG RUN HOME—excellent story!
~Sheridon Smythe, author of Shane's Hideaway

LONG RUN HOME is page-turner that won't let you put it down till you've reached the end of it!
~Mandy Jameson, reader

Long Run Home

by

Lynn Romaine

This is a work of fiction. Names, characters, places, and incidents are either the product of the author's imagination or are used fictitiously, and any resemblance to actual persons living or dead, business establishments, events, or locales, is entirely coincidental.

Long Run Home

COPYRIGHT © 2008 by Judi L. Romaine

All rights reserved. No part of this book may be used or reproduced in any manner whatsoever without written permission of the author or The Wild Rose Press except in the case of brief quotations embodied in critical articles or reviews.
Contact Information: info@thewildrosepress.com

Cover Art by *Kim Mendoza*

The Wild Rose Press
PO Box 706
Adams Basin, NY 14410-0706
Visit us at www.thewildrosepress.com

Publishing History
First Crimson Rose Edition, 2009
Print ISBN 1-60154-532-0

Published in the United States of America

Dedication

Long Run Home is dedicated to my older sister,
Gay,
who died too young
and never had the opportunity to fulfill her life.
This book is also dedicated to
Red Pants for the World,
to every young woman who finds a way
to live a creative life
and make a difference in the world.

Acknowledgements

I'd like to acknowledge a lifelong friend, Lorraine Weglarz, who made this book possible by her simple suggestion that we check out Pyramid Lake on our travels.

I'd also like to acknowledge my sister, Debbi Wilkes, and my niece, Emily Wilkes, both of whom always are generous and supportive with everyone in their lives.

Prologue

Omaha, Nebraska—1990

The silk scarf tightened around her neck. She shuddered as the climax rippled through her body like a sidewinder.

Pleasure abruptly collided with fear as the scarf twisted and tightened. She gasped, shoving against his sagging weight, clawing and tearing at his hands. The faces of her children swam in front of her, dissolved into darkness and disappeared.

Chapter One

Nevada—Present Day

Sam held her mail, the top letter catching her attention immediately. Tearing it open, a news clipping fell to the floor. The two-inch high, black headline stared up at her, a chill chased down her spine.

"WOMAN'S BODY FOUND IN RIVER"

She leaned down and snatched up the paper with trembling fingers. Suddenly, Sam Neally melted away and again there stood little eleven-year-old Catherine Bell, the daughter abandoned by her mother.

Omaha World-Herald—

"A two decade old mystery appears on its way to being solved. Yesterday, workers on the I-80 bridge repair project pulled a submerged car from the Platte River.

Inside was the body of a woman tentatively identified as Marilyn Bell, a 32-year-old Omaha native who disappeared two decades ago. According to the medical examiner, the depth and coldness of the river makes a positive ID possible. Final toxicology results are pending and the next of kin have been notified."

Sam let the thin sheet float to the table and turned over the mailing envelope. Two hand-written pages from her sister, Mary Beth, slid out.

Sam. Yes, it's our mother. I'm sorry I couldn't be there to give you the news in person—I know you're suffering. As you can see from this clipping, it was big news in Omaha.

The police called me two days ago to give me a heads-up. They called back this morning to say they had positively identified her. There's no doubt it's her.

The police said her death was due to drowning. Oh, and they mentioned something about possible suspicious circumstances. I'm not sure what that means.

The thing is she didn't abandon us. Or run off. She died! I know you hate this. So do I. But it's better than believing she could just drop us with strangers and take off.

Sam wiped at the blurred words on a corner of the page, probably from Mary Beth's tears. Her hands shook as she pressed out the page. Spots floated in front of her eyes, as if someone had sucked all the oxygen out of her, leaving a huge vacuum.

Call me as soon as you can. Make it nighttime so we can talk. I have to tell you, I'm getting freaked by the reporters pestering me! Call me! I love you—Beth

Sam slumped against the chair. She stared at the pages but saw no words. Images collided with questions in her mind, whirling and leaping from thought to thought. She'd dedicated herself to a throwaway life based on the belief she'd been abandoned at eleven. The most dangerous expression of the resulting anger and despair had been the protest bombing she'd gotten tangled up in at eighteen. That had been followed by twelve wasted years hiding out in the desert, running from the authorities—a throwaway life. Only the original event had been a lie. Her mother hadn't abandoned her; she'd died.

Rereading the letter, Sam forced her attention to one tiny sentence; '*they mentioned something about possible suspicious circumstances.*'

She sat down at her computer and began

searching on 'Omaha private investigators.' The fourteenth name down the list looked nondescript enough.

She pulled her little red cell phone out of her pocket and dialed.

"Robert Mathias."

"Mr. Mathias? My name is Sam Neally. I'm calling from out of state, Nevada. I'm looking for an investigator to do some research for me—in Omaha. I saw your advertisement on the internet..." She hesitated. The words sounded like someone else's

"Yes?"

What should I say? That it's been almost twenty years since I dissected any thought of my mother from my life, but now I've reconsidered and I'd like to know what happened to her.

"Mr. Mathias, I want to hire you to do some research on my mother. She disappeared nearly two decades ago in Omaha. I'm living in northern Nevada now. I can't get back to Nebraska myself, but I'd like you to find out what happened. My sister received a call from the Omaha police a few days ago saying they'd found her remains..." she stopped, waiting for the flurry in her chest to subside. "They mentioned there was some evidence of possible foul play."

"Go on." She'd caught his attention now.

"My mother dropped my sister and me off with a babysitter twenty years ago and never came back for us. We always assumed we'd been abandoned." She took a deep breath. "The police found her car last week in the Platte River with her remains inside."

"I know the story; saw it in the paper last week." Mathias coughed, a smoker's hack. "And what you need from me is to find out what happened, if it was an accident, or murder?"

"Yes."

"Okay, give me what you've got, everything you

can remember from twenty years ago. I'll tell you if I think I can help. Then we talk price."

She told him what she knew, answered his questions, but left out her recent history. He took it all in with a grunt and a cough.

Fifteen minutes later, she'd placed a $250 retainer in his Paypal account and promised another $500 in a week. She emailed him every piece of information she could think of, her contact info and then hung up.

A brief phone call, a few simple actions and she'd hired herself a PI.

What Mathias couldn't get from the data was the impact of one event twenty years ago on two little girls, dropped off at a stranger's house, never to see their mother again. Acquaintances of Marilyn Bell explained it easily enough; she was a mother who was so lonely she brought strange men home with her. And many nights she hadn't come home at all, forcing her children to cringe in a dark closet behind clothes smelling of cheap perfume. When she didn't come back that night twenty years ago, Sam had thought her mother sold her out for a man.

Sam carefully folded up the letter with the news clipping and tucked them both into a folder in her desk.

She remembered clearly what betrayal felt like. It had hit eleven-year-old Catherine like a car careening around a blind corner as she stepped off the curb. The pain knocked her flat and left her confused and afraid. She and Mary Beth crouched together at a greasy window, two gangly little girls, staring out at the street, waiting for a mother who would never return. Sometime around the second day, a pale-faced, dour woman from Child Protective Services arrived. Offering no explanation, she swished them away in a big tan sedan. One month into the foster care system, a family came and took

Mary Beth, leaving Catherine Bell behind. Within a year, her life fell into a routine of foster homes. The fear gradually dissolved, leaving behind the throbbing expectation of betrayal.

****

Three days after she'd hired Mathias his first email popped up; a terse one liner: *"Call me tonight. I've got something. Mathias."*

Reaching into her pocket, she'd pulled out her little red disposable phone with trembling fingers.

"Mathias."

"This is Sam Neally. What have you got?" She forced herself to take deep inhalations, getting used to the knot in her stomach.

"Don't get too excited. I've only had a day or two, only got some basics for you so far. I've got the police report and a copy of the post mortem."

She pictured a Sam Spade kind of guy, dressed in a pinstriped suit, hat shoved far back on a round head.

"What else do you need from me?"

"Nothing right now. I'll forward everything as I get it. The cause of death stands at accidental, by misadventure, with a notation from the post mortem of a crushed larynx, which brings up the question of foul play."

"So what do we do now?"

"I'll start digging into the background stuff you sent me tomorrow, do a check on her driver's license and taxes, her last place of employment, etc. You recall anything more about the guy she left with that night? White? Black? Age? Anything."

"Old, but from an eleven-year-old's perspective anything over fifteen fits that bill. I think he had brown hair, was pretty big, kind of burly maybe; and he laughed a lot."

"Remember any neighbors' names? Or where

she worked?"

"No. She changed jobs every time we moved. She did accounting. I think she liked her last job, and her boss."

"What about men?"

"There were a lot of them. What I can't understand is why the man who left with her wouldn't have notified someone if something happened to her."

"There are a lot of possible reasons for that. The one I'm most interested in is whether he did something to her himself. Right now, the police seem eager to write it off as accidental so they can close an old case. But I'm not going to let that happen, especially if it ain't right."

"Good. Thanks for being persistent."

"No problem. The police and I don't always have the same agenda. Let me get back to you." His words came out Iowa flat, where the Midwest meets the real West. "I'll need another $500 in my account. Is that going to be a problem?"

"No. It's fine."

The data he'd collected showed up immediately in her inbox. The police report stated the Army Corp of Engineers working on the Platte river revitalization project had spotted the submerged car. They'd had the car raised, and, inside, the remains of a woman were found.

But how much of the body could be identified after two decades in a river? Sam's eyes widened as she read the postmortem report.

Remains have undergone adipocere.

Unsure of the word's definition, Sam typed it into her computer. The Wiki definition was 'a tissue event, different from regular decomposition, occurring in twenty to thirty percent of submerged bodies over time.'

Pressing a fist to her mouth, Sam dragged

Mathias attachments into a file on her desktop marked 'Omaha.'

Three more days passed before another of Mathias' short, terse emails popped up. This time he reported tracking down a last known address, her mother's employer, and found a few of her former co-workers. He'd finished up with an enigmatic,

"I'm onto something. Will get back to you in a few days. I think we've got ourselves a murderer."

That was five days ago. Sam sat staring at her email, fingering her red phone.

Should she call him?

What the hell? There was nothing more to be done right now. She'd done a good job of taking action on her mother's behalf.

A heady whiff of freedom swirled about her. The need to toss off the past and break free overwhelmed her. She'd misinterpreted what her mother had done, so who could say she hadn't also overreacted twelve years ago. Maybe the FBI wasn't even after her. Or more likely, they'd written her off as a stupid, idealistic kid playing with fire and shoved her case into a cold file years ago.

She needed a normal life, like most woman her age—fun, friends, even a family. She shut down her modem and reached for her jacket. Hope flickered in her as she headed for Benton; maybe she'd even find an understanding man who'd overlook her past and care about her.

Chapter Two

Roper caught a snapshot glimpse of his suspect. She jerked down her red baseball cap and grabbed a bag of corn chips as she disappeared behind a pyramid of cereal boxes. He moved cautiously, keeping twenty-five feet back.

She looked smaller today, thinner, not gaunt, but with the kind of muscle tone he associated with honed athletes. A sliver of something stirred in his groin.

He threw a quick roadblock around his mind. What the hell business did he have feeling attracted to her? Or even curious? Getting the job done depended on keeping his perspective.

A few stragglers wandered down dreary aisles, the worn wood floor a product of busier times. But the world offered too many choices these days and a dingy little grocery store in Benton, Nevada could not compete.

Roper waited two heartbeats before circling past the Rice Krispies. He stopped short. She stood at the other end of the aisle, staring at dog food bags as if the choice was the decision of a lifetime. As she bent down, her Navajo jacket rode up, revealing the backs of strong thighs.

Dog food. Aside from her German shepherd, she lived alone.

There was the neighbor, Charlie Lemon, who ran a small ranch a mile and a half up the road from her. A full-blooded Paiute, the man clearly was on the down side of sixty. Charlie was her only visitor in the past three months of surveillance. The Bureau had dismissed a sexual relationship between them.

Craning her head, she took Roper in with a quick glance but continued studying dog chow. From a distance, she looked tough, like any woman resilient enough to survive alone in high-country desert. Bundled up against early September cool weather, she seemed indifferent to her own appearance.

Roper frowned, took another look, and turned to survey dusty condiment bottles. He'd never felt threatened by tough women, those who punched and kicked their way through life. But he had a problem with those who didn't include men in life's survival kit.

Odd bits of black hair stuck out from under her cap. From his research, he knew the color was dyed. Sam Neally, a.k.a. Catherine Bell, twelve years in hiding and still afraid to let her hair go natural.

Heaving a twenty-five pound bag of chow on her shoulder, she went around the end of the row. Roper snatched up a bottle of green olives and trailed along behind her. So what if curiosity mingled with a hint of desire? Who the fuck cared? None of it had anything to do with what he needed to do: make contact, engage her in conversation, and figure out a way to get inside her house.

Neally sidestepped a teenaged girl dragging a crying child by the arm, and headed toward the checkout counter. She walked with an odd rolling gait, coming down hard on the outside of one foot.

He ignored the twist of empathy knotting up his stomach, pulling him toward her like an emotional magnet. It got worse with every job, that tug of concern women evoked in him—Roper, the savior of the world, Don Quixote of the FBI. He pulled back hard against the urge. Sympathy was as dangerous as desire, and both spelled disaster.

He'd been put on warning. This time his job, as

well as his integrity, was at stake.

Roper studied the row of Butterfingers lining the shelf by the cash register, his pulse shifting into third gear as he waited for her to finish her business.

Pulling cash out, she planted it on the counter. Roper moved in closer, his ear cocked.

"That'll be it?" The clerk's eyes never wavered from the images scurrying across a TV screen three inches from his nose.

"Yes." She spoke quietly with no anxiety in a voice pitched lower than he'd expected. Yesterday, she'd sounded different, but she'd been outside, fighting the wind.

Dropping her change into a pocket of her fleece jacket, she hefted up the dog food and headed for the front door without a backward glance at Roper.

Taking his turn with the zombie running the cash register, Roper plopped down the green olives and the candy bar on the warped counter. He shoved four bills toward the clerk, who grabbed them up, no android when it came to money. The kid looked young, sixteen or seventeen, at most. Humming along with a heavy beat pulsing from the TV, he stuffed the cash into a drawer and turned his attention back to the screen. A stranger in town caused no concern here.

Roper strolled to the door. He pulled up his collar and stepped outside. A strong gust wrapped around his body and carried him along the sidewalk. Shit! He hated these assignments in the land of nowhere. Benton-fucking, Nevada. It was too goddamned cold for September.

Nothing moved in the empty street, no concerned citizens ready to raise an alarm at his first direct assault on the sanctuary of Sam Neally, a.k.a. Catherine Bell.

She stood beside her pick-up truck, an old Chevy

three-quarter ton, minus most of its blue paint. It matched her basic survival clothes and her life.

Juggling her bags, she yanked at the truck door.

This was it, his third encounter with her. He hoped to God today he'd hit the jackpot. Three days ago, he'd intercepted her jogging. Playing lost, he'd asked for directions. With no more than a shush at her dog and a quick check of his Department of Transportation vehicle, she'd answered him readily enough.

Manufacturing a second encounter yesterday involved a lot of wasted time. He'd resorted to using his NDOT connections to set up a makeshift detour, a put-up job at best. It'd been a helluva way to spend five listless hours, playing with his keys, wishing he were home with Joey, his son.

About ready to cash it in, he'd squinted down her road. Finally, there she came; her dented Chevy barreling toward him in a swirl of dust. He made damned sure she got a good look at his face that time, so she'd remember him. He'd hauled himself out of his vehicle, just another harmless highway employee directing traffic around a temporary detour.

But today was the real start of play.

Roper wove his way around a broken piece of sidewalk in his path. He loped toward her, his accelerating pulse keeping pace. The cold air smelled of something pungent, sage maybe. Or juniper. It reminded him of better times, camping as a kid with his parents, or last year, searching for lizards at Great Basin with Joey.

He pulled up short a few feet from her truck, his heart racing. "Excuse me."

She flinched slightly but turned toward his voice. "Yes?"

Bright sunlight reflected off her skin, turning it iridescent. He knew the shape of her face and mouth, knew them too well. He'd spent eight weeks peering at a grainy black and white photo, searching for the criminal hidden behind the shy smile and startled eyes. He'd never spotted it. Today was no different. Tough she might be, and a little wary, but without pretense. She had no look of a perpetrator.

"Sorry, I didn't mean to scare you." He held his breath. Now was the time for the brush off. Standing inches from her, he caught something subtle in her expression, grave and enigmatic. Her eyes matched the burnt umber hills behind her, already cast in late afternoon shadows. Up close, her strength dissolved, leaving a fragile, Madonna of the desert, potent enough to attract most men.

"I ran into you a couple of days back out east of the reservation. I was lost and you gave me directions. Then I saw you again yesterday. I was the guy freezing his butt off directing traffic around the 447 detour."

A ghost of a grin replaced her slight frown. She didn't smile easily, but then who the hell would, with her life? She couldn't have had much to make her happy, hiding out in the desert. And not much of anyone to smile with.

"Joe Thorp." Roper used his alias while holding out his hand. "I'm with the highway department." He yanked a thumb toward his NDOT truck. "Here on loan from the Vegas office for a few weeks."

The stiff breeze caught at her cap and she yanked it down, hiding part of her face. "Sam Neally." She spoke her name slowly, leaving each word hanging separately in the air.

He glanced down at the hand she gave him. Callused, narrow fingers, tinged with dark smudges on the tips. But she smelled good, a mixture of something sweet mingled with herbs. Thank God. He'd spent too many hours in the company of back-to-the-earthers, dirt punks or whatever the hell they called themselves. Most of them were kids who'd swore off hygiene as a badge of honor, a demonstration of their commitment to save the earth.

He'd assumed she'd look the same as all of them, earnest and passionate, but in her case, more worn out, beaten down by years in hiding.

Instead, up close Sam Neally looked as perfect as a desert flower with her unblinking eyes fixed on his face. He slid his gaze away from hers, preferring to focus on her beat-up truck, more in line with his expectations.

Considering his track record with women, he suddenly felt damned grateful he didn't need to rely on his own perceptions of her to do this job. He didn't know her. Just a brief encounter, maybe a couple of days, and he'd have his business completed. From then on, she'd be the Bureau's responsibility.

From his viewpoint, the whole thing was a practice in futility. Since the establishment of Homeland Security, he'd run his butt off chasing after idealists who, on paper at least, looked like threats to the country.

Twelve years ago a bunch of stupid college kids set out to protest governmental lumber policies by setting fire to a cabin in the El Dorado National Forest. In normal circumstances, they'd have gotten off with six months to a year in jail max. By now, they'd be well beyond the statute of limitations and home free.

But since the passage of the Patriot Act, all that had changed. A tiny, obscure paragraph of the Act entitled Section 809 said offenses perpetrated against government property resulting in possible bodily injury was retroactively punishable. Since a fire fighter with the National Forest Service had been hurt, this made it just cause to pursue indictment and spend the taxpayers' money nailing fugitives in a twelve-year-old case.

All bitching aside, breaking the law was breaking the law, and as an FBI agent, he had a job to do.

Roper searched for a friendly expression to push the distaste off his face. It was simple enough: Set the bait, get into her life and toss a net over her before she recognized the trap. She might be innocent as hell these days, but Catherine Bell's situation in the desert within reach of the Bureau of Land Management made her a tasty carrot to dangle in front of her former friends.

He shivered and yanked at the zipper of his bomber jacket. "Is it always this cold around here in September?"

"It's normal. By now, we can have snow." She searched the sky and turned back to study him, a little reticent but not afraid. "Where you from? Somewhere warmer, right?"

"Yeah. Twelve years in Phoenix. Las Vegas these days." He stepped back, taking up the dance; one step forward, one step back, wait for her to relax, then another step forward, then back if she showed signs of nerves. Do-Si-Do. "It's cold at night in Vegas, but nothing like this. And the wind here is damned annoying."

He'd lived in Las Vegas for ten years. The only time he'd spent in Phoenix had been courtesy of the Internet, memorizing facts about his cover story fabricated by the Bureau.

She transferred the dog food onto the other hip. He saw uncertainty cross her face followed by a flash of fear, maybe her basic survival instinct kicking in. He kept his smile reassuring, ready to change tactics if she showed signs of fleeing.

But she took another nibble at his line. "The weather grows on you. If you stick around long enough, you might even start to enjoy it."

"I'll be here a couple of weeks; but, if it's this cold, I'm sunk. Just a city boy at heart." Aw shucks. "How about a cup of coffee? Somewhere warm?"

"I really need to get back." Uncertainty laced through the words as if she'd stumbled into a place she didn't know.

He lifted a shoulder to ease a cramp in his back and drodged up another polite smile, followed by a rampaging bullet of remorse that zigzagged through his brain. Shit. Pretense cluttered his world, leaving him sick to hell of deceit. He made a quick promise to himself that once he finished this job, he'd cash in the undercover work. "A quick cup of coffee can't hurt."

A moment of yearning flickered over her face. He watched her resolve crumble.

"Well?" Balancing on the balls of his feet, he zeroed in for the kill.

"All right. A quick cup." She slid the groceries across the worn vinyl seat and slammed the truck door with a shriek of rusty metal. "Don't expect much when it comes to coffee around here. The stuff's barely drinkable."

Benton, Nevada contained nothing more than a handful of buildings, the remnants of a great civilization dwindled down to a hundred and fifty people, mostly Paiute, clutching at the leftovers of their culture.

They crossed the deserted street and stepped into a dingy little hole of a diner. The letter 'C' had fallen off the 'afe' slashed across the mud-streaked window.

A tongue of hot air lashed out at him as he stepped inside. At the far end of the narrow room a lonely waitress sat at the counter. Head resting on her hand, she flipped through a magazine, not even bothering to look up when the door opened. She wore a dark blue U of N sweatshirt; her faded blond ponytail curled limply over muscular shoulders. Just another cheerleader stuck in the past, lost in the future.

Roper trailed Neally toward a booth half way back. He frowned at the white scar crawling out from beneath the hem of her denim skirt and down her leg. It twisted along and disappeared into a boot. It wasn't an innocent kind of scar from childhood—from a leg caught in her Schwinn. It looked more like a memento picked up in Iraq from an IED.

What the hell? There'd been no mention of any injury in her files.

A few rays of daylight fought past the mud on the window and spot-lit the forlorn booth. He took the seat facing the two foot wide hallway with an exit door at the end. It left Neally facing the sun.

"Good pie here?" Roper asked.

She squinted through the weak rays of sunlight hitting her in the eyes. "I don't know. I'm not a pie eater, myself. Why don't you ask the waitress?"

On cue, the woman sauntered over and plopped two menus down on the scarred table. If she knew Sam Neally, she hid it well.

"Pie any good?" He asked the waitress.

"I like it, but hell, I'm the baker." The woman's passive face didn't prepare him for the creative rejoinder, a tenfold improvement on her surroundings. "I'd try the chocolate. It's pudding filling. No way can I screw that up."

"Okay. I'll give it a shot." He grinned and looked at Neally. "Coffee?"

"Black."

"Nothing else?"

"No. I'm good." Neally gave him a half smile back, and he caught a glimpse of straight white teeth. Whatever his little terrorist had been up to for twelve years, she'd managed to attend to basics. His smile froze on his face and left it feeling stiff. All his tension suddenly focused on a single place between his eyes. Undercover work, by its very nature, presented a damned mine field; but in the past he'd played the cat and mouse game well.

He sighed, feeling closer to fifty than his forty years.

Histories like hers were common; he'd seen a hundred suspects' files over the years. He could recite Sam Neally's without checking his notes; a splintered family, she and her sister abandoned by their single mother. Condemned to years of foster homes, she'd still managed to do well in school. She even won a scholarship from some do-good service club in one of the many anonymous small towns she'd been shuffled through.

In the end, she'd become one more statistic promoting the general belief that chaotic childhoods produced dysfunctional adults. She hadn't even survived her first semester of college before joining an environmental group with a stupid idea. Only idealistic college kids could believe setting fire to a pile of wood would make a big corporation change its logging policies. What they'd ended up doing instead was burning down three cabins in El Dorado National Forest—Catherine Bell's first and last protest, forcing her underground.

So here she sat, twelve years later, still hiding in the desert, her life in ruins.

And what about his own life? He felt sick of it all—sick of people's wasted existences and sick of himself for using the pitiful circumstances of peoples' struggles to twist and turn them for the sake of justice.

She slid out of her denim jacket and whipped off her baseball cap. Her strange hair stood straight up, refusing to be tamed. In the only picture he had of her, she'd looked anonymously attractive, her light hair curling over thin shoulders. No longer conventional looking, she had appeal, with her quiet, heart-shaped face and smoke brown eyes. Her plain white t-shirt revealed tanned, well-toned arms. She'd kept herself in good shape. By design? Part of some strategy to survive by keeping herself fit and ready to run at every moment? She sure as hell didn't dress to attract a man's attention. In fact, she looked as though she went out of her way to stay well under male radar. It hadn't worked.

"So what do you do?" He asked.

"I sell plants, mostly herbs, to a few small nurseries around Nevada. And some e-commerce sales." She ran her fingers through her hair. "Not very interesting for most people, unless you're a botanist. Or maybe a shaman."

The flash of wit surprised him. One thing he counted on with his job was consistency. He didn't like surprises. Contradictions could be dangerous. Wanted by the law for twelve years, living in this godforsaken place? What kind of a life did she have where she could make jokes? Her situation belied humor. He narrowed his gaze, struggling with this added dimension.

The waitress slouched over and slid a sad piece of pie toward him. She dropped two mugs on the table, slopping coffee over the rims. "There you are. Go for it."

Roper waited for the woman to saunter away, took a sip of the liquid and grimaced. "Not exactly Starbucks, is it?"

"I warned you." Another odd pause followed. Small talk apparently wasn't her strong suit. He said nothing, accommodating himself to her pace. "You said you work for the highway department. Is it usual practice for someone from NDOT to get lost?"

"What can I say? I'm a desk jockey."

She took another sip. "Hard to figure why they

call this coffee."

"Sure you don't want me to order you something else?"

She shook her head, and Roper forced himself to lean back. He stabbed at the anemic ridge of crust, searching for the natural flow of conversation, for a clear path into her trust. Roper traced the line of her white throat as she took another swallow of coffee. Hell, he felt as awkward as a sixteen year old on a fucking blind date with the prom queen.

"Why'd they bring you all the way from Vegas to work in Washoe County?"

"I'm an engineer; they needed survey work done for the new Highway 50 extension."

"Really? They're going ahead with that project? I thought it was put on hold for a couple of years. You running into much resistance?"

"We've gotten a few letters, complaints about the route mostly." She'd turned the conversation exactly where he wanted to go. He studied the room, downshifting his eagerness. "What kind of resistance are we talking about? Some environmentalist group worried about the highway destroying nature?"

"I doubt if you could call it anything as organized as a 'group.' A lot of folks might have concerns about land rights, but most people around here are too busy trying to survive to spend time saving the earth. The few who do have time to protest are focused on the law-makers in Carson City." She hesitated. "Or the Department of Land Management. I've never heard about any protests directed specifically at the Highway Department."

Moving right along. She made it almost too easy. "Land's not a big issue around here, then?"

"It's an issue, I suppose. Isn't it most places? But the wild horse problem is the big environmental story these days."

"Yeah, so I've heard. You see much of the horses

yourself?"

"Almost every night, roaming free around my place, but I'm a good five miles off the main highway."

"You live out there in the desert where I ran into you?"

She nodded, rotating the mug in her fingers, her eyes intent on his face, watchful.

"Pretty isolated isn't it? Must get lonely so far from friends and family."

"I'm not lonely."

"You grow up around here, then?"

"No. The Midwest. But I've lived here a while." Her voice turned husky. "I inherited my place from a relative."

In the early hunt for Catherine Bell, there'd been no mention of any aunt. Two months ago, the Bureau connected the dots with Anna Novak, the only sister of Catherine's mother. She'd lived forty years in the desert as the common-law wife of a Paiute with the strange name of Tilo Taase. No wonder there'd been no record of her aunt. The woman had maintained an invisible existence, hadn't trusted banks or the government, paid taxes, and gotten a social security card. Even in death four years ago, Anna Novak left nothing behind to connect her to Catherine Bell, except a thin paper trail of an irrevocable land trust, deeded to Sam Neally. Like her aunt, Catherine Bell had left only faint footprints behind when she transformed into Sam Neally

"You feel that at home in the desert?" The question came from true curiosity.

"I do. I've been here long enough. Sometimes I even forget I've lived anywhere else." She frowned. "But you don't want to hear the boring story of my life."

He'd term her life as chaotic, desperate, and

probably lonely, but definitely never boring. "Give me a try. I'll stop you if I start to fall asleep."

The name of Sam Neally turned up three months ago as indiscreet chatter on one of the various eco-sites tracked by the Bureau. Some young, eager special agent spotted it in a discussion of the unsolved El Dorado cabin fires twelve years ago. From there, the search moved to the Bureau's cold case warehouse in Rockville, Maryland. That many years ago, standard record keeping meant hard copies. It took three days to dig through the dusty papers and evidence folders before connecting Catherine Bell with a woman named Sam Neally living on a small ranch in Northern Nevada. Digging deeper into family history turned up the aunt, Anna Novak.

At that point, the Bureau called on Roper and sent him in pursuit. It seemed like a simple plan to round up the Consortium, put a stop to any future protests and close an old case.

He glanced at the quiet woman sitting across from him. Neally's current activities were easy enough to unravel. All it took was putting a trace on her Internet provider and lurking on her emails.

Now came the hard part; pulling together enough solid evidence to rope her into betraying her old friends. Who the hell cared if she'd never done another illegal act for the past twelve years? A dense weight spread across his chest and pressed against his heart. Sometimes he hated his fucking job.

He traced a crack in the table with an index finger as his eyes followed the movement of her coffee mug to her mouth and back down. Small talk equaled social garbage in traditional law enforcement, but in undercover work, the give and take of casual conversation was the key to success. After endless hours of digging into the ashes of Catherine Bell's life, what did he know about her?

Nothing more than a brief sketch of the woman sitting across from him in this last-stop cafe in Benton, Nevada.

He forked the last bite of pie into his mouth. "You really enjoy living in the desert that much?"

"For the most part. Why? You planning on turning into a desert rat yourself? I doubt if you'd like it."

"You're probably right. But as someone used to a softer life, I'm curious about what it takes to live without the usual crutches of civilization." What bullshit. He knew exactly what it took. In her case, desperation and the determination to survive.

She shrugged. "Maybe just different crutches."

He had no quick comeback for her. In his normal life, if a woman tossed out a philosophical query, he'd be out the door. In this situation, it kept the conversation moving right along to where he wanted to go. For some reason, it also engaged his personal attention, the last thing he needed. But he forged ahead. "I don't suppose you'd like to go out for a drink sometime?"

"That was sudden. Was it something I said?"

"Dunno." He replied. "Maybe it's the depth of conversation. I haven't had a real one in over a week. Let's just say I'm sick of talking about surface drainage and highway grading. So, do you want to join me at Porky's for a beer Saturday night?"

"You've been here a week and already know about Porky's?"

He shrugged. "It's the only bar within ten miles. I've grown fond of the place. It has a certain atmosphere I find appealing. But the bottom line is there's not much to do at night around here except sit in my motel room and watch TV."

"Or sit around discussing traffic flow?"

He grinned, hating the pretense.

"You could have found something more

entertaining in Reno than Porky's. And someone far more entertaining there than me."

"Maybe, but I doubt it. You and Porky's are as far from Reno as the moon, thank God." He shoved aside his mug. "A couple of hours, a drink, some entertaining conversation, a dance or two?"

"I'm not much of a dancer."

"Then we'll sit and talk." He stretched out his legs under the table, avoiding hers. "I'd like the company. No strings."

Her pause was shorter this time. "Look, I'll agree to meet you there, okay? But give me a phone number where I can reach you in case something comes up."

"Sure. Let's say ten on Saturday, then? That too late?"

"No, probably too early for Porky's. I don't think the place gets going before midnight. After that, it escalates pretty fast, with the clientele falling down drunk in the street by two. You really sure you want to go there?"

"Yeah. Sounds like an evening of surprises."

Chapter Three

Nebraska

Knock, Knock.
Mathias stumbled to his feet. "Wait a minute!" He fell sharply to his knees, tangled in a heavy satin bedspread.
Knock, knock, knock. The rapping grew louder.
"Hold your horses." Mathias made a second try. This time he tripped over his shoes beside the bed.
"Goddammit." He pulled angrily at the triple locks and yanked open the door. Mid-morning sunlight hit his eyes and briefly blinded him. "Yeah?"
"I'm looking for Robert Mathias."
"That's me." His mind moved like sludge, too much booze and too little sleep. "What do you want?"
"My name's Parry. I believe you've been asking around for me."
Mathias knew right away this man was out of his league. Who the hell dressed in a fancy gray suit at eight a.m.? He even had on a tie, for God's sake. Mathias glanced down at his own rumpled pajamas. What the fuck? Entertaining in his Sunday best, he wouldn't look any better. Besides, the number of zeroes in a man's bank account never stopped Mathias. This man had something at stake, or he'd never be visiting a sleazy motel in Council Bluffs, Iowa at this hour of the morning.
"Come on in," Mathias said.
The guy had to be in his mid to late thirties, neat in the extreme, with the kind of body that'd

turn to fat in ten years without a lot of gym time. While the man's ready smile shouted politician, he clearly wasn't here to campaign a vote.

Mathias didn't bother to offer his hand. "Push over my stuff and take a seat. I've got a few questions I'd like to ask you."

Parry glanced about him without appearing to lower his gaze to the mess in the room. "I'll stand."

"Suit yourself," Mathias sat down on the ugly green easy chair. "I'm investigating the death of a woman by the name of Marilyn Bell. She worked for your father twenty years back. You recall her?"

"My dad's dead. He died twelve years ago." His smooth features showed nothing.

"Yeah. I understand Marilyn Bell was his accountant back then."

"Yes?"

"You run Omaha Park Corporation these days, right?"

"I took over when my dad died."

"And I hear you've gotten yourself elected to the state legislature?"

"Yes." He shifted back, frowning at Mathias. "What's this all got to do with me?"

"Sure you won't take a seat?" He pointed to the only other chair again. The guy lowered himself down and perched on the edge. "You knew Marilyn Bell, right?"

"I was only a kid, but I knew most of the people who worked in my dad's office."

"You read the recent news story that her body was recently discovered in the river?"

"I believe I read something about that."

"From what I hear, she was quite a lady, made the bedroom circuit of most of the men in your father's company."

"If you're implying my dad slept with her, you couldn't be further off the mark. My dad was as true as they come. He'd never have an affair with a woman like that."

"I wasn't talking about your dad, sonny boy. Why bother with the old man when the kid's dick is ready and waiting?" The words echoed off the walls before landing on the guy, putting a dent in his calm.

Parry stood up abruptly but didn't make a move for the door. "What the hell is this about?"

"I've been talking to a couple of those former employees of Omaha Park who claim you and Marilyn Bell had a thing going. Until she disappeared."

"I'm a state senator. If you're setting this up to blackmail me, think again. I'm not buying. I was barely eighteen. Even if I did have a relationship of sorts with her, all kids screw around." He ran his hand over his bald head as though he still had hair. "If anything, she was the one to blame, seducing a goddamned kid. I don't care if you have twenty people talking to you, it wouldn't make even the local gossip column. So who hired you, sleazebag?"

Mathias ignored the comment. He pulled out a pack and held it out. "Smoke?"

"I don't smoke."

"Of course you don't. Well, look here, Mr. Parry, you may be a big shot, but that isn't going to stop the police once they get the toxicology report back on Marilyn Bell's cause of death. I happen to know they're seriously looking at foul play. You were the last guy in people's memory to be doing her; it won't be hard to connect you to the dead woman." Flicking his lighter, Mathias squinted up at the man. "We can do this the hard way or the easy way." He pulled on the cigarette and exhaled slowly. The lazy trail of smoke circled up and around Parry's head. "Ever heard of the Preppie murder case that happened in New York City about fifteen years ago? Well, I believe we just may have ourselves another one of those Preppie murders right here in the Midwest."

The man's cheek twitched, the only sign he'd heard Mathias.

"Here's what I think happened: I think you and her were hitting it. Probably doing a little experimenting, a young guy who suddenly discovers he's a stud. You get stupid and *bam!*" Mathias hit the desktop with his palm, pleased with the sharp retort. "You've got a dead woman on your hands. See? I'm givin' you the benefit of the doubt. We could even say you both got carried away; a little too rough, she stops breathing. Being the dumb kid you were then, you panicked. You got behind the wheel of her car, drove it to the embankment, and shoved it into the Missouri River. *Kaboom!* No more problem." He took another puff and waited. "Toxicology says she died of drowning, by the way. You probably didn't realize she was still alive when she went into the river and that by trying to cover your tracks, you committed murder."

Parry's eyes widened and beads of sweat started to appear on his brow. "That's the craziest story I've ever heard. What proof do you have? The word of a couple of old ladies who worked for my dad a million years ago? They probably made up the story about me and Marilyn Bell after they saw the news item. Makes a good tale at the nursing home. Puts them in the spotlight and brightens up their lives." He checked his watch.

"We'll see. I have quite a few names to check out, some of them other men who spent time with her. With that kind of information, who knows where it will lead me? Sure it wouldn't be easier to come clean right now? You were a kid. You can claim it was an accident, and you freaked out. Save us both a lot of time and trouble. You could even spin it to seem like you're the good guy, turning yourself in twenty years later."

"You have no proof. Not one damned thing to connect me to her disappearance." Parry paced to the window. "And what's in this for you? How much?"

"Are we talking bribery here?" Mathias shook his cigarette at the man. "I don't think so. I've got a real, honest to God client who cares what happened—someone who I'm positive doesn't want this swept under the rug, even if it involves a state senator."

"I see. And who might that be?"

Mathias stubbed out his cigarette and stood up, ignoring the question. "Either you and I come to some agreement here and you turn yourself in, or I lead the police to you. Your call."

Parry's lips drew back in an imitation of a smile. "I'd call it checkmate, myself. You've got nothing, except threats. And if I find out you're in any way libeling me, you'll be hearing from my lawyers." He smoothed down his pressed trousers and straightened his tie before heading to the door without another glance at Mathias.

Smiling, Mathias flipped through his list of names and began calling.

Six hours and a lot of grunt work later, he had three meetings set up, the seedlings of enough evidence to earn a subpoena. The grand jury would do the rest. A better ending for one Marilyn Bell.

****

Parry parked his car on the street close to the alley. It was eight o'clock and getting dark. He hadn't eaten since breakfast and he was hungry.

Digging around in the door pocket, he pulled out a bagel he'd stashed there yesterday. Peeling back the cellophane, the cream cheese oozed out over his fingers. "Hell." He chewed automatically, wishing he had a cup of coffee, anything to wash down stale bread.

In the middle of swallowing the last bite, his phone vibrated. Carefully wrapping the bagel back up, he laid it on his soft leather seat. He checked the number; his daughter.

"Hi! What's up, peanut?"

"Daddy. Are you on your way home?"

"Nope, sorry, I have to work tonight. What do you need?"

He heard her sigh. It was getting familiar, the sound teenagers made as they learned the sad lesson that life didn't always turn out their way. "I was going to the movies, and I said I'd drive. Mom doesn't want me to take her car, so I thought you wouldn't mind if I used yours."

"Sweetie, I'm in the middle of something. Put your mother on, and I'll see what we can do."

Ten minutes of deliberation later, his wife surrendered her Porsche. He rang off, smiling. The image of his sixteen year old, nose-pierced daughter driving up to her friend's house in a metallic gray showpiece was too much. Leaving the smile in place, he squeezed his eyes shut and forced himself to relax back and to wait.

Two hours later, Mathias stepped out the back door of Willie Joe's, a small, no-nonsense bar that sat squeezed between a pool hall and a pawnshop. An insignificant street corner in Council Bluffs about to be the scene of a murder.

The man lurched down the narrow alley, swayed around a dirty puddle and turned north. Parry stepped out of his warm car. He kept himself fifty yards back, staying in shadows.

It was too easy. The man might be good at digging in the dirt of other people's lives, but getting himself shit-faced by ten at night would be his eulogy.

Shit! It'd turned damned cold in the last hour.

Parry felt about in his jacket and pulled out rubber gloves. He slipped them on. Reaching into his pocket again, he found the wire, tangled up with the $50 silk necktie he'd worn to a business meeting two hours ago. His hands trembled as he struggled to unravel the garrote. It would be messy but guns were noisy.

Mathias turned down Henry Street, heading west. Halfway down the block, he veered into a city lot. He staggered up to an older model maroon sedan and fumbled in his pockets. Parry took a quick glance around, nothing but a dark parking lot, not even security lights. He moved up behind Mathias quickly, not giving himself time to consider. With a flick of his wrist, he slipped the wire around the thick neck and jerked back. Mathias never heard it coming.

They slid around like apache dancers, fighting for footing on filthy cement. For all his soft fat padding, the jerk put up a surprising struggle.

The wind shrieked now, as if orchestrated for murder. Damn, it was taking too long. Frustrated now, Parry pulled himself up to his feet. He gave Mathias a quick shove forward, and the guy fell face down on the pavement. Holding tight to the wire, Parry bent over him. Using both hands, he twisted and yanked back, using his own two hundred pounds for ballast.

A gurgling gasp escaped from Mathias, the wet, sticky sound of a man suffocating on his own blood. He twitched and his legs flailed once, twice. Then nothing.

Parry stood up almost casually, but his legs betrayed him. They shook like a toddler's taking his first steps. He reached down and released his garrote, holding the sticky wire in one gloved hand. The parking lot remained empty. Not even a forgotten car in sight. Parry scanned the dark until he spotted it; a gray whale of a dumpster that loomed in the far corner of the lot.

He bent down and retrieved Mathias' keys, discarded in the fight. He did a quick one-handed pat down of the dead man's pockets and retrieved a room key card.

Fluorescent lights cast strange blue haloes about the perimeter lights, but the rest of the lot lay in deep darkness. Parry sighed once and caught hold of the man's heels. He cursed and fought with the body. It took a long five minutes to get the dead weight into the back seat of the sedan.

Sweaty but shivering with cold, Parry scrambled around and climbed into the driver's side.

Five more minutes and the Olds sat beside the dumpster, the body of Robert Mathias buried under burger wrappers.

Parry strolled down Henry Street. He snapped off the bloodstained gloves and tossed them into a waste can with disgust. The next steps were easy. He found his own car and headed for Mathias' motel. The only thing left to do was find the name of the person who'd hired Mathias.

He regretted the necessity, but he didn't like leaving loose ends.

Chapter Four

Northern Nevada—Present Day

Sam frowned after Thorp's retreating back. His swagger was all cowboy, but his chinos and the blue oxford shirt screamed buttoned-down engineer. He swung his legs up into the battered NDOT truck and headed down the road, churning up dust.

She yanked her baseball cap further down over her face and watched the brown cloud dissipate. The NDOT van disappeared behind an abandoned fishery, heading east toward the lake.

What the hell was that all about? A man not only attractive, but interested in her?

And she liked him!

Eleven years without sex, until Keddie introduced her to Graham Rawlings last year, which led to a handful of dates with a man she found marginally attractive. The evenings always went the same; a barely edible casino dinner complete with overpriced wine and boxed cheesecake followed by twenty forgettable minutes in bed. The nights were predictable and mildly entertaining. Graham was a man of convenience at best and until now, as good as she could expect.

She shifted her leg about, avoiding the jagged edge of the seat cover. With a twist of the ignition, the engine struggled to wake up. Double clutching, she shoved the gear stick through first into second, hauling down the road in the opposite direction. A minute later, she accelerated past the last solitary house of Benton and headed for open desert.

The highway lost its pavement two miles south at the boundary of the reservation. She cranked the window down an inch and gripped the steering wheel with both hands. Squinting ahead, she sucked in the cold air, letting the familiar landscape wrap about her like a cocoon.

Coming on winter, tourists abandoned the high desert and its claustrophobic mountains, leaving the desert to the hearty. The shabby town of Benton lay against the southeast tip of Pyramid Lake. The lake was a secret few tourists discovered, a four thousand foot deep gem of pastel blue with mountains for a backdrop and no houses to mar the view. Primordial alkaline waters supported the cui-ui, a hulking skeleton of a fish too ugly for most fish lovers, except the Paiute and a few other brave fishermen.

She followed the highway easily enough, slowing automatically at blind curves and potholes. The wild horses posed a bigger problem. Even with the weekly Bureau of Land Management round-ups, twice as many stallions showed up the next week. She slowed down and kept her eyes moving from side to side. In daylight there wasn't much danger, but late afternoon heading toward dusk, coming up fast on a herd was a bitch. Ghost horses, the remnants of another time, like the people barely clinging to their lives out here in the desert.

Like herself.

Her mind circled back to Thorp. A nice guy, attractive, steady, direct. The sort of man she'd never known.

Men, she mused. What the hell did she know about them, anyway? No father figure around. All there had been were dark shadows and booming voices moving in and out of her mother's swinging bedroom door. Then, a few dates in high school and finally college. But that hadn't lasted long.

Rounding the last familiar curve of road, she

slowed to watch the sun sink below the western peaks. Shadows left her house in sepia tones that blended into the backdrop of the eastern ridges, making the place disappear in shadow. Miles from the main highway, the house sat alone, except for Charlie Lemon's, his lights barely visible in the distance.

Her ranch looked like every other one scattered around the reservation, lying in a shallow arroyo, low to the ground, and covered with worn clapboard, circa 1920's. The electricity came courtesy of Charlie Lemon, who fed it to her through a single line strung the mile and a half between the two places. The phone line, put in ten years ago by her aunt, had one purpose, to provide Internet access for her herb business. Heating and cooking came from propane tanks, supplemented with wood gathered by special permit on the reservation.

The Trinity Range loomed up behind her land. Five miles the other side of Trinity sat the Forty-Mile Desert, her avenue of escape at her back door.

She turned down her furrowed drive. There sat Dourcet, his yellow tail wagging.

The truck slid silently to a stop, inches from her corrugated out-shed. For the first seven years, she'd hidden the truck behind that structure, fearing every strange car zigzagging down the road. Old habits died hard. She'd never quite believed they wouldn't find her. Her first months with her aunt, she'd spent hours working through every possible scenario, unsure if she feared the FBI or the Consortium more. She mapped out all avenues of approach and carefully orchestrated the sparse information about her life she passed on to her aunt.

She yanked on the hand brake and slumped back. So what about Thorp? He claimed to want nothing more than a few hours of conversation and maybe a dance or two. Why the hell not accept the invitation? Her first big chance to step outside of a twelve year sentence in solitary. A week or two of fun, maybe even something more. She did like the look of his body, solidly built, not too showy.

With a few clicks of her mouse, she could check up on Thorp and his story easily enough, put in a call or two to the Nevada Highway Department. If he checked out okay, just maybe she'd give herself a break and a night out.

She hopped down and locked up the truck. Nothing stirred around her but the shivering of wind through the cottonwoods. Dourcet stood guard, his wagging tail hitting the door of her truck. It was one of those perfect autumn nights, with the scent of juniper filling the air.

"Come on, boy. Let's go eat." Her leg throbbing, she limped up the dirt path, working out the stiffness as she sidestepped small bunches of herbs laid out to dry that morning.

In its early years, someone had attempted a paint job on her house, but the wood wouldn't hold paint for long in the arid climate. Blotches of faded blue still lingered like haphazard polka dots, matching the scarred blue of her truck. The bright red front door stood out, protected by a low-hanging porch from the constant assault of wind pushing down the valley. Every plant and tree around the place had a job as a windbreak.

She avoided the hole from a missing board in her porch and fished for her keys. Dourcet panted happily beside her. Huddling close to the door, Sam jiggled the lock.

The pungent scent of drying sage and the crooked rocking chair sitting by the fire were the strongest reminders of her aunt's presence. Well-used white mugs still crouched on the window ledge from a time when her aunt's friends filled the room.

Twelve years. She'd never lived anywhere so

long. The sense of ownership warmed her, even though the last four years were empty.

The low-slung house had four rooms, an open kitchen with the living room running off of it, a utility room adjacent, a small bath, and a single bedroom at the back. The best feature of the ranch was the long front porch cradling the entire west side, keeping watch over the desert. On clear days, the sleeping purple snow-capped Sierras of California rose up a hundred miles to the west.

She went through her routine, turning up the heat, storing the groceries, checking every window as she roamed the empty house. She fed Dourcet before pulling out her little red phone and dialing Keddie Silva.

"Ked."

"Hey! What's up?"

Sam and Keddie, the odd couple. Prowling around a grocery store in Reno two years ago, she'd spotted a creature dressed in red satin bustier cut to the navel. She'd been picking over the avocados.

Keddie had immediately started up a monologue about the similarities between men and fruit, and Sam succumbed to the friendly banter. They'd finished shopping, gone out to dinner, and become unlikely friends.

"What do you think about pickup dates, Ked?"

"You know me, any port in a storm. You, I'm not so sure I can picture in a port. I need details."

"Highway engineer, early 40's, nice, a stranger come to town."

"Stranger. I like that. And I know it'll appeal to you since you're the world's best-kept secret. What are you proposing with this engineer?"

"He asked me to go dancing Saturday night in Benton."

"Benton? An engineer at Porky's? What is he, a closet cowboy?"

"He likes the place. Says he's lonely and just wants to have a few drinks and talk."

"So they all say." The name 'Silva' suited Keddie. She was quicksilver; slight, dark, and never still. But for Sam, a big part of the attraction to Keddie was the family stories. The youngest of a brood of six, her father, Manuel was a Portuguese fisherman from northern California. He'd come to America with no English, hopping freight trains until he landed in Eureka. From there, he'd struggled for forty years to turn a small dingy into a fleet of salmon fishing charters. The salmon gone, the six kids were the main source of income for the parents. Keddie did her part by dealing blackjack at Reno's oldest casino.

"So what's the problem, aside from the fact he's an engineer," Keddie retorted.

"Should I go out with him?"

"You're asking me? Of course I'd say go, especially if he's halfway more interesting than Graham, who probably puts you to sleep in the middle of an orgasm with his enormous ego. Even an engineer has to be better than that."

"I've set myself a new agenda these days. I'm going to get out more, but I still need some reassurance I'm not desperate."

"Ha! I'd like to see you get desperate once in a while around a man."

"Listen, I've gotta eat and take Dourcet out for a run before dark. More later."

Sam and her dog ate together each night, sharing the silence. She chewed slowly, watching the barely visible twin lines swaying in the wind. Thank God for Charlie's electrical hookup. And thank God for the phone line that brought the world to her.

She cleaned up dinner and booted up the computer. Nothing from Mathias. Damn! Where the hell was the man?

The tiny propane heater blazed away, but wind rattled the panes and found a way in through the cracks, stealing the heat. It was getting colder out. Googling Joe Thorp could wait until after a run.

"Let's go get some exercise, boy." Dourcet barked once and trotted to the door.

Daylight faded fast in the desert, especially as winter got closer. Six o'clock. Another hour and the hills would toss a shroud over the shallow bowl where her house sat.

They started out slow, trotting along the dirt road meandering around the boundary of her small plot. They rounded a butte and headed due east, taking aim at her neighbor's ranch.

A few months after she'd sought refuge at her aunt's, she'd gotten the idea to try running. The untreated wound to her leg healed poorly, leaving her with a limp. The first attempt at jogging, she'd barely made it the hundred yards to the shed. Her determination to keep working at it came more from fear than anything else; she could always get away if she could run fast enough—and far enough. As the years passed, running became more about pleasure and quieting her mind.

Following the slender thread of sunlight outlining the horizon, she ran instinctively, avoiding stones and ruts. She could manage five miles easily without getting winded, ten miles without feeling exhausted. She knew her loping, bobbing gait looked strange, but it worked.

A mile beyond Charlie's house, Sam pulled up. She reached into her jacket and pulled out a doggie treat. "Stay, Dourcet."

He knew the drill, waiting as she took off, zigzagging cross-country. The game was always the same. Dourcet would find her before she'd covered more than a half a mile.

Twenty minutes later, twilight turned the road

lavender, too dark to go further. Sam turned and headed for home.

The wind had picked up significantly, and it felt like snow. She buttoned up tight around her neck as she ran, keeping an eye on Dourcet's yellow coat, barely visible ahead.

He pulled up short, his ears perked. Closing the fifty yards between them, she caught hold of his collar. "What is it? What's out there, boy?"

The dog stood quivering, no sound coming from him.

A hundred feet away, all form disappeared into darkness. Sam turned to watch Dourcet, waiting for some further sign. A rabbit? A wild horse? The dog's behavior, added to the day's surreal quality, spooked her.

"Come on, boy. Let's go." She gave a sharp tug on his collar, released it, and began a slow jog down the black chasm of road ahead. The nape of her neck prickled, and she picked up her speed.

Rounding the last curve, the dim bulb above her shed door came into view, a swinging beacon in the desert. Shifting into high gear, she took the last twenty-five yards full out.

The single lamp she'd left burning in her living room window cast weak light. The rest of the house lay dark and silent. She took a deep breath and let the tightness in her stomach ease.

Inside, she moved from room to room, flicking switches as she went. Completing the inside tour, she grabbed her flashlight and headed out for a fast circuit of the exterior. She only did it when nervous and tonight she was.

The quick house check left her trembling and mentally disjointed. Inside, she dropped the flashlight on her white lacquer kitchen table and grabbed water from the refrigerator. Dourcet waited patiently on the front porch. She dropped down beside him. Safety.

"Hey, boy, how was the run? Good, huh?" He whined once, still sitting guard duty. Sam sipped at her water, gentling Dourcet with slow strokes. Her thoughts turned back to Joe Thorp, with his crinkly eyes and the clipped voice at odds with his smile. He could be a friend, even a temporary lover. She'd be happy with that, her first real experiment with trust in twelve years. She'd have no need to firewall the relationship and weave a blanket of lies around her past. He'd be here for a few weeks and then he'd be gone.

She studied the darkness, smiling. Her aunt loved this place. Or rather, she'd loved Tilo Taase, who loved the land. Anna, with her quiet voice and quick step, gone four years, but her absence felt palpable on nights like this. Safety.

An icy flurry of air whipped around the corner of the house, straight at her. She pulled out the hood of her sweatshirt from inside her fleece coat. Yanking on the strings, she relaxed back against the newel post. Safety.

The cottonwoods on either side of the yard began a swaying dance with the wind. The only other vegetation in this part of the high desert was juniper and some rabbit brush, too low to the ground for protection. It definitely felt like snow tonight, but the wind could howl all it wanted to; she was safe at home.

Ten minutes later she finished off her water and stood up resolutely. "Come on, Dourcet. Let's go inside."

Most of the warmth in the house settled about the propane heater, leaving the farthest edges of the living room cold, but she left the precious wood untouched. It would be needed more in a few days when the snow came.

She sat down in front of her computer. She

opened a browser and tapped in the name Joe Thorp, moving slowly through the hits. An hour of searching turned up the usual basics about a life; forty-two years old, he held a valid Arizona driver's license, and no outstanding tickets or warrants.

She pulled up an alumni list from San Diego State where he'd majored in structural engineering; nothing there. She stumbled onto a few recent articles relating to the NDOT Engineering Corp's survey of the new access road between Highways Fifty and Eighty; no mention of Thorp.

Oh, well, tomorrow was Thursday. She'd call the Highway Department, make up some complaint, and wheedle information about him out of the office staff.

She mentally shook herself for the coward she was. For God's sake, it was insane to still be in hiding for a stupid act committed at eighteen. Why sentence herself to a lifetime of paranoia? The statute of limitations on the crime had come and gone, no one had found her. A law never applied retroactively, but somewhere in her internet searches, she'd seen a reference to the Patriot Act that put her into a cold sweat. Had the damned lawmakers managed to sneak in a small footnote somewhere that was retroactive in certain cases? Did the FBI really care that much about a twelve year old crime committed before 9/11?

With all the time she'd wasted worrying the Feds would find her, who'd have guessed it'd be her old friends instead who turned up? Four months ago the emails from the Consortium had started; requests for money, friendly enough. She'd hesitated only a few minutes before half-heartedly responding with some cash.

She paused, hands poised over the keys. Somewhere out back a dull thud sounded, probably the wind hurling sagebrush at her house. It seemed fitting tonight.

She stood up and wandered to the front door. Restless, she pushed it open. The single lamp from the living room cast strange shadows on the front porch. Her battered truck glowed in the distance, but nothing moved. Cracked and peeling, her house and truck were as worn out as she felt, struggling for twelve years to survive.

She breathed deeply of juniper, with it the sweet expectation of something good about to happen between herself and Joe Thorp. She needed to trust someone and Saturday was her first and best opportunity. Whoever the hell Thorp might be, for sure, he was no threat to her freedom.

Chapter Five

Porky's was the last of the true cowboy bars. Inside, tinny music would be streaming from a sad jukebox that kept company with a few brave dancers shuffling across the floor. A makeshift combo would show up at ten, and the dance floor would instantly be crammed with squirming bodies.

Sam felt lost in this place. She'd lived less than ten miles outside of Benton for twelve years but had been in the bar only twice. Both times, she'd tagged along behind her neighbor, Charlie, who knew every worn table and scarred chair like his own hand. She'd avoided dancing both times, instead, hiding out in the darkest part of the room, drinking tasteless chardonnay and wishing she were home.

Rounding the corner of the building, she stepped over a broken chunk of sidewalk. Parking behind the building was risky, the lot no place for the timid at night. But the chance of cars boxing her in made her choose expediency over safety and she'd parked her truck by the back exit, the darkest spot in the lot.

She paused under the red and yellow flashing "Porky's" sign and watched Thorp striding toward her. He had on a bomber jacket and worn jeans that clung to him like an old friend. Without speaking, he took her arm and led her inside.

A rotating spotlight illuminated all the defects of the gyrating couples on the dance floor. Like a Friday night regular, Thorp circuited scattered tables and headed for a small one in the shadows. He pulled out a faded green chair for her and waved at two burley men nearby.

"Beer okay?" Thorp asked her. With his broad features and tanned skin, he looked like every other cowboy in the place. Only better.

"Sure."

A waitress strutted up to their table, a peacock in sapphire blue, her bright red hair fanning down her back. Annoyance pecked at Sam as the woman leaned a broad shoulder past her and flashed cerulean covered cleavage at Joe. Clearly it was Thorp she planned to service.

He smiled blandly and ordered two bottles of Bass. Ignoring Sam, the woman sidled off. Checking Thorp's face, Sam caught his quick smirk.

"She doesn't seem to know you." He hooked a thumb after the waitress, disappearing into the crowd. "You don't come here much, do you?"

"I'd rather have a lobotomy." Her voice sounded too tight to her ears, too significant. What the hell was that about? Jealousy? Of a bored waitress, dangling worn-out charms in front of this man she barely knew? She couldn't remember a time in the past twelve years she'd felt anything close to being covetous of a man. And she didn't like it—didn't like the woman's flirting, didn't like her own reaction. Most of all, she didn't like the ache in her chest that felt too close to need.

She crossed her legs and forced her hands to relax in her lap. "Sorry, if that sounded harsh. I've been dragged here a couple of times by a friend, but I'm not much for partying in public." Her eyes wandered to faces hidden deeper in the shadow. "Even Charlie, my neighbor, hesitated before issuing a second invitation, but his desperation won out."

She shrugged out of her jacket and tossed it across the chair back. "But I doubt if the waitress would notice me, even if I were a regular. I don't register on her radar."

The room continued to fill up, a mix of townies, a few Paiute, a couple of tables of Bureau of Land Management people, some stray wranglers, and a pair of young females, trolling. Sam studied faces and recognized no one. Not a disappointment.

Thorp leaned back, his long legs sprawled out in front of him, looking completely at ease: no strain, no need to rush into conversation. She liked that about him, the way he let things go the direction they wanted to go.

"Here you are, cowboy." The waitress winked this time as she pushed two bottles across the table, her smile broadening when Thorp smiled back. At least she'd brought two beers.

"Thanks."

Sam watched as he took one gulp and then another, as though his thirst was the most important thing in the room. She sipped once at her bottle and sat it down resolutely inside its sweat ring.

"So, this isn't your scene, huh?" His words floated toward her over the growing clamor, riding on the smoke lingering above their heads.

"Nope." She moved her bottle around, creating concentric circles of condensation. "But it seems to be yours. I'm surprised, actually. I pegged you for someone too civil for this bedlam. But, I believe I may be wrong." She watched to see if he was embarrassed, but his face didn't change. Her words slid right past him. He was the kind of man who, at first glance, looked ordinary, innocuously so, but on second take, he began to radiate a powerfully latent sex appeal. "Every woman in this place spotted you when you walked in the door. And the men are keeping track, as well, curious about the competition."

"That's some analysis for a woman who doesn't like public partying. You think I draw that kind of attention, huh?" He looked around. "I don't see a lot of women here. It looks more to me like this place attracts lonely men. You're drawing more sideways glances than I am."

She took a quick check over her shoulder but no eyes met hers. "You're dreaming. No one in here is looking for a woman like me, who'd rather be digging in dirt than dancing. Like I said, I'm not much of a mixer."

She took another small sip of beer, swallowing quickly to avoid the taste, like somebody's day old ham sandwich, fermented and shoved into a bottle. At least it didn't leave the aftertaste of warm piss like the chardonnay she'd ordered last time.

"So if this isn't your style, what do you do for company? Or don't you need to be entertained? A self-contained woman of the desert?"

"I have a dog."

He barked out a laugh and the sound forced a grin from her.

"Oh-oh. I don't think I want to follow up with a tag line. I'd hate to suggest a comparison between my company and your dog's."

Another waitress wove past the table, giving Thorp an extra swing of her hips. Sam shifted in her chair, yearning suddenly to be anywhere other than in this place tonight with this man.

"So you spend your time gardening?"

She blinked. "It's not gardening. I harvest herbs from the desert, I don't grow them."

"Like gardening though. You're still digging around in dirt, as you said. Have you always liked doing that?"

"No. Growing up, there was no time or place for it." Rundown houses and apartment buildings with trash-littered, weed-infested yards didn't make good gardens. "I got interested in herbs when I moved to Nevada."

"How long ago was that?"

"A long time now. I moved here to be with my aunt. She was married to a Numu, the name Paiutes gave themselves. My aunt was the one who started me digging around in the dirt.'" Sam stopped short of launching a monologue on Indian medicinal plants. It would bore him under the table.

"Your aunt? Is she the one you inherited your place from?"

"Yeah. She's dead now. Four years." She shifted her shoulders to ease a sudden tightness in her neck. She didn't want to talk about her aunt. Not with a stranger. "You said you're from Arizona?"

"I was born in upstate New York. My parents moved to Phoenix when I was a kid."

He sketched out his childhood for her, anecdotal accounts of his family and friends. It all sounded so sane. The soothing timbre of his voice took her briefly out of the strident sounds around them.

She followed his words for a few minutes longer, but eventually lost the thread, focusing instead on the rhythm of sounds accompanied by his body movements. He moved easily, loose-limbed and fluid.

What was so appealing about him? His nondescript brown hair was cut military style, his eyes the same shade of brown, but the crinkles at the corners made her want to respond to his smile.

"So what do you think?"

She flushed. "Caught me."

He held out a hand. "Wanna dance?"

The music was slow now, most of the couples on the dance floor stumbling around in some version of the Texas Two-Step.

"I don't dance." She looked down at her leg.

"Your limp? You seem to do okay walking. Dancing isn't much more than that, especially the way I do it."

"All right." She stood up slowly, reluctant, but a

desire to be touched by him overrode her embarrassment.

His hand was cool, barely making contact, but his palm placed against her back radiated heat through her blouse. He'd lied. The way he moved around the dance floor was a world apart from walking. Her head reached his shoulder, leaving her within inches of his neck, burned brown from the sun and contrasting sharply with the white of his t-shirt. She focused on the tan skin two inches from her nose, edging closer to inhale his smell.

They made a few circuits around the floor before he shifted back slightly. He was too close, his eyes piercing into her. "Not politically correct? Mentioning your limp?"

"I'm not that easily offended, Joe." It was the first time she'd said his name out loud. The sound hung in the small space between them. The tension grew, as palpable as the pulsing music. She turned her head away sharply to watch the swaying dancers.

When the tempo shifted, his touch stayed light, but she felt the tautness of back muscle straining against his cotton shirt where her hand rested. Instinctively, she glanced up and caught a remoteness drift over his face, something close to distaste. He glanced down and smiled. Maybe she'd imagined it.

They finished the dance, sat out a line dance, threaded their way through the tightly packed sweaty bodies for another slow one, then sat out two more. The volume steadily rose to a football stadium roar. It echoed off the tin roof, drowning out opportunities for conversation.

Cigarette smoke mingled with the hot air in the room sucking up the oxygen. Sam watched the band members lay their guitars and fiddles on chairs. They stumbled to the bar, as drunk as most of the people in the place.

Thorp leaned forward. "You mind leaving? I've about had it."

She nodded, relieved.

They stepped out into the hushed night, the back door shutting out the cacophony of heat and sound. An array of poor man's vehicles overflowed the parking lot, some rusted out sedans but the majority battered pick-ups. They'd been jammed helter-skelter into the small space as though abandoned by a gang of carjackers.

Faint laughter drifted out of the darkness behind them, interrupted by the tinkling of breaking glass. Sam studied the end-to-end vehicles, searching for her truck. "You park on the street?"

"Yeah."

"That was wise. Looks like most of these are stuck here till closing."

"My third visit. I'm learning. You blocked in?" he asked.

"No. I parked near the back exit. My neighbor's a regular. He taught me something about this place." She started toward the rear of the lot, but he reached out and caught her arm. They stood between two beat-up half-tons.

"I'll walk you to your truck."

"Okay, but it's too early for the drunks to be out yet."

"Let me be chivalrous. It'd make my mom happy."

They found her truck, wedged in on one side by a Bureau of Land Management truck, the other side flanked by a juniper. Squinting at the space, it looked like just enough room to squeeze by if she aimed straight.

"How about some coffee?" he asked. "The diner open?"

"Nope. Everything's closed this time of night,

except Porky's."

"You got any pie at your place?" He flashed a quick half-grin and her heart skipped. Was he flirting with her? God, how long had it been? Graham Rawlings never made the effort. His hefty ego determined it unnecessary.

She held up her watch to the light. "It's after midnight. Sure you want to drive that far out of your way?"

"Yeah. You're only about fifteen miles or so from Fernley, aren't you? My motel's five miles east so it's a snap. I'll follow you home to make sure you get there safely. Then beg some coffee for the road."

He helped her easily up onto the seat with a hand under an elbow. Her stomach fluttering, she pulled the door shut. The tension had followed them out here, but it felt less ominous and more sexual now, with an undercurrent of fear that flashed through her. Why the paranoia? The guy mentioned stopping by for coffee. That was all, for God's sake! He was a state highway engineer, not some stalker.

Thorp made a circling motion with his index finger, and she cracked the window.

"I'm driving the white NDOT truck."

"I'll meet you out front. I can promise better coffee at least than the diner. But no pie."

He stood there a moment before he nodded, then shoved his hands deep into his pockets and strode away.

She twisted her key in the ignition. It took three tries before the engine caught, followed by another two minutes of sitting in the dark to nurse it along.

Thud!

Something hit the top of her cab, vibrating the roof. She wrenched around in time to catch a flash of movement with her peripheral vision. Silhouetted briefly against her headlights was a man, dressed in black. He darted around her passenger side and disappeared behind her truck.

Her heart sped up, pounding in her ears. She fumbled with the gearshift and the engine stalled. It took four tries before her trembling fingers caught hold of the key and yanked at it.

Grrrrrr. Grrrrrr. At last, ragged but holding, the truck hummed to life.

Suddenly a bodiless, black-gloved hand reached inside the cab and seized hold of the steering wheel, wrenching it to the left.

One short scream escaped from her. She grabbed blindly for the gear again. Battling with the phantom arm, she shoved the gear stick into first and punched down the gas pedal. The truck bucked forward, stuttering along. *Thud!*

"Fuck!" The man's voice rang in her ear. She trod down on the gas pedal. The truck accelerated. It leapt forward and glanced off the juniper tree. She pushed harder at the arm this time, and he caught hold of her jacket collar and yanked hard.

Wham! Her face hit the window. Sharp pain stabbed at her cheek.

Desperate now, panting with fear, she caught hold of the crank and fought to raise the window.

She clawed at the fingers gripping her coat, digging her nails into soft leather. With another curse, he pulled back, his fingers barely clearing the window as it closed.

"Shit!" he snarled through the glass. Sam turned, catching the glimpse of a face that looked like an attack dog.

She stomped on the gas pedal. The truck jumped free of the tree and hit the curb with a thud. She met the street with a louder crash. After peeling around the corner, she headed for the bright lights.

Main Street.

Thorp's white truck sat idling quietly, his parking lights flashing.

She roared up to him, hit the brakes, and squealed to a stop.

Thorp leapt out of his Cherokee and raced across to her. He yanked open her door. "What the hell's going on?" he yelled.

She tumbled out into his arms. "God!"

He held tight, keeping her upright when she would have slid to the ground. "What's going on?" he shouted again.

"Someone tried to grab me. He tried to get in my truck!" The words burst from her like nonsense syllables. A second rush of adrenaline surged through her as she stumbled forward, clinging to Thorp.

"Are you hurt?

"No. I'm okay. Just freaked out."

He nudged her toward his truck. Boosting her up onto the seat, he took her chin in his fingers and turned her head. The cab light threw strange shadows on his face, and she drew back. He paused, staring down at her, then briefly reached out and touched her cheek.

"What happened to your face?" Joe asked.

"He grabbed my jacket. I think I hit the window."

Joe skimmed light fingers down her face, moved both hands to her shoulders and down her arms, searching for injuries. "Are you sure you're okay?"

"Yes. I'm all right. Really."

He leaned back but didn't move, watchful. "Okay. Stay here. I'm going back to take a look."

With a quick check around the empty street he shoved the door shut.

"Lock the door," he shouted through the glass and was gone.

She sat staring straight ahead. Who'd attacked her? A drunk? Someone she knew? Who? She squeezed her eyes shut and forced herself to lean back. It was cold inside the truck. It smelled of leather and smoke.

A mile of useless thoughts passed through her head before Thorp rounded the corner of the building and jogged back to her.

"Open up."

It took her two tries to work the lock. "Did you find him?"

"No. Nothing." His frowned down at her. "What exactly happened?"

"I was warming up my truck. I heard a loud bang, like something hitting the cab. I put the truck into gear and started to drive off but my window was down. He reached inside and yanked at the steering wheel. I tried to drive away, but I hit the tree. When I started winding up the window, he caught hold of my jacket and pulled. That's when I hit the window."

"Did you get a look at him?"

"No, not really. It was too dark." She swallowed.

"Did he say anything?"

"I think he said 'shit' when I rolled the window up on his arm. That's all."

"Good job. Stay here, Sam."

"No, Joe wait—"

Thorp ignored her protests as he trotted over to her truck. He did a slow circuit of it before he opened the driver's side door. At last he came back, cell phone in hand.

"What are you doing?"

"Calling the sheriff to report this."

"I'd rather you didn't. I'm okay. The guy was probably just drunk."

"He attacked you. He could do it to someone else. Let me put in a quick call and get someone out here."

She shook her head. "No, please. Let's just go. I'm tired. I don't want to hang around another hour to answer questions. I just want to go home."

Avoiding the police for twelve years had been easy. She made sure she stayed away from trouble. There was no point inviting it into her life now.

He looked ready to argue, but gave it up. "Can you drive?"

"Yeah. I'll manage."

"I'll follow. Pull over if you feel like you can't make it."

Thorp helped her to her truck. She started it up as he stepped back slowly. He nodded once, unsmiling, but seemed satisfied she could drive.

She accelerated cautiously, feeling the headlights of his truck at her back. Taking big gulps of cold air, her pulse slowed and grew steady.

****

Roper stayed fifty yards behind as she accelerated and headed down the empty road. A mile outside of Benton, he pulled out his cell phone and stabbed in a number.

"Buchanan, Roper here."

"Yeah, Joe? What's up?"

"I'm heading south out of Benton behind Catherine Bell. Someone jumped her in the parking lot of Porky's, the bar here in Benton."

"She okay?"

"Yeah, just shook up."

"Did she make the guy?"

"If she did, she ain't telling me. Claims she didn't see his face. Where are her friends tonight?"

"Still hunkered down and out of sight in Oakland. Word is they're getting ready to move out soon. Want me to send someone out to Benton?"

"No, don't bother. It's too late. The guy's long gone. I didn't try too hard to find him since I can't afford to break cover right now. You might as well put in a call to the sheriff's office here, though. Just report it as a possible assault. Don't encourage them to investigate but make sure there's a record of it on file. I'm following her out to her place right now. I'll get back to you in an hour."

Her broken taillight made it easy to follow her Chevy as it bounced along ahead of him on the dirt road.

Roper relaxed in the dark, letting his mind wander. He thought about Joey. One night four years ago when a stakeout got boring, his partner and he got a little too friendly. Not ready to be a mother, Angie Petroski paused only long enough to give birth and drop the baby off on his doorstep before heading for LA, a promotion, and a new partner.

Joey, the perfect product of his own not so perfect rules of good conduct. Roper, the stud, ready to jump in at the first sign of an unhappy woman. He'd comfort her, to hell with his ethics. But that time they'd produced Joey, the best thing in his life.

He steeled himself against the rising impulse to offer comfort again. Catherine Bell had been taking care of herself for twelve years. She might look fragile tonight, but she didn't need him for reassurance, especially in her bed. He was going to her house for one reason, to look for evidence.

Chapter Six

A few scattered houses illuminated the dark drive through the desert. It was a thirty-minute trip to her place.

Roper sat hunched over the wheel, loneliness his companion. He missed home. He especially missed his son.

He followed her taillight around a butte and the house came into view. It was no surprise to him. He'd spent four days perched on the hill behind it, freezing his butt off. He'd passed the dreary hours puffing on stale cigarettes and rereading Catherine Bell's files, with periodic visits into nearby sagebrush to pee.

Even more ramshackle up close, her house fit his expectations. This was it then, after months of digging and days of maneuvering. A jolt of apprehension, like a straight shot of caffeine, pulled him from the drowsy lethargy of driving.

He pulled to a stop behind her truck. He shifted his shoulders to ease the tightness. Shit, he was as nervous as a new agent fresh from Quantico.

Sam didn't wait for him but loped up her path in that strange gait of hers. She paused on her front porch, holding onto her dog's collar until he joined her. "This is Dourcet. Dourcet, this is Joe."

"Hey, boy." Roper let the dog sniff his hand and then gave him a perfunctory pat. She turned and smiled, an invitation into her world. If the woman could read his mind, she'd toss him out like a mold-infested leftover in a New York minute.

While the exterior of her place was predictable, the interior surprised him. He was used to people on the run, their houses as rebellious as their lives, but she kept strict order here. The white kitchen displayed minimal adornment, except the small brown, stenciled figures marching along the borders of the cabinets. Two chairs faced each other on either side of a white table.

Roper turned from the kitchen and took a quick survey of the living room. He watched her move about, switching on a table lamp, kneeling beside a propane heater. An oval red and yellow woven rug dominated the room and warmed it. A drunken-looking rocking chair sat between the heater and a cold fireplace. Bunches of plants hung drying on hooks at one end of the room. It felt safe here, almost like home. Hell.

Sam looked up at him, and he spotted the blotch of red spread over one cheek. "Your face looks pretty swollen. You sure you're okay?"

"It stings a little but I'm fine."

She turned back to the heater, and he continued his study of the house. It offered few clues to her past or her present life; no photos, no personal trophies scattered about. Industrial shelving lined with books covered one wall flanking a desk with a computer. Green and yellow folders hung from one shelf. There were no loose papers, no clutter to be found. She managed her environment the way she'd managed to hide her former life, presenting a tidy façade.

Keeping his expression casually interested, he wandered about, cataloguing the layout. The corners of the room lurked in shadows, but the center of the room was wide space, too exposed, with too few places to hide, too damned dangerous for a thorough search and seize operation, especially with the dog on guard duty.

Roper stopped beside a yellow flower blooming from a prickly cactus, a bright orphan amidst faded herbs. "Well, there's no missing the fact that plants are your business."

She stood up from the heater and rubbed her palms on her jeans. The look on her face was that of a proud mother. "They do have a tendency to take over." She met his gaze with a smile that was almost shy. "Let's get you that coffee for the road."

It seemed like a good time to stop digging into her life, except it was his job. Maybe he was getting too old for this 'hide and seek' crap.

He followed her into the kitchen and pulled out a straight-backed chair. He sat down, resigned to plow on. "You said your aunt got you interested in plants. How did it turn into a business? Or was she already running one?"

"No. We started it together." A copper-bottomed kettle sat on the stove. She turned her back on him and picked up the matches. It took her three tries to get the fire going. "Those first few months when I moved in with my aunt, we were strangers. She'd just lost her husband." She lifted one shoulder in an odd gesture, like shaking off a bad memory.

"My aunt loved the desert. Plants became her solace. At first I was only mildly interested, but they turned out to be a way we could find a bond." She grabbed two mugs, juggled them like thoughts, and set them down on the counter. "Eventually, I got very interested. Now I love them as much as she did."

He sighed, his gut tightening. Hell. She'd just handed him over a piece of her private world and all he could do was file it away, ammunition for the future.

She ground the coffee with a small hand grinder, another sign of the bare basic life she lived. Her face remained composed, with a stillness he was beginning to recognize. He followed each movement, hypnotized by them.

"My aunt's husband was Paiute. Those plants she dug up were used by the tribe for hundreds of years. They're still used." She grinned.

"So you stayed on to keep her company?"

"In a way." She answered more cautiously now. "It was mutual. I needed a place to live, and I was happy to find something stable after a lot of years of being shuffled around."

"You moved a lot growing up?" He knew the answer; he knew almost everything about her childhood.

"Foster homes." She made a face. "Psychologists would have a field day with my history. I suppose I stayed here because I needed a constant in my life." She made a gesture toward the dark window. "You can't get much more constant than the desert."

"Did it give you stability?"

When the kettle hissed, she grabbed it and poured the coffee. The question seemed to hang between them, almost too personal. He wouldn't be surprised if she didn't answer.

"Yes, I got stability here and a lot more. I didn't know my aunt at all before I came here. But she turned out to be about the best thing in my life."

"How did you end up in foster care?"

"My mother disappeared when I was eleven."

She offered no further explanation, but he didn't need any. He already knew the story of her mother's disappearance. The woman dropped her two kids off at a stranger's house and never came back.

Sam pushed a mug toward him; the subject clearly closed.

The padded kitchen chair squeaked as he leaned back and eased his legs out in front of him. He pushed down his impatience. Two, maybe three days was all the time he had to feed her questions and set the scene for her life to unravel.

"Want to sit on the front porch?"

Hell, no! He'd freeze his balls off out there. He nodded and stood up slowly, yanking at the zipper of his jacket.

The wind had eased up but the air felt damp, not the kind of desert high country weather he expected. The unfamiliar smell of sage hung close to the ground. No acrid Las Vegas smog out here.

Neally settled herself on the stoop, the dog at her feet. Roper eased himself down, leaving three inches between his leg and hers. He clutched his mug with fingers already stiff from cold. "You expecting snow?"

"Yes. Is that a guess or did you hear the weather report?"

"Guess." He sipped at the coffee. It was strong enough to haul his brain cells upright on full alert. "So what about the guy who attacked you at Porky's?"

Her leg jerked, hitting his. "What about him?"

"Are we going to just ignore it happened? You sure you don't want to report the jerk?"

"I'm sure."

"Why's that?"

"Those kinds of things happen at bars, especially cowboy bars. It's one of the reasons I don't spend much time hanging out there."

"Just a bar incident, huh?" The faint light from the nearby window cast high relief on her face.

"Yes." She sounded final.

Roper sighed and gave up. "So you think it'll snow tonight?"

"No. Tomorrow, probably late."

Snowstorm. His eyes followed the swaying dance of a single light bulb on her shed as he rearranged his plans. Tomorrow. It had to be tomorrow, one day to get inside, another to do a thorough shakedown of the place.

He sat forward and studied her closer. The cheek looked swollen, even in dim light, but she looked less tense, as though darkness soothed her. She leaned back on an elbow, looking almost comfortable. She said nothing.

It was a relief to sit in silence with this woman. The women in his life tended to be talkative and lively, while he hated small talk. He let them talk while he tuned out. In the bedroom it was different. There, he had no problem providing the entertainment.

Her stillness surrounded him like a blanket, a cocoon against the biting wind blowing across her porch. If he hadn't known about her past, he'd have believed she was exactly the person she presented herself to be; an independent woman who chose to live out here because she loved the desert and the solitary life.

His groin stirred and he sat up. He pulled in his legs and hugged his knees. He'd done some distasteful things undercover, but never sex with a suspect. Who was he kidding taking the high moral road? From a man who'd had sex with his partner during a stakeout because she was bored.

Roper gulped down the last of the cold coffee. Time to get the hell out of here. "I've gotta be getting along. It's a bad idea for someone like me to be wandering around back roads in the middle of the desert at night."

He made no mention of seeing her again. Off stride and a little unsure was where he wanted to leave her, eager enough to let down her guard.

****

Roper drove slowly back to his motel. Things had gone pretty much as planned. Except for the incident in the parking lot. He rubbed at the dull pressure growing behind his eyes. He still felt tense, despite the success of the evening.

His phone vibrated and he yanked it out. Buchanan. "Roper."

"Joe. Our agents are still sitting on our friends holed up at that motel in Oakland. Nothing there and no one's checked out when we weren't looking. Unless we missed one of the perps along the way, it wasn't our boys who went after your lady there."

"Shit! It can't be just a coincidence."

"What do you need from this end?"

"Have our man there sit on them and keep updating you. If anyone moves out and comes within range of our target, let me know."

"Will do." Buchanan paused. "How'd it go tonight with her? Anything new?"

"Not much. I did get inside her place for an hour. No time alone for a search. It all looks as innocent as a newborn babe. She's got no personal items hanging around in view, nothing to connect her with Catherine Bell."

"Watch your back. Something about that parking lot attack feels weird. Could it be she set you up with that?"

"Only if she banged her head against the glass herself, and I can't see her doing that, especially since it seemed to scare the shit out of her. I'd bet my left testicle she hasn't made me, but I'll stay alert."

Twelve years ago the Consortium had been nothing more than a fringe group of the ELF, the Earth Liberation Front. With El Dorado National Forest, the group tried out their fledgling wings by setting fire to a forestry cabin. Catherine Bell was the least consequential player on the team. An unexpected gas leak in the cabin had blown it sky high and the stupid kids had all split, leaving her behind.

"What's your next move, Joe?"

"Give her a day, then get inside her house for an extended visit." He didn't like it. Nothing about her life matched up as well as he needed it to; her place was too tidy, her behavior too straightforward for someone with something to hide. It was a tight fit to picture her still involved in some way with eco-terrorists. But she lived only twenty miles from the Bureau of Land Management pens, and he'd put money on that being the place where the Consortium had something planned.

Roper switched phone hands and downshifted, squinting at the veil of black bordering the road. He unconsciously searched for stallions. "There's a snow storm heading this way. Tomorrow, she says."

"You're figuring on using that to get inside?"

"Yeah. Stranded by a storm is one hell of a grand excuse for making myself at home. I've gotta make it good, Jack. We're getting too close to our target date and we've got zip." One member of the group fled to Canada, one dead in a car wreck, five players out of eight still at large—and Catherine Bell.

"Take it easy with her, Joe. There's no point in antagonizing her, especially since she's probably not even a member any more."

"No problem, except with all the BLM chatter online and it being just down the road, she's got to be our link—our one and only at this point. I'm pulling into my motel. I'm bushed, Buchanan. Give me a ring in the morning with anything new. Did you get hold of the Washoe County Sheriff's office?"

"Yeah. They're checking around. They weren't too happy to have the Feds out here in their territory reporting on some crazy bar scene event without a single witness."

"Hell. Do the best you can with them and see if they get wind of any fights tonight."

"Get some rest, pal. I won't let the foxes get close

to your little chickie in her henhouse."

Roper grinned and pulled up to his motel door. Buchanan was okay, even if he was a stiff. Roper shut his vehicle up tight, grabbed his stuff and sprinted across the icy pavement to his room.

The motel heater was on high but the tinny wall unit was blowing out a continuous stream of cold. It felt like a meat locker in the place.

He tossed his laptop down and took up a spot in front of the heater. The drab scene was a fitting backdrop for the throbbing pain having a field day in his head now. The hell with this undercover crap.

Gritting his teeth, he fidgeted with the blower knobs but cold air kept coming on. Still in his jacket, he yanked back the faded chenille bedspread and threw himself down, easing back against the headboard. Shit. Sleep was what he needed.

Flipping open his phone, he studied his three messages: one from his mother and Joey. He checked the time and sighed. Too late to phone a three year old. Two calls from Jackie, two calls too many. She'd started checking up on him routinely in the past month. She was pushing for more time spent with her, and it was driving him crazy. By most standards, she was hot—a long legged, blond, always dressed to kill. She wasn't looking for commitment, but liked him, or rather, liked his expertise in the bedroom and liked the idea of having him around. Lately, he'd become slower in his performance, and she'd turned inventive, wooing him with her proficient mouth.

He was tired of making bad choices, tired of short-term relationships. He was just tired. He deleted both of Jackie's voice mails.

Reaching across the bed for his laptop, he balanced it on his legs and booted up. Eyes on the monitor, his mind played tricks on him, the mirage of Sam's face fading in and out.

He connected to Carnivore, the FBI's elite tracking satellite with its daily reports. The trace on Sam Neally's email had turned up two questionable messages of interest to the Bureau. The first one dated, September 10th, at 0900, he'd sent on to the Reno office for analysis.

"Suspect S. Neally email interception to Robert Mathias, birth date 10/31/59, Nebraska PI License #813410-B, expiration date 05/2010. No history of arrests, no ties with Consortium or other terrorist groups."

He scanned down the trace on Mathias, not sure what he was looking at. She'd forwarded the guy $500 last week. Who the hell was Robert Mathias?

The second message, sent to the lead player with the Consortium, had turned up ten days ago. Roper's eyes slid down the contents of her email: "You had your last $200. The well is dry. Leave me alone."

He read it over for the tenth time, frowning. Blackmail? Something to do with tonight's attack on her? The quicker he got inside her house and got things moving, the happier he'd be.

He logged into the National Crime Database and punched in 'Robert Mathias.' It was a hundred to one chance, with nothing on the guy, but he had to check. Who the fuck was he, anyway? Some plant lover who happened to be a private dick? And why was she wiring him big bucks?

Still no damned heat in the room. He'd probably wake up in the middle of the night in a sweat lodge, the heat suddenly deciding to work and going at it full force.

Roper blew on his hands and kept them moving over the keyboard. He had a couple of days left to get what he needed. The next few days should be interesting.

Chapter Seven

The sun's last hurrah rimmed the hill with gold. It flashed once and disappeared, leaving the desert a deep purple. In Nevada high country, nature liked sudden dramatic transitions, day to night, light to dark, heat to cold.

Sam stretched out on the hood of her truck and soaked up the lingering heat from the engine. Nature's changes might be daily dramas, but she was used to the predictable. In the past few months all that had changed. First, came the reappearance of the Consortium, with their surprising emails, leaving her uncertain what they wanted. Even worse, she'd been left with a vague sense of someone watching her.

With the discovery of her mother's body, the interpretation of the past as she knew it had been all wrong. If the past was false, what was real?

And then there was Joe Thorp. He'd wandered into her world, and what the heck did she do with him?

A coyote howled somewhere in the night, and Sam sat up to listen. She sat there, unmoving until the mournful sound faded away. All that was left was the whistling of wind through the sage.

Sam eased herself back against the windshield. The snow was still hours away, but tiny shards of ice began to fall, stinging her cheeks. The contrast between sleet on her face and the feel of engine warmth through her jeans was almost sensuous.

The first year she'd come to the desert, she felt

the constant threat of the miles of open space with no place to hide. But like the Wallace Steven's poem about "the mind of winter," she'd eventually found solace here in the loneliness. The smell and feel of it comforted her. Gradually, the fear faded and she began to trust the open spaces wedged between buttes. Unlike Colorado and California, where the mountains overran and suffocated everything, Nevada provided room to breathe.

Sam hugged her sheepskin jacket closer and pushed loose strands of blowing hair under her hood. Dourcet barked at something a long way off, followed by the sounds of scuffling. Damn. What was he up to?

A gust of wind shook the truck, rattling the loose crates in the bed. She rubbed her numb hands together and struggled to hold on to her single sheet of paper she'd been working on. More of an incidental poet than an avid one, the writing urge usually came on with change. Tonight it was the restlessness before the storm. The poem she'd written was for her mother.

She pushed the paper and pen into her pocket and slid off the hood.

"Dourcet! Let's go!"

Where was Joe Thorp tonight? Working with his emergency crew to get the roads ready for snow? His goodbye last night had been careless, giving her no sign he'd ever call again. It left a slightly dead feeling in the center of her chest, probably not a bad thing, all in all. She was a fledgling when it came to men. It was best to step slowly.

She frowned and searched the dark for the faint outline of her dog.

What was the big deal? A nice guy, better looking than most around here, but nothing to her. God, but he smelled good, the scent of laundered t-shirt mingling with the sweat and smoke of Porky's.

It quickened her pulse, and she wondered briefly if she should make a trip to Reno soon.

Woof woof!

"Dourcet!"

Sagebrush rustled below her, interspersed with successive *thunks*, like small stones tumbling down the hill. Her dog was moving fast, scuffling up the frozen earth toward her voice.

This was followed by quiet. Nothing, but the moan of the wind. Then a faint whimper, the sound her dog made when he was pleased; someone he knew.

"Hey! Sam. You up there?" The familiar voice rose up from below.

She couldn't suppress a quick grin. "Joe?"

"Yeah, it's me."

Dourcet barked twice, followed by more scrambling.

"Sorry if I startled you. My pick-up broke down." Thorp's voice was so close she could hear his heavy breathing. "Stupid thing to do. I think I hit something. I should know better than to drive off the road after dark."

"What were you doing out there?"

"Looking for you. I thought I'd drop by for a visit. I stopped at your place. When you didn't answer, I drove over to your neighbor's. What's his name? Charlie Lemon?" Thorp stood beside her now, nothing but a dark form. "He pointed me down the road with some vague instructions about where you might be."

"There are phones, you know. I gave you my number."

"I tried your cell. No answer."

"I don't have it on me out here. I get so few calls I usually don't take it with me on quick trips. Besides, who wants to be interrupted watching the sunset?"

"That's what your neighbor said."

"He knows me well." She spoke at his shadow, the wind picking up her voice and carrying it behind her. "You were lucky to find me. I was just getting ready to take off." She allowed herself one small sniff of him. Tonight it was leather jacket.

"Like I said, a stupid move on my part. I could easily have ended up wandering all night in these hills."

"Not likely. If you're wearing the same kind of clothes you had on last night, you'd be stretched out dead long before morning, probably under a foot of snow."

"Well, hell, I always was lucky." The truck creaked and dropped a few inches, as if he'd propped himself against it. "So no cell on you, right? How was I supposed to call?"

"Earlier. Or later. Like I said, I don't like interrupting the sunset."

"What happens if you have an emergency?"

"I make sure I don't have them. The signal's undependable, anyway, in these mountains."

To stay anonymous but meet her business needs, she'd devised a complicated, meandering procession of ghost addresses, dead-ending at a post office box in Fernley, Nevada. But staying available to her sister had been a necessity. The disposable cell phone was darned inconvenient as it was, buying a new one every three months.

Sam shoved her hands into her pockets. "Dourcet. Come!" He scampered over, panting, apparently pleased as hell to have a visitor, a rarity. What she really needed was an animal who felt less like man's best friend, maybe a Doberman or a pit bull.

"You're a fine dog, aren't you? Who cares if you can't tell the good guys from the bad." Thorp made a slight sound and Sam turned. "Sorry, I didn't mean you." She reached down and scratched behind Dourcet's ears.

"When did you call me?"

"About an hour ago." He laughed. "My phone's in my truck—dead. I was recharging it when I crashed into that boulder or whatever the hell it was."

His laugh had a nice, easy sound to it, not forced. He was the kind of guy who didn't push the conversation toward his own agenda and didn't wear her out with talk about himself.

"How about a lift to your place so I can use your phone?"

"Sure. But I can't guarantee you'll find anyone willing to come out here and fix your truck tonight."

"I was thinking of phoning NDOT. They should be around."

She shrugged. "You know better than me, but I'd have bet all available personnel are on snow emergency tonight."

"You're probably right, but it can't hurt to give it a try. I was thinking along the lines of finding a tow, maybe. Bad idea?"

"Sounds even more unlikely to me. The only tow service close by is in Fernley. There's no service in Benton or Wadsworth. And with the weather closing in fast, you might have trouble talking someone into making a trip out here ahead of the snow."

"Got any other ideas?"

"I don't suppose you have a friend who'd be willing to risk coming out to get you?"

"Nope. I barely know the guys at the highway garage." He paused. "It would be pretty inconsiderate of me to ask you to give me a lift back to my motel and risk you getting caught in the storm."

"I wouldn't mind if I had a dependable vehicle, but I don't think it's a good bet with my run-down truck."

"How big a storm are we talking here?"

"Oh, probably up to a few feet in the first eight hours, then it depends on the wind. Maybe a couple of more feet after that if the front hits us direct. It'll take another day before things get moving again. All in all, we're looking at snowbound for two or three days." The sleet had turned to soft snow. Sam turned her face up and felt the first velvet flakes hit her cheeks. She pulled her coat tighter around her. "It's started snowing. Let's go back to my place. If worst comes to worst, you can always bunk on my couch."

She didn't wait for a reply but edged past him around to the driver's side. "Dourcet! Come!"

Thorp pulled open the passenger side and slid in. He'd dressed for Las Vegas's weather again, not the desert, in lightweight bomber jacket and worn jeans.

"At least you're wearing boots tonight."

He grunted. "Yeah, I'm freezing my butt off, but my feet are warm."

****

The gloom of the porch encircled them like a coffin, the only relief coming from a single dim light shining out one window. Her back to him, Sam fumbled with the key and shoved the door open. She took a step inside and stopped short. The dog followed her in but halted as well. He let out a low keening sound that sent a shudder through Roper's body.

Sam stumbled back against him as a strong whiff of gas rushed past his nostrils.

"Let's get out if here!" he yelled, catching hold of her from behind and lunging backwards. The two of them fell off the porch, landing in a heap in the sagebrush.

"Let go!" She fought him hard, kicking at his legs, and it took an effort to catch her under her arms and shove her upright.

"Let's get to your truck and get the hell away from here!"

"Dourcet! Back!"

The dog danced about on the porch, whimpering, probably confused whether to attack Roper or lick him.

Sam leapt up on her steps, grabbed hold of the dog's collar and began dragging him toward the road with Roper at her heels.

The entire comedy skit took all of a minute that seemed like ten. They jumped inside her cab; she did a quick 180 turn and jammed down the accelerator. The snow was accumulating now, almost an inch deep in places. It swirled about them as they roared down the road away from danger.

She drove only a hundred yards before pulling to a stop.

"Got a flashlight?" he asked.

She opened the glove box, grabbed a large commercial lamp, and passed it to him.

"I'm going back to see if I can get the windows open. Where's the gas coming from?"

"LPG. Propane runs my stove and is my alternate heat source for the house. It's stored in the mud room, behind the kitchen. The pilot light on the stove must be out."

He leapt out before she could argue with him. "Stay here. If I'm not back in fifteen, head for town."

"I'm going with you."

"No! Stay the fuck here! The dog will follow you, and all hell will break loose if he tries to get inside!"

He didn't bother to argue further but took off running. The house sat waiting, a ticking bomb ready to blow.

Sprinting full out now, Roper made a quick circuit around back and stopped at a large tank nestled against the wall. He flashed the light over it, found the off knob and yanked at it. It took three tries to get it closed.

Startled, he turned at the sound of heavy breathing behind him. "I told you to stay put."

"I'm going in." Ignoring him, she turned and disappeared around the front.

Roper followed, skidding around the corner. The porch was already covered in a thin coat of snow, turning it into an ice rink. Sucking in a lungful of oxygen, he sprinted inside.

She moved quickly from stove to refrigerator to heater, flipping knobs. The smell of gas already seemed to be dissipating.

"All the burners on the stove were turned on full," she gasped. He flashed the light on her face in the dark. She looked scared.

"We need to get some windows open and get out of here until more of this gas clears."

"All right."

They stormed the house as a team, yanking at windows, inviting in heavy gusts of snow driving sideways.

The cold smell of winter mixed with juniper quickly turned the air sweet.

At last, with every window wide open, they headed for her yard. Pausing at the gate, they turned simultaneously to stare at her house.

After checking her face, he began herding her silently back down the road, kicking at the growing mounds of snow as he went.

The truck was almost invisible through the white. Dourcet's wild barking could be heard fifty yards away.

"Come on! Let's get into the truck and get some heat going." Reaching the driver's side, Sam pushed the dog aside and climbed in. Roper went around and got in himself. It took three times to get the engine going.

They sat without speaking. Their hands

outstretched, they waited for the heater to turn warm and then hot. The dog sat between them, silent.

"God." She said at last, the word almost a curse.

"What the hell happened?"

"I don't know. I'd never leave all the burners on full throttle."

He frowned down at her. "So someone else did this?"

"I don't know."

Dourcet whined quietly, and she leaned over to shush him. "It's okay, boy. We'll get back home soon."

"Let's head over there now."

She steered carefully down the road, the snow deeper. With each swipe, the windshield wipers left small clear patches that disappeared almost immediately. Visibility was a foot in front of them. She steered the truck up beside the shed.

Like survivors from a shipwreck, the three of them climbed out and trudged up her path. Only Dourcet seemed happy to be home now.

Roper followed her inside, sniffing the air. His skin prickled, making the hairs on the back of his neck stand up. What the fuck had happened here?

They moved from room to room, shutting windows against blowing snow, then flipping switches to flood the place with light. The temperature inside the house was only a little warmer than outside.

Roper studied the ground as he went, searching for signs of something or someone out of place. He patted at his jacket pocket, his Glock, a comfort tonight.

They returned to the living room where papers and plants lay scattered about on the floor.

He glanced around. "This mess could be from the wind or from a break-in."

She shrugged and slowly began gathering things up. He saw her hands tremble as she set some tiny bunches of plants to one side.

They worked together, picking up papers and stacking them beside her computer. She took infinitely more care with her herbs, laying them out like injured birds on a low table.

"Any idea why someone would break in?"

"No." She answered without looking up at him. "People don't do that on the Reservation. We all know each other."

He watched her straightening things, wondering what kind of woman she'd become alone out here who didn't scream in fear when someone broke into her home. Not the sort of female he spent time with. He felt more removed from her than ever, yet with a sense of admiration he'd never have believed four days ago when he'd stalked her through the grocery store.

She looked up suddenly, as if sensing his thoughts, her face unreadable. "Can you check the mudroom and see if everything's all right there?"

Roper opened the little red door off the kitchen. He fumbled along the wall until he found the switch. Two walls were lined with neatly stacked boxes; another wall had a sink and small generator. Pieces of broken glass lay below a single window on the far wall. Blowing snow had coated the glass and left a three-foot swatch of white on the floor in front of it.

"The window's broken in here," he yelled. She came through the door and watched as he felt about the windowsill. "It's unlocked. You usually lock it?"

"Yeah, especially this time of year."

"Let's get this window boarded up now, and we can talk about what happened later. Got any planks around I can use?"

"I'll get some."

She came back with a few thin sheets of plywood

and a hammer.

"I'll get some dinner going," she said, and went out without looking at him.

Roper finished up quickly and joined her in the kitchen. He studied her as she worked at the counter. The swelling over her cheek had gone down, leaving a blue-black splotch that cut diagonally across her cheek.

"You're not going to report this one to the sheriff either, are you?"

"What do you mean, either?"

"The parking lot attack, now this."

She shrugged. "Not tonight at least. We've got a big snow storm on the way. Who'd care?" She broke eggs into a bowl, her movements precise. "The county sheriff's office doesn't have much jurisdiction over here. I'll call Charlie in a bit and see if he saw anyone hanging about."

"You're not a fan of the sheriff, I take it?"

She hesitated. "No. Like I said the other night, the people on the rez' and the sheriff's department don't have a lot to say to each other."

"Will you call the Bureau of Indian Affairs?"

"We don't have a BIA office here. Just the local Washoe Tribe Police. A man in Benton."

She beat the eggs with a whisk, pulling out bread from a dented red box decorated with white horses. "Eggs and toast okay?"

"Sure. What can I do?"

"Make some coffee."

"I can do that."

The eggs went into the pan, and Dourcet got fed while Roper worked on the coffee. He glanced over at her, the urge to call Buchanan pressing down on him.

"You seem pretty cool about all this."

"You think so?"

"Yeah. Especially since we're both sure someone

broke in here, right?"

She shifted out of her jacket and flung it across the chair back. "Leave it alone, Joe. I don't need you telling me what I already know."

Pushing the chair back, she sank down in it. "I'm sorry," she muttered, "That was rude. I've had a bad couple of weeks. Give me a minute to get myself together."

He pulled a chair up beside hers. Cautiously. and against his better judgment, he reached over and pushed a strand of hair away from her bruised face. "Take your time."

In an unexpected move, she leaned toward him, and he reached out, meeting her half way. He pressed her face against his bomber jacket. The instinct was automatic, the same sort of comfort he'd offer his son after a nightmare. He pulled her closer to give her some warmth. She smelled of herbs, a mixture of juniper and sage, like her house, but mingled with something sweeter. He took a deep breath, wondering when in the last hour, he'd begun the slow tumble down a hill of caring about her. It grew steeper by the minute, but below lay danger. Here he sat with his arms about a woman who had no clue the man in her house was her worst nightmare.

Chapter Eight

Charlie Lemon stepped inside the kitchen, hat in his hand. The man had a face like a desert lizard. His midnight black hair hung down to his waist over a worn sheepskin coat. Roper watched, curious, at Neally's exchanged greetings. Lemon towered a head and a half over her. She motioned him toward a chair but he shook his head, the briefest question crossing his face.

"Charlie, this is Joe Thorp. I think he stopped by your place earlier tonight. He works for NDOT and he's stranded." She offered no other explanation and Lemon didn't ask for one.

"So you had a break-in. Any damage done?" Lemon asked.

"A broken window out back. Nothing else. You didn't see anyone hanging around tonight, did you?"

'Nope. Except your friend here." The man made a motion with his hat toward Roper.

"The house was dark when I pulled up, no smell of gas and no sign of anyone." Roper stopped, feeling like a fool, needing to justify his activities. But this guy had the feel of a watchdog about him.

"Smell of gas?"

"The propane tank was running full out with all the burners open and no pilot light when we got back here. The house was full of gas."

That brought a frown from Lemon. "What do you need from me?" The question was not rhetorical. The man definitely was someone geared for action, not words.

"Nothing for now, Charlie. Thanks for stopping over to check on me, but with the storm coming, there's not much to be done."

"I'll take a look around and see if I spot any signs of intruders."

Roper cleared his throat. "I did a check around the house when we got back here, so there won't be much left of someone else's presence."

Lemon shrugged. "I'll take a gander anyway." He headed out the door, but turned back to Sam. "Need anything else before the storm hits?"

"Just some wood, but we'll manage that."

Lemon nodded once, stepped off the front porch, and disappeared into the snowstorm.

"I need to get that wood before the storm gets any worse."

"I'll get it. Where's it at?" he asked.

"In the shed. It goes under the tarp on the front porch. We'll need at least another day's worth." She held her hand out waist high for measure. "Sure you want to handle that in the dark?"

"Yeah. Earn my keep." He zipped up his jacket and pulled his collar around his face. "Hand me that flashlight, will you?" He turned back once more. "Your friend, Charlie, isn't going to think I'm some intruder and jump me, is he?"

"Don't worry. He's like Dourcet; he can see better in the dark than in daylight."

The wind came in gusts, playing tricks with the snow. It lay about him as gentle as a baby's blanket, then suddenly ripped across his face like a razor on dry skin.

Five feet away from the house, it disappeared from view. He moved cautiously, keeping his sight fixed on the faint bulb swinging crazily above the shed door.

The roar of the wind deafened him but the moment he stepped inside the shed, it turned into a low moan. Ten minutes of tossing logs out the door left him with a good three-foot high pile, already icing up with white.

Roper reached into his pocket for his cell, checked the time, and punched in Buchanan's number.

"What's up, Joe?"

"I'm at her place. Someone broke in tonight and left the damned house full of propane gas."

"No shit! You sure it wasn't an accident?"

"Not likely. But what do I know? I'm standing outside in a fucking snowstorm calling you." He shook a little pile of white off one foot, already numb. "We got the house aired out and I'm stuck here for the duration. What's the weather like there?"

"Expecting a foot, probably not as much as you'll get out there."

"Any likelihood that tonight's incident was connected to our perps?"

"No. We're on them like fleas on a dog. They're nowhere near you. Unless they've got friends doing work for them."

Roper glanced out the door, searching for a faint glow that might be her house. "See if you can get a hit on anything. This whole show is starting to stink, what with the attack on her the other night and now this. I'll get back later when I can. Don't initiate further contact with me."

"Right."

Roper flashed the light around the shed. It was filled with nothing but garden tools and boxes. "Just make sure our friends are sitting tight."

"We won't let any of them get to her, Roper. She's not gonna be out there much longer anyway."

"Yeah." He switched hands and stuck his colder one in his pocket. "I'll get back with you in a couple of hours. I'm going to ask her if I can use her computer. I'll forward anything I come up with."

"Will do. Watch yourself, Joe."

"I should finish this up and be ready for you in two days, three at the worst, if this damned snow keeps coming down."

Roper buried his phone deep inside an inner pocket, next to his Glock, and went back to tossing wood.

Fifteen minutes later, he'd secured the tarp over the porch stash and finished another circuit of her house. Nothing.

Stepping inside, he brushed snow off his jacket and bent down to remove his wet boots. The dog stood nearby, panting happily. Roper shifted out of his coat and hung it carefully with the gun pocket pressing against the wall.

"What's with all the wood? I thought there was a 'no-burning ordinance' in most Nevada counties."

"The tribe has separate laws. Inside the reservation, things are handled differently. The wood is a little hard to come by, but someone hauls it in each autumn from out west, and it gets shared by us." She rubbed her hands down her sweats, pulling the gray flannel tighter across her hips. "Get out of your wet things and I'll make a small fire. There's more coffee."

"I take it this means you're not tossing me out into the storm." Roper removed his damp socks. "You think it's worth my time to call a garage tonight and put in a request for a tow?"

She looked up, the bruised side of her face hidden in shadows. "Up to you. At least you'd be on their list, but I wouldn't get my hopes up you'll get a rescue any time in the next day. Not until it stops snowing and the roads get plowed. You might have more luck with the highway department, since they've got a vested interest in you."

"Yeah, well, I doubt they care much, except they

probably need every available hand right now. I should let them know where I am, though." He wandered over to her sink and washed his hands. "Can I borrow your phone?"

"It's sitting on the counter."

Keeping up the pretense of leaving his phone in the truck was damned inconvenient, but at least he'd get a look-see at her recent messages. "Mind if I make two quick calls? I need to check in with NDOT and put one in to my family."

"Where are they?"

"In Vegas. My mother and stepfather moved there last year from Phoenix. She's not used to the winters yet." He reached for the coffee pot and poured a cup.

"You're close to them?"

He glanced up at the yearning in her voice. "Yeah. I am."

She poured herself coffee and retreated to the back of the house. He heard a door shut quietly.

"Dispatch."

Roper left his callback number and punched in his mother's number. He got the answering machine, thank God. She had no qualms about calling him, even during a stakeout. "Hi, mom. I'm fine—I know you're worrying about the storm, but I'm safe. I'm out of cell reach for now so call Buchanan in case of emergency." Roper laid the red phone back on the counter.

The lights flickered and went off, leaving him in the company of a small lick of flames in the fireplace. Sam stepped out her door and headed for the red door.

"Need help with the generator?"

"No. I'm used to it."

She disappeared into the dark. Thirty seconds later, the generator rumbled, the lights flickered and then came alive. She came out wiping her hands.

"Nothing to worry about. Always happens in a storm. It's a little noisy, so I usually make due with an oil lamp and the firelight when the juice stops."

He knew she mostly survived off the grid. He'd tracked down no electric bills, but someone had rigged out the electricity, hooking up with her neighbor. A local company handled her propane deliveries. The only real utility bill he'd found had been basic phone service, still in her aunt's name, her Internet dial-up service.

"You're one cool character, Sam. I've never known a woman who could handle a generator. You did it in five seconds flat without a whine."

"I doubt if you know a woman who has a generator," she replied. "How was your family?"

"I left a message. Being a parent's a hard business sometimes. A kid's always a kid to his parents." He dropped the subject; there was no way he was discussing his own kid with her.

The fire threw tall shadows on the walls, gyrating dancers. She'd changed her clothes, shedding her loose sweats for some sort of leggings that clung, topped by a heavy sweater hanging mid thigh. The combination drew his gaze to her legs.

He grabbed up his wet socks and laid them out on the hearth, keeping his eyes on the fire. She moved about in the kitchen.

"What did the highway department say?"

"Didn't reach them either. I left them your number."

"You want dry socks? I've got some of my uncle's stashed somewhere. It's going to be a cold night. There's ice forming on my bedroom window."

"You seem pretty well prepared. Does your electricity die on you often?"

"It's unpredictable, but I can usually count on it happening in every storm. The line gets weighed down with snow. The generator works okay, just noisy."

Dourcet wandered over to Roper and nosed him in the back. "Hey, dog. What's up?"

"He's happy to see a new face around here."

"I set your cell back on the counter. Great phone. Haven't seen one like it before." He'd seen a shit load of them, disposable, impossible to trace, every perp's favorite toy.

"It works fine for my purposes. I don't need anything fancier. Believe it or not, my life's normally quiet, despite the two recent incidents."

"I can see how quiet it could be out here on your own. I'm sorry I brought you more complications by getting stranded."

"You're not much of a problem. As it turned out, you're actually reassuring to have around tonight, what with the break-in. That's why Charlie left without a protest. He didn't feel like he'd have to keep watch on me."

"I suppose I can look threatening if needed.

"No worry. I doubt whoever broke in will be hanging around in this weather."

He wandered over to the couch. "Is this my bed for the night?"

"Yeah. I'm afraid it isn't too comfortable, but I don't have another choice for you. It looks a little short."

"It'll do, or the floor in a pinch, if you have an extra blanket for padding."

"You won't like the floor, once the fire burns down. This place is drafty. You're going to need the couch and plenty of blankets."

Hell, yes. Cold air circled about his bare ankles. "Just as long as I don't wake up covered in snow."

"Nope, I promise you that but I hope you don't mind cold feet."

"Huh?"

"Sticking off the end."

"Don't worry about it." He had other things on his mind tonight besides sleep, cold feet the least of them. Drifts had started piling up against the windows; there was no way she'd kick him out now.

She made another trip down the hall and came back with arms loaded down with bedding. She moved to the couch, and he got a whiff of that sweet sage again. Uninvited desire slammed into him and left his knees a little weak. Fuck. He could do this. Just keep focused on his plans and ignore his body.

She held out the blankets. "Here. These should do. Want a cup of cocoa to give you a push to sleep?"

"Sure, if you're fixing."

Dourcet trailed her into the kitchen. Like a parade, Roper followed.

The wind had died down and she'd switched off the generator, leaving them surrounded by silence. They sat side by side in front of the fireplace, sipping cocoa companionably. Seduced by the sudden stillness, his anxiety moved to the back burner.

As he sipped, he searched for entry points into her personal history, ready to find the lies embedded in her story. "I think I'm starting to get the appeal of living out here."

"Really? Wait a few hours 'til the storm is howling so loud your ears are ringing, you'll think we've been struck by an avalanche." She grinned. "Let's see how appealing it is then."

"Well the sense of privacy out here is a treat. My house in Vegas sits so close to my neighbors, I can reach out and touch their shrubs. And the houses are so alike, I have trouble finding mine." In the moment, he could almost picture himself living this way, in a place quiet enough to think, with no traffic jam every time he went out to buy milk.

"I do have neighbors, you know, besides Charlie. There are ten ranches within fifteen miles of me, Benton's close, and I can make Reno in thirty minutes in good weather."

"What really made you move out here, Sam? Aside from your aunt needing you. You must have had other reasons. Something drives most of us to live close together, since the majority of Americans choose crowded cities. Or suburbs. Not a lot of us put thirty miles between ourselves and the masses."

"I like being able to see the sky. It keeps me humble."

"You're looking to be humbled?"

"I think it's good for me. But who knows why we make the choices we make? I can't give you a definite answer. It wasn't something I planned as a kid, you know. I don't believe I ever sat around speculating on where I was going to live when I grew up." She cradled her cocoa with both hands, like a child. "What about you? Did you dream of being a highway engineer?"

"Nope. All I can remember is wanting to play football with the Chargers."

"The Chargers? I thought you grew up in Phoenix."

Pay attention, Roper. "When I was a kid, there was no Phoenix club. The closest team was in San Diego." He hoped to hell he was right. "You follow pro ball?"

"Some, but not seriously."

"Most kids have some kind of dream for the future. You're telling me you didn't?"

"All I can remember is waiting to grow up and get out on my own." Her words had a certain amount of lightness about them, belied by her face. She looked stoic, but something close to hopelessness dulled her eyes.

He'd grown up with people who always loved him, while she'd spent her childhood circulating through the revolving door of foster care. He could only guess at what sort of a dent that put into someone's dreams. Her profile fit every perpetrator he'd met—unwanted, probably abused, turning her back on society.

He studied the shadows on her face. She was the worst kind of woman for him; strong on the outside, with brief glimpses of a shy child dancing in her smile, dragging out all his protective instincts.

"Any sisters or brothers?" He watched her shift about with that question.

"A sister. She lives back East. We don't see much of each other."

He knew everything there was to know about her sister as well. They'd watched her closely those first few years, after the Consortium made front-page news. But gradually, with no surprises turning up, and no clues, the Bureau eased back the watch on Mary Beth.

The sister didn't live back east, though. She worked as a nurse in Chicago and lived in a north suburb. Her life looked normal; no suspicious friends, no record of illegal activities in her past, and no links to The Consortium. Clean as a newborn baby.

"Tough not having family close. No one else?" He held his breath, wondering if he'd stepped too far over the line into interrogation.

"No. No one. It's hard to make friends in foster care. I went to college for a couple of years, back east, but I've lost contact with them. Just my sister. What about you? Any other close family?"

She'd taken a sharp left, away from something—college and the Berkeley crowd. He was getting too close.

"My stepfather, we're pretty close." He sailed the ball back into her court. "With your aunt gone, you don't feel a need for friends or family?"

"Whoa. I didn't say that. I have friends, you know. In Reno. And Charlie."

"Charlie's a full-blooded Paiute?"

"Yeah. He's my work back-up when I need him and a great neighbor. Probably the most straightforward person I've ever known. I'd trust him with my life."

He needed to have a longer conversation with Charlie Lemon, but it could wait.

The small fire burned low, losing the battle with the cold air creeping into the room. Roper stood up and wandered over to the front window. The snow had abated, but the wind had picked up once more. He watched the woodshed light boogie back and forth.

Rrrinnngg! It echoed off the walls like a gunshot. Sam leapt to her feet and reached for the phone.

"Hello?"

Roper turned, watching her.

"Hello?" She didn't speak, but snapped the phone shut.

"Who was it?"

"I don't know. A heavy breather." She smiled briefly but her hands trembled as she tossed the phone on the table. "I turned it off. I'll take a risk no one will try reaching us tonight."

"Do you have caller ID on that phone?"

"No."

"Like I said before, you're a pretty cool character, Neally. I think you've got a lot of guts."

"Let's forget it."

Roper turned back and studied the world outside for movement; nothing but blowing snow.

She came up behind him, and he held his breath, not turning. That scent again.

"It's going to be a long couple of days." She spoke aloud the words he'd just been thinking. "You're going to get a taste of why you'll be happy to be heading south in a few weeks."

He grunted. "I don't have to be convinced. You've probably noticed I lack the basic skills for cold weather. Lucky for me, most of my outside work gets done in the summertime."

She turned her head to look at him and the warmth of her breath grazed his cheek. Standing in deep shadow, a sense of expectancy crept over him and he waited.

Did she feel the tension? In the normal world, stranded with an attractive woman, he'd have made a move by now. Well, not the hell this time. His body might be eager, but the warning bells going off in his head rang loud and clear. He didn't intend to go where his body wanted to lead him tonight. He had things to do with little time to check out her place and get into position.

He kept his gaze fixed out at the night. Whatever her relationship to the Consortium was now, the past cast a long shadow over her present life. People didn't change their beliefs like changing clothes. They kept them around, feeding salt into wounds that they refused to let heal. Every idealist he'd ever met was an expert at making sure his beliefs were plausible and his actions justifiable.

There were plenty of fools on his side as well, blind followers of the party line. The only difference was the justice side of the fence was about controlling rather than disrupting; probably not so dangerous to the world. Or so it seemed.

The electricity flickered and came back on, throwing light over his desire and deflating it like a burst balloon. As though reading his mind, she moved away quickly, leaving him standing at the window. His next move would come later, when she slept.

****

Sam pointed Thorp toward the small half bath in the hall and made a final check of doors and windows, her heart slamming in her chest. What had just happened? In another minute, she'd have made a fool of herself and invited him into her bed. But the moment had died a sudden death.

The electricity stayed on, and she moved about the house flipping off light switches. She banked the fire, gave Dourcet a pat, and shut off the last lonely kitchen light over the sink. The desperate wind began another attack on the house, wailing in frustration at the walls.

With a last glance around, she limped toward her room. Three steps down the dark hall, she ran into a wall of warm skin. Dressed only in his jeans, steam spilled out behind him and circled his wet head. He had a towel around his neck, leaving his chest bare.

Dressed, he deserved a second glance. But clothes were deceiving and without them, he was something else. His body looked hard-packed, his well-defined muscles sprinkled with a dark mat of hair over impressive pecs.

"Goodnight," she whispered. Sidestepping him, she fled to her room, not waiting for a response.

Hell.

She undressed slowly, standing in front of her mirror, shedding one item at a time. The muted pink light from her bed lamp threw her into stark relief. She liked the way she looked; the utilitarian nature of her body suited her, except her leg, a constant reminder of the single night that had sentenced her to this life.

Until two weeks ago, it had seemed perfectly plausible to blame her choices at eighteen on her childhood. She'd even managed to ignore the fact that her sister had grown up balanced and lived a normal life. What could she blame her failures on now? Was something from the past, true or not, really a justification for bad choices? Or was it just an accidental wrong turn in the road? She wished she could believe it, but that was too easy. She'd made the decision that sentenced her to a twelve-year dead end.

She closed her eyes and took in a shaky breath. The sudden discovery of her mother's body, the attack in the parking lot, the gas leak tonight. All these threats to the life she knew.

And then there was Joe Thorp and his grin.

The jagged scar on her leg throbbed, and she rubbed at it mindlessly.

She pulled back the shower curtain and turned the knob, watching the small bathroom fill up with steam. Flinging off her robe, she stepped into the tiny stall. Water plastered down her hair and over her. In five minutes it ran cold and forced her out.

Toweling off quickly, she pulled on a nightshirt. She wiped a small spot in one corner of the fogged mirror and stared at herself. Her face looked untouched, the pain in her life never having put in an appearance. Even with the weird black hair, it always surprised her that distrust had never made itself at home on her face. She grimaced into the mirror.

Joe Thorp. She wanted him, and she knew he wanted her. She could see it in his eyes and read it in his body, despite his casual words. The opportunity was here, lying out on her couch, a guy who was sexy as hell. Stranded together for however many days, why pass up the opportunity? Why not take it?

Sam slapped off the light, scurried across the cold floor and slipped beneath the covers to curl up in a ball. She'd let this one play out and see where it led.

Chapter Nine

Roper lay with his feet dangling over the end of the couch. Ignoring the scratchy blanket, he kept himself as still as a mummy and waited for quiet to settle over the house. The wailing wind pierced his thoughts like darts to his brain.

The biggest problem was electricity to boot up her computer. If the power went down again, he was fucked. And then there was Dourcet, snoring at his feet; not much of a watchdog. Did she actually have the damned animal for protection?

It was ten after two. About an hour and a half since she'd turned in. Time to get going before the electricity crapped out again. He shoved back the blanket and sat up. Pushing forty and sleeping on a couch was hell. His heart sped up with a rush of adrenaline.

Standing, he shifted his weight from one socked foot to the other, getting acclimated to the icy floor.

Dourcet whimpered softly, having a bad dream or fighting off an imaginary attacker in his sleep? Roper bent down and scratched behind an ear. "It's okay, ole boy."

The fire had died out in the past hour, but the room glowed with reflected white from outside. Roper stumbled over a chair in his path, swore silently, and paused to listen. Nothing but the wind.

He crept across the floor and felt for his jacket slung over a chair. He fumbled with cold fingers in one pocket for his flashlight, then the other, where his camera phone lay buried. He briefly ran a finger over his pistol, but let it lay.

He needed to put in a quick call to Buchanan. The small bathroom was the only safe room. He paused outside her bedroom. There was no sound. He shut the bathroom door silently and flicked a switch, blinking at the sudden brightness. At least the room was warmer.

"What you got, Joe?" Buchanan answered in a slurred voice.

"Sorry to wake you, buddy. I couldn't get free 'til now. I've got a trace for you from her cell phone. See what you can get on a call coming in around midnight. Could be one of our friends."

"Who'd she say it was?"

"No one. A heavy breather."

Roper sat down on the toilet seat. "Got anything new for me?"

Buchanan sighed, bad news. "Yeah. Ever come across the name Gab Weir?"

"Not that I can recall."

"He's an ELF member from Portland. He's got vague connections with the Consortium."

"Shit!"

"We picked him up in Susanville about an hour ago."

"What the hell's going on, Jack? How'd this guy slip past us?"

"The report came from a first office agent. It got lost in transit last week."

Roper slumped back against the toilet tank. Fuck it. A new agent. He should have expected that; the Reno office overflowed with them, just a barrel of suited up monkeys.

"Okay. See what you get from him and stay close with our marks. Leave anything urgent in my voice mail. I'm turning off my phone for the night. I'll call you tomorrow."

"Take it easy, Joe. Things are going well."

"Yeah. You're right. But, I've got a favor to ask. Can you put in a call to my mother tomorrow? Just pass on my love to her and Joey. Tell her I'm fine."

"Sure. Will do. Have fun in the snow."

Roper snapped his phone shut and switched off the light. He stepped out and stood next to Sam's door, listening.

One small push and the door gaped open an inch. She'd left a light on by the bed, and it cast a glow over her as she lay sprawled out on her back, her hands flung over her tousled hair. He stood transfixed. As though in response to his gaze, she moaned and rolled over before returning to the even breathing of deep sleep.

He jerked the door shut. He flicked on his small light and moved quickly down the hall to her computer. She had a Mac, ten times harder to hack into than a standard PC. If she'd set a password, it would slow him down too much to do anything tonight.

Above the monitor she'd hung a scaphoid-shaped tack board. He flashed his light over it, studying the calendar with the picture of Chicago and a note for next week, "Mary Beth's birthday." She'd tacked up notes in a neat row, and he studied them briefly. Orders. Nothing else. No time tonight to look closer. He'd recheck them in the morning in better light.

He booted up and waited. Bingo. No password protection. He was in. He clicked on her dial-up connection and held his breath. Click, click, click. Cursing the sound of the ping as it searched for a signal, he waited.

He had a ready story in his mind, if needed. Bored, unable to sleep, he decided to check his email. But nothing stirred inside the house.

He opened her mail and scanned down fifteen new messages, watching the addresses without opening them—nothing there. Would she notice the messages popped in? Probably not. Most people were unconscious as to when new mail popped into their inboxes.

Roper moved to Sent Mail. She was careless here, as well, three hundred plus messages she hadn't bothered to delete; some business stuff, a message here and there to her sister. The familiar names of Consortium members popped out at him three times. He read each one and moved on. There was nothing the Bureau hadn't already intercepted, a shit load of wasted time.

He checked his watch. He'd been at it fifteen minutes. The wind cried louder, a freight train hauling ass through open country.

Finally, he sat back, rubbing his T-shirted arms. The room was freezing. Just a couple of more things to do and he'd call it a night. He logged off her email and did a quick run through recently opened files. He flipped open his camera phone, clicked away at her monitor and hit the send button.

Her browser cache was full. Careless. The computer screen flickered and went dead. Hell! The electricity had wimped out again. Roper stared briefly at the dark screen, punched blindly at the off button and stumbled back to his couch.

No time to hide his phone and flashlight, he buried them under the blanket as something creaked in the hall. Shit!

Dourcet whimpered, rose and headed toward the sound. Roper reached down and yanked up his blankets around his feet. Too damned close.

She moved silently, an apparition gliding into the living room. His breathing rasped loudly in his ears, and he willed himself to slow it down. Damn. He'd wasted too much time and gotten nothing.

She moved to a window, turned, and looked over at him.

"What's up?" he asked, sitting up slowly.

"The electricity shut down again. You okay? Warm enough?"

"I'm good."

"Come on, boy. Let's make it a quick trip, okay?" The dog trotted toward the door, knowing where he was going.

Roper reluctantly pushed back his covers. "Want me to do it?"

"No. I'll do it." She was already at the door but turned and grinned back at him. "You'll freeze out there, City Boy."

She yanked on boots and a jacket, then pulled hard on the door. An icy blast rushed across the room at him like a Chicago Bears linebacker.

Dourcet trotted outside, as cool as a gentleman at a garden party, Sam glued to him like an appendage. The door slammed shut.

They dallied long enough for Roper to stumble to the window and watch her struggle to keep her balance. Blowing snow had left three foot high drifts on the front porch. She yanked at the dog's collar, interrupting his yapping at snowflakes and pushed him inside ahead of her.

"Atta boy!" She dropped her boots and dripping coat by the door. The dog trotted over to lie down by his bowl, staring at it gloomily. She grabbed up the familiar twenty-five pound sack he'd seen her tote out of the grocery store and filled the bowl.

"He always eats in the middle of the night?"

"Not usually," she shrugged. "But since I'm up. And besides, he didn't keep me waiting out there."

The hem of her blue nightshirt was damp. It clung to her knees, leaving a foot wide space between the hem and her thick socks. As if she was conscious of his gaze, she grabbed a couple of sticks of wood from the box and headed for the fireplace.

The house was a deep freeze now. Sam knelt down to stoke the fire, her skimpy shirt showing the outline of her body. Roper couldn't drag his gaze away from her kneeling there watching the fire grow. Heat gathered in his groin. Hell, his body knew what it wanted. The atmosphere in the room was as thick as fog.

Was he the only one feeling the sexual energy?

She'd left a sweater hanging over the back of a chair. She reached out and grabbed hold of it, pulling the bulky material over her head awkwardly.

"You staying up?" Roper asked at last.

"For a while. Restless. Probably the storm." She got up and went to the rocker, leaving Roper alone by the fire. The silence stretched out around him, and he held his palms out for meager warmth, staring at the flames.

Only Dourcet moved, wandering from the window and back to Sam, butting her with his nose. She reached out to stroke his ears.

Roper stepped from one cold foot to the other, torn between wanting her to respond to the tension in the room and wishing she'd go back to bed. He glanced over at her sitting huddled in the chair. "Storms bother you? I'd have thought you'd be immune, living out here so long."

She fingered her sweater absently. "Storm or not, I often get restless and roam around my house at night like everyone else when sleep escapes me."

"Guilty conscience?" The words popped out, too raw and direct for his purpose.

"Maybe. We all have things we regret in life, don't we?"

"Hell, yes. And I've had a lot more years than you to accumulate them."

"I'm almost thirty."

"I'm thirty-nine—avoiding forty." He answered without thinking, searching for a question to slice through her reserve while smoothing over his bluntness. "Regrets are from the past but what about the future? What do you see for yourself? Do you have dreams?" What kind of dreams could she have, a woman focused on keeping out of the way of the law?

"Are we back to that conversation?" She pressed her face into the dog's thick fur.

"No dreams, then?"

"Maybe, but I don't share them, except with my dog. He doesn't ask me philosophical questions at two a.m." She pulled her knees up under her, and he caught a flash of pale thigh. "I'll admit to a few dreams these days. But if you asked any drunk lying in a gutter in downtown Reno if he had dreams, he'd spout them off like he'd just won the lottery."

"Sounds pretty cynical."

"It does. But people don't ask those kinds of questions around here. It's not cool in a place where locals don't trust authority and are always checking over their shoulders to make sure Uncle Sam isn't creeping up from behind."

Roper waited for her to elaborate. She was going where he wanted her to.

"We don't stick our noses into each other's business." Ouch. The warning glance was softened with a slight smile.

"Sorry if I sound nosey. Just making conversation. It's called being friendly in California."

"I thought you were from Arizona?"

"I learned all my social skills at college. You might not believe it, but I used to be a party boy. And look at me now, a buttoned-down bureaucrat." He raked his fingers through his hair. She'd turned the conversation around again when he got too close. He didn't like it.

"As far as dreams go, you'd find mine pretty boring," she said. "Like finding a plant everyone thought was obsolete. What a thrill, huh?"

"So your business is a passion as well as a job?"

"I suppose so."

"I don't know much about desert plants. Why do people buy them?"

"They're Indian herbal remedies mostly. Some very old, even prehistoric, used by tribal people long before the white man arrived. Some of them you've probably heard of; stinging nettles—the Indians call it *kcvcbanyoa.*" She paused. "Sorry. I get carried away. Just interrupt me with a yawn when you want me to stop."

"I'm not bored. You know the Paiute language?"

"A few words. It's obsolete for the most part."

He stepped closer to the fire, his feet absorbing the little bit of heat permeating the tiles. The more she spoke, the more she distorted his picture of Catherine Bell. Why the hell couldn't life just turn out as he expected?

She stood up and pulled her sweater tighter around her. "It's getting too cold to sit around my struggling fire."

He glanced at the small clock sitting beside her computer. "And too late. It's heading toward three a.m."

The wind howled about the house like a cry for help. Roper followed Sam into the kitchen, watching her check the heater. "So you've got the propane and the generator. Have you ever had them both go out?"

"Yes. Once. It's scary but not really dangerous. We have a lot of miles between us, but the neighbors watch out for each other. Other than the weather, there are few real dangers out here."

"You don't consider someone breaking into your house," he paused, "or some crazy cowboy attacking you in the parking lot, real dangers?"

She stared at him. "Those are real, but it's a waste of energy to sit around and worry about them tonight."

"You're right. Hell, I'm the last one to comment

on how someone runs her life."

"I'd have pegged you as a guy who's got life pretty well handled."

"Everyone's got something that nags and won't let go."

"What's yours?"

"Well, for one thing, I'm divorced."

"But you've got a great family. Your mom sounds wonderful."

"You said your mom disappeared when you were a kid. Did you know your dad?" he asked.

"I never knew him. Is your dad around?"

Roper shook his head slowly, conscious of that lingering sense of loss even after thirty years. "He died when I was a kid. I don't remember much about him, except he was a good father, a kind man. I do have it made with my step-dad. Right now they're living at my place in Vegas."

"Sounds like you had a great childhood. It shows."

"How's that?"

"Well balanced, no obvious hang-ups. Most people with solid families turn out to be pretty good adults."

"Yeah, well things aren't always what they seem." He shifted his gaze from hers. "If I look like I'm doing okay, you'd have to give the credit to my mom." And her good son was about to destroy the life of a woman who'd had the worst of childhoods. "Sounds like you had a rough time, but you seem like you're doing okay now."

"Thank God for my aunt, and a few good friends." She smiled. "And my dog. How long did you say you've lived in Nevada?"

"About six months." Las Vegas had been his home for more than six years.

"You like it?"

"Yeah. Enough to get my mom and step-dad to

move up." He stifled a yawn. "Sorry, I guess I need some sleep."

"You're right." Her smile was almost shy. "Goodnight, Joe."

Through the confinement of the storm, they'd established an unexpected bond tonight. He watched her disappear down the dark hallway, the sense of intimacy tugging at him uncomfortably.

****

Sam leaned against the headboard and thought about Thorp. Hoarfrost coated the window, leaving the room feeling colder than usual. Her bedside clock said three fifteen a.m. She'd shut the bedroom door tight, shutting out all temptation as well as any residual heat from the fire.

She sighed and slid deeper under her comforter. Distaste made her squirm. The only sex she'd had in the past twelve years had been with Graham Rawlings, thrusting into her with syncopated grunts, accompanied by the squeak of the mattress. A slight flurry in her chest, a quick spasm or two and that was it, the grand finale. His response would be as fast—a short gasp, a quick pat on her rear, and he'd hop out of bed. With a silent sigh, she'd always turn away, relieved she didn't have to take him home.

But Joe Thorp was another story, larger-than-life in her mind, she pictured him looming over her in the dark. It wasn't hard to imagine, especially after a glimpse of his bare-chest. She could almost see that affable grin of his transform into a look of desire.

She sighed again and shifted about. She wanted him and her body was not going to be stopped. It was only a matter of time.

****

By morning the snow had crawled up over the front windows. The drunken fence posts fifteen feet away were invisible now, leaving a white world uninterrupted. And the electricity was off again.

Roper stood, sipping on coffee, his hands cupped around the warm mug. He watched her work on a three-foot high pile of snow on the steps, clearing only enough space for Dourcet to do his duty. The generator pulsed dully in the background,

The dog finished, and Sam was left to do battle with the front door. She fought gale wind gusts, a twenty below wind chill, and the dog's reluctance before finally struggling back inside.

"You made it. I was betting on the dog."

"Funny man." Her cheeks glowed. "I didn't hear you offering to take him out."

"Yeah, I know. Remember, I'm a City Boy, a putz in this weather." He grimaced down at the coffee. "Strong."

"The stronger the better." She slid out of her boots and sheepskin jacket.

He watched over the rim of his mug as she toweled Dourcet down. Midway through the ritual, the dog pulled away and did a shimmy, leaving Sam and the floor littered with ice crystals.

"So what's on the agenda today? You think it's going to stop soon?"

She glanced outside. "Not today."

There was an edginess about the place this morning. They stood like two birds sitting on a high tension wire, the air crackling between them. What the hell was going on? Nine in the morning and lust had already gotten the better of him? One night alone with her and his penis was working hard to take his brain hostage.

He gulped down the coffee, pulled his gaze away from the white line of skin above her leggings as she bent down to swipe at a puddle.

"Want breakfast?"

"All right." He settled into a kitchen chair and

watched her fumble with cartons of food. She looked as jumpy as he felt.

"Can I cook? I'm pretty good at it."

"You don't have to earn your keep," she mumbled, breaking eggs into a bowl.

She had on the same outfit this morning, those tight-fitting leggings, but instead of the loose sweatshirt, she wore a pale blue denim work shirt, too often laundered and too tight for her.

He leaned past her to take the bowl out of her hands. "I gotta do something here. Omelets are my department."

Sam moved aside but stood watching him. "The herbs are in the cabinet over the sink; the bread's in the bin. What else do you need?"

"I'm good." He reached for the cutting board.

Twenty minutes later the table was set, the eggs flipped.

"Here you go." He slid the omelets onto plates. Just an ordinary couple enjoying breakfast together.

They ate in silence, serenaded by the gale rattling the windows. Dourcet ignored it all.

"What do you usually do on snowy days?" Thorp asked, balancing his mug on his knee.

"Work on my orders. Read. Meditate."

"Meditate?"

"Yeah. Nothing fancy. I took up meditation when I first came here. It calms me down. Not as profound as it sounds. Just sitting, watching my breathing, being grateful for what I have."

"Okay, let me see if I've got this right. You meditate, you run, you live conservatively, almost monastically. Sounds like some sort of penance to me."

She frowned. "Why do you say that? A lot of people do the same nowadays. Minimalism is common, getting more so. Why the surprise?"

He shrugged. "No reason. I'm just used to people

who like indulging themselves."

"Are you? Someone who indulges himself, I mean?"

"In some ways. I'm not a monk, if that's what you're asking."

"And you're inferring I am? Or trying to be?"

"Nope. You just seem to be leading a purer life than most people I know."

"I have my vices."

"And what might those be? Or is that too personal?"

She picked up her plate and stood. It looked to him like the end of the conversation, but she surprised him. "I'm not adverse to fulfilling some of the basic urges we all get from time to time."

His heart sped up. Hell! Here it comes.

Chapter Ten

The bedroom was cold, with only faint light seeping in through the single small window. He led her to the bed and stopped beside it, turning to her. The heat from his body pulled her forward; and she leaned into him, her arms encircling his waist. He put his arms around her, one large hand cradling the back of her head.

He bent down and kissed her slowly. She could feel the sharp edges of his lips against hers. Even the shape of them felt sensual. He tasted of coffee, with a tang of smoke about it.

Pulling away from the kiss, she looked up at him in the skimpy light. The smile he gave her was reassuring but his pupils were narrowed.

Her heart pounded. He slid his hands around, palms down, running them slowly down the front of her sweatshirt, skimming lightly over her breasts. He reached about her waist and drew her up against him, letting her feel his erection pressed to her belly.

He bent forward again, this time he kissed her neck. She could feel his tongue flicker over the small dent below her ear. As if on a signal, the game suddenly turned desperate. They were holding each other tightly, her kisses covering his neck, her fingers working at his back, digging into his flesh.

A hand here, another there, as clothes came off. Greedily they tore at clothing until they both stood bare and trembling. The last barrier was his jeans and he pulled them off, leaving her gasping at the feel of him against her.

They tumbled onto the bed, lying facing each other, sealed together with a hundred small touches; her hand moving down to grasp and explore him, his mouth finding a swollen nipple and pulling on it, his fingers sliding through wetness to probe her.

She kissed his chest hungrily, running her tongue over coarse hair, finding a nipple to lick, her hands weighing the size of his sac, taut in her palm.

He moved suddenly, as if he could wait no longer. He rolled her over onto her belly. She felt the roughness of his tongue as he kissed her back between her shoulder blades, down her spine. His mouth found the indentation at her waist, teasing her lightly, leaving her tingling.

With another quick move, he rolled her onto her back, pinning her there with a muscled arm. He took up his kisses again, this time moving down the front, starting with the swollen tip of one breast, leaving a wet trail over her belly. She waited, her heart thudding, he spoke low, saying something that sounded to her like a promise. Now he paused, leaving her in heated anticipation, then moved back up to her lips. The kiss he gave her was soft, gentle.

He pulled back and met her eyes in the dim light, the heated question in them making her pause.

"What's the matter?" she whispered.

He stared down at her, and she could feel his breath on her cheek, see the flecks of light in his pupils.

"Tell me," she begged.

"Are you okay with this?" he asked hoarsely. He searched her face, his eyes moving over her, looking for something. She reached out and ran her fingers down over his rough cheek, tracing the line of it. She found his mouth and touched the sculptured upper lip, her thumb moving down and over the dent in his chin.

As if her touch was the next sign, he lifted himself up and over, moving between her legs, wedging them apart. He was on his knees, bent forward, still staring into her eyes with a question there. He moved a hand down. She felt his penis, probing at her body, searching.

Raising her legs further, she spread herself wide for him, giving him access into her. "Yes," she whispered back.

It was the answer he needed. With one fierce thrust, he penetrated her, impaling himself deep inside her with a grunt. He was hard, huge, stretching her. She must have cried out, because he paused again, this time hanging over her, his arms trembling with effort on either side of her head.

"Just do it! Now!"

"Sam," he cried out roughly and began pumping into her. The soft squeaking of the bed springs mixed with their groans, the cries of two animals in heat. He pushed at her legs impatiently, heaving them up even further and pummeled her bucking body, again and again.

His eyes never left hers, their gaze locked together, as they melded into one body.

A long time later, the thin curtain still fluttered at the single window, the filtered light unchanged. Heat mingled with cold air, washing over their bodies.

She lay on her back, her legs trembling. Thorp lay silently beside her, still watching. The game had turned serious.

Sam shut her eyes, not ready to answer the lingering question written on his face.

The storm had ebbed off and the room brightened, leaving their bodies unexpectedly vulnerable to the light.

Finally, she opened her eyes and looked across into his face.

"Sam?"

When he reached for her, she went. His mouth found hers, and she accepted his tongue, probing, waiting until she responded. She opened her mouth and drew him in and they began all over again.

****

Sam awoke with a start. The electricity was back. The bedside lamp shone a spotlight on rumpled bed covers tossed aside, on Thorp's back, shiny with sweat. She reached out and traced the sinewy muscle on either side of the grooved column of his spine. He didn't stir, but some subtle shift of tension in his body alerted her to the moment he awoke.

She eased up on one elbow and watched him. She followed the line of his back with her eyes; down to his waist. The sheet draped over his hips, leaving a glimpse of strong buttock muscle.

With a quick move, he rolled over, eyes narrowed and stared back at her. Never losing eye contact, he reached out and with one finger traced a line down her throat, over her bare breast, just brushing her nipple, then sliding down her belly to linger low, hidden by the sheet.

She swallowed convulsively, holding her breath. Again he made it too personal, and it left her swimming in uncertainty. What was she doing with this stranger?

Creack. Creack. The sound cut through her tension, pulling at her from outside. *Creack. Creack.* It came again, like something swinging back and forth just beyond her window.

Thorp paused mid caress, and her pleasure stuttered to a halt. She fumbled to make sense of the shift from physical to mental.

"It's just the wind." He spoke low, as if he'd read her mind and saw her struggle.

Ignoring him now, she rolled away and stood up,

grabbing for the comforter. She made her way to the window. Snow covered everything in sight.

"Sam. Come back to bed. It's probably just a loose board."

Instead, she made her way to the bathroom, stumbling over the cold tile floor. The room was like a closet, with a narrow shower cubicle, a tiny mirror hanging over the corroded sink. It was even colder than the bedroom here. She closed the door firmly and turned to stare at her image in the raw light from the bare bulb. With flushed cheeks and wild hair, her face looked as naked as her body.

She bent over and scooped water from the tap into her parched mouth. She wet a cloth and pressed it over her eyes, inhaling the cold.

Her thighs were sticky. She used the damp washcloth to wipe them down, wincing at the soreness there. She almost welcomed it, a reminder that pleasure was temporary and always had a corollary the morning after.

A day and a night lost. Again the question came up for her, how had she gotten to this place with this man?

She took her time, gently washing the raw splotches on her thighs, toweling off all the guilty evidence of the past fifteen hours.

It was impossible to prolong confronting the rumpled bed any longer. She stepped outside, avoided his watchful eyes, dropped the blanket beside the bed, and slid under the sheet.

"You okay, Sam?"

"Yes," she lied. "Maybe. I don't know."

"Come here." His words were gentle as he reached out and pulled her to him, pressing her tightly against his belly. He was aroused again.

The smell of desire filled her nostrils and heat pooled between her legs. Her throat pulsed. Another question rippled through her mind; where was this going? Expectation hung in the cold air, as dense and deep as fog but she pushed aside the question and surrendered to his need.

****

Thorp sprawled out against the headboard, an arm thrown over his face. He looked almost peaceful, except for the muscle working in his jaw that gave him away.

"Joe," she whispered. He lowered his arm, and she searched his face. It was impassive.

They'd separated instinctively after the last climax, as if burned at last from too much contact. The smell of sex filled the cold room. The small lamp still shed too much light on their exposed bodies.

He closed his eyes and she lay there, watching his chest rise and fall. After a long time, his breathing grew regular and she thought he slept.

She pulled another blanket up around her and slept as well.

****

Dourcet's tail beat a tattoo on the bedroom door; time for another trip outdoors. Dragging herself out from under Thorp's leg, Sam stumbled from the bed and grabbed up jeans and shirt. She grabbed at the temporary escape from this man next to her.

She was no good at this. Sex was one thing, intimacy was another. It had come too quickly, leaving her unbalanced. Where did trust begin and end?

Sex with Graham Rawlings was as uneventful as a stop for a Big Mac, without the extras. Sex with Thorp pushed her into a pool of need with no way back.

Sam limped down the narrow hall to the kitchen, leaving the lights off, feeling blindly for her jacket and boots. Dourcet trailed along, whimpering in expectation. Opening the door, the sharp gusts swept the lingering haze from her brain.

Thunk. She froze, her pulse racing. Dourcet looked up, only mildly concerned. With a quick sniff of the air, he turned back to his business.

Thunk. She searched the dark silhouette of the building behind her and found the source. Metal hit the worn-wood slats of the house. She could just make out the drainpipe, overloaded with snow, swinging back and forth like a metronome

Inside, Thorp still lay naked in her bed. It was time to go back in and face him.

Head down, she fought the blowing snow back to the door. Leaning heavily against it, she reached for Dourcet and dragged him inside.

"Sam? You okay?"

Thorp stood at the stove, bare feet spread on the freezing tiles, clad only in jeans with a teakettle in his hand.

"Yes. Just cold." She hung up her coat and bent down to remove her boots. The question came too late. Feeling as exposed and raw as her body, she wasn't sure if she'd ever be okay again.

"Will you look at me?"

She glanced up.

The small light over the sink left his face in shadows. Where was the nice, simple man she'd eaten breakfast with fifteen hours ago? He'd been replaced by an enigma whose physical presence filled up her kitchen.

"Want some tea?"

The words were too innocuous, and she laughed out loud at her musings. "All right."

They sat at the table, silently sipping their tea.

"Look," he said, at last, "I'm sorry. I didn't plan for this to happen. Things got a little out of hand."

What had he planned? She sank back in her chair, mentally moving further away from him. "Joe, please don't apologize. You didn't go anywhere I wasn't willing to follow." The lukewarm tea suddenly tasted bitter.

"All right. Then, how about thank you? For the night. That work for you?"

"Yes."

He surprised her by reaching out and brushing a strand of hair off her forehead. "It sounds like the storm may be over." He stood up. "It's cold as hell in here. Let's get some sleep. I'm going to have to see about getting myself out of here in the morning. I've got to get in to work."

Shivering, she let him guide her down the hall to the bed. He lay down and pulled her up against him, her cold back pressed against his chest. She let her body relax and soak up his warmth.

****

Roper moved about the room, stepping over tossed-about clothing. It was still two hours until dawn, but they'd left the bedside light burning. He glanced out the small window. The storm clouds had blown over, leaving the moon in charge of the quiet desert.

Lethargy was a thousand pound weight, pinning him to the spot. Sex never made him sluggish, but he'd never participated in fifteen solid hours of it before. He slowly pulled on his pants, his eyes on Sam.

She lay on her stomach; the sheets pulled up over her hips. She'd dragged on a nightshirt against the cold. It rode up, leaving a narrow expanse of white skin glowing like a pearl in the dim light. His groin tingled at the sight but he ignored it. He was finished. His body just hadn't gotten the message yet.

How the hell had a quick tumble turned into a marathon? She wasn't a pro, there was too much uncertainty in her touch for that; but, the chemistry between them, or whatever the hell it was, had blown up in his face. He hadn't been able to stop until he'd gone way past recreational sex, crossing the line into something he couldn't name or even identify.

Reaching down, he gathered up the rest of his clothes and stepped out into the hall. He eased the door closed, leaving it ajar two inches.

The house had turned into a deep freeze overnight, and he gritted his teeth at the icy floor on his bare feet. Dourcet lay burrowed in a pile of blankets on the couch. He whined low, pulled himself up reluctantly and ambled over to where Roper stood. A couple of days of kind words and Dourcet had turned into his best friend; one more betrayal for Sam.

He patted the dog's head, yanked his shirt over his head, and grabbed up his jacket. He checked his watch, shivering. After five. He had two hours, if he was lucky, before she surfaced. It should be long enough. The only side effect of Haldol was a headache. She'd wake up with a giant one, but hopefully wouldn't realize she'd been drugged. Until he got the hell out of Dodge.

He moved easily around the place, mentally ticking off the order of search. He began with her desk, where every bin and file was meticulously labeled. He sat down and dragged out a tidy folder marked 'mail.' The systematic way she managed her life made his job easier, but it pissed him off. Fifteen hours tangled with her between sheets reeking of sex didn't fit into the punctilious world of her desk. He hated it when things didn't fit.

Wrapped up and insulated by the whiteness outside, it was eerily quiet as he worked. The generator was off and without the sound of the wind, the house vibrated with the low hum of the propane heater and the low sighs of her dog as he sank heavily back into sleep.

Roper's stomach churned as he pulled out his

small flashlight and began sorting her mail into two piles, possible—not possible. He pulled out his cell phone and sat it on the desk.

Click. Click. Click. The sound of the security clicker echoed too loud in the stillness. He worked painstakingly but fast, double-checking the 'possible' pile for addresses before stacking them into a third pile 'to be opened.' It took thirty minutes to sort, photograph and reseal his keeper pile. Only three pieces screamed out evidence, but he took the precaution of copying everything. Next came her desk. He slid a drawer open.

Thump. Thump. Roper jumped as the dog's tail hit his leg. He reached out automatically to pet him. "What is it now, boy?" Dourcet nosed his way between Roper's legs. He raised his snout within inches of Roper's face.

"Hell." Roper stood up abruptly, catching a pile of mail as it tumbled off the desk. "Come on." The dog followed obediently, trailing him around the kitchen, until he had his food.

Six drawers and thirty minutes later Roper found her accounts book. It yielded the biggest prize so far. Hard proof of the $200 she'd sent the Consortium. The date was August 10th. He rifled backwards through the ledger and found three more $200 checks made out the same. Fuck. He snapped photos of each page.

Shoving everything back in the drawer, he made his way to the mudroom. Another thirty minutes were wasted searching boxes stored there. He flashed on a single photo buried deep in a box of knick-knacks; Sam or rather Catherine Bell, looking younger than the four bearded skinny kids around her. Dressed in skimpy t-shirt and shorts, her unruly honey-colored hair wildly framed her face. He turned the photo over and checked for a date; 1999. Holding her head down, she gazed up shyly into the camera. It was the same way she'd looked at him last night.

Click-click.

Roper switched off his flashlight and shut the mudroom door. Mentally ticking off his evidence—account book, photo, emails—he punched auto dial and sent the images to Buchanan.

Exhaustion hit him, sudden and unexpected, a mixture of intense relief at the job finished, mingled with a deep sense of guilt.

Rubbing his burning eyes, Roper moved back to the bedroom. Sam still lay sprawled out as he'd left her, except she'd turned her head away, leaving the tender flesh of her neck exposed. He drew the door shut, cursing his job. Time to get busy and find something that would send this woman to jail.

Chapter Eleven

Roper sipped lukewarm coffee and stared out at the silent, pale dawn. Snowdrifts covered the west windows, but a shift in the wind had cleared the front porch, leaving him enough maneuvering space to slip away. He hoped to hell his Jeep hadn't disappeared under the fucking snow.

Jack Buchanan sat thirty minutes away in Fallon, waiting for Roper's call. He punched in Buchanan's cell, sure his partner would get here, even if he had to hire a plow to clear a path.

"Jack. I'm ready for a pick-up."

"Where do you want me?"

"Take 447 to her road, then north about two hundred yards, no closer. There's a bend with a butte running adjacent to the road on the eastern side. There's an old 'No Trespassing' sign there; the only sign on that stretch. Make sure you don't come any further, or the neighbor may spot you. My cover story for her is someone from NDOT is bringing a tow truck to dig me out."

"How'd it go?"

"I've got enough for a search warrant. Can you get the damned thing rolling right away?"

"I'll get it to Maxwell, but give me a couple of hours. You know how the ole boy hates being wakened early. It should be ready by the time you get yourself back to the office. What've you got?"

"Not a helluva lot. Some bank statements with four payments of $200 a pop to the Consortium. And a twelve-year-old picture of young Catherine Bell with our friends. It's all sitting in your inbox."

"Sounds like you've been busy, man. I'll get on it. You want me to pull the team together now?"

"Yeah. She's meticulous about her records, and she's already nervous as a cat. If she spots anything out of place, she'll bail on us." Roper looked down at Dourcet. "And watch out for the dog. He's protective, but not dangerous. Just bring something to tranquilize him."

"You want in on the bust?"

"No. Leave me out. I'll work on things in Reno and wait for you to bring her in."

"All right. I'll see you in thirty. Where's your Jeep?"

"It's a half mile down on the other side of Highway Fifty, at the intersection of 447. It's parked off the highway about thirty yards. Probably hard to spot, but I'll find it. Drop me there, and I'll meet you back in Reno to sign the warrant. I need to stop by my motel and grab my bags on the way."

"Sure 'nuff. Gonna need help digging the Jeep out?"

He sighed. "I hope not."

"All right. Suck it up, Buddy, and see you in thirty."

Roper snapped his phone shut, feeling grim. Right now victory tasted as bitter as his last sip of coffee. On top of that, Buchanan had known him too long and could read him like a guilty six-year-old.

Jack was as straight as they came. He never had second thoughts about doing his job. And he'd never had woman problems. Hell, he was a married man with six kids, and he loved his wife.

Stories about Roper's bedroom exploits began flying around the Vegas office four years ago when Angie had herself transferred to LA. He'd gotten off with a sharp reprimand and a vague warning about getting beached if caught fraternizing again. But everyone knew he had custody of their three-year-old son.

The stud stories were bogus, but made for good office gossip. His urge to comfort females in distress was more a fatal flaw than a gift. But he'd never fallen so far as last night, having sex with a suspect, especially one he was about to send to jail.

Roper laid his jacket and shoes by the door, checked his watch, and for the third time that morning wished life was easier. The Haldol should be wearing off soon. Time to bring down the curtain on this charade.

Morning light filtered into the dim bedroom. He sat down on her bed. He held a mug in two hands.

"Sam."

She moaned and rolled over, bumping his arm.

"Wake up, Sam. I made you coffee. Here, take a slug. You'll feel better."

One eye stared up at him, blinked, and the other one popped open. Her gaze traveled slowly down his arm to the mug. Reaching out for her coffee, the sheet fell away, revealing a twisted t-shirt riding up under her armpits to expose one bare breast encircled with a red splotch. He'd made that mark.

She yanked up the sheet, took the mug, and leaned back. She studied the far wall as she sipped.

"I've got to get going, Sam. I've managed to round up a tow from the Highway Department. They're on their way out here to get me." His hoarse voice rang false to his own ears, but he saw no distrust in her face. Instead, she looked resigned.

"Sure." She turned and gave him a brief smile. "You're lucky, having an inside with NDOT. They wouldn't be coming way out here in this weather for just anybody." She took another sip, her eyes not meeting his. "You probably have a lot to do, what with the storm."

"Yeah. All the emergency crews were called in,

and they want me over at the main garage." Fuck, did they even have a main garage within a hundred miles of here?

"In Reno?"

"Yeah." He bent over and brushed a swatch of hair off her face, keeping it simple, but his hand shook. "Nice do."

"Don't rub it in, Joe. I'm sure I look like hell."

"You look sexy as hell." He forced himself to stand up, his chest tight, feeling the need to get the crap out before he did something stupid. Something else stupid. "There's more coffee on the stove."

A piece of clothing under her nightstand caught his eye. It turned out to be his abandoned underwear. He leaned down and retrieved it, then took another survey of the room.

This was it then, the last scene. Without another word, he strode out, the quiet of the house screaming in his head. Even the dog lay silent, splayed out by the door, not reproachful, but like her, resigned.

He picked up his jacket and waited for her, wondering how to get out the front door gracefully.

Five minutes later, she marched into the kitchen, wrapped in a white robe, cradling her mug.

He turned to study the weather beyond her porch. He couldn't meet her eyes. "I'll probably spend most of the day getting dragged around the county to look at snow emergency set-ups." In a hurry now to leave, he pulled on his boots quickly and patted down his pockets for cell phone and pistol.

Giving a final pat to the dog, he made for the door. "I'll call you." Her dog got a pat, and she got one last lie. The smile she gave back was as tight as his felt.

The next time he saw her, she'd be in Reno, in shackles.

Slamming the door behind him, he inhaled, letting cold air rip through his chest like a straight shot of whiskey. The first step off the porch sent him into knee-deep snow. He struggled to stay upright, moving drunkenly down the path to her gate, conscious of her eyes at his back.

The snow got even deeper beyond the front fence. It took ten minutes to make the two hundred yard walk down the road and around the bend.

Jack sat waiting in a dirty white Durango, squinting into the bright sunlight reflecting off the hood.

"Everything okay, Joe?" he asked.

"Yeah. As good as can be considering the circumstances." Roper replied, climbing up into the truck.

"Sorry, Buddy." Jack pulled out slow and gathered speed as he hit grooved snow tracks. "Sometimes this job is shit."

"You've got it there." Roper muttered.

Neither of them spoke again until they reached the main road.

"Everything still a go?"

"Yeah. It's on." Roper pulled his phone out and checked his email. "I have back-ups of all the shit I sent you sitting in my mail if you need it."

They drove the few miles in silence, theirs the only car on the side road brave enough to face the snowdrifts.

Jack drew up along the apron of Highway Fifty where a few emergency vehicles sat making ready for duty.

Roper climbed out. "I'll meet you at the Reno office in an hour." Right now all he wanted was to get his gear and get back to his anonymous desk.

****

Sam stared after Thorp's back, her bare feet numb, a sense of doom fixing her to the spot. The pounding behind her eyes was the beginnings of a migraine.

At last, trembling with cold, she stepped back. In tune with her mood, Dourcet followed mournfully.

What bothered her most was the way he'd looked at her, or rather hadn't looked at her when he'd left. No gentle smiles now, just a cool nod and a wave goodbye.

What was wrong with her? She'd grabbed at an opportunity for some fun and great sex, nothing more. So what if he'd bailed mentally long before he'd made it out her kitchen door? Men did that all the time, didn't they? What the hell did she have to be depressed about? She'd gotten what she wanted. And fifteen hours in bed with Joe Thorp was way better than thirty minutes of Graham Rawlings' robotics.

Chock it up to one small step down a new road. Trust could be a bitch when one wasn't used to it. But the real problem wasn't trust, it was need. She'd come close to begging him to stay. Like mother, like daughter.

The memory was too sharp of her mother sitting by the door, flipping ashes from her cigarette with nervous fingers. She'd be waiting for some jerk, sure he wouldn't show. It had happened too often, the guy would stay around long enough for a bang in bed and then disappear, never to return.

A gray wall of desolation rose up like a vacuum sucking the life out of her body, leaving her limp. People always left. The words spun around in her brain, burned over most of her life. First her father, then her mother, then every foster parent she'd ever known, come and gone. Even her aunt had left. And now Thorp.

Sam pressed the brake down on her thoughts. Why the hell beat herself up? This was a first try at meeting a relationship half way. What more could she ask? Brief encounters were romantic, weren't they? And usually tragically doomed? It sold well in books and movies; it was entertaining in a way. In real life, it hurt too damned much.

So now what? Joe Thorp was a nice guy, a hot guy, not looking for anything long-term, no threat. Whether she saw him again or not.

She shivered and looked around. He hadn't bothered to light the fireplace. She knelt on the icy hearth, pulling her robe under her knees, the familiarity of it reassuring.

But God! She felt as if she was drugged. Drugged on despair? On loneliness? She pressed cold fingers against the middle of her chest where the deep ache was centered. The rest of her body felt numb, consumed by a strange lethargy that pinned her down in front of the fire like an old woman, unable to gather enough purpose to rise. She tried not to think about her mother and tried not to think about Joe.

Coffee. That was it.

Pulling herself up, she lurched to the stove. He'd left the pot simmering on a back burner, ready for her. Suddenly, she didn't want it.

She flipped off the gas, fed Dourcet, and automatically moved through her chores, leaving the computer for last.

No surprises there either; there was nothing new from Robert Mathias.

She logged off and stumbled down the narrow hall. It was cold enough in the room for her breath to gather and hang like a cloud above her bed. She drew the blinds shut against the bright sunlight that seemed to be celebrating her loneliness and fell onto her bed. A sob escaped her throat at the scent of him, lingering there on her pillow. Rolling into a tight ball, she pushed away images of Joe and fell into a deep sleep.

Chapter Twelve

The ringing of the cell phone vibrated her bed, pulling Sam out of a nightmare. She forced her eyes opened and grabbed for the phone under her pillow. The clock said eleven ten. She glanced at the window. It was still daylight. She'd been asleep less than two hours.

"Hello."

"Sam. It's Keddie. You survive the storm?"

"Keddie. Oh, God. Give me a minute. I was asleep." She punched up her pillows and shifted about.

"Asleep? It's almost noon. You sick?"

"No, I'm fine." She stifled a moan as she rolled over onto her back, her body aching.

Of course, if anyone would be surprised at her sleeping this late, it would be Keddie.

"I was with someone. Not Graham." Not Graham was a given. She'd never brought Graham out to her place.

"Ah-hah! It's the engineer, right? Tell momma." Keddie wasn't going to let go of this one. "I'm assuming we're talking serious sex here, right? Since you're in bed at noon. Is he still there?"

"No. He left a couple of hours ago. He got stranded in the storm."

"Yeah, right. Refresh my memory. He's with NDOT, a construction sort of guy? I'm picturing someone with a lot of muscles."

"Like I told you the other day, he's an engineer, a surveyor actually."

Keddie blew a raspberry into the phone.

"All right. No more."

"So, let's review this and see if I get it straight. He picked you up at the grocery store and somehow did the impossible and managed to make it into your bed? It took him less than a week to accomplish that feat?"

"Yes. The rest you can guess at. I'm not going into more detail."

"Come on. At least give me a few vignettes. This is some sort of historic event. I want the details. But I've gotta tell you, while I like a highwayman, I can't quite get engineer into the same scene with serious bed moves. So he got himself stranded at your place and hit it lucky. You said two nights ago, how much of that was serious action?"

"It was a little more than one night—more like a day and a night."

Keddie let out a howl. "Come on, Sam. Tell me something more here! I'm dying."

"He's a very nice guy from Vegas who's only here for a couple of weeks. The whole story boils down to a few lines. I met him at Ticutta's, he asked me out for coffee, we went dancing Saturday night," she muttered, "and to make a short story shorter, he got stranded and we both got bored. In a moment of insanity, we looked at each other and headed for the bedroom."

She stared at a ray of sunlight forcing its way under the blind. "It's no big deal. I did what you've been urging me to do. I had the opportunity and went for it." Dourcet pushed the bedroom door open and wandered in, sniffing the air.

"So when are you going to see this man of wonder again?"

"He was a little vague about that, or if I'll ever hear from him again." The last sentence was for her own sake, speaking the words out loud made it a little less painful.

Silence from the other end. "Was it worth it?"

"Oh boy, ask me tomorrow. Right now, I feel like I've been drugged. Once I get up and get the sensation back in my lower body, but I may be walking funny for a day."

"Well, hell. I'm jealous."

"Yeah, I doubt it. As for the soreness, it's probably from disuse. But I really do need to drag myself out of this bed and do some work. And poor Dourcet has been stuck inside for two days."

"So what's this guy's name again?"

"Joe Thorp."

"Description?"

"Average height, a bit taller, medium brown hair, body in good shape. Great shape, actually. Close to 40 and like I said, a nice man."

"So what happened? I've known you eight years, and you've never pulled a one-nighter, as far as I know. He's a nice guy, but you've said that at least twice. What's this guy got that made you choose him? And why now?"

"I don't know." She'd never mentioned her mother to Keddie, and there was no way to quickly explain she'd set out a plan to reverse twenty years of decisions by trusting one man. "He was here. I was bored. After all, Graham's not the most exciting man around."

"He'd be so disillusioned to hear you say so."

"Probably. At any rate, the man's only in the area for a couple of weeks, and there's no possibility of anything permanent." She pictured Keddie's grimace. The woman knew her too well.

"Well, congratulations. And I don't know why the hell you can't consider something further with this guy. Las Vegas is only eight hours away, not the other side of the moon. And please don't tell me to mind my own business. You know I never do." There was a longer pause. "So was it worth it while it lasted?"

"The sex was amazing." She wasn't going to be able to keep the truth from Keddie. "But I got myself into something way more complicated than I wanted."

"How's that?"

"The way he walked out this morning. It was so abrupt, so cold."

"Sounds like most men to me. Especially those engineers whose minds have gotta be competing with their dicks for attention."

"What does that mean?"

"Just that any guy who's so focused on the cerebral is going to be running for the hills if his cock suddenly takes over for a day and a night. "

"Well, I'm left feeling like an idiot."

"You'll get used to it. Feeling like an idiot the morning after, I mean. It's woman's lot in life."

"Maybe he's just not really interested in me."

Keddie hooted. "Could be, but a day and a night of bed time doesn't sound like he's not much into you. He might just be a player."

"He's forty. I never heard of a forty-year-old player. Anyone over twenty-five described that way has got to be stuck in adolescence."

"This from you, who sees the player-of-all-players every other month for sex. I don't have to tell you Graham has a woman in every layover on his fly route."

"You set me up with Graham."

"Yeah, well, it was a desperate situation, and you were willing to settle. Speaking of which, if Joe Thorp is really, really good, I hope you got more than a couple of positions out of him."

"I already told you I'm not doing a blow-by-blow."

"Oh well. Now that you've got me all wrought

up, I guess I'll have to go on the prowl tonight. What are you up to this afternoon?"

"Sleeping some more. I don't know when I've felt this sluggish. I guess I'm out of shape." She stood up and tried her feet. They seemed to hold her. "I have a lot of orders and I need to get out and check my plants." And check up on Robert Mathias.

"Are you coming into Reno next week or are you sated?"

"I don't know."

"Do you mean to say you're holding out a hope this Joe guy might come back for more?"

"Again, I don't know, Ked. Probably not, from the look on his face when he left." She hesitated. "Look, this is alien territory for me."

"Oh-oh. Tell mama."

"Sometime in the past twenty-four hours I let things get away from me. With a stranger."

"If we're still talking about morning-after awkwardness, I think it's something to do with the light of day. Prince Charming turning into a toad at dawn," she said. "I've learned to keep it light, even in the midst of all the moaning and groaning." Keddie stopped. "But somehow, I don't think it's what you're asking me."

"No. Hell, Ked. I don't know anything right now. Whether it was just lust or something more, it was too fast for me. It left me feeling lost."

"Welcome to the club, kid. Look, take it easy and get some sleep. Things will look better tomorrow."

"Promise?"

"Sure."

****

After wasting forty-five minutes digging out his vehicle, Roper crawled along behind a snowplow. The normal fifteen-minute drive had grown to thirty minutes.

Bleary-eyed, Roper turned into the Old Fifty

Motel lot. Inside his room, he grabbed bunches of clothes, threw them into his suitcase, snapped up his laptop, and headed for checkout.

He edged down Sierra in tight traffic, standard for this time of day, reviewing in his mind the past three days. He cursed himself until he was stupefied, so stupefied he almost missed the turnoff for the FBI office. He swerved into the parking lot just dodging a garbage truck.

Sleeping five of the past forty-eight hours, Roper was depressed, exhausted, and dragging his tail.

The warrant sat on his desk, the only paper in sight, neatly folded into thirds, waiting for his signature. He threw down his laptop and jacket, rifled through the pages and dashed off his signature.

Six feet away, Jack sat, legs propped up on his desk, following Roper's every movement. He reached out, and Roper passed the warrant into his outstretched hand. Buchanan slid the paper into his pocket, grabbing his cuffs and gun out of the top drawer.

"I'll see you back here in two hours with your friend in tow if we're lucky."

He pictured Sam stumbling into the interrogation room, her legs shackled; those same legs she'd kept wound about him most of the past two days. The urge to leave was almost physical, anything to avoid the accusations he'd find in her face when she realized she'd been set up.

Roper swiveled his chair around and stared out the window. Less than five inches of snow sat on the ledge, already melted, and not even deep enough to slow down the steady stream of Wednesday afternoon traffic. Roper reached for his laptop and blindly pulled a pile of papers toward him. He rubbed his gritty eyes, sliding his hand over his stubbly chin. Damn, he needed a shave, too. Yanking out a form from under the stack, he dove into the legalese miasma.

An hour into the mess, his cell rang. "Go."

"Joe. You made it."

"Jackie." Gut clench. "How are you? How's the weather down there?"

"Sunny and clear. Your storm missed us. I called yesterday, but they said you were stranded." At 35, her showgirl body belied her toughness, and she lived for her job as Assistant D.A. She'd been transferred to the Vegas office from Carson City a year ago. Roper asked her out two weeks after she got her desk assignment.

He sighed. Two months of plotting ways to end the relationship painlessly had failed; the more he planned, the more determined she was to up the ante. Not that she was after something long-term with him, but for now she was getting everything she wanted from the relationship: a respectable dinner date for Saturday night, good connections within the justice system, and sex on demand. She never seemed to mind whatever part he chose to play. As long as they both enjoyed themselves, the more impersonal the better.

The last time he'd seen her, it had been to drop by her house to pick up his bomber jacket. He'd barely gotten the closet door shut before she'd reached for his zipper, had his cock out and dropped down to her knees. Fumbling to get his gun out of the way, he'd pictured the headlines: FBI agent shoots himself in the balls getting a blowjob.

Was that all he'd been? A drive-by fuck? It had gotten bad enough that he'd been relieved to get to the undercover assignment in Reno, anything to gain some distance from her.

Jackie cleared her throat. "Joe. I asked how it was going. Is your case closing down?"

He checked his watch and sighed. "They're

taking her in just about now."

"Why aren't you there?"

"I was too close to it. She'd have made me if I came in with the backup team."

"So you got enough on her to get a warrant? How'd you get so close?"

Oh shit. Here it comes. She'd hear about it, anyway. "I got myself stranded at her place for forty-eight hours in the storm."

She snorted. Not a real laugh, he knew pretense when he heard it. "So what else did you do to kill time, Joe? She good-looking?"

"Passable. She's a former terrorist, Jackie, living off the grid, in hiding, dyed hair and all. And she's crippled." The last word tasted unpleasant. Why not tell her the truth and use this moment to end the relationship? I slept with the suspect, and it was something way beyond entertainment.

"She's crippled?" Jackie echoed his words.

"Yeah. Probably injured during the bombing. One leg's shorter than the other. It didn't show up in her file."

She didn't respond, but he could read her thoughts as easily as if they'd been written on the wall opposite, above the wanted posters. A crippled, unpleasant suspect, no threat to her stake on his life. Jackie could be a paper cutout of Angie Petroski, the mother of his son. Both strutted around in traffic-stopping bodies, so focused on their lives they'd suck the air out of anyone within fifteen feet of them. Sam Neally was a different type of female. Whatever motivated her to let him into her bedroom, he knew for certain it wasn't about her getting ahead in life.

"So when are you getting back to Vegas?"

"Maybe this weekend for a day or two. I won't be around until this case is wrapped." He yawned, too tired to play the game or care. "Listen, Jackie. I need to go. I'm really beat, and I've gotta get some food in me. I'll give you a call when I get back in town."

He flipped his phone shut and turned back to the deep snow of paper cluttering his desk. The day was a fucking train wreck, worse by the minute, and it annoyed the hell out of him.

Chapter Thirteen

There were four of them, guns drawn, dressed in black, standing in her yard. She knew they were the law. Awakened from a deep sleep, she stood in her kitchen, barefoot, with Dourcet barking frantically beside her. It was two p.m. and her life was about to fall apart.

"Catherine Bell." They shouted repeatedly, fanning out around her house, giving her fair warning. "This is the FBI. We have a search warrant. Leash your dog and come out with your hands above your head."

One of them stepped up to the door and pounded hard enough to make the house shake. Dourcet barked louder, nonstop, as if he knew what was coming.

"Open the door and step back!"

"Please, wait! Don't hurt my dog! I'll lock him up!" She grabbed Dourcet's collar, slid back the deadbolt on the door and backed away slowly.

Her gaze got stuck on the gun pointed at her.

"Please. Let me lock up my dog." She raised a pleading hand and began backing away, pulling Dourcet to the mudroom. She tied him up quickly and stood there, tethered to the spot herself.

Through the door, she saw the nightmare of a man in her kitchen pointing his gun at her. He was young, no more than twenty-five, and nervous. He motioned silently with his pistol for her to step into the kitchen. She clenched her trembling hands and lowered her arms.

"Keep your hands up!"

"All right."

His face looked nondescript beneath his black knit cap, but she could smell his fear as she edged closer to him. Her mind tumbled over the scene and its inevitable outcome; the dreaded future had arrived. They'd finally come for her.

She stepped into the dazzling light flooding the kitchen. Sparkling snow decorated the world beyond like icing.

It was a good day to go to jail.

From there, it went quickly. Someone grabbed her, did a U-turn with her body and cuffed her shaking hands behind her back. Their precautions were so absurd in the face of her sense of defeat that she almost laughed out loud.

A hand shoved Sam down to the floor, pressed her face into cold tiles and patted her down. Cold dread spread through her body. She turned to find a woman towering over her, mid forties, large framed, with short brown hair under her black cap. She held a big gun and smelled of sweet lilac.

"Get up!" The woman's voice, strangely high pitched for someone with her bulk, was as piercing as a police whistle. Grabbing hold of the cuffs, she yanked Sam to her feet, flashing a badge. "FBI Special Agent Forrester."

The woman kicked at a kitchen chair with one foot and caught hold of it as it tipped backwards. "Sit down."

An older agent sidled through the door, as loose limbed and casual as a friend dropping by for dinner. His calm quiet put a blanket on the agitation in the room.

"Special Agent Buchanan." He held his badge up and slipped papers in front of Sam. "Search warrant." The white sheets landed in a small pool of spilled coffee. Sam watched a dark brown stain edge its way across the page like a trail of blood. "Damn!" He yanked the warrant up, took a swipe at it, and placed it back in front of Sam. Small letters marched across the page like ants at a picnic, but they formed no words she could understand. She raised her head and looked around at the invasion of her familiar kitchen.

The other agents moved away, spreading out through her house. She watched as they pulled open drawers and shoved aside furniture, rifling through her life. The woman, Agent Forrester, unplugged her computer, dumped the contents of her desk into a box and dragged the carton to the door.

"I'm being arrested?" A stupid question since she knew the answer.

"No. Brought in for questioning."

No other explanation was offered. What happened to the Miranda law? Or did the FBI have its own code of conduct?

The door stood wide open, letting frigid air filter through her house. She shivered in her thin t-shirt and leaned forward to ease the pressure of her arms behind her back. Her head drooped down onto the table, heavy with the weight of reality.

Time slowed to a wiggle as the search continued.

The sound of Dourcet's frantic barking caused Sam to lift her head and crane her neck. One of the agents stood at the door to the mudroom.

"Fuck. The dog's going crazy." The man backed quickly out and turned to Sam. "What's this room used for?"

"Storage."

"Calm your dog down, or we're going to have to disable him." Buchanan issued the order.

Sam's head throbbed. "If you'll give me a phone, I'll call my neighbor over to take the dog. Please!" She clenched her hands into tight fists to keep from yelling out the demand. She'd have to start learning how to beg in this new phase of her life.

"What's the neighbor's name?"

"Charlie Lemon."

Buchanan paused, then nodded at Forrester. "Call him."

The agent whipped out her cell phone. No one could accuse Agent Forrester of being part of any sisterhood of women. If she ever did decide to join, there was no way she'd recognize Sam as a member of her chapter.

"This is Special Agent Forrester with the FBI. We're at your neighbor's, Sam Neally's place. We need you to come over here and get her dog."

Charlie would ask no questions. He'd do what worked for her, one friend amidst all these enemies.

"Bring some ID." The last was an order. Forrester snapped her phone shut and gave Sam an unreadable glance.

Charlie must have dropped his phone, grabbed his jacket, and sprinted over. In less than five minutes, he pulled up short face to face with a black clad Bureau commando guarding her door.

"Stop where you are. Put your hands up. Slowly."

Sam spotted Charlie, his head craned, looking in through her open door. She watched him pull his hands out of his pockets and raise his arms.

"Reach down and take your ID out for me. One hand only please."

"I'll show you mine if you show me yours."

Sam smiled grimly. Intimidation rarely worked with the tribe. They'd been confronted one too many times over the years by the law.

The pink-cheeked agent surprised her by whipping out his wallet. Charlie, in turn, reached into his pocket. The move was too fast for the kid, who grabbed hold of his arm.

"Whoa, son. Let me get my ID out, will ya?"

Charlie met her eyes as he stepped inside. "You okay?"

"Yeah. I'm all right. I..." She stopped. "I'm going to have to go into Reno. Dourcet's in the mudroom chained up. He's a little upset. Will you take him over to your place?"

"Yeah." Going on sixty, he could easily pass for forty if you looked beyond his sun-weathered face. His black hair, always braided tightly down his back, hung loose today, spread out on his shoulders. She'd never seen it unbound.

He followed Dourcet out of the mudroom, holding a rope tied to the dog. Dourcet stopped in front of Sam, reared up on his hind legs and pawed at her. Charlie let go of the dog and all the agents scattered, cutting a wide path between themselves and Dourcet.

"It's okay, Boy. Go with Charlie." Sam whispered, bending over him.

Charlie steered Dourcet toward the door, turned back, and they both gave Sam a last long look. "Any idea when you'll be back?"

"I don't know. Maybe in a day or two, maybe a lot longer." She cleared her throat. There was nothing else to add.

"Can I call someone for you?"

"Yeah, Keddie. Call Keddie."

Charlie turned to Buchanan. "Where you taking her?"

"Downtown for questioning. If she's charged, she'll be moved to City Detention."

Charlie didn't even bother to ask the charges. His face was somber. He knew it was serious.

****

Sam studied the black glass facing her, knowing there were people behind it, waiting for her to do something. She turned her back on them and stared out the single window where the shadow of an adjacent building provided only a sliver of bright sunshine and a snow-covered mountain.

The interrogation room had less personality than the ladies room in a bus station; overheated air absorbed all the oxygen in the place, leaving her gasping. Along a windowless wall sat a desk with an out-dated computer terminal. They'd settled her at a scarred wooden table, centered in the middle of the bare expanse. Three straight backs stood close by, ready for musical chairs during her questioning.

Sam leaned forward and shifted her cuffed hands about her back.

In the past hour and a half, the memory of those last few hours with Joe Thorp dissolved into a pleasant dream, no part of her real life playing out here. If he'd stuck around a little while, he'd have been caught up in her nightmare, but if so, she was sure he'd have moved out as fast as his NDOT truck would take him.

The door opened and two agents in shirtsleeves walked into the room. One of them leaned over and removed her cuffs. They both pulled out chairs and sat on either side of her.

"Do I get to make a call?"

The man who'd tangled with Charlie Lemon in the ID exchange had lost his pink cheeks. He sported a big gun strapped to his leg. Without answering her directly, he went and came back cradling a phone with a dangling cord. She took it silently and waited as he plugged it into an outlet. It was so quiet in the room she could hear her heart slamming in her chest. She knew she was not going home soon.

Sam dialed one of two numbers she knew by heart and Keddie's voice mail kicked in. "Hi all. It's Keddie, leave a message."

"Keddie, it's Sam. I'm hoping Charlie reached you so this won't be such a shock. I'm at the FBI office in Reno. I think I'm being arrested." It sounded like a silly game. "I have no idea what time it is but I need a lawyer. Your friend, Deckard, maybe."

She glanced at the two men encircling her. Neither of them met her gaze. "I think I'm going to be spending the night in jail." She rubbed her chafed wrists together. One of the agents wordlessly spread papers out on the table in front of her. "I hope you can get someone here tonight. If not, tomorrow will have to do." Sam whispered. "I'm sorry to get you involved in this, Keddie."

Special Agent Ed Buczek, his nametag said, was as burley as a long haul truck driver. He relieved her of the phone and drew a card from his breast pocket.

"You have the right to remain silent. If you give up that right, anything you say can and will be used against you in a court of law. You have the right to an attorney and to have an attorney present during questioning. If you cannot afford an attorney, one will be provided to you at no cost. During any questioning, you may decide at any time to exercise these rights, not answer any questions, or make any statements."

And so it began.

The men took turns, tossing laser fired questions at her:

Name?
Your real name?
What's your relationship to the Consortium?

The same three questions again and again and again.

"Samantha Neally. I refuse to answer any other questions until my lawyer arrives." And on it went.

Desperation pressed hard on her chest but she managed only an hour and a half of resisting before fear won out. "Catherine Bell. My name is Catherine Bell."

The two men exchanged glances, the goal line in

sight.

"What's your association with the Consortium?

On four separate occasions this year you gave the Consortium $200. What was that for? What do you know about the 2000 Bureau of Land Management bombing?

How long have you been part of the Consortium? What's your role with the organization now?

Tell us what happened twelve years ago at the El Dorado National Forest."

Her mouth was dry and her replies turned to glue, getting stuck on her tongue. The wound they dug into continued hemorrhaging out her life and her fear of the future escalated. She pushed it all away and kept answering their questions.

It was dark outside now and the small table sat under a spotlight in the center of the room, leaving the corners in subtle shadow.

The door opened, someone stepped inside and shut it softly. Both of her flanking agents stood up, one of them rubbing his eyes. The other ran nervous fingers over his shorn head.

Sam looked around. Two men stood in the shadows, watching; one of them was Joe Thorp.

He moved slowly toward her, grim, and she saw he was with them in her nightmare.

A flurry of panic broke loose in her chest and the wound there turned into a small, red-hot knot of rage that swept through her body like a wildfire. She stood up as he reached her, lifted her clenched fist and swung at him. It was a glancing blow that caught him in the jaw and chaos broke free in the room.

"Fuck!"

"Grab her!"

Rough hands caught at her arms and swung her face down onto the table, recuffing her hands behind her back. The smell of rancid coffee permeated her nostrils, and she tasted blood.

Someone yanked her upright and pushed her into a chair. She recognized Joe Thorp's calm voice amidst the mayhem, "That's enough! Leave her alone."

"I'm going to be sick." Someone close by swung her around, shoved a wastebasket between her legs, and pushed her head down. She bent over and surrendered, retching until there was nothing left but bile. As she fell forward to her knees, someone caught her and eased her down.

Defeated, she rested her head against the side of the wastebasket, the smell of vomit gagging her.

A long time seemed to pass, the silence in the room interrupted only by occasional murmuring, a question, a response, then more silence. Someone caught her carefully from behind, eased her up and into her chair.

"Uncuff her," Thorp ordered.

More incoherent murmurings followed while she sat rubbing her wrists, refusing to look up.

He pushed a paper cup and tissue at her. She took them silently, still not meeting his eyes, but she wanted to put her head down on the table and weep.

The door opened and closed. Sam looked up. The room was empty now, except for Agent Forrester, standing at the window. Joe Thorp had disappeared.

Chapter Fourteen

The silence lengthened and time stretched out. Sam sat, staring at the table, trying hard to think of anything but this room and her mute guard. At last, the door opened, and this time Agent Buchanan stepped out of the ring of darkness, followed by Deckard Stewart. "Hello, Sam."

At forty, Deckard was an unlikely Galahad. A casino manager, he'd gone to school nights and moved himself into the world of law. Once Keddie's boss, he was now her lover. And apparently, now he was Sam's lawyer as well.

Agent Buchanan held a chair out for Stewart and inched his own closer to the battered table. It was probably the middle of the night, but Buchanan had transformed himself into the man in the grey flannel suit with matching tie. He glanced over at Stewart. "We've already Mirandized her and your client has agreed to answer our questions. Can we get started?"

Deckard nodded. "You all right, Sam? Need anything?"

She gave Deck a brief, humiliated smile. "No, thanks, Deckard."

"Ms. Neally. May I call you Samantha?" Buchanan interrupted, his smile as friendly as a Midwest high school principal, welcoming a new student.

Sam sat up straighter, wary of this new Buchanan. Ruthlessness behind impeccable manners and good will posed the worst kind of threat. "Sam."

"What?" Buchanan's eyebrows formed a single line. "Oh. Sam, of course." He drew a small recorder from his breast pocket, pressed a button and laid it down in front of her.

"Please state your name."

"Before we begin, what happened to Thorp?"

Buchanan looked confused. "Thorp?"

"The man I took a swing at."

He hesitated. "That would be my partner, Agent Roper."

His partner, her bed partner. She didn't miss the quick glance he tossed at the mirror covering one wall. Squeezing her burning eyes shut, she pictured Joe Thorp standing there, watching. "I see. Joe Roper."

Buchanan cleared his throat and turned to Deckard. "We had a little incident before you arrived, Mr. Stewart. Ms. Neally got a bit upset at my partner. We're not going to press charges. Agent Roper is against it and under the circumstances, I agree. Just make sure your client keeps herself under control, all right?"

Deckard sat forward. "What circumstances are you referring to?"

"Special Agent Roper has been undercover this past week, and Ms. Neally knew him as Joe Thorp. She was understandably upset when she found out he was part of our ongoing surveillance."

"Hell." Deckard grunted.

"So let's see if we can make a go of it now, all right? We're all getting pretty tired. I've sent an agent out for some food. In the meantime, can we begin?"

Buchanan started down the road she'd been traveling the past ten hours—name, real name, relationship to the Consortium. She answered haltingly at first, staring out the window at the lonely night.

Deckard refused the food when it arrived, but Buchanan handed her a sandwich and unwrapped one for himself. He fed her questions as he chewed.

Sam studied the man with the slightly askew necktie, a contradiction to his precise movements and speech. She answered his questions slowly and gave him what he wanted; the truth. "I took the name Sam Neally twelve years ago. Before that, I was Catherine Bell, a Midwest hick, college my first step into adulthood. Someone introduced me to the members of the Consortium. I was eighteen."

The dam burst and words spilled out, tumbling and tripping over each other. She leaned back, shut her eyes, and went over her past like a review of a bad movie, starting with her childhood, the years in foster care, Berkeley. The Consortium was nothing more for her than a group of friends, bonded together, doing something exciting for the world. Until it all went bad.

She recited the events on the night of the bombing. She'd gone along as lookout in a game that seemed closer to Dungeon and Dragons than eco-terrorism. With minutes passing, hearing shouts, she'd jumped out of the VW bus and the world exploded around her. It was just one more betrayal when they left her behind as she limped out of the flames after the fleeing van. The next thirty-six hours she'd struggled to find some sanctuary through a fog of pain. At last, dirty and bleeding, she'd managed to hitch rides and landed at her aunt's ranch, thirty miles northwest of Reno.

Buchanan and Deckard leaned forward, food forgotten. Neither interrupted her.

The simpler details of the past twelve years were easier to recap; recovering from her injuries, her new identity, her business, her fears of being found by the Consortium as well as the FBI.

The silence in the room was punctuated by a furnace kicking on somewhere in the bowels of the building.

Deckard sat back, watching Buchanan. The questions became more specific, focusing on recent activities. Sometimes Deckard stopped her mid sentence, coaching her in the responses. Mostly he sat listening and taking his own notes.

"We have emails from you to the Consortium starting about four months back. Who contacted who?" Buchanan asked.

"I had no contact with any of them for twelve years. Until this summer."

"So what happened?"

She glanced down at her fingers, picking at a corner of her sandwich. "As a fugitive, they've had a potential hold over me for twelve years."

"Why'd they start emailing you now?"

"Money. I got the first email in May, asking for money. The message was friendly, I suppose. They mentioned they knew I was living in Northern Nevada." She dropped her sandwich on the crumpled wrapper and rubbed clammy palms against her thighs. "I'm still a fugitive, even if the statute of limitation has passed. I don't know how significant the new Homeland Security laws are, or how committed the government is to tracking down old cases. I don't know what these guys are up to now, whether they're even protesting or if they would turn me in to the FBI. They never said directly they'd do that, but I sent them the money they asked for, $200, and hoped they'd lose interest."

"What would guarantee they wouldn't keep asking for money?"

"Nothing. They did, keep asking for money. I went along for the past few months, dumb of me but it seemed like the simplest thing to do."

"You don't have that much money, do you?

Enough to make it worthwhile to keep coming back to the well for more?"

She shrugged. "I have some; what I got from my aunt. The point is, living in hiding turns into a way of life. It's automatic for me to keep protecting myself, any way I can." She paused. "I don't even know if they were really a threat but a few hundred bucks seemed like the easy way out. I did some searching the internet for them but didn't find much."

"Actually, it was Consortium chatter that led us to you. But, what's the point of all this? A few hundred bucks at a time isn't much. Are you sure they're not after something more?"

"Like what?"

"You tell me."

"I don't know what you're talking about." She shivered, a fragile growing trust in this man dissolving.

He let it drop and moved on. "So what about your sister? Is she involved at all? Is the Consortium posing any threat to her or any other family members?"

"No, she says not."

"You sent them a second $200 on June 15th?"

"Yes. I did."

"And since then you've received six more emails, five of which you responded to, and two more payments of $200, the last in August."

"Yes."

"And have you gotten any direct threats?"

"You apparently have access to my emails. You must have read them all. Nothing specific, just some vague innuendos that since I've done such a good job hiding, I might consider joining them again."

Buchanan pushed away the remains of his sandwich and took a sip of Coke, in no hurry. "Those recent events—your house filled with gas and the parking lot attack. You think they could have been instigated by the Consortium?"

"Joe Thorp reported those, I suppose?"

"Roper. Were you lying when you told him you didn't get a look at the man in the parking lot?"

"No, I really didn't see him. Or what I saw of him, I didn't recognize."

Stewart shifted in his chair. "Agent Buchanan. It's very late, as you have indicated, and my client is exhausted. Since you seem to know the answers to these questions you're asking, can we curtail this until tomorrow?"

Buchanan checked his watch and glanced at Stewart. "It's after three. Too late to set bond. We'll keep her overnight in the lock-up. Tomorrow we'll see what kind of deal we can work out and ask the court to set bail."

"What's she charged with?" The overhead light made Deckard's features stark.

"No formal charges yet. Held for questioning. You can see her in the morning at the Detention Center."

Buchanan stood up and straightened his tie.

"Is your partner going to be interrogating me tomorrow?"

Buchanan turned, his expression unreadable. "Roper? You'd prefer he ask the questions?"

"No. I refuse to talk to him."

He nodded. "All right."

"Deckard, do you need anything from me? Some money for a retainer?"

Stewart shook his head. "Keddie covered it. We can deal with that later."

Agent Forrester reappeared and indicated for Sam to stand. She reapplied the cuffs and began on the shackles.

"I'll see you first thing in the morning?"

"You have my promise." He headed toward the

door. "Try and get a little sleep for a couple of hours, and we'll see where we're at tomorrow."

They took her by van, cuffed and shackled. Two miles of flashing neon, still a scattering of people on the streets of Reno, all of them too busy throwing money away to watch one more police car zip past.

Sam watched the lights streak by and wondered where Joe Roper was and what he was feeling. The worst had happened. Where did she go from here, alone?

Chapter Fifteen

Roper sped out of the empty parking lot and headed for the city limits. Buchanan had led her lawyer, all dressed up in Armani, into the interrogation room as Roper pulled on his jacket and headed out.

Four hundred and fifty miles to Las Vegas, eight hours of solid driving with too much time to think. Roper reviewed the past week, culminating in the ugly picture of Sam Neally hanging over a green metal wastebasket.

Once the lights of Reno were at his back, giant patches of white showed up, like specters waiting for the dark of the desert. A rare headlight leant a solitary sadness to his trip. An hour south, the snow still iced the peaks but disappeared from nearby hills, with only a rare dirty patch springing up alongside the road.

Roper sucked in air laced with pine. He'd beat it out of the Bureau as fast as his reports would allow.

Once again, he'd strayed over the line of duty and fallen victim to lust. He could have just drugged her earlier, avoided her bed, and kept his conscience intact. Instead, he'd given way and let his cock lead the charge.

Where the hell was the good guy his friends and family knew? Having sex with another agent was ethically questionable, but sex with a suspect was reprehensible. Everyone at the Bureau knew the FBI general policy was 'don't ask, don't tell,' but he'd have sworn he'd never go far enough where he wondered if he'd crossed the line.

Roper forced his attention back to the road. He searched the darkness. Two worlds—his personal life, his job. Keeping them separate was about as easy as jogging through quicksand. He was suffocating as a result.

Neally'd initiated it. He hadn't coerced her, but he'd been a willing enough participant. The hell of it was he liked her. But, it had turned too personal for his taste, too far outside his comfort zone for sex.

He flipped on the radio and scanned the channels. Country. Jazz. Blues. Perfect; blues set the tone tonight. Too personal? What the hell was sex about if it wasn't personal? Seeing, touching, tasting every part of a stranger's body was sure as hell personal. Except with Jackie and Angie, it had never been more than functional.

So what about it, Roper? It's okay to have a quick lay with a suspect but keep it impersonal? The real problem stemmed from the fact that he'd taken a suspect to bed and discovered a human being with a soul there. She'd been awkward, but oddly charming and winsome.

Gripping the steering wheel, he clenched and unclenched aching fingers. Nina Simone paused a beat and whispered the last raw line of "Little Girl Blue."

He reached down, flipped the heater switch off, and punched at the window button. The window slid down further and biting air poured in, flooding his mind, steering him away from another replay of the bedroom scene.

His cell jarred him upright. "Go."

"Roper, Buchanan here."

"What's up?"

"We just finished for the night. She's on her way to the lock-up. We've come to an agreement of sorts, and we're definitely headed in the right direction."

Roper's last view of the interrogation scene had been something from a film noir, with Sam Neally sitting, head bent, under a single spotlight.

"How much longer do you need?"

"Things are moving fast. She's going to be ready in a day or two. She's been operating from the notion the Consortium's been blackmailing her all along." He paused. "Could be, but I read no real specific threats in their emails; just requests for cash."

Roper drew in cold air and let the sharp pain assault his lungs as penance. "So what's the latest on her friends?"

"They're sitting tight in that funky motel over in Susanville, but the chatter online is getting louder. I think we need to get in gear this week. Sounds like they're focused on the BLM's northern headquarters. Could be something big, or just blowing air, but we need to move on it."

"I'll be back in Reno Thursday night, Friday morning at the latest. Have Neally ready to roll. We'll use her place for set up. Let's keep things quiet if possible."

"Hell, Joe, that's unlikely since the press is already sniffing around trying to get a line on the woman we've rounded up."

"Do your best. I'd like to keep the Consortium from getting nervous by moving her around too much. We need to avoid any more incidents."

"I'll get the team in place, get her briefed and ready for you." Another of Buchanan's famous pregnant pauses followed. "You get some R&R. While you're there at home, pull your head together. And say hello to Joey."

"Will do. I'll get back with you tomorrow. Let's say by one." Roper sighed, wishing for a shower, but it couldn't wash away the smell and taste of his betrayal. He never wanted to face her again, but the hell of it was, he was going to be spending the next week with her. He wondered if he'd survive.

Roper flipped something less morose into the CD player, flicked the light on the dashboard, and checked the time; almost four. *Stop wallowing in it, buddy. You did the deed, now take the consequences and stop sucking on the guilt.*

Instead, he thought about Joey, the big eyes staring up at him unhappy since Daddy would need to leave again. He'd been gone too much lately.

His tiny, black-haired baby had turned up on the front porch in the arms of a Child Services woman. Terrified by the small, thin, creature flailing his fists about, Roper's only hope had been his mother, who'd flown in hours later from Phoenix. She'd come without a word of complaint, leaving Lester behind in the comfortable ranch house he'd sweat bullets to buy for her.

Roper pictured Lester Hernandez, his mother's second husband, showing up two months later, smiling broadly. Loving Roper's mother the way he did, he'd barely blinked an eye when she told him she had to move to Las Vegas. Lester only wanted whatever Dorothy wanted. And what Dorothy wanted was to be with her grandson. So, he'd sold the ranch house on the golf course in Phoenix, done all the heavy work of packing, and followed Dorothy to Vegas without protest.

Joe pushed the accelerator to the floor.

Four hours later, he sped past the sprawl eating up the desert north of the city. His small house sat two miles north of the Strip. Built in the early days of the boom, it was close enough to downtown for convenience but far enough away for relative quiet. The previous owner had been a croupier at the El Rancho, the first casino on the Strip, back in the Fifties when crowds of out-of-staters flocked to Vegas for work.

Years ago someone had painted it pale beige

with turquoise trim. The place still had the circa 1950 breezeway and semi-open carport. He pulled in and flipped off the motor, staring at the lawn tools Lester kept lined up on the back wall like a regiment of soldiers. Lester and his routines were always reassuring.

Roper shrugged out the tension in his shoulders. He shoved the door open and heaved his body out of the car. Two small hands caught at his trousers. He looked down at his son, standing with bare feet protruding like a penguin's beneath too-short, striped pajamas. In the past year Joey's hair had lightened up, matching Roper's, and tousled at this hour of the morning.

"Hi, pal! Where's your coat and shoes? It's cold out here." He dropped his bag and reached down to pull his son up into his arms. Roper buried his face in the thin stalk of a neck and inhaled Sugar Pops.

At three, Joey was small for his age but he'd make up for it soon, leaving a trail of outgrown clothes for Dorothy to pack away as she contemplated a hope for more grandchildren.

"Daddy! Did you bring me anything?" What he lacked in strength, Joey made up for with vitality. Roper tightened his grip on his son.

"Course I did. Just let me get my bags, and we'll get inside out of this cold. You shouldn't be out here without a coat, you know."

"I know. Grandma said so. But I was in a hurry."

Holding Joey, Roper grabbed his bags and staggered into the house.

"Joe! You made good time." His mother leaned out the breezeway door, hugging herself. At eight in the morning she wore full make-up. Roper smiled. Home.

"Mom." He eased Joey down and dropped a quick air kiss by her ear, avoiding brushing his stubbly chin on her pink cheek. "Where's Lester?"

"Gone for donuts." His mother never wasted words on basics. She had better things to talk about than waste time on small chit-chat.

Joe grinned. It was great to be home. Donuts. There wasn't a homecoming without donuts. Lester carried on the tradition started by Joe's father without protest, the most natural thing in the world. And Lester loved those donuts.

Dorothy peeled off Roper's coat and gently pushed him into a chair where Joey took his place on his lap immediately.

"Rough case?" His mother's eyes bored through him even as she poured coffee. There was no place to hide from her. She knew him too well. She scooted a mug across and sat down to wait for an answer.

"Yeah."

"Yeah? That's it? Nothing more?"

He shook his head and stroked his son's soft head. The only comfort he wanted right now was the weight of the small body against his chest. He refused to meet his mother's eyes. Talking with her was easy if you didn't mind being drilled into like a Nevada silver mine, but tonight his responses stuck in his throat. "Not right now, Mom. Maybe later." He shifted in his chair and turned to Joey.

****

Lester stood tall at five foot four, with a lean and handsome way about him that had nothing to do with his body and everything to do with his character. Right now, he carried a giant white box, bleeding grease on all sides. A childhood of little food had turned Lester into a man who bought three times more donuts than needed, making the local wildlife very happy with leftovers.

"Hey, Joe. Whadda ya know?" Lester reached over and caught Roper in a quick hug. The man was a contradiction, the face of a Colombian cartel hit man, hiding a heart as full as a new mother's. Roper had no problem returning the guy's warmth. He liked the man, especially because Lester made his mother happy.

"Not much, Lester, but it's always great to be back home with Joey." He grinned. It was bravado, nothing but show for Lester, and Dorothy knew it.

They sat around the chrome rimmed Formica table, and Roper listened as they reviewed the best moments of the past three weeks. He'd missed Joey's first day at nursery school, the tooth he'd lost last week, and the Tex-Mex grocery store opening two blocks away.

A half empty box of donuts later, Joey scuttled off to watch morning TV and Lester headed outside. Dorothy barely waited for the door to slam before she began again.

The voices of cartoon characters seeped into the kitchen and flittered about Joe, who refilled his coffee at the counter.

"So, before you tell me what's going on, Joe, you should know Angie called last night."

"Hell, that's all I need right now. What'd she want?"

"I think just to talk to you. About Joey."

He'd barely known Angie Petroski, a new agent, assigned to the Vegas office, they'd only gone out a couple of times. A quick interlude to spice up a boring stakeout, and they both lost interest. A month later, she'd transferred to L.A. without so much as a backward glance.

She'd never bothered to tell him she was pregnant, but six months later, she rang up Jack Buchanan from an L.A. hospital, two months early but in labor. Roper had been on special training assignment in D.C. Jack finally tracked him down, relaying the news: Joe Roper was a father. He'd been standing on a busy street in the thick heat of

Washington when he got the call. Clutching the phone with sweaty hands, he'd listened to Buchanan's account of Joey, lying in the Neonatal ICU two thousand miles away, not expected to survive.

It was one of those rare events when time stops. The smell of diesel still brought back the memory for him. From then on, being a good father took over his life.

One brief phone call later, Joey belonged to Roper, signed away like a puppy dropped off at a shelter. They heard from Angie at birthdays and Christmas.

"She said she's gotten married and wanted to say hello and see how Joey's doing."

"Did she talk with Joey?" Fear clutched at him and Roper jerked back, knocking over a pitcher on the table. Cream poured over the metal edge and trickled onto his pant leg. "Shit!"

"Hell's bells." His mother reached for a dishcloth, calmly wiping down the table and his pants, giving him the same look she gave Joey when he spilled his milk.

"Yes. Joseph, they spoke and all's well. She just wanted to talk with him. What has you so jumpy?"

He sighed and rubbed his face with both hands. He was losing it. "Mom, I'm sorry. I'm coming down off this case. I've had about five hours of sleep in the last thirty-six. If you want a sane conversation from me, you'll have to wait until I get some rest."

She'd never let it go so easily. "Joseph, what's going on? You don't let your work get to you."

"You know I can't talk about the case, not in the middle of it. Especially when I'm UC." He reached over and caught her hand. "Look, Mom, give me a couple of hours, and I'll let you have all the details. Or most of them." *Funny man.*

"You'll feel better if you tell me." As single-minded as a pit bull, she was the most focused woman he'd ever known. Joe pulled the white box with red letters "The Donut That Ate Vegas" toward him and reached for the last chocolate covered jelly. He took one bite, then another.

"Joseph," she paused to take another swipe at a spot on the table, "is this something to do with a woman?"

He stopped chewing and stared at her.

"Don't look so surprised. All your problems seem to have to do with women but that doesn't make you a failure. Relationships are tough. And I know you, Joe. You can trust yourself." She wasn't a woman who fidgeted, and she didn't now. "What is it? And don't use the UC thing to shut me out," she added. "You were up in Reno the past couple of weeks on a case. And you had an arrest last night, right? Well you're home now, so you're not UC."

He dropped the last bit of donut on his plate queasily. "I got involved with the suspect. Inappropriately involved." He pushed back his chair and reached for the coffee pot, tipping the last of it into his mug. Without waiting to see her reaction, he turned and stared out the window. Lester was busy scattering birdseed and donut crumbs on the ground, oblivious to the drama in his kitchen. "Shit. I hate this."

"Come on, Joe. What do you mean by 'involved'?"

He turned back. "I slept with her."

Married to his father thirty-one years and career FBI when he died, she'd heard it all. She knew the rules and knew what got an agent benched, the two major ones being booze and broads. OPR, the Office of Professional Responsibility, was the most dreaded acronym in the Bureau. Nobody wanted to get called on that particular carpet.

"Okay. So what happened?"

"She's a potential inside source, so my job was to

get myself into her life as fast as possible and search for ways to pull her to our team. I didn't need to have sex with her to get information. I liked her. I felt compassion for her circumstances, and I was attracted to her, so I slept with her. Then, I had her arrested."

"She's in jail?"

"Being held for questioning, until she takes the deal we're offering to cut her. If she works for us, she's promised a clean record and freedom."

"Are you still on the case?"

"Yeah. I'm scheduled to run her as my inside source."

"So she knows you were the one who turned her in?"

"Since last night. When she found out, she took a swing at me." Silence.

"And is she going to be willing to work with you?"

"She doesn't have a choice. If she wants her freedom, she'll work with us. With me, in particular."

"So you're going back up to Reno?"

"Yeah. I'll set up the sting operation with her as bait."

"Then what's the problem?" She stood up and began sweeping tiny crumbles of donut onto her open palm.

"The problem is I feel like crap. And I don't want to feel that way."

She loaded her dishwasher with the precise, quick movements he'd seen her use for forty years. "Joseph, your problem has always been too much conscience. Even as a kid, if a bunch of your friends toilet-papered a house, you'd be the only one to confess and be punished. It's an admirable, if overworked, character trait of yours. I just wish you'd stop beating yourself up for being human and admit you're a guy with a sensitive heart who cares too much about protecting women. The only complaint I have about you is that the women you pick don't demonstrate the best of character themselves."

Roper turned back to the window, watching Lester taking swings with his five iron. Ten a.m. and he felt beat, too damned tired for the day to only be starting. "Well then, I guess you could say I may have disappointed you again on that score. This one's wanted by the FBI."

"What was her crime?" Her question caught him off guard and he didn't reply at once. "What was her crime?" she repeated.

"Twelve years ago, when she was eighteen, she got herself involved with an environmental terrorist group who set fire to some cabins in a national forest." He watched Lester put aside his club and pick up a shovel. The man smiled, thrilled to be digging a hole for one of Dorothy's plants. "It was a bunch of college kids. When the protest went south, she ran. She's been underground for twelve years. We found her a couple of months ago, tracked her to Reno and, like I said, are going to use her as an inside source. That's all I can say." Roper opened the dishwasher and turned his mug upside down on the rack. "Look, Mom. I've gotta get some sleep."

She came over and reached up to kiss him on the cheek. "All right, Joseph. You've got clean sheets, and there are towels on your bed. Joey and I are going shopping."

He gave her a brief hug. "Thanks, Mom. Wake me if I sleep longer than noon."

"I will. And don't worry. Things have a way of working out, even the worst of things. You'll do what's right."

He drew the shades in his bedroom, threw off his clothes, and hit the shower for two minutes. Still damp, he slid under the cool duvet and was asleep in two more minutes. But even in his sleep he chased Sam Neally down a deserted road into a bottomless black lake.

Chapter Sixteen

Jail turned out to be a bizarre mixture of fun house and insane asylum. At three thirty she'd been booked in with a group of women in various stages of fancy undress, her holding cellmates. A weed amidst orchids, she'd sat in her jeans and sweats at the end of a line of exotic ladies, waiting to be mugged and printed.

One after the other of the women made funny, distorted faces for their grainy mug shots. Fingerprinting dragged on another hour, slowed down by their recurring games. It was dawn before the guards moved them all to the block. Sam followed dutifully. The strange camaraderie she felt with these women left her with an ache in her chest.

The fun continued as the women chanted and banged on bars, calling the guards, who responded as eagerly as puppy dogs in a nursery school.

By ten a.m., the ladies were gone, one by one bonded out by their lawyers. Sam stayed behind, left with the meth addicts and habitual drunks. She was the only one with a fancy lawyer and any hope of being released.

With two hours of sleep, Sam stumbled along the gunmetal gray hall, following the painted red line behind her guard. She walked carefully to avoid the hem of the orange jumpsuit two inches too long. A thin rod of pain ran down her bad leg from ankle to thigh.

She shifted her shoulders and eased the accompanying ache in her neck. Her body was adaptable, but sleeping hunched over in a corner of an airless cellblock with only a cold cement wall for a pillow was barely surviving.

Until last night, jail had been nothing more than a concept, a place where criminals belonged. Now it was a world peopled by women like her, whose blind actions in moments of powerlessness changed their lives forever.

"Your lawyer's here." The guard's words fell out automatic and flat. He wasn't unkind, just worn out from a thankless job done in dehumanizing conditions.

The lawyer's room consisted of a three by three foot cubicle. One folding chair sat on either side of a clear partition. A useless phone dangled from the wall, leaving the lawyer and client the only option of shouting at each other through thick glass like angry neighbors.

"When can I get out of here, Deckard?"

He sighed, ran a palm over the top of his shaved head. She could barely hear his Brooklyn-accented voice as he reviewed the charges against her: Conspiracy to commit a terrorist offense involving a foreseeable risk of serious bodily injury, involving the destruction of government property; courtesy of Section 809 of the Patriot Act of October 26, 2001.

"Sam, twelve years ago setting fire to a cabin might have seemed fairly innocuous, but it's a different world today. Terrorism is serious business, as in Homeland Security." He pulled a cigar out of his breast pocket. She almost smiled at the strangeness of a world where she had a lawyer who wore a designer suit costing more than her entire year's income.

Deckard gave a quick glance around and lit up the stogie. It was definitely illegal to smoke on county property, but no one stopped him. "When they take you over to the FBI office later today, I'll be there to make sure your rights are protected, but you're going to have to play their game. It's your golden door out of this mess."

She frowned. "Do they think I've been working with the Consortium all these years?

"I don't know, but I made a point of reminding them you've been victimized here. The money you shelled out to the group is as good of a defense as evidence, depending on how you spin it. Let's sit tight and see what they want. They have something in mind. Otherwise, you'd have been charged by now. Instead you're just being held for questioning."

Sam nodded, holding her breath against the foul cigar smoke seeping in around cracks in the glass. "Deckard. Can you get Keddie in to see me?"

He took two more puffs. "She'll stop by when she gets off work tonight. Or early tomorrow. Do you want her to bring you anything?"

"Some money to get some food from the commissary. And a phone card. I can make some phone calls, can't I?"

"Yes, just don't make any calls you don't want heard. I'll make sure Keddie gets in."

"When do I get out?" That was the real question.

"Maybe tomorrow. They need to get your statement down and offer up their deal. Let's wait and see what they have to say."

She sighed and leaned over, resting her forehead on the cool metal table. "I'm not sure if I can take another night sleeping on the floor."

"I'll see what I can do about getting you a separate cell. They're overcrowded as usual, but maybe we can get the Feds to spring for a single."

"Just see what you can do. And thanks, Deckard. I appreciate it."

****

It was mid afternoon before they came for her. Her transport van was white, the good guys car. She watched the surreal world fly past, the random gray-black heaps of snow looking like tattered bodies, run over and left alongside the curbs. They'd allowed her no shower, just a quick sponge bath after a lunch tray. Her orange jumpsuit reeked of overcrowded jail, a mixture of perspiration, government issued rations and disinfectant.

Buchanan glanced up calmly as she entered the interrogation room, followed by Deckard. No Joe Roper today.

"Take a seat, Ms. Neally. Samantha. And Mr. Stewart." Buchanan opened a white paper sack and extracted a plastic box filled with cut fruit. "I know food can be a bit of a problem at the jail, so I brought you something." He slid Starbucks cups toward them and uncapped his own.

"Now, let's get back to where we left off. You haven't had any contact with your former friends until recently?"

"No. Not for twelve years. Until about five months ago." She snapped open the fruit box and picked up the fork he pushed at her. "I'm not sure . Maybe they only recently located me or maybe they had no use for me before. Since they're thinking about protesting the wild horse problem..."

"They told you specifically they were going to do something in northern Nevada?"

"You said you saw the emails. They mentioned they were interested in the BLM and the horses. That's all. The emails started casual at first, except they mentioned where I lived."

"And you replied?"

"No, I ignored it."

"So they didn't ask for money the first time?"

"No. The first few emails were conversational, as if they were trying to reconnect. It took them three tries to ask for money."

"How long before they did ask?"

"About a month."

"At what point did you feel threatened?"

"From the beginning. After all these years, having someone tell me they knew exactly where I lived was disconcerting when I put so much effort into remaining anonymous. But when they started asking for cash I began to get seriously afraid. I tried blocking their mail, got a new user name." She rubbed her eyes. Shadows hugged the room, even in daylight, lack of sleep causing images to flicker in front of her eyes. Her face felt shrunken, as though she'd aged ten years in twenty-four hours.

"It took them a week to find my new email. And it began again. They sent me a web address. I checked out the site and found references to me there, as Catherine Bell. Not where I lived at first. They saved that for the next link. The web site belonged to another group, an offshoot of the Consortium."

"Green Justice?"

"Yes." She raised her eyes. "They rambled on about my past, nothing specific," she said, "so I paid them the $200 they wanted. Within three days."

"Why'd you pay them the money? They're on the run themselves. Anything close to criminal activity on their part would bring us down on them. And aside from money, why would they want to reconnect with you?"

"I don't know. I barely know them, but it was frightening to see my name on the internet and know people were talking about me. I felt completely exposed." She sank lower in her seat, already exhausted. "I didn't know if it was even the Consortium contacting me. It could have been the FBI. Or someone else." The last word floated about the room.

"So you took a chance if you gave them some cash, they'd leave you alone?"

"I was hoping they'd let it go with the first payment." She grabbed the coffee and snapped off the lid, avoiding his eyes. "There was nothing from them for a month. They said they would come see me in Nevada, and they could use some help from me. I sent them another $200 and told them I wasn't interested." Sam smiled bitterly. "Why should I believe them? No reason, but I was trapped. I ignored the next email." She sipped at the lukewarm coffee. "They asked for more money in the next two months, and I jumped both times. Finally, I had enough, and last week, told them I was done sending them cash." His serve.

Deckard cleared his throat. "I'd like to know, Special Agent Buchanan, what you're looking for here? My client is exhausted. She only got a couple of hours sleep last night lying on the floor of your overcrowded jail. I need to get some sense of where this is leading."

Buchanan shrugged, so slight a move she almost missed it. "We have enough evidence to call a grand jury for Ms. Bell. Ms. Neally, that is. But I feel fairly certain at this point she's telling the truth and hasn't been involved for the past twelve years. Like you said, Mr. Stewart, the evidence we've got could go either way. We're not interested in wasting our time and money on your client. We are interested in getting something on the Consortium and putting a stop to their current plans."

"And do you have an idea of exactly what they're planning?" Deckard, the pit-bull in Armani.

"As your client indicated, we believe they're going to make a big move here in Nevada. That's all I can say for now."

"And you want to use my client as bait?"

"I prefer to call her an inside source. They've been in contact with her recently. We think she could offer them money, offer her services even, and we'll pull them in. We're not going to put your client in any direct danger. We'll have an agent with her at all times and can promise there won't be a repeat of the incidents last week."

Deckard turned to Sam. "What incidents?"

"Someone jumped my truck in the parking lot of Porky's last week. And someone broke into my house a couple of days later and turned on the gas. There's no proof it was the Consortium, but it could have been, I suppose."

"We've got the group under surveillance a good distance from your client's place right now," Buchanan said, "and we're keeping close tabs on them." He turned to her. "You don't think the man in the parking lot was one of your former friends?"

"I have no idea. I didn't really see the man's face or recognize his voice, but it's been twelve years." She sat her cup down. "And I have no idea who broke into my house."

Deckard held up a hand, stopping her monologue. "Before we go any further with your questions, what are you offering here, Agent?"

"We're ready to give Ms. Neally immunity, if she's willing to cooperate with us."

"Cooperate how?"

"Give us everything she can recall about her friends and the events of twelve years ago, be willing to testify against them as to what she knows and what they're currently proposing. We'll set her up to work with our agents to bring the group in. We don't have a lot of time to get this going. We need her assistance now. If she plays, we'll give her full immunity in return, and once we complete our operation, she'll be free to go."

"What guarantee does she have she won't be in danger?"

"We'll insure her safety. She won't be dealing face to face with any of them, just email or phone contact to get things rolling."

"I want to make sure my sister has protection also," Sam interjected.

"You'll have it."

Deckard stood up and went to the window, his back to them. "We're going to need to see all of it in writing before she answers any more questions."

"We can do that, but we need to get this done soon. We're ready to go on this, and we need your word you'll give us complete cooperation."

Deckard turned and looked over at Sam. Her call.

"If you'll promise you'll leave me alone once this is over, then you have my word. And some sort of protection or guarantee the Consortium won't come after me in the future."

"Agreed." Buchanan stood up and motioned to an agent. "You'll have to spend two more nights in jail, but I'll see what I can do about getting you more privacy."

"All right. Let's get started."

Four hours of questions and paperwork later, she made the trip back to jail and a new cell. It was her game now, as long as she cooperated; hers and the FBI. Where things went after that was the real question.

Chapter Seventeen

Sam stared up at the single light bulb dangling overhead. She pictured the world outside and tried to imagine freedom, but she'd already forgotten how it looked and felt. Here it was, the opportunity to salvage her life. She'd failed miserably so far, spending twenty years avoiding the world.

The cell belonged to her but it was too cold and too brightly lit. The smell of jail, unwashed bodies and bad food, hung in the air and permeated her clothes.

Unable to sleep, she tried not to think about Joe Roper. Instead she wondered what Robert Mathias had turned up about her mother.

Her mother. Twenty years of faded memories, most of them painful. As far back as she could recall, the three of them, her mother, herself and her sister, had moved from one disreputable Omaha neighborhood to another. Her mother's jobs, usually bookkeeping, had kept them barely going, always moving on, searching for something better.

With so many men's faces coming and going, she and Mary Beth knew when their mother didn't come back that she'd finally found something better. On that hot summer day, she'd dropped them off at a small brick bungalow on a street crowded with dirty, wild kids. Kissing them goodbye, she'd caught up the arm of the man beside her and strolled out of their lives.

Sam pushed the thin pillow behind her back, avoiding the damp cement seeping through the thin cotton jumpsuit. She stared at a dull worn spot on the floor of her cell, evidence of all the other desperate women who'd been there before her.

An hour after breakfast, a guard came to get her. A visitor.

The surroundings had a frightening sameness about them, a world of gray and orange. Keddie was the only break in the decor. She sat like an exotic bird at the scarred gray table, flashing smiles at the guard.

"Sam."

Sam reached across the table to touch her hand.

"No contact, please."

"Keddie. Thanks for coming."

"Of course I'd come. What'd you expect?"

Sam shook her head. "I don't know. Why should you be eager to visit a friend who'd lied to you? A fugitive?"

"Oh, well, that. It was a one-time event from what Deck tells me. So what's the big deal? You were just a kid."

"I suppose the FBI has been all over you."

"Well, not exactly all over me, but they pulled me in for questioning, as they say in CSI. But, what the hell? It's the FBI, for Chrissake! Not the Mafia. They didn't use a rubber hose. Just thumbscrews."

"I'm sorry, Ked. You know you're my lifeline, one of my few friends. You and Charlie." Sam made a face. "So they questioned you. Was it bad?"

"No sweat. If I can handle a belligerent drunk at my blackjack table, I can handle a couple of young FBI dudes." She drew a newspaper out and held up the Reno paper. "I don't suppose you've seen this? Your story made the front page. The FBI making an arrest on a twelve-year-old cold case is big news, especially ecoterrorism. Hell, Sam, you're famous."

"I thought I already had my fifteen minutes of fame twelve years ago. No fair." She leaned over to study the page and her orange jumpsuit twisted about her like a straight jacket.

"So tell me what's happening? Deckard's being discreet. All he would say is that you're getting out, probably tomorrow. A plea bargain or something."

"I'm going to be their carrot dangled in front of my old pals. Once they get things wrapped up with them, I'm free."

"Is it dangerous?"

"They say not. They're giving me protection until things are safe."

Keddie shifted in her chair. "How did they find you?"

"The FBI? The internet."

"So aside from getting caught, spending time in jail, what else is there? There's something you're not saying."

"Joe Thorp. You remember him, the man I spent twenty-four glorious hours with in bed? Well, it turns out his real name is Joe Roper, and he's an undercover FBI agent. The whole thing was a set-up, meeting me by chance in town, taking me out, getting stranded at my place."

Keddie leapt up, knocking over her chair. "Hell!" The guard moved quickly to her side and caught hold of her arm, Lancelot of the lock-up.

"I'm fine. Just a teensy bit clumsy is all." She smiled up at the guard, in his early twenties, probably a nice kid who regularly opened doors for women. He stepped back, looking uncertain, and watched Keddie pull her chair upright.

"Dammit, Sam! I mean, God, talk about sleeping with the enemy."

"Shh! Not so loud, Ked. I don't want every person in this place to know what happened."

"I'm sorry. I know it's gotta feel real bad, but he's nothing but a fucking loser. Especially pretending to be a nice guy. The least he could have done was be the jerk he is."

Humor. Sam smiled. Keddie brought a joke to every situation.

"So what do you need? I brought you a phone card and some cash. It's downstairs with the guards. Anything else I can do?"

"A key? Or maybe a cake with a file in it." Sam flashed a weak smile and glanced at the guard. "Can you call Charlie Lemon and see if Dourcet is doing okay? And ask him to keep an eye on my place."

"Don't worry about your place or Dourcet. I'll give him a call, but not to worry. Charlie loves that dog. While I'm at it, I'll go dig up some dirt on your FBI guy. Roper, is it?"

"Don't call him 'my FBI guy.'"

"Okay, that bastard, Roper." Keddie looked startlingly alive in the gray room, wearing a chartreuse tank top under a black see-through blouse.

"Don't bother. My poor judge of character is to blame, or maybe my lack of practice over the last twelve years."

"You're okay, babe. He's the spitball, remember? You'd think a Federal agent sleeping with a suspect would be frowned upon."

"I have no idea what's frowned upon by the FBI."

"Well, it certainly seems like it worked out fine for him, doesn't it? He gets sex on the job, captures a fugitive, and he's a hero."

"Why dig up more on him? What's the point?"

"To get even. Maybe you could file some sort of class action suit against him—conflict of interest, or maybe sexual misconduct. Hell, I don't know, but everyone's filing civil suits these days."

"You've been spending too much time with Deckard. How would someone like me, with no ready cash and few friends, be able to bring a law suit against a Federal agent?"

"Well, there's definitely got to be something illegal about sleeping with a suspect. He can't do it and get away with that crap. We'll turn him in, have his badge, and get him sent to Gitmo. Or whatever they do with bad agents."

"Keddie, I know you're on my side, but I don't want to prosecute Joe. I just want to forget him."

"Well at least let me pass this on to Deckard. As a fall back plan, in case the immunity thing goes bad. Deck will love it."

"I don't care. I don't have the energy right now to bother with it. I'm too busy trying to survive jail."

Keddie's face crumpled. "Oh, God, Sam. I'm a jerk. I have no idea what it's like inside these days."

"You've spent time in jail?"

"Well, not me exactly, but one of my brothers. You know. Marty. He spent two weeks in the Eureka jail when he was fifteen. Car theft. He loves his cars."

Sam grinned. Keddie would defame her entire family to make Sam laugh. Martin was studying for the priesthood. He did love cars, though.

"So is it dangerous? What they're asking you to do?"

"Well, I'm the worm on the hook dangled in front of my former friends. But they promised no risk." Sam reached out a hand to Keddie, stopped again by the frowning guard. "At least I'm not running any more. I don't think I could manage it. I'd have so many people on my tail; between the FBI and the Consortium, it would look like a traveling circus. Twelve years in hiding is enough." She reached up and parted her hair, showing the lighter roots. "Underneath this black mess is the real me."

"What color is it?"

"I think it was sort of a light brown then, but who knows? Maybe I've gone gray over the years from worry."

"I always did wonder why you had the Goth thing going, but, hey, who am I to question somebody's look?" Today, her own hair had fuchsia streaks. "How's the food in here?"

"Well, I'm not used to eating things I can't identify, but other than that, it's fine. I think it's been a lot of meat. So much for being a vegetarian. The vegetables are gray and mushy anyway. At least I think they're the vegetables. And fruit doesn't come with the jail kitchen repertoire."

"I'll bring you some fruit, okay?"

"Sure. Hopefully I'll be out of here before you have time."

Keddie stood up to go. "Sam, what about your sister? You've been in touch with her?"

"No. The FBI have. I'd like you to call her and tell her I'm okay. Don't worry her, just make it sound like I'm being questioned and things are going to be better."

"Give me her number."

Keddie pulled out a pen and wrote it on the edge of the newspaper. A bell rang and the guard stepped forward.

"Don't worry, Sam. I'll handle everything."

"Thanks, Keddie. Give my love to Mary Beth."

"Sure."

"You've managed to brighten up my day, as usual."

Sam stared at the door, her stomach clenched into a small, hard ball. Her life was coming apart but the newfound longing for something or someone beyond her empty life kept her company.

Chapter Eighteen

Lingering in Las Vegas. It sounded like a bad movie, but Roper felt only relief slipping into the familiar combination of Mr. Mom, GI Joe, and Son of the Year. Soon enough he'd have to head back to Reno and his job.

Roper slept six dreamless hours and woke up ready to spend the rest of the day catching up on the three weeks he'd missed of Joey's life. Even his mother refused to spoil it, throwing him no more questions and offering no more philosophical evaluations of his character.

Instead, she filled him with food and kept him busy with errands. His only reality check was Buchanan, eager to get Joe back by Friday.

Wednesday played out happy with his family, but Thursday he began to lose the fight with his demons. The next day, he'd have to go back and face Sam Neally. He ate breakfast with Joey, drove him to his nursery school, and roamed around town doing mindless tasks he didn't need to perform. But nothing kept his mental battle quiet for long.

Two hours later, he tossed in the torture towel and went home. He pulled out his laptop and stared at the white lid. The house was silent, his mom and Lester off at some sale or other, leaving him free to torment himself in the quiet of his small study. The room was full of his past—photos of him playing football, his baseball trophy, his diplomas. And more pictures of Joey.

Hell. Roper put in his call to Buchanan.

"How's it going, Jack?"

"Same ole. How's the weather down there?"

"Cold. Looks like snow, must have brought it with me." Enough bullshit. "Where are we at? How's she doing?"

"We're gathering data from her today. She's cooperating, looks tired but seems determined to carry this through. No BS from her.

"Yeah, well that's no surprise. She might be cautious, but when she shoots, it's straight at the mark"

A long pause followed. "You okay with being her handler in this operation, Joe?"

"Yeah. We already set it up. We're going to have to get past the bad feelings, but I'll manage."

"All right. I think we can agree she's at some risk from someone, maybe a renegade member of the group."

"I'll watch her. No one's getting close again."

"You'll be back tomorrow?" Buchanan sounded worn out himself.

"I'll be there by two, three at the latest. How's the stakeout in Susanville going?"

"I've got Cramer and Jacobson on it. They're so bored staring at the parking lot of that crappy motel, they're actually talking to each other. We're gonna have to get the show on the road, Joe, or pretty soon they'll be in love."

"That I'd like to see." Roper waited but Buchanan didn't sign off. "Something else, Jack?"

"Yeah, there is. Be careful, Joe. You gonna be okay spending that much time with her?" Roper knew it for what it was, a simple warning between friends. "You looked like hell when you left. Whatever it is, I just want to know you can keep your personal feelings out of this operation. That's all."

Roper sighed. "I'm struggling a little, but I can

do my job, I promise you I won't blow this thing."

"Okay. Just checking."

"It's a go, and I'll deal with my personal shit."

"Enough said."

"Did you do some checking on that PI in Nebraska she sent dough to?"

"Did a quick background on him, nothing there I could find. The guy's reputable, runs a low profile operation, no red flags in his history to raise any warning around terrorism. What do you make of it?"

"Don't know. Want to put out some feelers to the Omaha office? And have them forward it on to me. What about the sister? Get anything new from her?"

"The sister freaked out. She's all set to come rescue her big sister." Buchanan rattled some papers.

"And the fly boy?"

"The pilot claims he knows nothing about her. He's only in Reno on layovers once or twice a month."

"And? He never got interested enough to find anything out about her? Never asked questions?"

"Nope. Seems all he did was take her out once a month."

"And the friend? The blackjack dealer?"

"She's pissed at us right now. We're getting nothing from her."

Roper sighed. He needed to get back and move it along before the whole operation blew up. "She's still in jail?"

"Yeah. You know the drill these days. With any mention of terrorism, we've got a green light to keep her locked up."

"So there's no possibility she'll slip away from you before I get back?"

"Nope. But get your butt up here tomorrow, Roper, and work your magic on her."

"Yeah, right."

Joey giggled from the kitchen. "I gotta go, Buchanan. My kid's back. See you tomorrow." Roper flipped his phone shut and looked up. His mother stood in front of his desk, looking unhappy. Damn.

Joey peeked around her legs, and Roper held out his arms to his son.

"How was nursery school, buddy?"

"Good. I drew a picture." Joey held up a paper with a pink something, maybe a flamingo, or an elephant.

"Fantastic! Let's see it closer." He held the picture up, avoiding his mother's gaze on him.

"Joey, you can tell your dad about school after your nap."

Joey looked ready to argue but Roper intervened. It was time to get back to being a father. He tousled his son's hair, bent over, and whispered to him. "Take a nap now, and you and I'll go out to the Mall when you get up. Is it a deal?" He kissed his son and aimed him for his bedroom.

It took Dorothy no more than ten seconds after Joe returned to call her meeting to order. "You okay to talk now, Joseph?"

"Sure. But if it's about my case, I've already told you everything I can."

"You had lunch yet?"

"No. You making?"

She motioned and he followed. They stepped into Dorothy's world, a kitchen yellow enough to blind a normal person.

"How was the sale?"

"Like they all are, a lot of old people wandering around looking to save a dollar on a useless piece of junk. You've developed a sudden interest in yard sales?"

The high gloss white chair printed with yellow daisies made him nervous, but it was the only seat available, so he sat down gingerly. Knife in hand, she returned to the business of the red, green, and yellow things huddled on the cutting board, waiting for the sacrifice. She gave the vegetables a piercing glance and then turned it on him.

"Just give me a general overview of the crime."

He took a deep breath, letting it out, a slow puncture. "Like I told you, a twelve year old cold case, a fire set by an environmental group. She was involved with them."

"And you were assigned to this one particular woman?"

"Yeah. Work my way into her life, get inside her house, and gather enough evidence to reel her in. Get enough stuff on her that she's willing to be dangled in front of her old friends. And turn states evidence against them."

Dorothy Roper Hernandez had been taught her questioning technique by his father, a pro at it, and she proved as relentless. She could have been an agent herself. It didn't matter if he evaded her questions, her intuition was too good, and she figured it out. "So, you've gotten into something here, Joseph." She rolled her eyes at him. "I won't say anything further, but I know you. You'll straighten it out." She shoved the vegetables into a bowl. "What about Angie? Did you reach her?"

Roper massaged his forehead. He was getting a headache. "I'll put a call in to her." For someone who'd had his child, it was ludicrous. He knew her about as well as he knew his dry cleaner. Worse, he could talk to his dry cleaner. Angie was a good woman in her own way, but he felt like he had to wing it every time he spoke with her.

His mother straightened her dress. It had pale yellow flowers all over it as well. Whatever the time of day, his mother was dressed for a garden party about to happen. "Joseph, it looks to me like you've got a few too many irons in the fire right now. I hope one of them doesn't burn you when you're not looking."

"I'll handle it. Don't worry, Mom." He leaned over and kissed her cheek, earning a smile.

"When are you leaving?"

"Tomorrow morning, by seven. I should be finished up there by Tuesday or Wednesday at the latest. I'll be back down here for a few days before I return to Reno to wrap things up."

She placed a sandwich on the table in front of him and poured him milk. "So she's something, huh?"

"What?"

"Well, you're shook up about this woman in Reno, so she must be something. Which brings us back to where we left off last night, Joseph. I have more things to say. You're my son and you're just like your father, a good agent and a kind man. If you got involved with her, you care about her." She tossed her next words over her shoulder, a reprieve. "We bought ice cream. Want some?"

****

Roper put off phoning Angie until six, assuming she'd be home by then, hoping she wouldn't. He didn't get his wish. Her voice sounded the same as always, with that throaty whisper he'd fallen for on his way into her bed. He searched his emotions for lust; nothing.

Their conversation took five minutes, but it surprised him. Either marriage had worked a miracle on her, or he'd gone through some sort of transformation in the last couple of weeks. They talked like casual acquaintances, even friends; she seemed pleasant, friendly and totally cooperative. His reassurances about Joey led to an even more surprising turn of events. He invited her to spend some time with his son, and she agreed. He hung up, scratching his head. Who'd have believed it?

Roper sat down and pulled his son's warm body into his lap. He dreaded telling Joey he was leaving again in the morning for Reno, one more separation.

The cell phone vibrated in his pocket, and Roper jumped. Jackie. He deposited Joey in his mother's lap and slipped into the kitchen.

"Joe. How are you? Glad to be home, I bet." She was one of those people who always answered her own questions, one of the many minor things that drove him crazy. Great in bed, and low maintenance in some ways, but she was getting to be more and more of an intrusion in his life.

"Jackie. I'm just about to put Joey to bed. Can I give you a call back?"

"Sure. Rather than calling, come on over. I could do with a little exercise."

One of the things he did like about her was her directness. No need to wonder what she was thinking. She made it clear what she wanted.

He looked into the living room where his mother sat holding Joey, her eyes glued to the TV, her ears tuned to his conversation. What he really needed wasn't exercise but to clean up his life. He took a deep breath, held his nose, and jumped into the pool. "All right. I'll be there by ten."

Two hours later, Dorothy took a final swipe at the counter and shut off the light. "Say hello to Jackie for me." Her words trailed him out the back door.

Jackie lived on the other side of the Strip, twenty minutes in the daytime, thirty on a busy night which meant most nights. She met him at the door in a silky wraparound garment slit to her navel. She was naked beneath. A heavy feeling circled about him, a vulture waiting to take a dive at the road kill of the guilt cluttering his mind. He sidestepped her arms and held up a hand. "Jackie. We need to have a talk."

"Oh-oh. I thought something was wrong. What is it Joe?"

"Can we sit down?"

The living room she led him into was unfamiliar. They never stopped there but always made for the bedroom. The decorating scheme was similar, moss green with a lot of fancy scrollwork and heavy flowers. Minimalism was not her thing and the room was as impersonal as their relationship had felt.

He slid his jacket off and sat down on the edge of a satin chair, feeling like a lizard in a lovebird's cage. As prim as a silk-clad schoolgirl, she drew her robe tightly together and sat down sideways on the chaise lounge opposite. He could read nothing on her face except concern. No pleasure, no joy, no satisfaction. He didn't blame her.

"Jackie. There's no way to say this except to just say it. We've had a lot of fun and some great companionship, but I don't think it's working."

"Who is she?"

"There's no one serious, Jackie."

"If you're calling it off with us, you've got to have someone else lined up. I know you, Joe. You're too into sex to just call it off without someone else out there."

"There is no one else. I'm not in the market. You know I've been working on this case the past four months and UC the past few weeks."

She narrowed her gaze at him. "Then why the sudden urge to end our relationship? I'm sure not wanting a long term commitment from you."

"I know that, Jackie. You and I have both agreed we've wanted to keep this pretty casual and the relationship's often a matter of convenience. You're a nice woman and we've had fun, but I'm feeling the need to get my life in order. Call it early mid life crisis or just getting my priorities a little more in line, but I'm feeling the need to make some serious changes. My son's getting older, and I need to focus on him. Getting together for an hour here and there, when we're both feeling the need, worked great for us, but I can't explain where I'm going to him. He's getting old enough to notice things."

"Are you saying you're looking for something solid for him?"

"No, like I said, I'm not seriously looking right now, but I have a lot of loose ends in my life. I'm committed to sorting out my priorities and where I'm focused. I guess you could call it putting some integrity and stability into my life."

"Well, if that's the way you want it, Joe. I have a feeling you have something going up in Reno, but if you feel it's time to move on, that's fine. It's been fun and you can always give me a call if you change your mind." And that was that. He was even more inconsequential than he'd assumed. "When do you leave?" She reached across and straightened a pillow, smoothing out the satin cover. He felt a strange kinship with it and about as useful.

"I go back tomorrow morning, early."

Roper slid his worn leather jacket on and searched for some lighthearted banter to end the evening. Nothing. Nothing to say except goodbye. Goodnight and good luck.

She stopped in front of him, adjusting his jacket, staring into his face intently. The first real look they'd exchanged. "Get your next girlfriend to buy you a new jacket, Roper. This one looks like something you picked off a perp."

Bending down, he brushed her cheek with his lips. "Thanks, Jackie. I'll let myself out." He turned at the door for a last look. "You're an amazing woman. I hope you get everything you want."

It was as cold as hell now as Roper drove home, shivering in the dark car. His mind spun around like an over-wound alarm clock, trying not to think about

Jackie in her tidy house, trying not to think about Sam in her grim cell. Like mirrors held up in front of him as he drove, the events of the past few weeks were repugnant reminders of what his life had become.

Roper's phone buzzed. He pulled to a halt at a red light, the only car in the intersection, shoved the gear stick into neutral and gunned the engine.

"Roper here. What's up?"

"I've got some news, Joe. We've gotten a line on another Consortium member who slipped below our radar. We're tracking the lead right now. He could be our loose cannon causing the problems with Neally." Buchanan sounded more exhausted than Joe felt.

"Fuck. Any evidence he's got a connection to her?"

"No. We're working backwards from a phone call made from Susanville. Looks like he's in Sparks, but there's no direct link with your friend. I've got Cramer and Jacobson on it. I sent Cramer out to Neally's place to keep watch, and Jacobson is following up with the motel clerk in Sparks."

"I'll leave tonight. Just give me an hour to say my goodbyes to Joey and my mother, then I'm on the road." Disillusioned and restless, he needed to get moving. A kick of adrenaline from his job sounded like a good thing right now. Tomorrow was Friday and he'd be back in Reno.

With all the distaste at the messes cluttering his life, there was a small corner of his mind satisfied that he'd taken the first steps toward straightening it out. Just behind that was an almost imperceptible sense of expectation at the thought of seeing Sam Neally again. He threw the car into first and hauled for home, making it through the light as it turned from yellow to red. He needed to get moving.

Chapter Nineteen

Deckard breezed into her cell, not bothering with the cramped lawyer's cubicle.

"Hey Deck, Where you off to? A Mafia picnic?" Deckard was wearing his best suit.

"You've been spending too much time talking to Keddie. Gather up your things, Sam. You're out of here."

Things? Sam checked about her cell to see what she might have hoarded. Her toothbrush?

It moved fast after that, from cellblock to holding area for processing with Deckard tagging along. He waited for them to push her personal items through the small opening in the cage and issued instructions as she signed the papers. Released into the custody of an agent, no bail required. Ordered not to leave the area. For a few minutes at least, she was free.

She pulled out the crumpled clothes she'd been wearing when booked into jail. They'd been tagged and bagged but left unlaundered. The distinct odor of fear still clung to them. Sniffing at a t-shirt, she wadded it into a ball and shoved it back into the sack. The cheap clothes issued all inmates on release would do just fine.

"I'm due in court in fifteen minutes, Sam." Deckard ordered her to sit tight, wait for her handler, and do whatever the Feds asked. "I'll be in touch. You'll be fine."

Yeah, right.

In egg yolk yellow shirt and matching polyester

slacks that hung on her at least two sizes too large, she wondered whose body they'd given her this morning. The shoes, standard jail issue sneakers, fit at least.

She clutched a small brown sack stamped with WCCC in one hand. Someone had forgotten her jacket, or lost it. She'd have to do with shirtsleeves. Little Orphan Annie out on bail. It felt more like three years than three days she'd been here.

At least the weather had turned warmer overnight, more typical of Las Vegas than Reno. No more little dirty piles of anything were left behind to remind people it was coming on winter.

She stood staring out the wide-paned glass window of the Washoe County Detention Center at the tiny cars racing by on the Interstate heading north, north toward Pyramid Lake and home. She'd be one of them herself, except there would be some FBI agent pulling her strings. But if she played their game for a week, she'd be home free.

Conscious of the guard's eyes following every move, she pulled her dignity around her and stepped outside into the sun. The circular drive sported concrete barriers, put in place after 9/11 against terrorists. No wonder the guards were nervous about her.

The scar running down her calf began to throb as if she'd gotten the wound yesterday. She stood on her good leg waiting for her keeper, the late afternoon sun searing the top of her head.

A black SUV shot down the side road toward her, darting around an elderly truck weighed down with dead tires. She squinted into the glare and watched as the vehicle swerved into the parking lot and around the protective barriers. The driver sat invisible behind tinted glass.

Sam bent down and looked inside. Joe Roper, with no incorrigible smile for her this time.

Apparently he'd lost his charm once he'd sent her to jail.

"Get in." He said roughly.

Sam straightened up and turned to look back at the Washoe Detention Center. She'd find no saviors there. She shivered in the heat and small rivers of perspiration ran down her back.

Shoving open his door, he unfolded his long body and climbed out. "Get in, Sam."

She took a step back, her heart slamming in her chest. What were the new rules of engagement? "Joe Thorp, or rather it's Joe Roper, isn't it? No one bothered to mention I'd be spending the next week with you."

"Yeah, well I'm sorry but I'm afraid it's a done deal. I'm your case officer." His lips stretched into a thin line. "Get in."

She took another step back, searching his face. It was unreadable, pure FBI with no bullshit allowed. She wondered how she'd missed it before.

"You can get in quietly or make a scene, but either way, you're coming with me."

"So you're it? My 'handler?' Well I suppose it's appropriate since you're already familiar with the territory."

He sighed, shifted his shoulders like an Olympic wrestler on his last try. "Call me whatever you want, but you've signed the agreement. Look, I'm not having this conversation with you standing out here. Get in!" He opened the passenger door.

She crawled in, clutching her crumpled sack like a five year old on her first day of kindergarten. This was going to be the last time he surprised her. From now on, she'd be ready. She'd pick her battles, not react to his war.

The inside of the Cherokee smelled like new car, a mix of leather and cigarette smoke. He'd left the motor running and a burst of frigid air hit her as she slid onto the seat.

Roper slammed her door, went around and got in. "Just so we're clear, I'm lead on the team for this case, and if you want immunity, you're stuck with me. Since my job is to make sure this operation succeeds and you're kept safe, I'm sticking to you like super glue."

She knew every part of his body, every scent, every sound he made, but his face had become a stranger's.

"You can hate my guts, but my recommendation is to put it away until after this is over. Otherwise, it's going to be a long week."

She sank back and shut her eyes. "I can shelve my anger, even be civil if it comes to that. My only request is honesty. No tossing the charm at me, no pretense of being a friend. "

He didn't answer for a long time, and she opened her eyes to study him. When he spoke, he sounded more like the Joe she'd known. "For what it's worth, I'm sorry. What happened between us had nothing to do with my job. I don't make a practice of mixing personal business with my work."

He wore the same leather jacket over dark t-shirt she'd seen him in and out of a lifetime ago. Instead of jeans, he wore khaki fatigues with heavy brown boots, more Special Forces than FBI. In need of a haircut, the shaggy ends looked sun bleached. The butt of his gun peeped out from under his jacket. She turned away and studied the white-topped mountains of home to the north.

Courage. It came down to two facts. She was the felon. He was the law.

Three or four days with a man who'd lied to her. Why the hell did she feel angrier with herself than with him? Someone with a lifetime of misunderstandings and lies couldn't be expected to immediately turn into a good judge of character.

He eased out onto Interstate 395 heading south, edged over and took the exit for Interstate 80 eastbound. Where was he taking her? They traveled in silence through the last of Friday's homebound traffic. At Sparks most of it fell away, leaving a few lonely truckers heading for Winnemucca and points east.

"Nice car. Yours or the FBI's?" She could play the small talk game.

"Mine. The truck I drove last week was courtesy of the Highway Department."

"Air conditioner works well. Does it have to be on? It's a little cold in here."

"Sorry. I put it on automatically." He flipped the switch.

The sun no longer followed them overhead, leaving a softer daylight. Sam relaxed against the cool leather, knowing she'd just crossed some bridge of cooperation with the brief exchange of words. "Enough civilities, Roper. What's the plan?"

"Roper is it now? Joe would be fine."

"I prefer Roper."

"Suit yourself. The press got hold of the story about your arrest."

"I saw it."

"We wanted to get it out to your friends that we had nabbed you."

"Please don't call them 'my friends'."

He nodded. "Okay. What about 'the suspects'?"

"That's fine. Go on."

"We also planted the story you were released, due to lack of evidence. As far as the Consortium knows, you're of no further use to the Feds." The man stared at the road ahead, as impersonal as a tax collector.

She rubbed clammy hands against her thighs. "So, this is going to be strictly professional, Roper? No sleeping with me as a perk of your job?"

His unflappable composure fled, replaced by a frown. "This is a purely professional arrangement. My job is to help you set up a meeting with the Consortium and keep you safe in the process. I promise you I have no agenda here but that. Ideally, it would be nice if we can have civil exchanges and that's it."

"All right." And that was that. She turned her gaze back to the window as he pulled out his phone.

"Buchanan, Roper. I'm about ten miles out of Reno, heading for Fallon. Any word on Cramer and Alexander?"

Ignoring the rest of the conversation, she watched the highway come toward them. It soothed her with its illusion of freedom. She shivered and wrapped her arms tighter around her body.

He snapped the phone shut. "We've got the suspects under surveillance. There's no need to worry about a repeat of the parking lot incident at Porky's. And we've got an agent watching your place."

The muscles in her jaw twitched. "All right. How long have you been keeping track of the Consortium?"

"We've had them in our sights for a few months. They've been under closer watch for a month. Right now we have them sitting tight in a motel in Susanville, but they've been making frequent trips to the Pyramid Lake area in the past few weeks."

"Have you followed them to my place?"

"No, just the BLM."

She waited for her heart to slow. They'd been in her area and she had been clueless about it. She might have even passed them at some point driving back and forth to Benton. "And what about my sister? Is she safe?"

"There's no likelihood they'll be traveling that far east. They've made no attempts to contact her.

Their focus is on Nevada right now. There aren't enough of them to bother with your sister in Chicago."

"Can I use your phone? I need to call her and make sure she's okay. And let her know I'm all right."

Roper reached over and touched her arm briefly. His fingers felt warm. "We'll be stopping in a little while. You can put through a call then."

"So what happens next?"

"The next step is to have you contact the group, let them know you're pissed with us and want to play with them again. I've got a script written out for you. You'll tell them you've been mistreated. Since you're no longer underground, you're ready to get to work. Mention you know the area around northern Nevada and know the layout of the BLM operations."

She was surprised. "That's the whole plan? They'll never buy it. After twelve years, I'm suddenly eager to get involved?"

"We think they will. You've given them some money in the last few months. We're counting on their being consumed with their plans. And the news release should soothe any fears. You'll email them and ask to be part of their next protest." He took a quick look at her. "It'll sound better when you read over the script we've written out for you."

"You're sure there's some sort of BLM thing already in the works? Otherwise, we could be waiting for them to make a move for months."

"We've been following two possible targets. One of them is the Sierra Army Depot. It's fifteen miles from Pyramid Lake."

"The munitions burning base, right?"

"Yeah. Not in Nevada but California, operated by a civilian contractor working for the U.S. Army. They're doing open burning of munitions. There've been a lot of scare stories about heavy metals, dioxin, PCB, and fiberglass, et cetera, being released into the air."

"You don't think it's true? I mean the pollution problem."

"Probably is. The Nevada State Health Division has been working on it, checking out the potential air quality threat. I don't think they've come to any conclusions yet. Anyway, it could potentially be the next target for the Consortium. But right now, our best guess from the chatter online is they're setting up something for the BLM."

"The corralled wild horses?"

"Probably. It may be they're using it as a distraction, but we're going to stop it there, before they can get into more trouble at the munitions site. We need to move on this now, while they're playing around in your backyard."

There was nothing more to say.

The two-lane highway rolled out empty and dark, night turning the hills purple-gray. This was her territory now, but the land looked different. Three days away and she'd become someone else.

She sighed. How could she have been so ignorant at eighteen? It probably wasn't that uncommon. Weren't most people looking for a purpose to life at that age? And she'd been particularly vulnerable, desperate for some way to discover the good person she wanted to be. Not a totally ridiculous thing to do, but foolish.

Sam watched for familiar signs as Roper turned off Interstate 80 and headed north. A large green exit board said 'Wadsworth 5 miles.' They were within ten miles of her place.

He waited, glancing over at her from time to time. "Well?"

"What?"

"You're okay with the plan?"

"I didn't realize you needed an okay since I've already signed the agreement."

"We don't. But I do. I don't want my name added to the list of people who betrayed you. I want your word it's a go."

It sounded like regret and made him too close to human.

"I'm not proud of jumping out of your bed and tossing you to the wolves as I headed out. Can we call a moratorium and get the job done together?"

They passed scattered, forlorn-looking houses signaling a town was coming up. "I've signed on for this, Roper. I'll go along with your plan. Let's get it over with."

"Agreed."

Eight hundred people, half of them Paiute, lived in Wadsworth, Nevada. Five miles off the reservation, the place struggled to stay alive by catching traffic hurtling west to Reno. Cars stood in a row outside the only two-story building in town, a combination restaurant/grocery store. A tour bus sat idling across the street.

Without speaking, Joe pulled out a map from his glove box, replaced it with his holstered gun, and twisted the lock. He glanced over at her, reached into his jacket and pulled out a phone.

"Here. We're still monitoring yours until we finish up the operation, so use mine right now." He opened his door. "I'll wait on the sidewalk while you make that call. You're phoning your sister?"

"Yeah."

"Make it brief, just a friendly hello. Let her know you're fine, but don't tell her where you are or where you're going."

"I assume I'm going home." The words trailed after him. He'd already slammed the door and ambled to the curb, lighting a cigarette.

She held her breath until she heard Mary Beth's

voice. "Hello?"

"Hi, Mary Beth. It's Cathy."

"Cath! Are you okay?"

"I'm fine. I can't talk long, just wanted to hear your voice."

Sam watched Roper, one hand jammed into his jacket. He stood under a neon light, sucking on a cigarette. He looked bored but she suspected he was following every person's move around him.

"Your friend, Keddie, called me a few days ago. She told me you were in jail. They let you go?"

"I'm free now and in a week, I'll be cleared of all charges."

"God, that's so good, Cathy! The FBI called me today. They told me you were working with them. Is that true?"

"For now. It's part of my plea bargain. It'll be fine."

"Well, they left me a number and told me to contact them if anyone called me from that group you were involved with."

"I know, Mary Beth. I'm sorry. I promise this is going to be it. Just do what they say and it will be over soon. There's no real danger for you, but they're making sure all's well. And making me feel better. I can't tell you more now. I need to go."

"Call me as soon as you can."

"I will. Mary Beth, I hired a private investigator to look into mom's death."

"Oh." Silence. "What good will that do?"

"Get some idea about why she never came back. Make me feel better, at least. I've spent so many years hating her, I don't want to leave it and forget about her. I want to know what happened. And I'd like to do a memorial. Is that okay with you?"

"Sure. I don't have as many memories of her, but I'd like to put the past to rest. She deserves something, whatever the heck kind of mother she was."

"We'll talk next week, and I'll send you anything the PI in Omaha turns up. Things are going to be good soon. I'll be able to see you. You can come out and visit with me now."

"At last. I'll finally get a look at that old ranch."

"You might even like it and decide to move out to Nevada."

"Probably not, Cath. I've got something serious going on now with someone, but I can't wait for us to have some real time together."

"All right. I'll be calling." So many years without seeing each other, the thought of what they'd missed hurt her throat. "I love you."

"Ditto! More later."

Sam climbed out and made for Roper. He stubbed out his cigarette. "Everything okay?"

"Better, at least. Not okay, not until this is over." She passed him the phone and followed him inside.

Friday nights kept the town of Wadsworth alive, the pit stop for tour buses filled with seniors eager to lose money in Nevada.

People in casino-wear crowded around dinner in the smoke-filled room. A beaded curtain separated the restaurant and adjacent grocery. She felt curious eyes pinned on her bright yellow prison wear as she trailed Roper into the back room.

He moved about gathering up jars and boxes while she stood silent, waiting, refusing to ask questions within earshot of the townies. She'd been in the place a hundred times over the past twelve years, but no one spoke to her.

The woman doing checkout knew her well. She was Paiute and an old friend of her aunt's. Her age was anyone's guess, somewhere between fifty and ninety, with permed, jet-black hair glued to her head. She wore a silky red dress that hit white stockings mid-calf and ended with patent leather Mary Jane's. Her face was as lined as a county map.

"Glad to see you're back, Sam."

"Hello, Alameda. Thanks."

The woman glanced curiously at Roper, but he only gave her a brief smile as he paid and quickly steered Sam out into the darkness.

The wind had picked up and the temperature was dropping. She stood back, bare arms wrapped about her shivering body, waiting for him to unlock the SUV.

"Where's your jacket?"

She shrugged and slid gratefully inside his car. "Someone misplaced it at the Sheriff's Department."

"What the fuck is wrong with them over there at the jail? Someone should have thought to find a coat for you." He shifted out of his own jacket and tossed it down on her lap. "Put it on."

"Yes, sir."

He slammed the door, did a quick study of the street, and strode around to get in. She hugged his jacket around her. It smelled reassuring, like the car, tobacco and leather. Reaching past her, he unlocked his glove box and pulled out his gun.

"Do you need to wear that?"

"Yes." Not bothering with conversation, he slid the pistol into the holster and laid it on the dash, then reached around and yanked out a pea green vest.

They drove north, leaving the lights behind.

"Where are we going?"

"I thought you knew. To your place."

She swallowed a hard knot in her throat and turned to gaze out into the dark.

Five minutes more of silence and he pulled over. Flipping on the overhead light, he plucked his map out from under the seat and studied it briefly. They started up again, moving through the desert toward home. The cab was warm, the silence calming.

"I checked up on Dourcet. He's doing fine with Charlie Lemon."

"Thanks," She replied, surprised that Roper had kept track of her dog.

More silence.

"Am I allowed to ask some questions?"

"Of course. What do you want to know, Sam?" His voice sounded tight. Did he think she'd get too personal? The last thing she wanted right now was to feel a connection to his life.

"How long is this going to take? When will it all be over?"

"The operation? We're targeting Tuesday. But it could be a day or two later. At worst, you'll be out of this by next Friday."

"And what happens then? Do I have to testify?"

He downshifted, slowing to a crawl and cracked open a window. Snow lingered on the sage and junipers out here, the scent of the desert riding on the cold wind.

"I'll do my best to go with a signed statement from you; but, depending on whether the group talks, we may need you to testify. It's a long way down that road before we get to trial. You'll be free, aside from a possible subpoena in the future, as soon as we've got the group rounded up. You'll need to keep us informed of your whereabouts and make yourself available when the time comes. If we call a grand jury, it'll be closed with no reporters or gawkers. Once you've testified, that'll be it." He glanced over. "We'll wipe your record clean. If you need protection for a while, we'll see to that as well."

"Protection?"

"Just a precaution. We've got our sights on all the active members of The Consortium. Don't worry, you'll be fine."

"I don't think these guys are a physical threat to

me, despite whatever happened in the parking lot last week. I'm not afraid they'll actually hurt me. My sending them money had to do with my being afraid they'd turn me in. From what I remember, they were gentle people and not at all threatening."

"Except for being responsible for ten fires over the past twelve years and some random tree spiking," he replied.

She searched in the dark for his face. "Whatever they've been up to since, the people I knew were innocent kids. I never felt personally threatened by any of them, and I can't imagine them doing harm to anyone. From what I've heard, there's no record of any environmental group ever killing someone."

"As far as we know, that's true but setting fires is dangerous and illegal. We've got to stop them, Sam."

"Yeah. I know, Roper. Will they be given prison time?"

"I don't know. Depends on whether we prove them guilty of setting those fires. We've got evidence on them. We'll see if they're willing to do some plea bargaining themselves."

She eased her aching leg out in front of her.

"Leg hurting?"

"A little. The jail forgot to add jogging to my schedule."

"We can do that. I wouldn't mind some running time myself."

He'd be there in her house again, a shadow this time, never letting her get more than a few steps away, his only purpose to get his business done. During those two days with him last week, she'd thought she knew him. What did she really know?

To the north, the white tops of the Sahwave Range stood out like a beacon. They were getting close to home.

"Will your agent be waiting at my place?"

"Yeah. He'll be around, watching our backs for the next few days. We've informed your neighbors to stay out of the way for now. Once I've got things moving, my guy will be heading back to Reno."

"What about Charlie and Dourcet?"

"I'm afraid Dourcet is going to have to stay with Charlie Lemon a while longer. He'd cause a problem barking at my man. More important, if our suspects do show up and get nervous, they'll want to get rid of Dourcet. You wouldn't want something happening to him, Sam."

She shivered. "I thought you said I'd have no direct contact with them."

"We'll do whatever it takes to keep them away. It's just a precaution. We need to be ready to roll if there's a change of plans, though, and the dog's one more problem with moving out fast."

"All right. It makes sense. He can stay with Charlie." Sam pulled the jacket around her. It reminded her of Thorp, not the man toting the gun beside her, but the one who'd shared her bed.

Sleep arrangements. Another problem. He'd be bunking down on her couch again, and she'd be sleeping in the same bed they'd made a shambles of five nights ago. She dismissed the irony of it. Her life was filled with too many paradoxes these days.

"You still cold? I can close my window."

"No, I'm fine."

"Sam. I'm not stepping over what happened between us. Waylaying you in Benton was a set up, but sleeping with you wasn't. As I said, I don't sleep with my suspects, except you. Look, I took advantage of the situation, and I'm sorry. But like you said, apologies can't change the facts. I wish they could."

"I don't blame you for the sex. I was more than willing to participate. In fact, as I recall, I issued the first invitation. Let's leave it at that and move on."

She inhaled slowly, letting the sweet smell of

home wash over her.

"I won't be involved with the actual arrests you're planning, right?"

"That's correct."

"You aren't going to have me staked out someplace in the desert, like a sacrificial lamb?"

"Very funny. You're not getting anywhere close to the actual sting operation. The meeting will take place a long way from here."

"Oh."

"There'll be no danger once we get things moving. It's only the few days before I'm worried about, as we wait and see if they bite. And then a few days after, to make sure we've got them all sitting snug in jail."

"Don't worry too much about me, Roper. I've managed for twelve years on my own."

"Humph." He pulled into her dirt drive.

There was no moon and the light over the shed door had burned out, leaving them in darkness. Sam put a foot on the ground and eased out, testing the weight on her bad leg. She limped slowly up her path to the house, a black empty shell with no Dourcet springing out to greet her.

Thud, thud. She stopped to listen. Thud, thud. Probably another loose board banging against the house, picked up by the wind. Thud, thud. It syncopated dully, like a tired heart beat, from somewhere around back.

She took another step.

"Wait," Roper barked, coming up beside her. He carried a small flashlight in one hand, something shiny in the other. His gun. "Stay back. I'll go first."

His flashlight, wavering and bodiless, moved toward the house. She heard his feet hit the loose step on the porch, then the click of the latch. There was the familiar creak as the door swung open and another flash as he swung the light around inside the kitchen. She tracked the phantom light through the house, a wobbly, faint trail moving toward the back and disappearing. Still she waited.

A very long time later he flipped on the kitchen light and motioned her curtly to come inside.

"No gas this time?"

Without a smile, he silently went past her and out the door, returning with the groceries. The house felt very cold, a numbing, dread-like sort of chill. She roamed from room to room, looking for signs of trespassers, flipping light switches in each room. In her bedroom, her clothes sat in neat piles on her bed, maybe the FBI's work or maybe Charlie Lemon's.

In the living room, the contents of all her cabinets had been restored, the bookcases meticulously straightened. Everything else was in order except a yawning space along the opposite wall. Her computer, her files, all her loose papers, even the things tacked to her bulletin board, had been removed.

Roper struggled inside, juggling a large brown box.

"Where's my computer and my paperwork?"

"Right here. Prop the door, will you?" He lowered the box to the floor in front of her.

"There are three more boxes outside." She followed him out, wordless.

It took six trips to empty the SUV: Her three boxes, three white plastic sealed cases of his stuff, one small black suitcase, and her sad brown jail sack.

They worked without talking, unpacking the computer, getting it hooked up and on line.

The cold house was next. Roper stood up, still wearing the hunter's green vest. "I'll get more wood and check on what's banging out back."

Ten minutes later he returned, his arms loaded with wood. "The sound we heard was a loose rain gutter. It was hitting the house, so I pulled it off. You'll need to get it fixed when the weather gets better." He dropped the wood in the box at the door. "Got any extra light bulbs? The one over the door is gone."

"Gone? Did your agent do that?"

"Take the light bulb? No." He answered, still grim.

"You think it was someone from the Consortium?"

He considered his answer as he hung up his coat and still didn't speak as he dumped splits beside the fireplace. "I don't know. Don't worry about it now since I just spoke with Buchanan. We've got every last one of them under surveillance still. If someone was here, it was much earlier today or even yesterday. Everyone's accounted for up in Susanville and beyond since three this afternoon."

"Can I borrow your phone again? Or better still, can't you just give mine back? If you're monitoring it, I can still make normal calls, can't I?"

"Sorry," he said, shaking his head, "it won't work. I need to know all incoming calls and keep track of the outgoing. You'll get it back soon."

"Well can I have yours? I'd like to call Charlie and see if he spotted anything unusual."

He grunted and passed her the phone. "I suppose he could have seen something. I've had someone watching this place for the past three days, but there's always a chance somebody could slip in under cover of dark."

Sam dropped into her old chair, the phone drooping in her hand. "Never mind. Take back your phone." She felt too worn out for any of this, right now. Charlie would call or leave a message if something unusual happened.

Roper eased the phone from her fingers. "Why don't you grab a shower and get some rest. I'll make a fire and get supper going."

"All right. I'm not hungry, but make yourself at home. You know where everything's kept." She met his eyes, aware how easy it was to slip right back into where they'd left off.

She stumbled to her bedroom and jerked off her clothes, tossing them into the darkest corner of her closet. Someone on the rez might like the mustard yellow. They wouldn't have a problem with prison gear but instead would think it was hilarious to taunt the law with their own standard issue clothing.

Charlie had faithfully kept the juices flowing into her house, and the shower ran beautifully hot. The water pounded the tin walls and onto her head, camouflaging her sobs. She wept both in relief at being home and from some raw place inside her that knew she'd failed to keep her boundaries high enough to stop Joe Roper from meaning something to her. She lingered in the shower until the water turned lukewarm.

Not bothering to dry off, she shivered in the cold, pulling sweats off the pile of clothes, stacking the rest on the dresser. Ignoring the lingering memories rising from the bed, she dragged the quilt over her body, curled up tight and let sleep settle over her like a narcotic.

****

Sam fought her way out of a gray sleep and sat up abruptly in the dark. The room was warm, the door ajar, letting a thin shaft of light and the smell of coffee push through. This was her bedroom. She let out a sigh and sank back. Thank God she was home. The rattling of pans from the other room brought her upright. Thorp. No, Roper.

She stumbled up and out to the kitchen.

He glanced up casually as he ladled something red into a bowl. "Feeling better?"

"Ask me again in a few minutes." She rubbed her hair. It was still damp. She'd stood in her shower a very long time, scrubbing the stench of jail off her, sobbing. She looked down. She had on pale blue sweats, her own clothes.

"Want something to eat? I made chili."

"Is it edible?"

"Sure. My stepfather taught me to make it. You'll never taste better."

She narrowed her eyes at the pieces of meat floating in thick sauce in front of her.

"I'm a vegetarian, remember?"

"I do, but I was hoping you'd give it up for tonight and give my chili a try."

"Okay. I did eat meat in jail. Or at least I think it was meat."

He gave her a half grin. "Want milk?"

"Do I need it?"

"I always think it works best with Hector's chili."

They spooned and sipped. The house was too quiet without Dourcet. She missed his sighs and moans, and the tapping of his pads on the tiled floor.

"You're right. This is good." She shifted her glance away from his gaze, too close. "Who's Hector?"

"My stepfather."

"Oh." The boundary between them continued to bleed together, blurring the lines where his personal life lay.

"He lives in Las Vegas with my mother and my son." He stood up. "Want some more?"

"No, thanks. I'm fine." She gulped down milk. "Your son?"

"Yeah. He's three. I'm a single parent."

"I see." She said. "From what you said before, it sounds like you have a great family, Roper," she said. "Look, Joe, I'm really uncomfortable here. I don't want to talk about your family or know anything more about your personal life. Okay?"

"You want to keep the conversation one syllable and professional, no small talk, right?"

"Yes. I'm returning to the scene of a meltdown of twelve years of my life. With the guy who lit the torch." She shrugged. "Look, I'm sick of pretending everything is fine. It's not."

He pushed away his bowl, keeping his eyes fixed on her face. "I know. Well, maybe I don't know, but at least I'm listening." He ran nervous fingers through his hair. "Hell."

With the propane heater working overtime and the fire roaring, it was too hot now in the house. She felt as though she stood beside a giant chasm, her past burning up fast behind her, staring down into an empty dangerous future.

"I don't have a clue what you've lived through these past twelve years. I sure as hell can't pretend to even try and imagine a world out here by yourself."

The knot in her chest loosened, releasing a tiny sliver of hope.

"Once this is over, I'd like to do what I can to help you find a normal life. I know it's asking a lot right now for you to trust me when you have the right to tell me to go to hell."

She didn't want to see this side of him. It was easier casting him as the villain in her life for a few days, and then he'd be gone. She pushed aside the food. "I don't know what I want right now, except sleep. Do you need anything from me tonight?"

"What do you mean?"

"With the case?"

"No. Let's leave it until morning. I've got to set stuff up tonight. Tomorrow we'll get the ball rolling."

"All right. I have a couple of personal things I need to handle tomorrow and figure out what kind of mess my business orders are in. Your guys did a nice job of dumping everything from my desk into a box."

"Yeah. I'm sorry about that, too. I'll help you with it tomorrow." He looked as tired as she was, a thin white line forming around his lips. He still wore his gun.

She took her dishes to the sink and looked out at the darkness. "The bulbs are under the sink if you want to put a light back over the shed door."

"I'll get to it later."

Sam shifted her weight to her good leg, easing the dull throb in her bad one.

"Leg still hurting?"

"A little. I'll need to do some running tomorrow."

"Fine. Why don't you get some sleep now?"

"I'll get you your bedding." She turned but he caught her arm.

"I know where it is. I'll manage. Go to bed."

"Goodnight, Roper."

She left him standing there. There was a question in his gaze. What did he want from her? He'd already stolen her trust.

Chapter Twenty

The wind whistled around the corner of the house like an old friend, but not loud enough to mask the sounds of someone or something moving about outside. No loose piece of gutter this time, it was a more sporadic crashing.

Bang.

There it was again.

Roper stuffed his bare feet into cold boots, reached for his Glock, and went to the front window. With no moon, the darkness was almost complete, just enough snow left beyond the road to cast faint illumination on the shed and dirt road beyond. Hell, he should have gone out and replaced the light bulb on the shed.

He checked his watch; it was after one a.m. He'd been asleep two hours. He held his breath and waited. His eyes roamed the horizon as he searched for something moving to catch his focus.

A large shadow shot out of nowhere and disappeared around the back of the shed. Roper ran for the front door. He grabbed his jacket from a hook as he slid silently outside onto the shadowed porch.

It was well below zero, cold enough to numb his fingers within seconds. He tightened his grip on his pistol and waited on the top step. Bang. And again, the shadow dipped and dodged as it disappeared behind his Cherokee.

Roper cautiously moved down the ice-covered steps. He crouched low as he crept up the path toward the fence. The wind groaned intermittently, like an old man in pain. He pulled out his penlight and flashed it toward the vehicle.

"You, there! Stop where you are!" He leapt forward, through the gate and around the cab of the Cherokee.

A blast of arctic air grazed his face as a flicker of something dark flew by. It passed just inside his field of vision—a horse's hoof. It had missed contact with his jaw by less than an inch. Adrenaline pumped through him, and he gulped in icy breaths.

"Damn!" Glued to the spot, he shivered. His gaze followed the pale outline of a horse speeding across snow-flecked open country to disappear into the night.

Roper pocketed his penlight and turned back to the house, gun in hand. Christ! It was freezing, and he'd almost gotten himself killed by a damned horse.

Sam stood in the doorway, a pale ghost outlined by the faint light behind her. She had on the same sweats he'd stripped off her five days ago.

"What are you doing?" She whispered.

He grimaced. "Apparently practicing for a part in The Three Stooges. I heard a noise and went out to check." He shut and locked the door behind her and turned on the overhead light.

"You took your gun?"

"That's what I have it for, Sam." He shrugged off his jacket and hung it up. He placed his Glock carefully on the kitchen table. "It was one of your wild stallions."

She stood close and smelled of apples. Without thinking, he reached out and stroked back a loose strand of hair. She flinched. "Sorry, your hair's sticking up." He took a step back. "You okay?"

"I'm fine. The horses are no strangers around here. We see them a lot. If I look nervous, it's because I'm not used to someone chasing them with a gun."

He grinned. "You know us city boys, scared of our own shadows. Since we're up, want some tea?"

"I don't think so. As I recall, the last time you made me something to drink in the middle of the night, it was drugged. Admit it, Roper, you slipped me a Mickey, didn't you?"

He shrugged. "It was Haldol, actually. I needed to do a thorough search of your place. It was the most efficient way to do it." He wasn't going to offer an apology. What was the point? It was his job.

Any shared humor evaporated. "I'm going back to bed." Head high, she went into her bedroom and shut the door firmly.

****

Watery light seeped into the living room, hitting Roper in the eyes. He blinked and rubbed his face as he glanced around. Yanking back the blanket, he staggered to his feet. The damned couch was still too short. The propane stove and fireplace blazed, but there was no sound about the place.

The bittersweet smell of brewing coffee mingled with wood smoke, and Roper stumbled to the kitchen. He poured himself a mug and sipped cautiously as he stared out the small-paned window over the sink. A light snow fell.

Where the hell was Sam?

A tour of the entire house proved it to be empty. At the front door, her boots were missing. Shit! She hadn't even left him a note.

Gulping down the last of his coffee, he exchanged the mug for his holster, slid it on, and hauled on jacket and cold boots.

Her tracks were clear in the fresh snow.

Fifteen minutes of trudging later, head down against the wind, Roper stepped up onto Charlie Lemon's porch. He was breathing like a fireplace bellow.

The dark wood door opened before his fist made

contact. Charlie calmly stepped aside to motion him in, unperturbed, as though the FBI showed up on his doorstep every morning.

"Roper, right?"

Roper nodded at the man in worn flannel shirt and jeans towering over him. "Yeah, formerly Thorp. You seen Sam?"

He motioned Roper inside and pointed at Sam sitting by the fire, nursing a mug. Dourcet sat like a knight in training at her side.

"You having a party here?"

Charlie Lemon grunted then waited as Roper beat snow off his boots and stepped across the entrance.

"Roper. You found me." She looked as unperturbed as Lemon.

"It's snowing. You left a trail."

"Have a seat. Did you have a tough time getting here? You look worn out." He caught the flash of a grin she suppressed. "Charlie can fix you up with a hot drink."

He shook his head. "You could have wakened me, you know. I thought we planned on running together this morning."

"You looked so peaceful, I hated to get you up."

"You should have wakened me." He didn't bother to hide his annoyance. "The point is, it's my job to make sure you're safe."

"I'm sorry, Joe. I wanted to see Dourcet."

Roper unbuttoned his jacket and sat in the closest chair. "How's the leg?"

"Better now that I've had some exercise."

"Yeah and I bet you didn't show up here huffing and puffing like me." He wiped sweat off his forehead with the back of a hand.

"You can blame it on the altitude, or the weather. You're out of your element. I'm sure you'd beat the heck out of me on your home turf."

Roper stuffed his hands into his jacket and forced back a retort. She needed a little time with her dog. A lecture could wait for the trip home.

****

With no wind, the snow covered the hard earth like white silk, silencing their footsteps home. She'd shown no hint of resistance as he chastised her about running off.

Inside the house, she hesitated at the kitchen. "Want something to eat?"

"No. I'm good. Let's get to work."

Shoulder to shoulder, they sat in front of the computer to compose an email to the Consortium.

Roper gave her a quick, sideways glance. She looked scared but purpose overrode her anxiety, and she kept at it. He liked that about her, a certain determination to plod on. It had probably been what served her best for the past twelve years underground.

The room was too hot, and her hair clung to her damp forehead. She pushed it back out of her eyes and sipped at her coffee automatically as she scanned what they'd written. The only change she made was the addition of a few personal references to events of twelve years ago. Her face looked grave, focused on her work. How the hell had he ever thought her plain?

"Ready?"

"We've included a time and place for rendezvous? Looks good." He watched her press 'Send.'

"Well, that's that. Now we wait." He stood up.

"I have some things I need to handle."

He checked his watch. It was almost noon. "Let's fix something to eat first."

"Okay."

They sat by the fireplace in stocking feet, eating in silence. His gun and holster lay on the table nearby, just another cozy morning at home.

"So what got you into FBI work, Roper?"

"Is it a joke or you really wanna know?"

"I really want to know."

"Ever hear of Jim Jones and Guyana?"

"He was some sort of cult leader who died in a mass suicide in the late 70's, right?"

"Yeah. My dad was FBI. He was there, in Guyana, protecting California Congressman Leo Ryan. He was gunned down, along with the Congressman and a couple of media people with them. I was ten at the time. You can understand where I get my distrust of ideologies or people on a mission to save the world. I'm the task force specialist for eco-terrorist activities in Nevada these days."

"I'm sorry. That must have been cruel for you."

Roper shrugged. "He was a friend of Leo Ryan's and went along unofficially, posing as a journalist. He didn't like the situation, but there was no way anyone could have talked him out of going." His voice cracked, the memories of his dad were like a series of old movie clips, a big man who liked to fish and laughed a lot. "Maybe we have that in common. You could say I've designed my entire life around a single event, my dad's senseless murder. And you've lived almost twelve years in reaction to an event that happened when you were eighteen."

"You feel okay, knowing you've got a career based in one horrible moment in time?"

"Maybe, or maybe I just admired my dad. Who knows? And isn't it what we do all the time? Respond to what we know? Head toward what's familiar? The sons of doctors become doctors. The sons of lawmen become FBI agents."

"Maybe. I don't know." She stood up abruptly.

"Why does that upset you?"

She went to her desk and dug through the pile of

loose papers sitting there. She brought a newspaper clipping over and dropped it into his lap.

"'Woman's Body Found in River.'" He looked up. "What's this?"

"It's my mother. Her body turned up a few weeks ago in a submerged car in the Missouri River. I didn't live my life on an event twelve years ago. It was almost twenty years ago my future got formed, based in a false notion, apparently. It seems she didn't abandon my sister and I when we were kids like I believed. She didn't come back because she died that night."

"Hell!" He reached over and caught one of her hands. Her fingers felt cold. "I'm sorry, Sam."

She left her hand in his a moment, before gently withdrawing it.

He stared down at the date on the newspaper. "Two weeks before I met you. The authorities in Omaha tracked you down?"

"No, they found my sister." She said. "She called me, frantic. I hired a private detective to see if he can find out what happened and report back to me."

Shit. "What about the PI? What's he got so far?"

"I've heard back a couple of times from the guy, but then you came along, and I got sidetracked. One of the things I want to do today is get in touch with the man and see what else has turned up."

"And how'd the police identify the remains after so long?"

"They had her VIN from the car. And Robert Mathias, the PI, sent me the medical examiner's report and all the rest of the records he could get hold of. There was some mumbo-jumbo in the toxicology report about adipose decomposing or something, making it possible to identify her body."

"Cause of death?" He waited.

"Drowning."

"I see. No evidence of foul play?"

"The post mortem said she had a crushed larynx, and inferred possible foul play. But Mathias said the police would like to call it 'accidental death' and close the case."

"What else are you after from this guy?"

"More background information on my mother and what happened that day, if possible. I feel like I owe her that."

"Where's he looking?"

"He's digging into tax and employment records, searching for our last street address, anyone who remembers her and can shed light on who her friends were. The idea is to reconstruct what happened the night she died." She swished her spoon around in her bowl. "Unfortunately, I'd gotten only two reports from him before you showed up. I checked my email this morning. There's nothing new from him, no emails. You guys took my phone, so I don't know if he called."

Roper shook his head. "No calls except your sister, and your friend, Keddie."

She frowned. "I dug out your phone this morning and rang Mathias, but he didn't pick up."

It was his turn to frown. Hell, she was digging into his pockets while he was out cold. He needed to get some good sleep. "Is that strange?"

"He said he'd be in contact daily. It's been a week since I've heard from him. I need to organize a memorial service with Mary Beth, but I don't even know if they've released my mother's remains or how I go about getting them released."

"I'll put someone in touch with this PI you hired if you like."

She nodded. "All right."

"And I'll see what I can find out about getting the body released to you or your sister."

"Thanks, Roper."

She got up abruptly and he followed, grabbing

dishes. She stood at the sink and he stepped up, leaving an inch of separation between them but he didn't touch her. "Anything else?"

She shook her head, not turning.

"It's going to be fine."

"Thanks, Roper. For the reassuring words and for offering to help in Omaha." She wiped a strand of hair off her cheek.

A simple acceptance of his help, it wasn't much, but it shifted everything for him, and maybe for her.

Leaning past her, he sat the dishes in the sink.

"I'll put in a quick call to get the ball rolling in Omaha."

It took ten minutes to get to the right person, ten more minutes for him to update the agent on the situation. Someone had to track down Robert Mathias and see what he'd come up with. Chandler agreed to follow up and call back as soon as he had something.

Stoking the fire, Roper glanced up as Sam entered the living room. "So tell me about your dreams."

She sat down in the closest chair, flashing him a rare smile. "As I recall, we've had this conversation before."

"Ah, but this is a new world now. You have your freedom, and the world's out there waiting for you."

Sam shook her head. "You're asking too much, Roper. I'll need a little more time before I can come up with some dreams."

"Who says so? Dreams can be created in a moment."

"Roper, for an FBI guy, you're pretty smart. And romantic."

"I never expected to hear those words from anyone but my mom. And my son. Never from someone I sent to jail."

"What about your son?" She asked.

"Sure you want to go there? I thought I wasn't allowed to share anything about my personal life."

She leaned back and shut her eyes. "I give up. I can't lie around here for two or three days and be a bitch. It's too much work."

"Thanks. I appreciate the concession it takes to let go of being pissed."

"I didn't say I wasn't pissed, but it's probably harder on me than you. You know the old saying, 'take poison and hope they die.'" She leveled her gaze on him. "So, about your son?"

"He's three, and he's the best thing in my life."

"He lives with you?"

"Yeah, and with my mom and step dad when I'm on a case. We live in Vegas."

"So that part of your story was true."

"Yes."

"The mother isn't around?"

"No. She's out of the picture, by her own choice."

She frowned. "I can't imagine doing that by choice."

"She wasn't ready to be a mother or a wife. It's probably just as well since we hardly knew each other. It would have been a train wreck of a marriage."

"You don't have to get married to give a kid two parents."

"I always wanted a regular family, mother, father and all that. But my mother's great with Joey." He studied the fire. "My instincts are sometimes faulty when it comes to picking women."

"Like me?"

"My old girlfriends are nothing like you."

"I can believe that. I can't quite picture you hanging out with a fugitive."

"That's not what I meant, Sam. They've all been career-driven women. I'm useful for entertainment and holding an arm on their way up the ladder."

"And you distrust your instincts? Especially succumbing to sex with me."

He gave her back her frown. "That's too simple of an explanation."

"You need an explanation? I always thought it was biology."

"I seem to recall the most recent theory on what makes humans tick is that we're just computers, mapping our present and future based on our past."

"I've sure as hell defined my life by my past. What other measure of reality is there?"

Roper stood up and wandered to the window, turning his back on her. "I don't know. Sounds complicated. And too philosophical for a mere FBI agent."

"Yeah? And who says FBI agents can't be philosophical?"

He turned and gave her a grin, "You may be right. Come on and let's see if anything's come in from the Consortium."

"Once they respond, what's next?"

"Make a request to meet, confirm the meeting, leave enough time to get my men set up and we round them up. Simple."

"So you think they're planning something to do with the BLM? What happens if it's the other target you mentioned?"

"We'll adjust. But none of that's your worry. You're not going to be part of anything out in the field."

"You really think I'm in danger with them?"

"No. But we're not going to let you get close to the operation itself." He reached over and clicked the mouse. "No news yet."

She started to move away, but he caught her arm. "Sam, there is one more thing I want to say. I don't want to beat this to death but let me just say that sleeping with a suspect could potentially cause me to lose my job." She looked up. "But I wanted you enough to chance that."

"Roper, don't go there. You were willing to chance losing your job for sex?"

"I'm not talking about sex alone, Sam."

"I'm doing my best to deal with this bizarre situation civilly. I can't talk about any of this now."

"All right. But there is something else between us besides sex. When this is all over, I'd like you to consider us spending some time together and really getting to know each other."

The silence was deafening. She jerked her arm out of his grip. "Are you nuts, Joe? You say you've made poor choices in women in the past, an ecoterrorist and an FBI agent spending some quality time together sounds impossible."

"Maybe. Call me stupid, but I am one persistent bastard when it comes to getting something I want."

"And that is?"

"Something's possible between us. I promised I wasn't going to go beyond the professional while we're confined like we are, but there is something. You're a good person who took a wrong turn. I'm a good guy. It's out of my comfort zone, too, but I'm willing to take a risk. Are you?" He leaned forward to search her face. "After this ends, I'm making a suggestion we consider seeing if there's something possible with us. That's all. I'm not asking for anything more than that and no promises right now."

She gave him a lukewarm smile. "I have to admit, Roper, you have charm, and you're damned persistent. And despite myself, I do like you. Who'd have thought it?" She turned away and headed for the kitchen.

"Coward." Roper stood up and wandered to the window. It was snowing just enough to obscure the long view and lend the house a sense of false protection.

He put in a quick call to Buchanan for an update.

"Sam." She looked up. "A second story's been leaked to the Reno paper reporting you've gone into hiding and are considering legal action against the FBI. We've got the motel set up in Stagecoach. Not a lot of traffic but close enough to the interstate. We'll be good to go by Monday, or Tuesday at the latest."

She nodded. "So what's next?"

He strolled over to table, removed his holster and gun and laid it on the table. "We wait."

Chapter Twenty-One

Joe stood directly behind Sam as she sat at the monitor and clicked on her email. A lemon scent tickled his nostrils, and he ducked his head and took a quick sniff of hair. Catherine Bell's lighter roots had gained some ground on the black mop of Sam Neally. She shifted her shoulders and he glanced down. Her face looked pinched this morning.

"You okay?"

She jerked around and his chin took a glancing blow from the top of her head. "Sorry. I'm okay. Why?"

"You look—pale."

"Prison pallor."

He searched her face.

"Joke, Roper. It's a joke." She swiped at strands of her hair stuck to the stubble on his chin. "Like I said, for a vegetarian, jail food is unpredictable." She straightened and this time bumped his chest.

He leaned down over her shoulder, refused to give way, and watched her email pop in. One of the six new emails was from the Consortium.

Catherine, or should we call you Sam now, how was jail? Are you serious about joining us?

She glanced up at Roper. "What should I say?"

"How did you relate to them twelve years ago?"

"I don't remember. I was young and naive."

"Well try 'still naïve' with a little age and cynicism from twelve years on the run. Can you do that? But make sure they recognize your sincerity."

"I can be irritated with the FBI. That's not too

hard." He watched her keyboard in a reply.

I'm interested. Just tell me what I can do.

"Add something about knowing they're working on something local relating to the BLM, and you've got useful information you can give them about the area. Make sure you let them know you're being watched by us, and it's hard to get away."

I hear you're planning something with the Bureau of Land Management. I've got inside information you could probably use about their set-up. She typed the line and sent off the email.

Where'd you hear that? The reply came right back.

The FBI. When they questioned me, they kept asking what I knew about the BLM.

"Good," Roper said.

I've got maps, a schedule of their hours. They're probably tracing my email, so I'm not going to chance emailing it to you. We've got to meet. Just once. No more. I can get away once, but they're keeping a close eye on me.

All right. Where and when?

Neally looked up at Roper as he slid a paper across the desk.

The Nevada Motel in Stagecoach.

Why the hell there? It's too far for us.

"Tell him it's the best you can do, that you can't slip out of our surveillance for longer. Stagecoach is thirty-five miles from here. We don't want anything closer to you at this point."

She keyboarded her answer, and Roper held his breath, waiting.

Okay. Pick a time and day. It's gotta be in the next few days. We're moving after that.

She looked up at Roper again.

"Monday night, 10 p.m. Tell him you'll get back to him with a room number."

She followed his instructions, and they waited.

All right. You've got it. Send me a room number when you have one. And for God's sake, make sure you let us know if something comes up and you can't make it. Or if you're being tailed, stay the hell away. Otherwise, we're SOL.

"Wait. Add a line asking if you can meet all of them. Everyone in the group," Roper added.

The response took longer.

Why?

"Tell them you need to know who they are. You don't trust them and want to make sure you've got some leverage."

I'm not in this unless I meet everyone. You all are inside. I need to have some leverage myself.

All right. Get back with us with the room number. If you're pulling some crap with us, it's not going to go well.

"That'll do it. We'll wait fifteen minutes and email them back with the room number I wrote down. Then we wait some more."

He moved away, restless, pulling out his cell phone.

"Buchanan. Roper here."

"How're things? She doing okay?"

"She's fine. I'm fine."

Silence. "All right. That's clear. If uncommunicative."

"We're set. We made contact with them, and they agreed to Monday night at 10 p.m. in Stagecoach." Roper turned to check on Sam and study her monitor. "I wasn't sure they'd go for it but they seemed almost eager."

"Good."

"I don't know. It's too easy. I don't trust it."

"What do you want to do?"

Roper stared out the window. Snow fell lightly, turning the emptiness beyond white. "Go with it. What else can we do?"

"So, it's Monday night, then. There's a gas station across the street from the motel. It's out of business. We'll pick you up in back of the station at 9:30."

"Will do. Call me in the meantime if anything comes up."

Roper snapped his phone shut, reached for his holster and headed for the door.

"I'll get more wood. We're running low," he called over his shoulder.

It was only Saturday night. Two days to get things in place, two long days. And nights.

****

Sunday dragged. The light snow stopped, leaving less than half a foot of white stuff on the ground. Sam kept tabs on Roper cautiously. For two days she'd watched him pass the time, putting in calls to his son and endless calls to Buchanan. Between these, he made routine searches of the premises, inside and out. And regularly, morning and night, he'd pull out a crumpled pack and take a few puffs on a cigarette, standing on her front porch with his eyes narrowed.

Each day Sam called Charlie Lemon to see how Dourcet was doing. Roper would take up a vigil at her shoulder to monitor everything she said. She smiled at the bizarre picture of Charlie hanging out with an FBI agent. Roper and Charlie were different, yet strangely similar men, who in another reality could have been friends.

The moratorium appeared to be working with Roper; but, by Sunday night, the seams of their apparent camaraderie were stretching apart with signs of strain. As she sat at her computer idly entering orders, the familiar ring of her own cell phone brought her to attention. He reached into his pocket, pulled out her little red phone and strode across the room. He held it up in front of her face.

"Know the number?"

"Yeah. It's Keddie." She reached out, but he pulled the phone back. "Roper, this is ridiculous. I'm not under arrest now. I want to talk with Keddie, and I want my phone back."

"I know you do, but I need to keep monitoring all your calls until the operation's complete. I'll take this." He ignored her protest and stepped away from her. "This is Agent Roper. What can I do for you?"

Sam smiled. Keddie's demanding voice echoed across the three feet between her and Roper.

"She's fine. I'll put her on for a minute, but she can't talk long." He leaned over and held the phone to Sam's ear.

"Ked? It's me."

"Where the fuck are you? Deck told me they let you go, but he wouldn't say anything more. Are you being held prisoner somewhere by those goons?"

Keddie's world. "No, nothing that dramatic—or entertaining."

"Well why don't you answer your own calls then?"

"They're monitoring them right now. I can't go into details, but I'm perfectly okay. In fact, I've got an agent guarding me day and night."

"What the hell does that mean? I'm not forgiving that jackass for turning you in."

"He's not a jackass, Keddie." Sam turned and flashed a quick smile at Roper who remained impassive.

"Well, how long are you going to have this watchdog?"

"A day or two. Then, I'm free and clear, a brand new experience for me." Roper did a circle with his index finger. Time to wrap it up. "I'll give you a call Tuesday or Wednesday and fill you in. Don't worry."

Roper slipped the phone out of her hand. "She says goodbye." He snapped it shut and slid it into his pocket. "We need to keep things simple, Sam, no calls with anyone now, not even family. Okay?"

Two, maybe three more days was all. "You want some dinner?"

"Sure. But before we shut down the computer, can you show me where those files are from the private investigator?"

"They're in my document file saved under 'Omaha.'"

Roper sat down and opened the folder. He clicked on the ME report.

"She died of drowning under questionable circumstances. A broken hyoid bone."

"It's in the report. I don't feel like going over the details with you, Roper. It was some sort of rope or scarf, they think, a ligature they called it." Her stomach did a dance, and she swallowed to steady it.

"What's the adipocere reference?"

She studied the wall behind the monitor and waited for the tightness in her chest to ease. "I looked the term up. Adipocere is what happens to some bodies in the absence of oxygen, in wet, cold environments, like the river. Based on bone marrow, they ruled it death by drowning, but there's a question, because of the broken bone, whether it was accidental."

"I'll forward this to Chandler in Omaha." He said. "The Bureau might be able to get something more from the local cops."

She stood up, turning her back on him.

"What's going on, Sam?"

"I thought I wanted to know what happened. Now I'm not sure I can handle it."

"Then why put the PI on it?"

"I don't know. It sounded simple enough. Just find out what happened. Really, I was more focused on Mathias digging up information on her life that would magically turn my memories of her into a happy, carefree person with friends who loved her." She sighed. "I was thinking it would be good to honor her memory and find out what happened, but I don't know if I can stand knowing it was violent. Or that she was probably terrified when she died."

He stared at her for a long time, ran one hand over his face and stood up himself. "When Chandler finds Mathias, I'll have him relay what the PI's got so far. I'll just get the basics. Then if you want to know more, or there's something Mathias hasn't found you want to know, we'll go there."

"Will you promise to keep whatever you find quiet? I don't want a horrible story to get back to Mary Beth."

"I promise." He pulled out his phone. "You're not going to punish yourself for whatever I find out, are you?"

She shrugged. "I don't know. I'm so used to feeling guilty and secretive, I'm not sure I know how to feel innocent."

"Well, we could both sit around tonight and feel bad together if you want."

She almost smiled. "And your enormous guilt is from what? Having sex with me and sending me to jail? That's kid's stuff, Roper, and a pretty flimsy excuse for feeling sorry for yourself. At least my guilt's twenty years old."

"I've left a slew of bad judgments along the way myself. I can count those. And then there's Joey." He stopped smiling.

"What's the guilt about with your son?"

"That he's been raised without his mother."

"Oh, well. I'll give you one guilt point for that, then, since I can relate to how bad it felt to be motherless. But at least he has a grandmother to step in. She sounds way better than a mother who didn't want him in the first place."

"Yeah, you're probably right." He held out his

hand. "Truce? No indulging in self-pity for now. Okay?"

She took hold of his hand and his fingers curled around hers.

"So let's make some dinner and while we're eating, we can pass the time entertaining each other with our bad deeds."

"You've already read all of mine."

"Yeah, well, I'll tell you the details of mine, then."

"Okay. Then when we get really bored, we can get out the cards, and I'll whip your ass at Texas Hold 'Em Poker."

He grinned. "Where did you learn that? I thought you had no use for bars?"

"Keddie. It pays to have a card dealer for a friend."

"You think you can whip my ass, huh? We'll see. Us suits have a lot of hang time on surveillance."

****

They stood side by side fixing dinner like old friends. Then they sipped wine as Roper entertained her with stupid jokes. They'd taken their dinner by the hearth, sitting opposite each other, her face glowing from the firelight.

"So talk, FBI man. You know a heck of a lot about me, and you're going to have to go some to catch up."

He took a bite of food. "First, tell me exactly what happened when your mom left you at the stranger's house. What you remember?"

"Why?" She sighed and leaned back. "I thought this was about you. Are you asking as part of this thing you're doing for me in Omaha?"

"Yes. No. Just tell me what you remember, Sam."

Sam sat her plate aside half-eaten and leaned forward; she gazed into the flames. "I was eleven,

Mary Beth was eight. We lived in Omaha. I was born there, grew up there. Seven different homes, always in Omaha." She looked over questioningly, but he only waited. "My dad left after Mary Beth was born. I don't remember much about him; just a shadowy figure with a loud voice, suddenly gone. I don't think he was married to my mother." She shrugged. "Mostly I remember a lot of small dreary places, staying with neighbors while my mother found odd jobs—she was good at managing money—for others." She frowned. "Funny, huh? Since we were always broke. The bookkeeping jobs kept her busy in the daytime, the men kept her busy at night."

"She turned tricks?" Joe asked.

"No, nothing so organized. She was just desperate to have a man in her life—any man who would pay attention to her."

He sipped his coffee. A slight ache had settled somewhere in the middle of his chest, and he didn't look at her.

"I couldn't even guess at the number of men who passed through our doors during those years." She took a deep breath. "On the last day we saw her, she picked up some guy and drove what seemed like hours before she stopped. It was a house on the east side of Omaha, in a crowded, dingy little neighborhood. We didn't know the woman where she dropped us off, but I remember her name—Mrs. Beck."

"Do you remember how your mother seemed? Was she upset? Agitated?"

Sam shook her head. "Happier than normal. She had a real date. She didn't say where they were going. She took her own car. I don't know if the guy didn't have a car or why she drove. We never went to babysitters, so it was unusual. She usually just brought the men home."

He frowned, picturing bringing women home

every night with Joey in the house. "So what happened?"

Sam shrugged. "She didn't come back. After a couple of hours, the lady got upset and started yelling at us. My sister and I finally fell asleep on the couch. In the morning, some people came and took us away. They said we had to go with them. That was it."

"What about friends or family?"

She rubbed her face. "No one. It was all like a nightmare. I don't think anyone ever came to see us; no one told me about anything but we realized pretty fast our mother wasn't coming back. I decided she'd grown tired of carting us kids around and took the easy way out. It was the only explanation I could come up with at eleven. Within 24 hours we were transferred to Nebraska Child Protective Services and within a couple of weeks we were split up and sent off to foster homes."

"Tough break for you." He shifted around, feeling the place in his chest expand and throb. "What about names from back then? Besides that woman Mrs. Beck?"

"I gave the only names I remembered to Mathias and the last street where we lived. I think he found some families around still. And he had income tax information filed by her employers over the years."

"What about your aunt, the one who lived here? No one called her to come and get you?"

"I don't think anyone knew about her. We didn't even know much except her name and that she lived somewhere north of Reno in the desert."

"So you grew up, despite the horrors of foster care, and managed to get yourself to college even. Not bad for an abandoned kid."

"Yeah. For about six months, until I stumbled onto the Consortium." She grimaced. "My aunt was the one who gave me a life."

"When you got here and met her, didn't she give you any information on your mother? Some way to track her down?"

"No, nothing. Anna said they hadn't spoken to each other in twenty years." She looked uncomfortable, like Joey when he was about to cry. "But that's enough, Roper, your turn. Let's hear your story."

"Where do you want me to start?"

"Are you really from Arizona?"

"I grew up back east, went to San Diego State on a football scholarship, studied law enforcement, not engineering. I served in the Gulf War as an MP. When I was discharged, I joined the Bureau. I've been with them for 14 years. Like I said before, my dad died thirty years ago when I was ten. My mother remarried about five years later. They moved to Sedona ten years ago when I was transferred to Vegas." Before that, I was in Denver. My son, Joey, is three. His mother and I had a brief fling, nothing more. I've never been married. Anything else?"

"How long have you been on this case?"

"Five months. I'm part of the Domestic Terrorist Task Team. I was assigned to track you down three months ago, right after an alert agent picked your name off the listserv." He waited. "What else?"

"Nothing. Not right now."

"Well, I have a couple more questions. What the hell do you see in Graham Rawlings?"

"Anonymity. He's a pilot, doesn't live in Reno, and isn't curious enough about me to ask questions."

"He's a slimeball."

"You know something about him?"

Roper shook his head. "We pulled him in briefly last week and got a statement. No doubt it's my ego thrashing around, wondering how you'd find a guy like him that attractive." He gave her his best piercing stare.

The silence grew, drawn out like a bowstring, ready to snap.

"I don't have anything to say. Why should I protect your ego when you didn't pick me up because you found me hot, Roper?"

"Not exactly true. Maybe I didn't pick you up because of it, but I did find you hot."

She hooted out loud. "Really? With my baseball cap hiding my dreadful dye job. I bet."

"About my ego, you could say something like, 'you were, by far, the better lover, Roper."

She laughed again.

"Hello. A laugh. What a surprise!"

Leaning forward, she punched him on the arm. "You were by far the better lover."

Unexpectedly she stood up and headed for the kitchen.

"What do you want to do now?" He called after her.

"Some Texas Hold 'Em Poker?"

"Your choice." He threw the words back at her, letting her feel the heat of them.

She turned back, studied him, watchful. "What do you want from me, Joe? I can't play games with you. Are you bored and thinking about sex as entertainment this time? Or did I misread that as a veiled suggestion in your voice?"

"Sam. I promised you I wouldn't mix my job with my personal life. I think the question you might ask is something like 'if we do this again, what does it mean and where are we going?'"

She took two steps back toward him, eyes narrowed. "Are we going some place? Other than our separate ways?"

"I'd like to hope we are."

Confusion spread over her face. He wanted to interpret it as a mixture of disbelief and desire.

"Don't bother tossing me lead lines, Roper. They

sound too much like typical female questions to me."

He stood up slowly and walked toward her. "They're not unreasonable things to ask, Sam. The answer for me is, I don't know where we're going, but I'd like to consider the question. I'm not just bored, not looking for more recreational sex. I've had enough of that in my life to last me a long, long time." He reached out and brushed hair off her damp forehead. "I do want to get to know you. My question to you is, what do you want? Are you willing to go beyond the lies I've given you? I don't blame you if you're not, but there is something there between us. I'm asking a lot, I know, and I promised I wouldn't bring up personal stuff between us, but I can't let it go. I've had a great time the last two days, the best days I've had in a very long while. I like you and I think you like me—despite my being a bastard and betraying you. And despite the fact that I'm a bureaucrat. Would you be willing to give me the benefit of the doubt and see where we could go from here? I've got no hidden motive, I promise. And I promise not to slip something into your drink, I'm not going to search your house, or leave tomorrow morning, or have you hauled off to jail." He held his hand out to her, an invitation only. "I would love to spend the night with you but it's your choice. If not, no problem, we're still friends."

She shifted her gaze to his outstretched fingers, hesitated and took his hand.

****

Roper sat upright with a start. He was a light sleeper but something woke him. What was it? The wind had let up in the night, leaving the room silent. Sam's head was turned away from him, facing the wall.

He eased out of bed and pulled on jeans and t-shirt. Her scent lingered on his body, a powerful aphrodisiac, urging him to forget his expedition and hurry back to her warm body.

Yanking on his holster, he stepped out into the hall. The silence in the house rang in his ears, a replay of five days ago, only this time he had nothing to hide from her. He prowled the rooms, stopped to pile a couple of stray logs onto the last embers in the fireplace. He checked his cell phone for messages.

Nothing.

He moved to a front window and peered out into the dark.

Nothing. The moon shone like a lantern on the desert beyond, and he stood there for a long time. When it finally disappeared behind her shed, he headed back to the bedroom.

He slipped silently in beside her, leaned forward on one elbow and studied her face in the semi-darkness. She lay curled up, a hand under her chin, relaxed and softened. He liked the look of her at night.

The explosive sex of five days ago came from a mixture of adrenaline and the illicit, but tonight had been better; unexpectedly better, with something more than lust to drive his senses.

He reached down and dragged the quilt over them both; he drew her into the circle of his arm. He placed the palm of a hand over her flat belly and savored the warmth of her bare back against his chest. She slept on.

****

The pale orange sky looked like an oil painting through the tiny bedroom window. Roper lay on his back with Sam's head cradled against his shoulder and watched the sun slowly clear the mountaintop. He pictured the morning two hundred miles away in Las Vegas. Seven a.m. and his mother would be up, a walking contradiction in her frilly housecoat as she organized the day like a Fortune 500 CEO.

He tried to picture Sam sitting at his mother's

breakfast table. How would they all respond to her? Joey and Lester would be easy; they liked everyone. His mother, on the other hand, could be a little difficult. She had nothing but disdain for the women he'd known who trod carelessly through his life as they searched for career steppingstones. That description would never fit Sam Neally. But the real issue was, coming from the pasts he and Sam brought with them, could they take a chance on a future together?

Chapter Twenty-Two

Monday the sun burned away most of the snow by mid morning, leaving the yard looking like a cotton field. Sam stood at the front window, staring out at her hills stretching to the north. She glanced back as the bathroom door opened and Roper emerged, his face impassive. His plain white t-shirt stuck to his damp body, his hair standing up like a schoolboy's. The eyes that met hers contained a silent question that she answered with a smile. She liked the look of him in the morning.

Moving to the counter, she poured coffee.

"Service. Thanks." He took a sip and pointed a finger at her. "Leg bothering you this morning?"

"Yeah. Probably too much exercise last night." His response was a thin grin.

The night had started out easily enough, but moved quickly to warp speed and eventually burned up the sheets.

He sat his coffee down, took a step toward her, and caught hold of her neck. His quick, hard kiss tasted of toothpaste and coffee. "Good morning," he said.

"Good morning to you, too." There was still a question hanging in the air between them.

"We're still friends?"

"Yup." She watched him over the rim of the mug. What was up?

"I just spoke with Buchanan a few minutes ago. Everything's set. The entire group, Josh Kennedy, Dennis Folverwiz, and four others were tracked to

Reno last night. They're holed up in a motel south of town off Highway 395."

"Good. Then things are moving fast." She pulled a chair out and sat down.

"Looks like it. We need you to make a call this evening. Reconfirm the meeting tomorrow. Make sure they've got the exact location and room number of the motel in Stagecoach."

"Sit down, Roper."

"No. I need to move around a little. I always get restless before a bust."

"Are you worried about something else?"

"I don't know. Yeah, maybe. I was expecting you to be upset this morning; but, instead, you're as cheery as a kindergarten teacher greeting a new pupil."

"So are *you* the one upset?"

He frowned, rubbing the back of his neck. "No."

"Good. I'm not either."

He sipped again at his coffee. "You want me to shut the hell up?"

"That would be good, instead of stirring up problems that don't exist."

"But there's still the question of what's next?"

The two words 'what's next' fell out of his mouth as alien as a meteor landing in the middle of her kitchen. Next? In another day, the suspects would be caught and jailed. And Roper would be out of here, headed back to Las Vegas and his real life, probably damned happy to be escaping the strange world she inhabited.

For now it didn't matter. Nothing mattered this morning except that the sun shone bright, the coffee tasted great, and the future seemed wide open. She stood up and faced him. "You know, Roper, this might sound insane, but right now I don't care where the heck we're going."

"I have a feeling I just got insulted."

Reaching up, she ran her fingers lightly over his damp hair. "No way. I'm tossing you a compliment, not an insult. I'm just happy enjoying my coffee. Let me have a little pleasure in the morning, without adding any questions, okay? I'm content with life right now, Joe, and you did that."

"Hell, I know I'm good."

She swatted his arm. "I wasn't talking about your sexual prowess. You know you're great in bed. I meant the whole thing; my getting hauled off to jail by you, being forced to confess my sins, and finally dealing with the past. For the first time I can remember, I'm sitting around having normal conversations and sharing my life without holding something back. No secrets. You did that for me."

"You're saying my tossing you in jail was a good thing?"

"You don't get it, Joe. The worst happened to me, and I survived it. I've spent the past twelve years waiting to be found out. It happened and not only did I survive, but I'm finally free from hiding. It's amazing. And then there's you, who betrayed me, but we're still talking." She paused. "Astounding! I like you, Joe. And you like me. That, by itself, is a miracle. Can you imagine? A former eco-terrorist and an FBI agent, hanging out, laughing, wherever the heck we're headed or not headed together?"

He shook his head.

"So what's your question, Joe? About the future?"

"Help me out here, Sam. You know what I'm asking. I've got a past littered with women who liked me fine for the sex, but always wanted to find bigger ponds. I'm nearly forty, and I'd like a word from you we're doing more here than just having great sex."

"Great sex. Great conversation." She grinned.

"Yeah, great sex and great conversation. Are we

done then? Men aren't supposed to be out looking for commitment, but what about a future?" His dark eyes shone startlingly clear this morning, like the butte outlined in the window behind him. "I want something more, Sam."

She reached for her mug, but he caught her hand, turned it up, and dropped a kiss on the palm before releasing it. It was that kind of thing about him that got to her, unpredictable, like the simple statement, "I want something more." It grabbed at her heart and rolled it over.

"I wanna see where we can go from here." He looked as unsure as she felt. "You game?"

She glanced around her kitchen, littered with his things. His blue shirt hung over the back of a chair, his holster lay on the counter, his cell phone beside it. His things. "If you're game, then I'm game, Joe."

"I'd like you to meet my son. You'd like him. And he'll love Dourcet. The little bugger's been pestering me for a dog for months. And you'll like Lester and my mother." He rambled on, filling in the quiet with expectations. She liked him even more for it.

"I'd like to meet them, but what do they know about me?"

"My mother knows I've been working on a case related to you."

"What did you tell her?"

He shrugged. "That I was working UC and got involved with my suspect, then had you arrested."

"And what did she say?"

"That I'd better figure out a way to make things right."

Mothers. She was walking unfamiliar ground here. "I like her already. But things have been put right for me if I get my freedom out of this and some peace of mind. And a life. There's nothing more you need to do."

"Yeah, there is," he replied. "Once we get you free of your past with the Consortium, as the father of a motherless child who never had a real honest to God mother, we're going to find out what happened to yours."

"Okay. I'll take that."

Roper cleared his throat. "So what about it? Are you game to come down to Vegas with me for a visit, once we've wrapped this up?"

"I've never been to Las Vegas," she said. "Well, I've never been anywhere, really, in the past twelve years except Wadsworth and Benton, and to Reno every other month. But since I'll be a free woman, there's nothing stopping me from making that trip with you. I'd like that, Joe."

"Good." He leaned over and placed a quick kiss at the spot where her t-shirt met her skin, kicking the heat up in the room a notch.

"Before we start something, I need food."

"All right."

"Scrambled eggs do you?"

"Sure." He picked up his holster and she watched him pull out his gun and go through the automatic steps of checking it over.

"You always keep it loaded?"

"Yeah. Standard procedure. I'm surprised you don't have a gun around this place." He looked up from his task. "Why not?"

"I don't like them. Nor did my aunt, or Tilo, her husband. I don't think they ever owned one." She pulled eggs from the refrigerator and broke five into a bowl. "Do you think you'll need it for tomorrow? I mean, do you know if they're carrying weapons?"

He shook his head. "Nope. They're not carrying as far as we know, but there's no way to be sure." A gun was just part of his world, Joe Roper, Nice Guy, FBI. "I've got a service pistol locked in the trunk of the car. I want to leave it with you tomorrow while

I'm gone."

"You worried about me?"

He shrugged, continuing to clean his gun. "No point in being careless. You refusing the offer?"

"Yes. I'd probably be in more danger with a gun than without one, since I don't know how to use it. Sit down, I've got your eggs on."

It took five minutes to cook them and five more minutes to eat them.

They stood up simultaneously without a glance at each other, placed their dirty dishes in the sink, and headed back to the bedroom.

****

The weather held. By late afternoon the last of the snow disappeared, leaving small torrents of water carving paths across the yard. They'd had sex, slept, and had more sex. Slow, side-by-side, face-to-face sex, watching every movement, the most mind blowing, erotic experience of his life. No rush, no embarrassment, just connection with another human being.

Roper stood on the porch, flexing his back, waiting for Sam to get ready for a run. He felt alert and clear, not stupefied like sex usually left him. Whatever was between them, there was no way in hell this was going to end tomorrow.

His cell phone rang. Omaha and Chandler. "Go."

"It's Chandler. I've got some news for you on Mathias. He's dead. His body turned up in a dumpster in a parking lot in Council Bluffs, his face the color of a cooked beet." He paused. "Someone slit his gullet nice and clean, probably garroted."

Roper expelled the breath he'd been holding. "Fuck. Any leads?"

"Nope. No one saw anything. Body turned up yesterday. Discovered by the dumpster guy. Mathias was on the bottom of the pile. They empty the dumpster every seven days, so he could have been there that long."

"Anything found on him? Cell phone? Address book, papers?"

"His wallet, his car keys were found in a late model Olds, obligingly parked next to the dumpster. Considerate of the perp to leave the keys for us. We found a receipt in his wallet for a motel room in Council Bluffs. Just searched the place. Someone shook it down, wiped it clean, but left the guy's clothes strewn around the room."

"Relatives? Friends contacted?"

"He was divorced, something of a loner. Haven't found any close friends so far. No one's claimed his body."

Roper sighed and watched Sam step out onto the porch to join him. She stopped short when she saw his face.

"Let me know the moment anything else turns up. Who's running the investigation?"

"Us. We just got called in, since the guy lives across the state line in Nebraska."

"In Omaha?"

"About twenty miles west."

"Why the hell was he staying at a motel in Council Bluffs if he lives in Omaha?"

"Dunno. Maybe his case was focused in Council Bluffs, and it was easier to stay there. Or he was on a stakeout. The two cities are so close it's only a fifteen minute drive."

"The guy's a PI. What about his office? Have you searched it?"

"We're on that next. It's over in Omaha."

"Hell. What a goddamned mess. See if you can find out whatever else he's been working on, but I have a hunch this is related to our case."

"Will do. I'll get back with you in a couple of hours with anything we find at the office. I've copied you everything we've got so far on him."

"Thanks, Chandler. Later." Roper snapped his phone shut. "Let's go back inside, Sam. The run can wait."

"What is it?" The alarm in her voice was palpable.

"Come inside."

He steered her through the door, yanked off his jacket, and pushed her down on the nearest chair. The familiar sweet apple smell of her assaulted him as he knelt down and focused on what he had to say. "They found your PI, Mathias. He's dead. Murdered."

Her face lost all color and she swallowed convulsively, three times, before speaking. "What happened?"

"His body was found in a dumpster in Council Bluffs, his wallet still on him, his car parked nearby. His motel room was sacked."

"It has to do with him investigating my mother's death?" She whispered.

"I can't say for certain yet."

"How was he killed?"

Roper paused, searching for the most remote description of the act. "Strangled, Sam."

"Oh, God!"

"His throat was cut with a wire."

She pushed him away and stumbled up, wavering. Roper reached for her, pulling her against his chest. Her fingers clawed at his arms.

"You think this is related to my mother?"

"I don't know, Sam. Let the agent in Omaha do his job. I've got him working with the local police. We'll see what they come up with in Mathias' office. And if necessary, after things get cleaned up here, I can fly out to Omaha myself." He said. "You know of any connection with your mother to Council Bluffs?"

"It was right across the river. We never lived there that I remember, but I think my mother may have worked there sometimes." She sat down again, very still, looking almost childlike in her pose.

"By the way, no one has claimed Mathias body. I wasn't sure if you wanted to do anything about that."

"God, yes, the poor man. Oh God! He's dead, maybe because of me."

He bent over and shook her shoulders lightly. "Stop it. Leave this alone for now. It could easily be some other case he's working on, or even a random thing. It was his job, Sam. It was what he did. Chandler's sending me everything he comes up with. All we can do for now is wait."

She got up and wandered from window to window, running a careless hand through her hair. "All right."

Roper waited, watching her until she pulled a chair over to the window and sat down, staring outside. He moved to the computer and pulled up his email. Chandler copied him photographs of the crime scene, photos of Mathias room and copies of his ID. He studied the close-ups of the body, fear grabbing hold of him like a cold fist. For the great way the day had started, this was a fucking surreal bad ending.

Chapter Twenty-Three

Keddie pushed two stacks of chips to one side with the back of her hand, straightening the cards with the other. Four years of dealing blackjack made for smooth moves. She watched as disappointed gamblers wandered away to find a better table. Thank God. Her two hours off hadn't come quickly enough.

She removed her billed cap and thought about a peaceful dinner with no one calling out 'Hit me' followed by a few minutes outside to sniff some real air. The closest restaurant with no kids running wild was a flight up.

Keddie slid across the cranberry red seat of the booth and pulled out her book. Erotica, a small indulgence, but it proved necessary when Deckard was too busy to give her his full attention. She couldn't feel too sorry for herself, since the man had fantastic mattress skills for an uptight lawyer.

Caught up in a particularly lascivious scene between a preschool teacher and a principal, she missed the approach of the man. In his mid 30's, he was better dressed than every other man in the place, his shaved head a contrast to the too long sideburns and worn out military cuts of regular patrons. Taking a second look, she realized he was closer to forty than thirty, with the sort of face reminiscent of powerful politicians. His large framed body looked like it got regular workouts, probably with a trainer, so as to not detract from his meticulous clothes.

"Sorry to disturb you. My name's James Arthur." He held out a card. "I work for the Herald Sun out of Chicago. If you don't mind, I'd like a few minutes of your time." He pointed at the seat opposite her. "May I?"

Keddie shoved her book to one side and motioned him to sit. "What can I do for you?"

"I'm on assignment, doing an in-depth piece on terrorism in this country, Homeland Security and all that."

"And what does that have to do with me?"

"I believe you have a friend by the name of Sam Neally?"

"You're wasting your time." Without missing a beat, she motioned the waitress over for her bill. "I've got nothing to say."

"Just give me a few minutes to explain." The waitress moved in, check in hand, but James Arthur cut her off neatly with his own order, demonstrating the same proficiency he'd used to snag Keddie's attention.

He ordered dessert for her and a coffee, ignoring her protests. "My treat, to show you I'm one of the good guys. I'm not out to crucify Sam Neally. Just the opposite. I want to tell her side of the story, kind of a Patty Hearst thing. How young she was, how she didn't know what she was getting into. I hope to raise some issues about the Patriot Act, since it's coming up for a vote again later this year." His smile was charming and impossible to ignore. "I have some questions about the appropriateness of the FBI's behavior during her arrest, and where they draw the line in cases like this."

"Or where they don't draw the line. As far as I'm concerned, there was no line."

"That's exactly the story I'm looking for. We can do this off the record and keep your name quiet if you want."

"I don't give a damn if you use my name. It's Sam's name I'm worried about." She reached across the table and held out a hand. "Keddie Silva, by the way."

He shook it. "How are you? You're a good friend of Sam Neally's, I believe. I'm glad I found you."

"You found me how?"

"When the story broke in the news last week, I started doing some digging and eventually got to you."

"So what are you looking for from me?"

"Some background on her life, her recent arrest. How she was treated, what's happening now, tell me how I can get an interview from her."

"I probably don't know as much as you do about her past history. Her arrest last week you can get in the news. What's not there and probably isn't going to be known is that the FBI agent who had her arrested was sleeping with her. There's your story. I'm sure there's some sort of FBI code of ethics code broken here. But hey, I'm only a blackjack dealer. What do I know about ethics?"

He pulled his notebook out and began writing fast. "Do you know this guy's name?"

"Not saying. I promised Sam I wouldn't mention details to the press. It might go against her chances of getting cleared, which is what they're promising her, by the way, if she goes along with them and turns states evidence."

"What do they want her to do?"

"After keeping her cooling in jail for three days, they let her go, but not really. They're using her for some sort of operation, and the agent who turned her in is her bodyguard. He's staying out at her place while they work out the arrangements of the agreement. She's pretty much a prisoner, as far as I can tell. I tried calling her earlier today, but Roper wouldn't let me say more than a couple of words.

Said it was too dangerous. Until they finish their investigation or whatever the hell they're doing." She grabbed a dish of tiramisu the waitress sat down and took a bite, darting glances around the room. "Hell, I shouldn't be saying any of this to you. How do I know you're even with the press? You might be one of Sam's former terrorist friends." She looked him over. He looked more like a Donald Trump wannabe.

He pulled out a wallet, the kind made in Italy that Deckard liked. Did eco-terrorists carry leather wallets? Weren't they into animal rights? He flipped it back and showed her a press card. "That satisfy you? Or do you want to see more? I have my driver's license here. Let's see what else I've got."

Keddie waved a fork at him. "No, it's okay. I can't picture you spiking trees, not in that fancy suit, at least." She paused. "Canali, isn't it?"

"You know men's fashions?"

"I have a friend who knows clothes. But how does a reporter afford Canali?"

"You caught me. I'm not just a reporter. My father owns the Herald Sun. The story I'm working on is going to be part of a book."

"Oh." She took of a quick sip of coffee. "Anything else you've told me that's not quite true?"

"I apologize. I thought it would be easier to get your attention as a reporter."

"Is the book really going to be about Homeland Security, or did you make that up too?"

"No, it's about terrorism in this country and the fear-mongering being tossed about by the last administration." He took another sip of coffee. "This man, Roper, he's with the FBI?"

She nodded. "But if you print his name, I'll deny I mentioned it to you. I promised Sam I wouldn't say anything about him directly."

"Okay, I won't use the name. Just a few more

questions. They're still holding her?"

Keddie shook her head and stubbed out her cigarette. "Not exactly. She says she's there willingly, but they're staying at her place, she and Roper. When I called out there today, he mentioned I'd be able to talk with her after tomorrow night. So it sounds like whatever they're doing is going to finish up tomorrow."

He kept writing. "So, do you have any idea what they're up to?"

"Not really. I don't think it's going to happen out at her place. He mentioned something about a meeting somewhere else."

"What do you think her role in this is?"

"Look, Mr. Arthur..."

"James, please."

"All right, James, I shouldn't have told you any of this. Sam's lawyer also happens to be my boyfriend, and he'd kill me if he knew I passed any information on to the press."

"I understand. I won't push you any further. Just one more question. You said the FBI was setting up some sort of sting around her former eco-terrorist friends? But she's not going to be directly involved with that?"

"No. Deckard said the agreement with the FBI was for her to use her past connections with the group to set up the meeting. Once it's set up, she's done."

"What about a contact number for your friend? She have a cell phone?"

"She's got a phone that's disposable, and she changes numbers every three months. I reached her yesterday on the latest one I've got, unless they changed it again today."

He pulled out his cell phone and tapped in the number, then whipped out a card and slid it across to her. "Here's my number in case you think of anything more."

"God, I should keep my mouth shut. If you mess up this thing for her, I'm screwed."

"Don't worry. I'm not interested in messing up anything. I just want a story I can use for my book."

"Well, I've gotta give Sam a heads-up about you. That's the only way I can justify my big mouth when I promised her I'd keep quiet."

"No need. When I set up an interview with her, I'll mention you had her best interests at heart."

"No. I think I need to give her a quick call."

He frowned and glanced at his watch. "I need to get going."

Keddie watched him pay the cashier. He turned and glanced back at her briefly before heading out the door. She poked at the last of the tiramisu, uneasiness making her queasy. It was after nine. She had thirty minutes to put in a call and 'fess up before getting back to her table.

She headed for the back door and stepped out into the deserted street running behind the casino. She punched autodial and waited, her heart pounding. Shit!

"Roper here. What do you want now, Keddie?"

"I need to speak to Sam. It's urgent."

"What is it? You'll have to tell me." She could tell by his voice this wasn't going to go well.

"I need to speak with her. It'll only take a few minutes. It's important."

She heard Roper mumble something and Sam came on. "Keddie?"

"Look Sam, I know I'm not supposed to call you, but I needed to tell you something." She paused and took a deep breath. There was only one way to say it, direct. "I did something stupid. A reporter intercepted me tonight at dinner. He wanted to get background for a book he's writing on Homeland Security and the abuse of power."

"What happened?"

"Well, you know me. I was pissed at your situation, so I sort of told him some of the story."

Silence. A very long silence. "What part of the story, Keddie?"

"Roper having sex with you and then having you arrested. And your being held by him now until his FBI case is finished."

"Keddie. You'll have to tell Roper what happened, before he rips the phone out of my hand. Tell him what you told me, so he can decide what to do."

Keddie considered hanging up. Or dumping her cell phone in the trashcan nearby. Neither seemed like a good idea since he knew where she worked. And hell, she didn't need to justify herself to this guy. Unlike Sam, he didn't have anything on her.

"Let's have it. Who did you talk to and what did you say?" His voice was too calm; it reminded her of her father the time she'd set fire to the boathouse.

"Like I told Sam, a man came up to me tonight while I was eating and introduced himself. He said he was a reporter from a Chicago paper."

"What paper?"

"He said The Sun, or something like that. His dad owned it. He told me he was writing a book about Homeland Security and had been following Sam's arrest."

"Goddammit, what else did he tell you about himself?"

"Not much. His name's James Arthur, he gave me his cell phone number to get in touch with him with anything more."

"Give me that."

"I can't read it out here in the dark. I'll call you back with it once I'm inside."

"All right. Now tell me exactly what did you say to him?"

She took a deep breath. "Only that you'd seduced Sam and then got her arrested."

He said something she didn't catch. "And?"

"And that she'd been released on some sort of plea agreement in exchange for information leading to some terrorists. Basically that you're dangling her as bait for them."

"And what else?"

"Nothing. I don't know anything more. I don't know the specifics of whatever you're doing."

"Where the hell did you get all the crap you told him? If it was Sam's lawyer, you'd better pray this operation goes down without a hitch, or you may have just been responsible for a violation of the plea agreement. Her lawyer could lose his license, and you could send Sam right back to jail."

Keddie tightened her hold on the phone, her hands shaking hard enough to drop the damned thing. "I didn't tell him anything specific. I don't know any specifics. He swore that since this was going in a book, it wouldn't be published any time soon. He wants to meet her and get an interview is all." God, how the hell did she get herself into this?

"Yeah, well you better pray to God he doesn't do anything more. Don't even think of calling him back. Just keep your mouth shut, and don't say anything to anyone else about this."

"What are you going to do?"

"I'm going to find out who the sonofabitch is and how much damage he can do. Call me back with that number, then keep quiet, mind your own business, and don't call here again. Sam will call you when she can." He snapped the phone off before she could say more.

The dark street was empty, with nothing but deserted warehouses lining the other side. Clutching her phone, she turned her head at a sound behind her, too late. She never saw where it came from, never even felt the blow that caught her in the temple.

****

Roper snapped her phone shut, pulled out his own and stood up. Without looking at Sam, he headed for the privacy of the bedroom.

God, Keddie. Stupid, stupid move, trying to be her protector.

The fire had been burning long enough to turn the room unbearably hot by the time Joe emerged, his face grim. Sam followed him into the kitchen and watched as he poured himself coffee before turning to face her.

"Your friend was supposed to call right back with a phone number but she apparently thought better of it. Where does she work so I can reach her?"

"The DeVille Casino."

He turned away and she waited, holding her breath as he made calls.

"Goddammit. Her phone's shut off and no one's in the office at the DeVille who can tell me how to reach her."

"What are you going to do?"

"I'm going to get someone to check on this James Arthur." He spoke with a finality that allowed for no further questions. Ignoring her, he punched in numbers.

Sam sat down on the couch and waited.

Thirty minutes of phone calls, interspersed with tense silence later and Roper's phone rang. Sam looked up. She was too far away to catch his words.

At last he came over and stood, looking down at her contemplatively.

"Well? Is it bad?"

"No. So far James Arthur seems to be exactly who he says he is. A freelance journalist, son of the owner of a small weekly out of Evanston. No criminal record, no connection to any terrorist group, and no connection to our case."

Sam drew her knees up to her chest, her stiff shoulders sagging. It was all too much. She needed sleep. "It's just the way Keddie is, Joe. She's got a mercurial personality, but she's loyal. Her main fault is she lets her passion rule her mouth, acts before she thinks. But she's not vindictive, and she hasn't really got a mean bone in her. She just wants to protect me."

"By jeopardizing a six month operation we're running and risking your freedom?" He spoke quietly, his voice tight.

"Will it mean I'm going back to jail?"

He sighed and shoved his hands into his pockets. "No. I'm not going to let you go back to jail, whatever the hell happens." He lowered himself down on the couch, but didn't touch her. "You didn't pass any information on to her earlier, did you, Sam?"

"Like what?"

"Anything about your agreement with us? The where and when of it?"

"No more than what you heard me say. You're the one monitoring my phone. The only other opportunities I've had to speak with her were while I was in jail, and I didn't know anything about your operation."

He sighed and leaned back, keeping inches between them. "Well, she may have just gotten her boyfriend's license revoked, if she passed on anything she got from him."

"Oh, God, Joe. If that happens, it will kill Keddie."

He shrugged. "We'll see. If things go as planned tomorrow night, I won't raise the issue. But if anything goes wrong, I'm going to have to put in a report about it." He watched her closely. "I've got to; it's my job."

She nodded. His job, her life. How could these two worlds ever get together for more than a couple of nights? "Keddie didn't understand. She only saw what she thought was happening, that you were taking advantage of me, and that you're still doing that."

"It's tough, isn't it, Sam? Friends with an FBI agent?"

His face was impassive again, the cop face. "Right back at you, Roper, only substitute fugitive. At some point, there's going to be something that can't be solved between us in bed."

He reached over and traced one finger down her cheek. "Let's not go there right now, okay? For now that's enough. When the time comes, we'll handle it however it needs to be handled." Catching her hand, he locked fingers with hers. "We are going to see this through, you and me. Former enemies we may be, but we'll work it out." He pulled her up, swung her into his arms and carried her to bed unaware that outside in the shadows someone watched and waited.

Chapter Twenty-Four

The phone rang insistently.

"Hell." Roper crawled out of bed, grabbed his clothes, and left Sam's back exposed to the cold. He yanked his pants up over his bare buttocks. He fought with the buttons with one hand as he grappled with his phone. "Roper."

Shivering, Sam sat up, a thin sheet over her, and listened to his end of the conversation.

"Yeah, got it....Okay....Yeah....No. Right, call me if anything changes." He dropped the phone back on the table next to his pistol, sat down on the edge of the bed, and dropped a kiss on her shoulder. Faint light shone in through the window.

"Well?"

"So far, so good. No contact between James Arthur and the Consortium. Everything checks out with him. He's been here about seven days, four days before the story broke about your arrest. According to rumors back home, he is writing a book about the government." He spoke the words automatically; reporting on his thoughts while his flared nostrils said something else.

Leaning forward, he slid one hand under the sheet and skimmed it down her naked body. Her eyes locked with his, she spread her legs and gave his long fingers access. Trembling, she leaned forward and set off on a trail of discovery down his damp chest to his belly, coming to rest on the bulge beneath his half zipped pants. He swore softly as she reached for the zipper.

"Roper?"

He pushed her backwards on the bed, pulling his pants down to his knees before rising up over her.

He gave her what she wanted and she took it, moaning. She fought his attempts to withdraw, desperate to finish what she'd begun. She choked briefly before catching his rhythm but managed to keep pace until his last hoarse cry dissolved and he fell to his side.

Panting like a runner at the end of a marathon, he lay still with his eyes closed. Sam quietly rolled over and put her head down on his heated chest. He slid his fingers into her hair, pushing it away from her damp face.

"Joe? You okay?"

"You may have witnessed my last hurrah here. Right now, I don't think I'll ever be able to move again."

"I doubt that. In another minute, you'll bound up off the bed, ready to field calls, panting for your big day to begin." Silently she wondered if this really was their last hurrah.

"Easy for you to say. I'm a man closing in on forty."

"We're already established you're great in bed." She grabbed hold of his closely shorn hair and yanked him down to plant one final kiss.

"Yum. You taste good."

"What an ego. I taste like you."

"Okay, that's it, woman. The final insult. I'm outta here." He rolled off the bed, got caught by his pants clutching at his ankles, and fell to the floor.

"Brrrrr. This room's cold enough to freeze my balls off."

"There's probably plenty of hot water for a shower."

"Then come on. Let's do it." He called to her and

stumbled into the bathroom.

Nude and shivering, she followed.

****

Yesterday's clear sky had given way to low-hanging clouds during the night, a sign of more snow to come. Sam stared at a slender finger of frost crawling along up the kitchen window. Both the fireplace and propane heater worked hard, but the house stayed cold. Today it would be too cold to melt the coming snow.

Roper sat at his laptop, cell phone in hand. He wore his holster. He finished his call, stood up, and ambled over behind her, legs barely touching hers. He reached around her and grabbed a piece of bread. "I'm glad to see you cook something else besides eggs."

"Why?"

"Job interview."

"For what? I'm not looking to be somebody's housekeeper."

"What can you cook?"

"Soy loaf. Tofu cheesecake."

"How about a nice rib roast?"

"Nope. Haven't you heard people don't eat that kind of stuff any more?" She caught his hand as he grabbed for another piece of bread. "Seriously, Joe, have you gotten anything more on the journalist snooping around Keddie?"

"No. Nothing on the guy. He's probably nothing other than one more jackass journalist, trying to work his way into a fresh angle on a story. That was Chandler from Omaha calling. He's tracked down a lead on your mother's case, someone she worked for nineteen years ago."

"Who?"

"The name's Bradford Parry. He's been dead for twelve years. Owned a bunch of shopping malls around Iowa and Nebraska. She did some accounting work for him. He filed a 1099 in 1989."

She frowned. "I never heard of him. I don't recall the name, but I don't remember the names of anyone she worked for."

"Chandler's following up on this. Seems unlikely the guy had anything to do with your mother's death. He was clean as a whistle, not even a tax audit in his past. Family man, two kids, grown now, a loving wife, no alcohol, no drugs, nothing on him. Chandler has a meeting set tomorrow with his former secretary. She's still alive, lives in a retirement village in Omaha. He might get something from her."

Sam took a deep breath. "Anything more about Robert Mathias?"

"Not much of anything useful in his office. No other active cases. A couple of recent ones completed. Nothing dramatic about them."

"So what happens next in Omaha?"

"Look, Sam. We don't have to go into that today. Let it wait until we've got the Consortium operation wrapped."

Sam shook her head. "I want to know now, Joe."

He put his arms around her from behind. She could feel his warm breath on her neck.

"You mother's case is being tagged as probable homicide with our push on the case. It'll stay open, cause of death still drowning, but with enough collateral evidence to leave the case open." He spoke slowly, as though weighing each word. "They're doing another search of her car, and we've called in a forensic expert on water remains."

"How much evidence can there be after so many years?"

"It varies, but there could be more. You've already seen the preliminary report Mathias sent you."

Sam shuddered and he stopped. "It just keeps

getting worse in Omaha, Joe. I just want to get my mother's remains buried, have the memorial, and get it over."

He tightened his hold on her. "Yeah, I know. I promise we'll get it complete when this case is finished."

"Anything more from Keddie this morning?"

"No. She's probably ducked out for now, turned her phone off, and hid out until this is over."

****

Monday continued to drag as the time for Roper to leave edged closer. Buchanan called every hour with updates on his agents moving into place.

The phone rang again and Sam watched, tense, listening to Roper's half of the conversation.

"Yeah? Where?" He sounded grim. "Did you make the car?" A pause. "Is it still there?" A longer pause. "Call me back when you get something on it." He flipped his phone shut and stood up.

"What's wrong?" she asked.

"Maybe nothing. We're checking. One of agents spotted a late model Ford 4x4 sitting a hundred yards up your road around the bend this morning."

Roper reached for his automatic, shifted it into the shoulder holster. "Know anyone who drives a truck of that description?"

Sam shook her head. "No. What are you going to do?"

"Nothing, for now. Getting ready. It could be some idiot who got lost, or could be anything, maybe even that damned reporter Keddie met. They're doing a plate check right now. They'll keep an eye on his vehicle, follow him if and when he moves. He's been sitting tight about fifteen minutes."

He roamed around the house like a caged cat, checking windows, leaving Sam in the middle of the room, following his pacing.

His phone rang again. "Roper." He frowned and

listened. "Yeah, okay. Track him for a few miles and see if he's clearing out." He jammed the phone into his pocket and sat down beside her on the couch.

"It's a rental car from the Reno airport. The name on the rental agreement is Paul Ost, Chicago license. Know anyone by that name?"

Sam shook her head. "Is this something I should worry about?"

"I'd say no. The guy just took off. My agents will tail him for a while, as a precaution, while they finish running his driver's license." He smiled. "Sorry, Sam. I always get tense at the finale." He pulled her against him. "Don't worry about it. We've got all our suspects covered so it's definitely not one of them. At the worst, it's one of those damned journalists calling my office with questions about you and the Consortium."

****

In many ways, life had become far simpler, and far more complicated. They ate in front of the fireplace one last time. Was this it, then, in the end, nothing but a brief interlude?

Roper did a final run-through with his team by phone and put in a call to his son. She washed the dishes, scrubbed down the counter, and tried not to listen in on his laughter. When it was silent, she wiped her hands and turned around to say a final goodbye.

He wore a black t-shirt, commando pants, and hooded jacket that broadcast 'FBI' in blocked white letters. He dominated her living room. Without taking his eyes from her face, he slid his arms into his bulletproof vest and checked his Glock.

With five quick steps, he cut the distance between them down to inches. "You look like hell."

It was the last thing she'd expected. "Roper, you say the sweetest things."

She clenched the Kevlar vest in her fists and

pulled him against her. "I don't know how to do goodbyes. The people in my life usually leave without saying them." She searched his face.

"Looks like a good time for a lesson. Say after me 'Goodbye, Joe. I'll see you in a few hours.'"

She pressed her face into his neck, inhaling one more memory, just in case. "You're coming back here tonight?" she mumbled.

"Yeah. It could be late, but I'll be back. Hell, I gave up my motel room, remember?"

"So is it usually dangerous? These stakeouts and shootouts and things?"

"Yeah, we're bad." She could feel him grin.

He pushed her away and ruffled her hair "When is this weird hair of yours gonna grow out? I can't wait to see the real deal."

Hair. Men. "A few months, maybe. I could get a buzz cut and it'd probably grow out faster," she laughed, "and then we'd have matching haircuts." Matching anything was inconsequential if they never saw each other again. "So you like long hair, I suppose? Like most men?"

"Well, that's a hell of a sexist thing to say for a feminist."

"Where'd you get the idea I'm a feminist?"

"It's obvious, self sufficient, running your own business, no man around to fix the garbage disposal. Sounds like a feminist to me."

"Except for sex, you mean?"

"Shit, you said it, not me. I wasn't going to touch that one. Your aunt swore off marriage, didn't she?"

Sam shrugged. "Not really. She and Tilo never married for a lot of reasons, but she was no feminist."

"And you?"

"I think you're showing your age, Joe. It's probably not a major concern these days between men and women; but, for what it's worth, I never said I didn't need men."

"So do you need a man?"

"I'd like to have a normal life, which probably includes relationships with men—or a man."

"So you're willing to give it a shot with me? See what we have going?"

"Yes. I told you I was willing. Are you?"

"Hell, yes. I'm more than willing. Just wanted to be sure we're both clear on where we stand. Once this thing is over."

He bent down and kissed her slowly. She slipped a hand beneath his vest and under the sweatshirt. His heartbeat was steady and reassuring. Turning her head, she brushed her lips against his neck, lingering on the pulse at the base of his throat to taste him.

They both drew back at the same time, measuring each other. Without speaking, he turned and walked slowly toward the door, grabbing for his jacket. He hesitated briefly, then strode back to where she stood in the middle of the room. This time the kiss was calm and resolute. "I'll be back late, probably after midnight."

Without waiting for her reply, he headed out. "I'll leave a couple of men around until everything's under control. And I've put in a call to Charlie Lemon. Once my men are pulled back, he'll check up on you until I show up."

"I'm used to living out here alone, remember?"

"Yeah. I remember. I'll call you as soon as things are clear." He pointed to the counter. "I'm leaving your red cell phone with you. It's sitting on the counter. Don't make any outgoing calls until I give you the all clear. And don't pick it up for anyone other than me." He frowned at her. "Remember, no calls. Unless it's an emergency. You hear?" He hit the door with the flat of his hand to get her attention. "Promise?"

"I promise. Don't worry, Roper, I'll be fine."

Uncertainty crossed his face. "Take care, babe." He turned quickly and left, leaving the last word hanging in the air.

"Good luck." She whispered to the door.

His dirty SUV disappeared into the dark as the first flakes of snow parachuted down to the ground.

Sam shut off all the lamps, leaving the firelight for company. She pressed her palms against the window, feeling the cold tingling her fingertips, watching snow turn into a thin blanket. Her leg ached, she missed Dourcet, and she missed Roper already. Life. Her life. She thought about calling Charlie, but her instructions were explicit—no calls. To anyone. It was going on half past nine. The curtain was set to go up on the big scene in an hour.

She roamed the house, picking up dishes and clothing, straightening everything in her path, checking the clock every ten minutes. In an hour it would be all over, an hour or two more and Roper would be back here, safe.

Chapter Twenty-Five

The Nevada Motel sat on the western side of Stagecoach, a town no one cared about. It was exactly thirty-seven miles from Sam's place, but the blowing snow made the trip a slow go. Roper spent a half hour sitting behind a jackknifed semi on Highway Fifty before a snowplow and tow truck showed up to clear a path.

The operation itself rolled out fast and was over in twenty minutes. They'd caught four of the five inside the room eating KFC, the fifth was nabbed behind a beat-up Ranger, loading hammers and wire cutters into the trunk.

The four men inside surrendered without a whimper, throwing aside their buckets of chicken in unison as the FBI burst into the room. Crying for their lawyers before the cuffs were on, they had their rights read to them and were led to the waiting van.

The fifth man was the only one who took off running, dodging behind his truck in the dark, and sprinting across the motel parking lot like a six point buck. They tackled him two hundred yards down the highway, heading west.

Roper stood outside, watching his agents handle cuffs and shackles, fighting the snow. A gust of wind rattled his truck and almost blew him over. He signed the warrants and passed them off to the deputy, watching as five shackled suspects shuffled their way into the Washoe Department of Corrections van, destination the county lock-up. He squinted as two agents shoved the last man, into the van. He checked the time, eleven on the dot.

Lifting a hand, he motioned them on. "Roll 'em out!"

The last two agents worked automatically, sweeping the scene, snapping photos, getting the site secured for the night. Maybe another thirty minutes work minimum before he could leave.

Roper climbed back into his Cherokee and would have breathed a sigh of relief, except for one big fucking complication, the local sheriff's department. They'd managed to get themselves included in the FBI bust at the last minute, showing up with a warrant in hand for one of the men wanted on assault charges, filed yesterday by a local woman. There was going to be a jurisdiction fight, and it was up to Roper to make sure the guy didn't walk on a technicality.

"Hell." Roper shoved aside the warrant sitting on the passenger seat, shrugged out of his Kevlar vest, and pulled on his bomber jacket.

He grabbed up his cell phone. "Mankowicz? Roper here. We've got our five in custody and ready to close it down for the night. Any activity out your way?"

"No, quiet as a tomb," his agent replied. "Except for a few stray drunks weaving down the highway."

"I'm going to be another forty-five minutes doing a final sweep here at the scene. Take a quick turn by her place, then call it a night, and head back to Reno."

"Will do."

Roper punched in another number.

"Hello."

Relief shot inexplicably through him like hot mercury. "Sam, it's Roper. Everything okay there?"

"Yes. Are you okay?"

"Yeah. Things went smooth. We've got all five of them in custody. No worries." Or almost none.

"Is that all of them?"

"Yeah. All except one inconsequential loose cannon with a big Internet mouth who's over in Sparks, but we've got a man ready to pick him up."

"Did you have to use your gun?"

"No. Look, I can't talk now, Sam." He leaned out and barked a quick order at the last agent, locking the place down. "I've gotta go. We're finishing up. I'll be here a while longer in Stagecoach, then I have to head on back to Reno. A little complication's come up with the sheriff's department. I don't think I'm going to make it out to your place before morning. I've pulled my man off your road, but I'll give Charlie Lemon a shout out to check in on you."

"No need. I'll be fine tonight, Joe."

"I'm giving him a call, anyway. I'd feel better if he brought your dog back to you tonight. I'll see you early tomorrow. After that, I'll be tied up for a couple of days, but once I get things cleared up in Reno, let's look at heading east to Omaha and get that mess straightened out. We'll talk about what's next." He paused, wanting to say more, feeling the pull to get moving. "I've got to get on the road. Go to bed."

"God, you're pushy sometimes, Roper."

He heard her grin and smiled. "Yeah, I know, I'm a pain in the ass, for a nice guy."

"You are, both of those things."

"Bye Sam." A dark shadow passed through him, and he held the phone a moment after she hung up, uncertain. He quickly dialed Charlie Lemon's number. His voice mail picked up on the sixth ring. "Shit." There was nothing to do but leave a request for Charlie to check up on Sam tonight, whatever time he got the message.

Roper climbed out of his warm SUV and started shouting orders to his man. All he wanted to do was get the hell out of here, head for Reno and get back to Sam.

****

Sam lay sprawled out on her couch, still dressed, staring into the dark. She was wide-awake, and there'd be no sleep for her tonight.

The shrill ring of her cell phone shot her upright in the cold room; probably Charlie, checking up on her, or maybe even calling to see if he could bring Dourcet over.

"Hello?"

"Is this Sam Neally?"

"Yes. Who's calling?"

"My name's James Arthur."

"James Arthur?"

"I think your friend Keddie gave you some information about me."

"Yes, she did. I really don't have anything to say, Mr. Arthur. I'm not giving interviews, and I doubt the FBI would appreciate it if I did."

"Ms. Neally, I apologize for manipulating your friend. I am a journalist, but I wanted to contact you about something else I'm following up on. I have some information for you about your mother."

Sam clutched the phone tighter. "What are you talking about? Who are you?"

"I picked up the story from the AP about your mother's body being found in Nebraska."

"You saw a news story and came all the way out here in the middle of the night to talk to me about it? What's that got to do with the story you're writing" She gasped. "Who are you really?"

"I'm a friend of the Parry family, I went to school with Evan Parry. Your mother worked for his father."

Parry. That was one of the names Roper had given her. Who was this man? "I don't know. I don't know anything about that." An expanding panic snatched and grabbed at her insides.

"Your mother worked for Mr. Parry around the

time of her death. I'm calling because I have some information I think you may want, about your mother's death."

"How would you even know she's my mother?"

"The news story about your capture by the FBI last week. The story said your real name was Catherine Bell. I'd like to meet you somewhere tonight and talk about this."

"I have no idea who you are or what you want. If you think I'm meeting you tonight, you're crazy. You can call me back tomorrow. You're a friend of the family she worked for, and you've had this information for almost twenty years? Why do you feel compelled to share it all of a sudden? If you've waited this long, I don't see why we can't have this talk in the morning."

"Because I didn't know where you were until I saw the story on your capture. I knew the Parry's, and I think I know what happened to your mother back then, but until I saw a piece in a Chicago paper about finding her body... Look, I don't want to go into it over the phone. I have the information if you want it, something I think you need to know and see. I've been searching for you for three days, but I'm not hanging around much longer. I've got an early flight back to Chicago in the morning, so it's now or never. Meet me now and I'll give it to you."

"And what do you want in return? Why bother with all this?"

"I want a story, for my book. Like I told your friend, I'm writing a book on Homeland Security and personal freedoms. I saw your name in the paper a while back, connected it with what I knew from Evan. So here I am, hoping to get a first hand interview. I took a chance and flew out to do a piece on you. I give you what I know about your mother, and you give me the story of your underground life and your recent capture. I get an exclusive, and you get your past back."

"That doesn't explain why it's so urgent tonight. You could contact me and set this up for the future." She clutched at the phone with trembling hands.

"It's hot right now. Someone else will get to you for a story before I get back here."

"Well, tonight won't work. I can't meet you tonight." Reason struggled and won out over a wild need to know.

"All right. You've forced my hand. Check your cell ID and tell me whose phone I'm using?"

Sam glanced at the caller ID closely. Keddie's phone. "How's you get Keddie's phone? Where is she?"

"She's not here. She's not going to need it right now and maybe not ever again."

"Where is she?" Her head screamed the words, her voice begged.

"I've got her safe and sound. She's a bit worse for wear; but, if you meet me tonight, I promise I'll let her go."

"You're crazy!"

"No, just desperate. Like I said, meet me, and I'll release her."

"How can I trust you that you'll release her?"

"I'll put in a call to her boyfriend, Deckard, isn't it? I'll promise you I'll make the call. I can make it before you get into my truck. How's that?"

"Then what? What do you want with me?"

"A couple of things, Sam. Like I said, I do have information on your mother. I'll give that to you and in return, I've got to have a few promises from you. I think we may even get your friend, Roper, in on this since I need the FBI to back off as well."

"Roper's not going to cooperate with anything you suggest."

"I think he might if you're in the mix. But if your friend isn't enough of an incentive," he paused, "there's always your sister. If I can't get what I need from you, I'll fall back on her for my plans. Your choice. We do it tonight, or I head to Chicago and your sister."

She swallowed down fear rising bitter in her throat. "You promise you'll tell me where Keddie is and let me call Deckard if I meet you?"

"I promise. I'm not interested in hurting your friend."

"And you'll leave my sister alone?" Sam waited for the awful tightness in her chest to ease. "Please leave her alone. She doesn't know anything except I've been on the run for twelve years."

"You have my word, if I get what I need."

Sam stared into the dark, sifting through what he'd said, sorting out what to do from what she desperately wanted. The fireplace had burned down to ashes. With the lights off, only the bulb from the shed beyond the yard shone in through her window, making the whirling snow into a menace. "Where do you want me to meet you?"

"I'm sitting over on Highway 447, where it meets your road. I'm in a white Ford 4x4."

She'd be a fool to meet him alone, but Keddie! She had to go.

"Like I said, it's tonight or never. Keddie or you."

Fighting the frenzy in her chest, she inhaled sharply, searching for sanity in a world gone berserk. "All right. What should I do?"

"Meet me at the highway. Come alone. If you bring any goddamned FBI, I'm out of here. And no calls to your friend, Roper before you get here."

Fear tightened her throat. Where was the truth in all of this? Roper had done a background check on this man tonight, and found nothing suspicious. Who was he really? "All right. I'll meet you. Give me five minutes."

"Five minutes, no more."

Sam threw on her shoes and buttoned her jacket. The snow had stopped, leaving a few clouds, but the moon wove its way in and out between them. A slippery layer of snow covered the ground. A gust of wind tossed a chunk of ice into her face. She climbed into her truck and blew on her icy fingers as she started the engine. She nursed the motor, revved it repeatedly while fingering the phone in her pocket. Her mind flew over her options.

The lights of Charlie's house twinkled to the north, and she almost turned right, overcome by a need for Dourcet. But she was afraid, for Dourcet more than herself even. She pushed back the need for someone to save her and pulled out onto her road, ignoring her fear.

She bounced along the road, swerving to avoid potholes, taking the curves automatically. James Arthur's white 4X4 was pulled off to the right side, a good fifty yards from the paved highway.

Sam pulled to a stop behind his truck just as the moon popped out, illuminating a pale figure sitting inside.

She shut off her engine and climbed down, making her way cautiously to the passenger side. Her heart hammered wildly. Anxiety turned to fear that lodged in the back her throat.

The overhead light came on when the door opened, revealing a large man with a shaven head and almost handsome features. His skin looked tanned, his clothes expensive.

She hesitated, searching his half-shadowed face. He motioned her to climb in beside him.

"No. Give me Keddie's phone and tell me where she is." She held a hand out waiting.

He smiled, not a bad smile, reached down and picked up the phone. He leaned over, and she took it from his gloved hand. "She's locked in the closet in room 910 of the Dupont Hotel."

"Aww!" The sound escaped her trembling lips, but she grabbed the phone. With numb fingers, she scanned down the numbers and found Deckard's. It took her three tries to hit the autodial and put the call through.

"This is Deckard Stewart. I'm unavailable right now. Leave a message. If it's an emergency, dial my service." Sam didn't bother to hang up and redial. She literally screamed her message into his phone. "Deckard, this is Sam! It's Keddie! She's tied up at the Dupont Hotel, room 910! Get the police and find her!"

A hand reached across and grabbed the phone from her fingers. With a quick flick, he tossed it out the door behind her. "That's enough. They'll find her. If they don't tonight, someone will in the next day. Get in!" He held a gun pointed at her.

She surged back, ready to run.

"Get in now! I won't miss from here."

Sam pulled herself up onto the Ford's bench seat and fumbled to shut the door, hands quaking. The interior went dark, and she heard the snap of locks. Pressing against the door handle, she stared at the gun reflected in the dashboard lights. "What do you want?"

He grunted something, started the vehicle, and pulled out. He juggled the weapon carelessly as he shifted gears. He handled it like a toy.

"Where are we going?"

"North, toward Pyramid Lake."

An arrow of fear shot through her, as powerful as if she'd stuck her finger in a light socket. She recognized it from twelve years ago; not fear, terror. Her mind flooded with uncertainty, sifting through one scenario after another, searching for some action to save herself. "Who are you? What do you want with me?"

"Evan Parry. Recognize the name?"

"Parry." She whispered the single word.

"Your mother worked for my dad." He drove fast, hitting the ruts too fast. Her thigh hit the door handle, and she winced, grabbing hold of the armrest.

"What do you want with me?"

He drove fast, making a sharp left turn that threw her across the seat. With his gun hand, he shoved her back. "Just sit there and keep quiet."

Snow covered everything with a thin veil, the night suddenly her enemy, but she recognized the landscape. They were heading north on the lower ridge road.

Her cell phone rang sharply. He caught her arm as she reached for the phone. He pulled up short, shoved the gear into neutral but left the engine running. "Hand me that phone," he demanded.

Fear had taken control of her mind and his words were just noise.

"I said give me your phone. Now!"

"All right." Confused, she did the automatic thing, reached in her pocket, and grabbed for the phone. It kept on, unrelenting, the shrill ring vibrating in her palm.

"Give it to me!"

She held it out, and he grabbed it, dropping it into his lap.

"Stay over on your side!" he yelled at her, pulling a sharp right onto another dirt road, shifting gears and climbing a steep incline. She recognized this road, as well, the upper ridge trail, running adjacent to the reservation for five miles between her place and Benton, less than five miles west of the Forty Mile Desert.

Suddenly Parry pulled to a stop. With the engine running, he turned; the gun gleamed in his hand. He pointed it at her as if it were a camera.

Involuntarily she grabbed at the door handle and yanked. "Let me out of h.....!"

Whaam! The gun barrel connected with her cheek and interrupted the scream.

She felt no pain, just a flash of black followed by a sense of swimming through consciousness, then the sharp stab of pain down the side of her face. Her head throbbed, and she fell back against the seat, fighting dizziness and nausea.

"Don't do that again. I don't want to shoot you."

He grabbed her hands and squeezed them together. Something cold encircled both wrists, and she yanked back, a reflex action. Sharp pain sliced across both wrists, displacing the throbbing in her cheek. Something warm trickled down her jaw.

Gloved hands grabbed hold of her jacket collar. She jerked back. He captured her shackled wrists with one hand, and she cried out as an agony of sharp pain shot through her arms. He pressed her face against the rough wool of his jacket. She inhaled the sickeningly sweet smell of cologne as she sobbed and gasped for breath.

"Stop fighting!" He shoved her roughly back against the door and another moan broke out. Pressing her lips tightly together, she focused on his face, trying to make out his words.

"Twenty years but I remember you, a skinny, little, freckled-faced kid."

The words floated toward her through a thick red haze that engulfed her body.

"You don't remember me, do you?"

"No." Her body shook and the word sounded slurred. "What do you want?"

"Well, for one thing, I'm going to have to stop you from investigating your mother's death. None of this would have happened if you hadn't stirred things up with your digging into the past."

She fought her way out of the gray reaches of

pain. "You were there the day she died? Did you kill her?" she whispered.

"It was all an accident; a little game we were playing, she and I. Just sex." He shifted toward her, and she shrank back further, the armrest dug into her spine. His tone sounded sincere, his strange explanation incongruous and unbelievable.

Bile rose in her throat and she swallowed it down. "Please, I don't want to know."

"I need to tell you so you'll understand. I'm not a bad guy. I didn't murder her. It was an accident," he said. "I was a kid, just eighteen. She was thirty, an older woman leading me on. I was her employer's son, probably some sort of trophy for her. It was her idea to play the game with the scarf. She told me about it. It was exciting with someone like her. I never expected it to be dangerous."

Drowning in terror, Sam sucked in air. She searched for some way to survive the images from his macabre tale.

"It was all a stupid accident. I'm not a murderer. I'm a family man myself now. I've got a daughter. I'm respected in my community. I recently was elected to the state legislature so now my reputation is at stake not just for my family but for the people of the state as well. She wanted me to put the thing around her neck. But then she died."

"Please, I do understand. Don't tell me any more. I wasn't trying to dig up something against anyone. I barely remember her. She disappeared when I was eleven, and I always blamed her. When I found out she'd died, I just wanted to discover what happened to her."

She could feel his mind's eye searching in the dark for the truth of what she said.

"I see. What about the private investigator you sent? And the FBI?"

"I hired the investigator but only to uncover the

truth. I wanted to know who my mother was, who her friends were, and what happened that day when she never came back. The FBI only got involved because I asked them to. When they found the emails to Omaha, they were investigating me, not you. They only dug further into it recently for my sake."

"Well, I'm sorry if that's the case, but it's too late now." He paused. "I regret the necessity, but I can't let you live."

Chapter Twenty-Six

Roper checked his watch. Twelve fifteen and he was finally on his way. Still no answer from Charlie Lemon, but it was probably a moot point now. He pictured Sam tucked safely away in bed an hour ago, sleeping soundly despite the fears swirling about in Roper's head.

It was cold as hell now, probably getting close to zero, but at least the wind had died down a little. Roper pulled out onto the highway and headed for Reno and a long night. Highway Fifty was lonely and dark as a grave, the only lights coming from an occasional truck, driving too fast. He followed suit and burned rubber, hitting eighty within five seconds. One-handed, he punched in another call to Charlie Lemon. This time the man picked up.

"Yeah?"

"Charlie—it's Joe Roper. I'm finishing up on a job and heading toward Reno right now. I wondered if you'd check up on Sam for me? I've pulled out my men watching her, but I don't feel good about leaving her alone all night. Can you keep an eye out 'til I get back there in the morning?"

There was a long pause, not rare for Lemon. "Any reason?"

"No. Yes. Maybe. Probably just my nerves. We've got her former friends locked up tight, so there's no threat there."

"Huh," he grunted. "I'll head on over there. I called her a couple of minutes ago, but she didn't pick up."

Fear, a great wave of it, washed over Roper, leaving his arms feeling weak. He gripped the steering wheel with tight fists. "Probably already in bed. I talked to her over an hour ago." He stopped. There would be no pretense with this man. "Can you drive over to her place and give me a call right back? I just made the intersection of Highway Fifty and Ninety-Five."

"I'm on my way. Any objections to my bringing Dourcet along?"

"No. In fact, I'd prefer if you did. I'd feel a hell of a lot better if you left him with her. Ring me back on this phone when you get there."

"All right." Lemon hung up without a goodbye. Roper relaxed back against the seat, brief but potent relief pouring through him. Lemon was an enigma, but a goddamned dependable one. And he'd do anything for Sam.

Roper passed every badass driver out tonight, leaving them in his wake. He was five miles south of 80 when his cell rang again.

"Roper."

Charlie Lemon didn't bother to identify himself. "I'm sitting in front of Sam's house. The lights are on, but she's nowhere around. Her truck's gone."

"Hell! Did you go inside?"

"Yeah, no sign of anything unusual. I tried her cell phone again, no answer."

Roper had tried her three times in the past ten minutes. He punched the pedal to the floor. "I'm on my way. I'll be there in ten minutes, fifteen tops. Is Dourcet with you?"

"Yeah." A whine sounded in the background.

Roper cranked the window down, reached up, and slapped the bubble light on top of his Cherokee. He punched in Reno dispatch.

"Roper here. Patch me through to the Churchill Sheriff's Office in Fernley."

"Will do."

Night dispatch picked up at the Sheriff's Department. Roper identified himself and barked quick orders at the confused woman on the other end to get a search party out. Then he redialed Reno Dispatch.

"Ruby, put me through to whoever's there in the office."

"That'd be Buchanan. Just a sec."

"Buchanan."

"It's Roper."

"Where the hell are you? We're ready to get things tied up here. I've got the Washoe Sheriff Department chomping at the bit to get hold of their suspect."

"That'll have to wait, Buchanan. I'm heading back to Sam's place. She's not there and not picking up her cell phone."

Buchanan cursed softly. "What do you need from here?"

"Get those Washoe guys out here to start searching and send me a couple of our agents, fast! I'm meeting Charlie Lemon at Sam's. I'm about ten minutes away." The urge to start shouting at Buchanan, at anyone, was overwhelming. "Her truck's missing."

"I'll send Sobiak and Kandinski. We're about done here. Whatever's left, can wait. Call me as soon as you find her."

Roper struggled to pull control toward him.

"Buchanan?"

"Yeah."

"One more thing. Can you get hold of the Bureau of Land Management tonight and see if they can put a couple of rangers on call, in case we need them?"

"Ease up, Joe. Maybe she just felt restless and took a ride?"

"Like hell! I've got a bad feeling about this. I've put out a call to the Churchill Sheriff's office in Fernley also. Make sure you send those bastards you've got hanging out there along, make them earn their keep."

"Will do. Give me ten minutes to see what I can come up with."

"Out." Roper rang off and focused on his driving. He'd just made the 447 turnoff when Lemon called.

"I'm at 447 and Sam's road. Her truck's parked along side the highway. Just sitting there. The engine's not cold yet."

"Stay put, Charlie. Don't touch anything else. I'm five minutes from you." He scanned the horizon, looking for other bubble lights. "I've got a call out to the local sheriff. Keep a watch out for them." He pressed down on the gas, and his tires spun before catching on frozen dirt.

Five minutes later Roper spotted Sam's blue truck, facing south, away from her house. He skidded to a stop, leaving a hundred yard distance between vehicles. His headlights hit Charlie Lemon, leaning against a battered army green truck with a barely visible BLM logo, covered over with thin black paint. He'd parked on the opposite side of the road. Lemon spotted him and climbed out of his cab. He turned and held the door ajar and Dourcet leapt out.

"Charlie!" The wind carried his voice away, and Roper added volume as he dashed across the road. "Anything new?"

"Nope," Charlie replied, a man of few words.

"Let me do a quick walk-around of her truck, and we'll head back to her house." His words were again grabbed by the wind and carried away.

Moving in concentric circles, Roper widened each revolution by a foot, watching the ground. Ten feet out he gave up and went back to Lemon, who lounged against his truck watching.

"You felt the hood of her truck. Did you do much walking around the perimeter or touch anywhere else?"

"Nope, just the hood, then I glanced inside her cab and came back across."

"Show me your prints."

Moving with the ease of a wolf on the prowl, Lemon slipped across the road and pointed at some footprints. "There."

"Good. The dog hasn't been over here?"

"Nope."

Roper pulled open the driver's side door with two gloved fingers and did a quick scan around the inside. He let out a quick breath. No blood.

A car, bubble light blinking, sped down the highway toward them. It squealed to a stop, and two Churchill deputies stepped out. Roper held out a hand. "Agent Roper, FBI. This is Charlie Lemon."

The men shook hands and nodded at Lemon. "We know Charlie. What's up?"

"How much did my dispatcher fill you in on?"

"Possible missing person."

Roper frowned. "Her name's Sam Neally. She's been in protective custody. We released her tonight. She's disappeared. Last word from her, she was going to bed, no plans to go out tonight. She was told to stay put one more night."

"You think she hightailed it?"

Roper shook his head. "No way. She was in the clear after tonight. No reason for her to run. Last contact was about eleven p.m. I spoke with her, gave her the all clear. She said she was going to bed." He pointed at her truck. "We've got a couple of sets of footprints." He stepped carefully into the perimeter of the truck and pointed down.

"These are Charlie's, those probably Sam's." He pointed to smaller prints leading away from her truck. "Tire tracks there." He pointed again. "Looks like she got into another vehicle."

Roper set them up to make a grid of the area and secure her truck. He pulled out his card. "Call me as soon as you finish—or if you get something. I'm heading down the road to her house. When you're finished here, I'd appreciate it if you'd come on down there and do a sweep of that area as well."

Roper gave instructions to her place and got into his truck. He led, Lemon and Dourcet followed, a caravan, making the dark journey in less than two minutes.

As Roper pulled up in her front yard, the cell rang again.

"Roper, Buchanan here. I've got something. Where are you?"

"I'm sitting in front of Sam's house. Her truck's been abandoned at the end of her road. What've you got?"

"Remember the white Ford 4x4 this afternoon? The rental vehicle we checked out for you? The name on the credit card came back registered to a James Arthur from Chicago."

"Goddammit!"

"You know the name?"

"Yeah, it's the journalist who's been poking around Sam's friend, Keddie, looking for a story."

"Yeah, well it's not him. This Arthur guy is still in Chicago. We contacted him. He is a journalist, but he says he hasn't been to Reno in years."

Roper cursed again. "And?"

"The rental agency had a local address for the guy. We did a quick search of his hotel room. It's registered to Robert Arthur, but the room still has his luggage sitting in it. One of the pieces of luggage has an ID tag—Evan Parry, Omaha, Nebraska."

"Shit!"

"One more thing, Joe. Sam's friend, Keddie. We

found her tied up in the closet of Parry's room. She's in ICU at St. Joseph's in Reno, her skull fractured."

"Goddammit to hell!" Every fucking piece of Sam's life was caving in. Roper forced deep breaths, repressing the urge to shout. "She conscious? Able to talk?"

"No, and there's no way to tell when she will be."

"How bad is she?"

"She's in surgery right now, but they say she's probably going to make it."

"Buchanan, get on the phone to Omaha and ask for Chandler. I don't give a fuck if he's in bed screwing his wife, get him up, and find out who this Evan Parry is and what the connection to Marilyn Bell is. Have him give you everything he's got on Robert Mathias as well."

"What the hell's going on, Roper?"

"I've had Chandler in the Omaha office doing some work for me on Sam Neally's mother, Marilyn Bell. She disappeared nearly twenty years ago. Her remains turn up three weeks ago in a submerged car in a river near Omaha. Sam hired a PI to track down details but he'd disappeared." Roper swallowed hard, fear pounding on him like a sledgehammer. "The PI, by the name of Robert Mathias, was found murdered a few days ago."

"Hell, Roper, this is some snake pit you stepped into. What does Parry have to do with all this?"

"Chandler was checking on a former employer of Marilyn Bell by the name of Parry."

"Watch your sixes, will ya? I'll get back as soon as I get something from Chandler. You want more men out there?"

"Yeah. Are Sobiak and Kandinski on their way?"

"They left fifteen minutes ago, should rendezvous with you by 0100. I'll round up a couple more men for you."

"Thanks, Jack. I've already got two Churchill

County deputies at the scene, and Charlie Lemon with Sam's dog are with me at her house. Any word from the BLM?"

"They're pulling in some men and sending them out to you. Take it easy, Roper. She knows the land out there. It gives her a big advantage."

"Hell!"

"I know." Buchanan's words had an ominous finality to them.

"Get back with me when you get something more from Omaha. Over."

Charlie Lemon sat in his dented green truck, Dourcet beside him, both of them statues. Roper glanced at the house. All lights were blazing but he was afraid of what they'd find there. And even more afraid his cell would ring with word they'd found her body. He didn't know how he was going to manage if it turned out bad.

"You hear anything more?"

"We're treating it as an abduction, rather than missing person, and we've got a possible suspect. Someone from Omaha. Sam ever mention Omaha to you?"

"No, not directly, except she was from there. And the other day when she came by my place, she mentioned she'd hired someone to get some information about her past back in Omaha."

Roper nodded. "Does her dog have the ability to track her?"

"Yeah. Dourcet can do it. Best to start him out by her truck and let him go from there."

"Right. Let me do a quick run-through of her place first."

Roper inhaled sharply, cold air and fear kicking his adrenaline into high gear. The front door was unlocked and he pushed it open and stepped across the threshold.

He inhaled again and went very still. The place

smelled like her. He'd grown used to it.

He skated silently from room to room, looking for anything.

Nothing.

Her computer was off, no cell phone in sight, nothing out of place. Pulling out his phone, he dialed up her number. The same, nothing. Even the fire had been banked for the night. Aside from a quilt tossed on the couch, it all looked normal.

He checked her bedroom. The bed was made. Again, normal.

Pulling on evidence gloves, he grabbed her nightshirt hanging on the bathroom door. It was unlikely Dourcet was SAR trained, so did he even know how to scent his owner? Taking the front steps in one leap, Roper ran for his Cherokee.

He motioned to Lemon to follow. "I brought something of Sam's. Can the dog follow a scent from her clothes?"

"Yeah. Sam and Dourcet have a game they play where Dourcet tracks her."

"Thank God for small favors. Let's get back out to the road."

The moon hung low, reflecting off the shiny spots on the top of her truck. The deputies worked to rope off the area, ignoring them.

"Did you get casts of the prints around here?" Roper called over.

The older of the two nodded. "Yeah. We got photos, too. Tread marks look new, a lot of wide spaced grooves. Some sort of off-road type vehicle."

"4x4?"

Another nod from the man in charge. Rotund, he looked like someone who should be sitting home in front of a TV watching the late news rather than freezing his ass out here.

"I'm letting the dog loose." Roper pointed back at Dourcet. "He belongs to Sam Neally. We'll see what he can do with finding her scent."

The deputies stood back as Dourcet bounded across to Roper, holding up Sam's nightshirt. Dourcet sniffed it and whined. He barked once, and Roper caught hold of his collar, tugged him over the tape and inside the truck. Holding his breath, Roper shoved the driver's door wide open and yelled, "Find Sam, Dourcet. Find Sam."

The dog bounded forward a few yards, stopped and sniffed the ground, raised his head to take another sniff, then continued on, head down. He stopped fifty yards out, beside a roped off set of tire tracks, looked up once, sniffed again and barked three times.

Hell, Roper cursed. What did they know, except Sam got into the other vehicle? At this point he was as lost as Sam.

Chapter Twenty-Seven

Sucking in air like a newborn, heart pounding, Sam forced herself to focus on Evan Parry's words. She needed time to think and plan an escape. "I don't understand what all this has to do with what you told Keddie, about writing a book."

"I'm not writing a book," he said. "I wouldn't know the first thing about that. James Arthur is an old college friend of mine. As far as I know, he still lives on the Gold Coast in Chicago and writes a syndicated column. His old man owns a newspaper."

Her cell phone rang for the fourth time, and Parry picked it up in one hand, switching his gun to the other. He glanced down at the number and held it out. "Who's this?"

"Roper, with the FBI. He's looking for me." She needed time. "How did you first hook up with my mother?"

Parry frowned and shoved the phone in the cubicle under the dash. "I was eighteen, getting ready to go off to Northwestern. I worked for my dad that summer. Your mother was a nice woman, but more important to me at that age, she was a pro when it came to sex."

Sam shuddered and inched further away, feeling for the door. Her fingers touched cold metal, the lock. She pulled at it but nothing.

"If you're trying to get the door open, forget it." He paused, reached over, and grabbed hold of her wrists, yanking her back.

With the car idling, heat filled the cab and sweat

trickled down between her breasts. Sam shifted around, searching her mind for anything to keep him talking. "You said it was an accident. What happened? How did the car get in the river?"

"I was a dumb kid, a teenager. It was your mother who brought up trying the autoerotic bit. You know, tying something around her neck and having sex. Just as you're about to pass out, whammo, a great climax." His voice trailed off. "We got a little rough but nothing out of the norm. She stopped breathing, and all I could think to do was to get rid of her body and her car."

Sam swallowed hard, tears smarting her eyes. Please, no more. She wanted to yell the words. Ask him questions about anything else but her mother's death. "You found me with the newspaper article?" She whispered.

"No, I found you through your private investigator. I came out here once I got a lead on where you were. I came after you that night in the bar parking lot, but you scampered away like a scarred rabbit."

"Were you the one who broke into my house and turned on the gas?"

"Yeah, sorry. I was trying to get your attention but, as luck would have it, the FBI had found you, and you were the headlines. When they released you I was waiting, hoping to get to you, but it got even harder with the FBI around. Keddie was a big help."

"Keddie?" Fear snaked through her again. "Did you hurt her?"

"I knocked her out, but she's alive. I had to stop her from giving you any more information or the FBI, until I got to you."

Her face felt numb again, but her wrists throbbed, the pain cut into her thoughts. "Why? What do you want? I'm not after you. I didn't even know about you. I just wanted to find out what happened that night."

He shrugged in the dark. "If you hadn't set up that private investigator, I'd never have tracked you down; and you wouldn't be out here with me. Then my secretary called a few days ago and told me the FBI had been nosing around, asking questions."

Sam sifted through her mind as he talked, fighting to push away his words that filled her with terror.

"I had no choice. I had to do something. I can't afford to have you ruin my reputation, especially right now. Having the FBI digging into my life just won't work."

She was drowning in sensations, going down for the last time.

"How did you catch me...alone?" Her voice broke.

"I watched. I was on your road earlier today, watching, waiting for the FBI to leave."

"Your friend was very helpful. She gave me an overview of your situation, everything I couldn't get from the newspapers. Or Mathias' papers." He shifted around.

Robert Mathias. Oh, God. "You killed him?"

"I had to. The man had no scruples; he was going to come after me. He threatened blackmail. At first I thought your sister hired him, but I searched his room and found your stuff there."

"Please, leave my sister out of this. She doesn't know anything about him or you. All she knows is the police found our mother's body."

"Mathias could have contacted her. I've got to make sure. I can't have loose ends dangling."

"What good will it do to kill me? The FBI will find you. They probably already have your name and know you're connected with Mathias' death." Reasoning with this man was like talking philosophy with a mad dog, but she couldn't stop, pleading was her only recourse. "Agent Roper is a friend of mine now. He'll find you. You can't win. The best thing to do is to turn yourself in and tell them what you told me. You can do that."

"That won't work. Any word of scandal and I'll be tossed out of the legislature. It will reflect on my family. I've got a kid myself. I'll take my chances I can get out from under this."

Joe. How could he find her?

"I don't kill innocent women. I'm going to put you out here in the desert. I've heard it isn't too unpleasant to die from hypothermia. I'll give you a little help, knock you out. Then you simply will lie there and fall asleep."

"Please, let me go! Just let me out here. I promise I won't tell the police anything. Just leave me here. You don't need to do anything else." A sense of foreboding circled over her like a very large bird, the weight of it heavy and dark, pushing her down toward an abyss. She wanted to weep, but there were no tears.

"I would if I could, but it's too late." He sank back, letting go of her wrists, his voice sad. "That night I didn't realize what had happened. I looked down and saw her eyes were open, but she wasn't moving. She wasn't breathing."

"Please, no more. Don't tell me any more." She began to shake. Nothing mattered now but to survive.

"Please, I'm going to be sick. Open the door, so I can throw up."

"Hell!" He reached for the lock and shoved her door open.

She lunged toward the cold air, pulling away from his hands clawing at her collar. Turning her head, she vomited out the door.

Frigid air blew loose hair around her face. Balanced on the truck seat, she twisted about, raised her bound hands and with one swift move, caught him under his chin. She yanked up hard.

"Ayggh!" His scream rained spittle on her face, and her ears rang. She grabbed under the dash for her cell phone. Holding it tight in both hands, she rolled out the open door.

Whomp. She landed on all fours, the frozen snow-covered ground battering her palms and knees.

Freedom.

Holding the phone like a lifeline, she scrambled up, stumbled away from his car, searching for anywhere to hide.

Warm liquid ran down her trembling fingers and over her bound hands. It had the coppery smell of blood about it. Hers or his?

She shoved with bound hands and struggled to her feet, tripping, clawing at the icy ground to gain a footing. Shrieking wind tore at her, pulling at her gaping coat, leaving her exposed to frigid air.

She reached up and touched her cheek. No pain, just numbness. She shivered as a trickle of warm liquid dripped off her chin. It ran down her neck and found a pathway between her breasts.

Fifty feet, a hundred, two hundred, three hundred she ran on, lurching and stumbling. The moon dissolved behind clouds, leaving the desert shrouded. She tripped and fell into a juniper bush, throwing herself down, still clutching the phone. Sobbing and gasping, she heard the sound of the engine revving up, somewhere out there in the dark.

Chapter Twenty-Eight

Roper and Charlie Lemon stood three feet back, watching Dourcet pace in a circle around Sam's truck. His nose to the ground, he snuffled at tire tracks, moved away, moved back, sniffed, and stopped. Suddenly, raising his head, he whined, a haunting plea echoing off the nearby hills.

"Find Sam, Dourcet. That's it, boy. Find Sam."

Nothing, they had nothing. No clues, no scent. Roper cursed, his body struggling for control. Time was running out. He felt it. They had to do something now.

His phone rang. Sam's number came up. He flipped it open and nothing. He'd lost her signal.

Roper turned and shouted at the deputies, who ran over.

"You got a signal?" he barked at a deputy.

"Not here. Move about fifty feet toward the highway, and you can get the signal back."

Roper ran the fifty feet and punched in Sam's number. An impersonal voice said "This number is out of service at this time."

He punched in Buchanan's number. "Buchanan! I just got a call from Sam's cell phone. I couldn't get to it in time. Now it says it's not in service. Can you get me a fix on that last call?" He spat out Sam's number. "Hurry, man! I'll hang on the line." He waited, pacing back and forth. Charlie Lemon came over and stood behind him with Dourcet at his heels.

Two minutes later Buchanan was back on the line. "We got it. We got a ping from a tower two miles east of Hill Ranch Road, five miles north of Wadsworth."

Roper yelled across to the deputy to take down the numbers and shouted out the coordinates after Buchanan.

"I know the area. Let's go." Charlie Lemon was already jogging down the road to Roper's Cherokee, Dourcet at his heels. Roper called out for the deputies to wait there for his agents and followed. He kept a running dialogue going with Buchanan to relay orders to be forwarded to his men heading for the scene.

Roper leapt into his truck. "Get in," he threw the words at Charlie Lemon.

The moon was under cover again. It turned him into a blind man negotiating a dirt path. Charlie Lemon repeatedly spat out directions, warning of a sharp curve or dip. Roper stayed focused on keeping the pedal to the floor. He tried not to think of Sam lying someplace in this cold hellhole of a desert.

Minutes ticked by and the silence in the Cherokee grew heavier, punctuated by an occasional whimper from Dourcet. Roper tightened his hands on the wheel to keep them from shaking and pushed forward.

"You got a fix on her phone?"

"Yeah, it picks the closest tower and pings it. The newer ones not only ping the tower, but squawk the latitude and longitude, which is a hell of a good thing, since out here, a tower could cover a lot of miles. Or none at all." Roper kept his eyes pinned on a faint outline of dirt road disappearing in front of him.

His own phone rang again.

"Roper."

"We got some more on the guy who rented the 4x4."

"Let's have it."

"The guy flew in to Reno seven days ago. Parry is the son of Marilyn Bell's former employer, one of the leads Chandler's been following. She worked for Parry for about nine months before she died."

"Shit." Nothing but bad news. "Go on."

"The guy's record is clean. The older Parry died years ago and the son's been running his daddy's business since. And get this. He's just been elected to the state legislature of Nebraska."

"What else?"

"The guy's married, has a kid. Friends and work acquaintances say he's a straight up guy, no gambling debts, a little bit of a prig, with zip relating to terrorist activities in college." Buchanan paused. "Then there's the PI. According to Parry's secretary, a Robert Mathias called and requested information on Evan Parry, which she refused to give. He wanted to schedule a meeting."

"And?"

"Nothing. No record they ever met—but Mathias is dead."

"Where are our agents, Buchanan?"

"Should be within range of you in five, ten minutes max. I've sent two more back-ups, and I'm out the door right now."

Roper heard his car starting.

"I've given another heads-up to the BLM and the sheriff's office in Sparks. They're rounding up as many men as they can get out there."

"We've passed the tower and within range of the GPS fix. Out." Roper snapped the phone shut but held it in his hand, a cold two-inch piece of chrome his only hope. He felt too damned tired to do anything but pray.

****

Sam knelt down, squinting into the night. She needed a better hiding place. The only lights in the dark came from Parry's truck. She shifted her wrists, still bound, fighting against the burning pain. She shivered against the arctic wind. She forced deep breaths to slow her pounding heart. Something cold and hard still lay in her palm, the cell phone. She thrust it into her coat pocket, a small piece of hope to keep for later.

Again, the moon slid out from behind a cloud. A friend and a foe, it lit the barren landscape spreading out before her. But she knew this place. It was within a few miles of her home. She'd been here often.

Moonlight caught the reflection of the 4x4 a hundred yards to her right. She'd crawled a full circle and was back to the dirt road, behind the truck. The interior light was still on but she could see no movement. She pushed aside a small burst of optimism. It was too soon to feel grateful she was alive.

She shook her head, clearing blood-soaked hair from her eyes. The move made her dizzy. She caught hold of a rock, steadied herself and kept her eyes moving. Where was Parry? He was out there somewhere. No lights from houses, no other vehicles, no one to rescue her but herself. Run. Home.

A small juniper lay to one side of the path, its gnarled trunk an old friend. Sam sank to her knees, grateful for the cold seeping through her thin jeans that revived her. She worked at the bindings on her wrists. The wire wouldn't budge. It must be close to one a.m. now and the moon, half full, hung well down in the sky, making that direction west. She gazed at the horizon, fixing her position by the moon.

A gust of wind attacked her, whipping at her bare skin. Parry had managed to rip off all but two buttons on her jacket, leaving shirt and flesh exposed. She worked with bloody fingers to fasten those two buttons. Her feet were cold and she worried over them. Keep moving; keep warm, keep the blood flowing. What about shock? Blood loss? How bad had she been hurt? Her mind seemed too slow, the cold catching her thoughts and trapping them.

She reached up and touched her face. Blood oozed from a sharp edge on her cheek, sticky and warm. She opened her jaw and felt a quick stab of pain, but she could move it. It wasn't broken. With numb fingers, she traced razor-like cuts on her wrists.

Her wrists. She pulled on the wires again and got back raw, wet pain.

But the lower part of her body was still good. Her leg ached a little, but not unbearably. She could run, even with bound hands, she could run at least far enough to get away from Parry. But first, she had to slow him down. Then, she'd have a long run home.

She began crawling south, moving behind and away from the truck, keeping a distance between herself and the vehicle. She turned back once and saw flashing red, the parking lights. Where was he?

Stay low, no running, keep hidden for now. It was a mantra, running through her head. She looked back every few feet to check. No sign of him. The moon had disappeared again, and nothing moved in the dark. No sounds. She couldn't see the car lights, but the idling engine still rumbled faintly. She kept moving, shivering from the blood-soaked shirt beneath her flapping jacket.

She crawled on, like a nightmare when the body moves but goes nowhere. The wind had picked up again, the air hitting her in sharp blasts, clawing at her with icy fingers. Too close to him, her mind yelled. Don't run.

The wind whistled about her ears, deafening her.

Then she heard it, louder now; the engine of the truck revving up. It grew louder, as if moving closer to her, then softer, as if muffled behind a butte, then louder, too loud. She glanced over her shoulder, confused. She was unsure what direction it came from.

Lights appeared, twin demons, this time less than two hundred yards behind her, coming at her fast. The roaring grew louder, lights bearing down.

To the right was a ledge, a small ridge. She knew it well, the rock outcrop running for more than a mile. Then would come a drop-off, not far down, but enough, ten feet in some places, thirty in others. She dragged herself upright and began to run beside the ledge, stumbling, always keeping it on her right. She left a few precious feet for safety between herself and the drop-off. On the other side of the narrow road grew a row of sage, a barrier to keep the truck from veering away.

It roared at her, lights blazing, a hundred yards back now, maybe less. She staggered on, panting, her bound hands stretched out in front of her.

When it was less than fifty yard away, she veered off into the sage.

Abruptly, the truck pulled up. She could see the lights wavering. The vehicle sat perched precariously close to the ledge. The car door opened with a screech of metal.

"Come out! There's nowhere to run!" He yelled but his tone was one of patience, like a mother calling for an errant child playing hide and seek.

His shoes weren't made for the desert in winter and each step hit the frozen earth with a loud thud. Squatting, she listened, searching for a way to get past him. She stood up and began moving, bending low, finding her footing amidst dense sage.

Making a wide arc, she began circling back toward the sound of the idling truck. Desperation made her quick and sure.

She could hear him, moving about, seeking for her.

The brittle crunching of footsteps grew fainter. He'd moved further away now.

Crouching low, she did a quick turn, heading straight for the low murmur of the engine. The truck's lights shimmered brightly in the cold night. He'd left the driver's door open and the cab light welcomed her. She had to suppress the urge to cry out in relief.

Twenty-five yards away, then twenty, then fifteen. She kept low, listening. He was still scuttling about some distance off. He hadn't realized she'd changed her course.

The open door yawned a mere five yards beyond her.

"Stop where you are!" he yelled. The sound of his voice felt like a knife stabbing at her.

She began to run, her bound hands held out as if in prayer. She stumbled. A shot rang out, the sharp ping ricocheting off something nearby. The bullet had hit a fender.

She tossed a quick glance over her shoulder and lunged for the door.

She looked back as she scrambled inside. He was close and coming on fast, thirty yards behind the truck, a devil in the red glow of taillight.

She grabbed for the gearshift.

With both hands, she shoved it into reverse. One foot left dangling outside the cab, she stomped on the gas pedal with the other foot.

The truck shot backwards straight as an arrow. The world sped by in a blur.

She caught a brief glimpse of his face, a smile turned to terror and then he disappeared, leaving only an empty road gleaming in thin moonlight.

Thump! She felt the wheels roll over him with a

soft squishy sound, leaving the springs bouncing slightly.

The truck swerved sharply and the door swung wider, her left foot still hanging outside. She felt frantically about for the brake, but not fast enough. The wheels skidded on frozen ground and the vehicle tilted crazily. The back wheels left the safety of land and the cab slid backwards off the ledge, bouncing and rolling.

Her world turned upside down and the truck came to a sudden stop on its top. She lay stunned for a moment then slowly opened her eyes. She was sprawled out against the roof of the cab, the steering wheel below her. The headlights still blazed, lighting up the topsy-turvy landscape.

Blinking, she turned her head slowly to survey what she could see. The ledge in front of her where she'd fallen from was a steep fifteen feet up. She sniffed and was relieved to smell only dirt and sage. No scent of gasoline, no smoke.

Easing sideways toward the open door, she paused to listen, then pulled herself forward.

Pain pulsed from every part of her body.

She ignored it and rolled out. Shivering and coughing, on hands and knees she crawled away from the wreck. Desperation pushed her along, the need to put space between herself and the truck.

The engine had died leaving an eerie silence that filled the night.

She twisted about and stared at the bizarre scene. The truck lay belly-up, its wheels spinning; an upended turtle.

Where was Evan Parry? Was he still alive? Was he coming for her?

She tried not to think about the soft sound his body had made when she'd run over it. Fighting and clawing herself up onto her knees, she bent over double. Her insides turned over and she heaved and wretched until only bile came up.

Gasping in the icy air, she shoved herself up onto her feet. She bent low, trembling. She listened.

The only sound was the drone of the truck's spinning wheels. It gradually slowed and then stopped.

But still she waited, panting, afraid to move. The wind picked up briefly and howled about her like a wounded animal. This subsided, leaving the whisper of sagebrush and then silence. Tiny chards of ice hit her face, taking away her breath. It had begun to snow again.

The pain was everywhere now, her cheek, her neck, her back, especially her wrists, and a new one in her side that throbbed like an abscessed tooth. Her shivering grew worse. A combination of shock and not enough clothing, her body was too cold. She knew that soon numbness would set in and with it would come the urge to lie down, to curl up and wait for death.

Instead, she pulled herself up. Unsteady as a toddler, she took one tentative step, then another. Where was Parry?

Chapter Twenty-Nine

Charlie Lemon leaned over and tapped Roper's arm.
"There."
Roper stared off to the right into the darkness. Something large and white shone in the moonlight. The truck.
It lay on its back, wheels up in death, hugging the ridge behind it.
Roper grabbed his phone. "Buchanan. Roper here. We've found a truck. It's lying just off the Lower Ridge road, a rollover. We're within maybe..." Roper checked the GPS, "200 yards of Sam's last cell phone coordinates. What's the likelihood of getting a helicopter service to stand by in case we need it?"
"That would be the Nevada National Guard. Hold on and I'll check." A pause, then "If we can get it set up, Sheila will get back with you."
"My signal's in and out. Can you get my coordinates off my GPS?"
"Got 'em."
"We're checking the vehicle. I'll get back with you. Over." Roper shoved aside sagebrush and juniper, moving stealthily toward the truck. Dourcet and Lemon were at his heels. "Keep the dog back, I don't want him messing things up here."
Lemon pulled out a leash and hooked it to the dog's collar. Dourcet danced about, howling into the wind. The mournful cry sent a shiver through Roper.
Splashing light on the ground around him, Roper approached the truck. Heart hammering, he

knelt down and illuminated the interior of the cab. The driver's side door was swung wide.

No one was inside.

Costly minutes ticked away as he carefully made his way around the perimeter of the truck, searching the ground.

The dog's whine grew more persistent. Lemon held him back, keeping a close lead. The dog's barking continued, high pitched, as if calling out.

"What is it?" Roper asked.

"He has her scent," Lemon answered. "He's telling us he wants to go."

"Hold it a minute." Roper came back around to the driver door and leaned down for a closer look. Dark splotches painted the sage at his feet, crushed by something. He reached out and touched a patch. He rubbed it between his fingers, sniffing. "Blood."

Picking up the scent of blood, the dog grew more restless. Lemon bent over and gave him a pat. "Hold it, boy. Give it another minute and I'll let you go after her."

Roper stood up and reached for his phone. "Buchanan. We're at the scene. We've got the 4x4 white Ranger here. It's rolled, with no sign of anyone but there's blood."

"A lot?"

"No, but enough to need that fucking helicopter. What's the situation with it?"

"They're restricted from doing night searches unless it's a national emergency. We can use them for medical rescue only at this point. At daylight, they can start a search and rescue by air. Want me to call them out right now for medical purposes?"

Roper sighed, struggling to find calm. "No. There's not enough to justify it at this point. Get as many ground searchers out here as you can." Roper stopped. "Hold it a second."

He leaned over to Lemon. "What do you think?

There're no tire tracks around the truck. Where do you think it came from?"

Charlie pointed up and Roper raised his head and looked at the ledge towering fifteen feet above them.

"Up there. Pipeline road."

Roper nodded and turned back to Buchanan. "Looks like the truck took a dive off the ledge above us. Pipeline Road according to Lemon. You got it on your map?" Roper waited for a grunt back. "I'm going up on the road. Have half the team head up there and send two men to the 4x4 below to start the CSI. Where the hell are you?"

"I'm about ten minutes from you."

"Right. Meet me up on top. Over." Roper snapped his phone shut and motioned to Lemon. "What's the easiest way up that ledge?"

"This way."

Barking and pulling at his leash, Dourcet led the way.

Five minutes south, a small foot trail led up a steep incline to Pipeline Road. Dourcet shifted from excited to distraught at the top, issuing one long, high-pitched howl, dragging Charlie Lemon along. The dog turned more frantic as they moved down the road.

Clouds covered the moon now but the light snow had stopped. In the dark Roper almost stepped on the thing lying in the path. Heart pounding, he ran his light over the mass of clothing at his feet; a body, face up, distorted and unrecognizable, the entire head blood-covered and misshapen.

"Keep the dog back," Roper barked. Trembling, he bent down and studied the head. It had no hair. Relief shot through his body and he fought the urge to vomit. The man was hairless, wearing dark clothing, with faint symmetric marks running down the front of one pant leg. Tire tracks.

Roper pulled off a glove, leaned over and felt for a pulse. Nothing. Turning his wrist against exposed skin, he paused. It was cool but not cold yet, maybe twenty minutes dead, maybe less in this weather. He pulled out his cell phone, watching as a bubble light, bounced down the road toward them.

"Buchanan, we've got a dead male lying on Pipeline Road, mid to late thirty's. Send a forensic team out with a body bag." Roper paused as a black van drew to a stop fifty feet away. "Looks like our agents are here," he said into the phone.

"Any sign of Neally?"

"Not yet."

"I'm five minutes away, tops. Over."

Dourcet barked nonstop now. Roper glanced over at Lemon. The urge to let the dog go was a thousand pound weight pulling on him. "Can you get going with the dog on foot, and I'll follow in five minutes?"

Lemon nodded, drawing Dourcet away from the smell of blood and excrement at the scene.

Roper pulled out his phone. "Take this. I'll call as soon as I'm done here, get a bead on where you are and follow with my vehicle."

"All right. I'm taking the dog below where he got the scent."

Roper watched Lemon and the dog disappear into the dark and turned to bark orders at his agents as they pulled up. "Work with the sheriff here, and when you're done, get down below and get started on the truck."

Sirens cried in the distance as two sets of lights shimmied down the road toward Roper. The first car pulled up and Buchanan jumped out. A Bureau of Land Management official leapt out of the second truck.

It took less than three minutes to review the situation with Buchanan.

"Where's the dog?"

"I sent Charlie Lemon to start tracking her. I'm going after them, Jack. Can you handle things from here?"

"Yeah. The forensic team's on the way." Buchanan moved closer to Roper. "You okay?"

Roper shook his head to clear it, a sense of dread hanging like lead in the pit of his stomach. "Yeah. Too much adrenaline."

"It's cold as hell out here. You're tracking on foot?"

"I'll take my vehicle to catch up with Lemon, then I'll probably leave it and go on foot from there. Have an EMS vehicle standing by. Give me your spare phone, Jack."

****

She had to keep moving or die.

Focusing on the pale landscape ahead, she staggered forward. The numbing cold settled over her and turned her thoughts sluggish. She needed a plan.

The night sky had cleared, leaving the stars overhead pointing her toward the southwest and home.

She started out with a slow jog, pain tearing at her side, punishing her head, but she kept pushing forward, looking for the familiar, a path or a trail.

Minutes later, an eternity, she found the extension of the dirt road Parry had driven her down. It came at her from a right angle. Once on it, at some point she knew she'd hit either the highway or her house.

She began to run now, the soft sound of her feet kicking up new snow too loud in her head. In her mind, it reverberated off the surrounding hills and she kept running. The frigid air turned her burning wrists icy, the aching pain no longer a problem.

Her attention wandered. She thought about her

sister in Chicago, then about her mother.

She began to count the steps each time her foot hit solid ground; one, two, three, four, five... Roper; her mind made a left turn toward him.

Where was he?

The cell phone! She reached into her pocket. It was there, waiting.

She pulled up short and fumbled with numb fingers in the stiff wool lining. At last she found the cold metal. A bubbling, incoherent joy caught in her throat and she laughed out loud.

It took four tries before her fingers found the right buttons. Nothing happened.

The phone shone like a diamond in the moonlight, just as useless to her.

It was dead, like she would be soon.

As if on a trip wire, her thoughts turned wild, despair taking over when hope died. "Mama, Please, help me get through this! Mama." The words echoed in the night, tumbling over each other out of control.

Clutching the cold metal with both hands, she staggered forward. The moon seemed to run with her now. It called out to her, *keep going, don't stop, keep going*.

Her legs moved on, ignoring her mind crying for them to stop. Each step became a giant one until it was as though she'd been running forever.

She ran until she could run no more. At last, her legs gave way. She glanced around one last time. In her mind, she saw her road, she saw Dourcet beside her. She heard him barking and tried to call out.

Finally, she knew it only a dream. She sank to the ground and closed her eyes.

Time slowed and she blended into the darkness about her.

****

Roper leapt into his truck and dialed up Lemon. "Just keep talking. I'm heading your way, and I'll find you with the GPS device."

Dourcet and Charlie Lemon had made it a half a mile, running at full speed like ancestral ghosts. It took less than five minutes for Roper to reach them. He pulled up and leapt out, ready to take it on foot from here on. "Go on ahead and let the dog do what he needs to. I'll keep up."

Lemon bent down and whispered something to Dourcet, who turned, sent a quick glance at Roper and took off.

And so it began.

They would go for five minutes before Lemon would stop and give Dourcet time to get another scent, then they'd repeat the pattern. The pace had Roper gasping by the third round.

Afraid he'd slow them down, afraid he'd seriously injure himself in the unfamiliar desert at night, he weighed his options. After a second stumble, he began a slower jog, his flashlight aimed low. He let Lemon and Dourcet manage their own pace.

The temperature had dropped but the wind had let up, making it bearable as long as he kept moving. Lemon stopped twice more to let Dourcet find the scent. At that stop, Roper called Buchanan for an update.

"Keep going, I'll catch up," he called out to Lemon who started up once more.

His feet numb, Roper pushed desperation aside, rubbed his hands together and focused on Buchanan. "Did you get an ID on the guy?"

"He's got plenty of it on him. The wallet says he's James Arthur, but I'd lay all bets on this being your guy, Parry."

"You ready to transport the body?"

"Just loaded it. We're waiting here for the other EMS to show up."

"Can you get more men searching?"

"Yeah, the BLM guy is already heading out. He's got a couple of officers meeting him at the intersection of 447 and Pipeline who know the terrain. Keep me updated."

"Right. Charlie Lemon's got my phone, so have the BLM people use that signal. Over." Roper shoved the spare phone into his jacket, fumbling in the cold. Dourcet was already out of sight and Roper headed out at a fast jog, following the sounds.

His phone vibrated in his pocket. Cursing, he pulled it out. "Go."

"Roper, we've got a fix on her phone again." Buchanan barked out the coordinates to Roper.

"Thanks." Roper pushed his cell phone into his pocket and began running, yelling after Lemon.

The man grunted at the information Roper gave him. He took off with Dourcet, leaving Roper to trail behind.

The snow had stopped completely and the moon peeped out, throwing blessed light on the long night. They'd been running for fifteen minutes when Dourcet made a sharp turn east. Roper, his body heaving and gasping for air, felt his spirits soar. He recognized the land. They had hit the dirt road between Sam's house and Charlie Lemon's place.

Dourcet gave two sharp barks and Charlie reached down to unhook the leash.

The dog charged ahead, followed by Lemon sprinting after him. The tone of Dourcet's bark was different now. It was both a call of a welcome, mingled with distress.

The hairs on the back of Roper's neck stood up. He shouted after Lemon, "What's happening?"

"Dourcet's got her scent. She's nearby."

The dog came to a complete halt, mid road. Roper made out a figure lying in the center, curled up.

He sprinted toward Lemon, who knelt down

with Dourcet standing guard over them, whining and pawing at the ground. Lemon caught hold of the dog's collar and pulled back as Roper knelt beside Sam.

He pulled off a glove, reached out with trembling fingers and felt a thin pulse beat in her throat. She was still warm. The smell of blood permeated the air around her. A shudder coursed through him. Her pulse was weak and thready, but it was there.

"She's alive." Roper tore off his jacket and cocooned it around her body. He ran his light over her. Her eyes were shut; her face streaked with dirt and blood; one side of her face was purple and swollen.

Using two fingers, Roper pried open her lips and checked her airway with his flashlight. It looked clear. She was ghost-like, even in the dark, her body too cold to the touch. He moved a hand lower, over the dark patches of wet and found her hands, bound.

He pulled out a knife and quickly sawed through the wires around her wrists.

"Give me your coat!"

Lemon shucked his jacket off and tossed it to Roper who eased it under and around her body.

The urge to throw himself down over her and make her warm overwhelmed Roper. He yanked out his phone again and dialed Buchanan.

"We've got her. She's got a pulse. We need the EMS, Stat! We're ..." He looked up and Lemon answered.

"A mile north of Sam's place on her road. The fastest way from Pipeline Road is the Lower Valley Road east to 447 and north."

Roper relayed the directions. "Any chance of getting the fucking Nevada National Guard helicopter to put down out here?"

"I'll put in a call to them but the EMS will be

there before the Guard copter even lifts off. Hold tight. We're going to get this done, Joe. Hold on the line. I'll have the EMS relay instructions to you as they go."

With the EMS on the line, Roper answered questions about Sam's condition, and they started the rewarming process.

He lifted her arms, rubbing them automatically, avoiding the wet places on her wrists. Reaching down, he dragged his jacket up over her chest and heart area, instinctively moving to prevent further cooling.

"Christ! Where the hell are they?" Roper shouted.

Lemon said nothing, but stared at Sam, steady and watchful, as if the power of his presence would keep her alive.

Seconds stretched out like a mirror, distorting time. At last, the moan of a siren hit them followed immediately by the lights of the EMS bouncing down the road.

Pulling up sharp, the support team leapt out, grabbing gear and moved in on Sam. Lemon pulled the dog further away.

One of them, a woman, checked for vitals, while a man wrapped Sam inside a thermal blanket. They set up a small apparatus looking like an oxygen tank, close by her head, a core rewarming machine. The man placed the mask over her face and started the motor as the woman called out vitals.

Roper stood, frozen in place, hands clenched inside his pockets. *Come on Sam, come on. Stay with us. Breathe!*

He followed her chest movements, rising sluggishly at first, then faster as she took in warmed oxygen. A minute passed, then another. They kept working. Roper waited. The woman ran back to the truck, pulled out packs and placed them under

Sam's neck, her arms and her hips as Roper continued to count the steady rising and falling of her chest.

"How's she doing?" Buchanan. Roper hadn't heard his jeep pull up.

"She's hanging in there." He replied tersely. "What's happening with CSI?" He threw the question at Buchanan.

"The body's on its way to Reno. The upper road site's been secured, and the sheriff's leaving a man out there. They're still working the truck scene."

They had her hooked up to a monitor now, followed by an IV as the women kept calling out vitals.

It took ten minutes that seemed like a lifetime when they finally lifted her onto the stretcher and moved her into the EMS vehicle. Roper stood at the door, staring at the face of the woman who mattered. They'd cranked up the heat and warm air poured out the door around him.

"Sam, wake up. Wake up now!" the woman kept calling at her.

Roper heard the moan first, followed by a mumbled word. He inhaled in relief; the first deep breath he'd taken in two hours. Dourcet let out a yelp, and Roper turned. Charlie Lemon smiled.

"She's asking for Joe," called out one of the EMS techs.

Roper sprang up into the truck and bent down to her. They'd removed her oxygen mask. "Sam, it's Joe. I'm here."

She blinked twice, and her unfocused eyes roamed about to finally light on his face. "Joe," she whispered.

"I'm here. It's going to be fine." He forced a smile, his face as tight as a mask. "Dourcet and Charlie are here too. Your dog found you."

Her lips turned up slightly, a wavering smile.

"Good." She closed her eyes. "I'm tired."

Roper reached out to touch her free hand, avoiding the blood soaked gauze wound about her wrist. "You're going to be okay. They're taking you to the hospital. I'll be right behind you."

He stood up and turned to the paramedic. "How's she doing?"

"She's stable. Should make the trip fine."

"Where're you taking her?"

"The Medical Center in Sparks." The paramedic held out Roper's jacket. "This yours?"

Roper grabbed it and backed out the door, watching them shut her in. He pulled on his jacket and zipped it shut, feeling no cold. The jacket was damp and smelled of blood.

Buchanan stood to one side, cell phone glued to his ear. Roper waited for him to finish. "Can you manage here if I follow the EMS into Sparks?"

"Sure, Joe." Buchanan dug into his jacket, pulled out a set of keys and dangled them in front of Roper. "Take my car. Where's yours? I'll get a ride there with the BLM people."

Roper gave Buchanan instructions, exchanged keys and motioned to Charlie. "You riding with me to the hospital?"

"Yeah. Think they'll let me bring her dog in there?"

"We'll get him in." He watched the EMS truck pull out, driving slow, following the red taillights until they disappeared behind a butte. He turned back to Buchanan. "Call me with updates."

"Will do. We should be getting something more on Parry. The Omaha office is working on it." Buchanan checked his watch. "Meet me back at the office, in, say, an hour and a half?" He hesitated. "Let me know how she is."

Roper nodded, made another motion to Charlie Lemon and headed for Buchanan's Jeep.

Neither of the men spoke as Roper negotiated the ten miles back to Highway 80. Pulling out onto the main road, Roper turned on the siren, stomped down on the pedal, and aimed for Sparks, thirty miles west.

"Any questions?" Roper threw the words out into the silence heavy between them.

"None of my business."

"You've got a right to know."

The man shifted around. "Any plans you have for that girl better not include any more hurting." Charlie issued the threat so quietly Roper almost missed it.

"I promise you; I'm not planning on hurting her." Roper kept his eyes fixed on the highway. At three in the morning, with the snow stopping, a lot of trucks were making up time. "When she's better, I'm going to take her down to my place in Las Vegas, if she'll go with me, so she can recover there."

Lemon grunted and looked away. They spoke no more until they pulled up to the emergency entrance of the hospital. Roper turned back to the man. "At least that son of a bitch out in the desert is dead. I promise you no one's going to hurt her again."

Chapter Thirty

The Medical Center staff surprised Roper. He flashed his ID at the information desk, exchanged a few brief remarks with the woman working there; she merely raised one eyebrow when Lemon brought Dourcet through the door and led him into the waiting room.

Lemon lowered his long body down onto a sofa chair, Dourcet settled at his feet. Roper moved down a hall restless, fighting a desperate tiredness. He found a Coke machine, and he pushed quarters into it.

Handing Lemon a Coke, Roper sank down in a chair beside him. "You need something for the dog?" he asked, "Didn't see any kibbles in the candy machine, but I spotted a convenience store across the street."

Charlie gave him a faint smile like an invisible bond between two men naturally at odds with each other. "We'll amble over there in a couple of minutes. Just need a short nap first." Charlie Lemon pulled down his hat and closed his eyes.

Five minutes more and Roper stood up again, moved to the desk and flashed his badge, just in case they'd forgotten. "Any word on Sam Neally's condition?"

The lady at the desk frowned at him but scurried down the hall, returning with a man in blue scrubs.

"How can I help you?"

Roper tried the badge again. "I need an update

on Sam Neally. Or better still, I need to see her."

The name plate said Ed Scovich, L.P.N. He hesitated only a moment before motioning Roper to follow him. They passed through double doors into a room crawling with white and blue coats hustling around a central desk. The nurse led Roper to a cubicle at the end of a narrow aisle.

"In here. We're still rewarming her, so she can't talk." He held the white curtain back for Roper to pass through. "I'll see if I can find a doc to come see you."

Sam lay with eyes closed, engulfed by an oxygen mask. Aside from the purple swelling on the left cheek, her color looked almost natural. They'd exchanged the blood and dirt on her face for a white dressing, extending from her scalp line down her forehead. She looked small, as though the night had stolen part of her away.

Sensing his presence, her eyes snapped open, and he moved to her side and gently took hold of her free hand. He let it lay in his palm, rubbing her fingers lightly. Sadness pooled in her gray eyes.

"Hi there. How you doing?" He held up a hand. "Don't answer. I'll do the talking."

She grinned faintly and he could almost read her mind.

"I've got Dourcet and your friend, Charlie, sitting out in the waiting room, scaring away all the other visitors."

Another smile lurked about the sides of the mask.

"I'll stay close until I get an update from your doctor." He squeezed her fingers. "Then I've gotta get back to Reno and get things settled for the night. I'll be back early tomorrow. I'm leaving Charlie and Dourcet to keep watch, okay?" She blinked twice, as if ready to speak. "I know you want to tell me what happened, and you've got a lot of questions, but rest for now and we'll get to all that tomorrow. Everything's going to be fine." He bent over and kissed her, ignoring her uncertainty. Shoving aside the curtain, he stepped out of the cubicle quickly.

The doctor was young and female, late twenties or early thirties. Roper stood by the central desk as she frowned over the chart, lips moving as she read. She looked up. "You're here about the hypothermia case, right?"

"Sam Neally. What's her condition?"

"We're still doing rewarming. As soon as we can, we'll move her down to x-ray and get some pictures of her head. She's alert, which is good. Probably a concussion, no signs of a fracture."

"What about other injuries?"

"Mostly minor. Some nasty bruises, a lot of blood loss with the head wound, shock adding to the hypothermia. And then the wrist wounds. Assault?" she asked.

"Yeah. Any signs of rape?"

"None. Mostly hypothermia combined with blood loss shock. Got any idea how long she was out in the cold?"

"An hour, maybe less. She's a runner, so she was probably doing her best to stay warm by running."

"Saved her own life. Kept her circulation going. You found her unconscious?"

"Yeah. Curled up in a ball. About five or six miles from where the attack happened."

"She was in the desert, some place south of Pyramid Lake, right? How'd you happen to find her?" She looked curious.

"We used her dog. He tracked her down."

"Good dog."

"Yeah. He's getting steak tonight." Roper smiled grimly. "I've gotta get into Reno. Can I leave my cell number in case of emergency?" He pulled out a card and handed it to her. "Her dog and a friend are in the waiting room. Any problem with letting her see the dog and the friend once she gets off the oxygen?"

Dr. Kidwell's eyes lit up. "I don't see any. We'll just bring him in the back way." She laughed. "Go on about your business, Agent Roper. She's in good hands with us."

****

Four in the morning and the lights blazed in the Reno office, six people awake and busy. Roper headed for his desk where Buchanan sat, bent over a report. It was still dark outside, dawn only a few hours away.

Roper threw his jacket over the back of a chair and pulled up beside Buchanan.

"Roper, how's Sam?" Buchanan asked cautiously, his eyes fixed on his partner's face.

"Good, better than expected for the condition we found her in. They were still working on warming her up when I left. She probably has a concussion. The rest of her wounds are superficial, a lot of blood, especially with the head wound. Running probably saved her. Not just from that bastard, but from freezing to death."

"Good, Joe. I'm really glad."

The words leapt across the invisible line Roper maintained. "Thanks, Jack. Yeah. I'm..." He stopped, unsure what words to use. "You're loving this, right?"

Buchanan grinned back at him. "I've been waiting a long time for it. I'm just surprised at the way it happened. If I'd known you had a penchant for the simple, alternative kind of woman, I'd have fixed you up with my sister." His grin widened. "She lives on an organic farm in Oregon."

Roper jabbed an elbow into his side. "Can it, Buchanan. Let's see what we've got here."

****

It took two hours to review evidence and fill out

forms. It took another two hours to finish up the Consortium report, which included trumping the local law's warrant for their head suspect with a court ordered Federal subpoena. The updates on Evan Parry's life kept pouring in, making the picture more complicated and sadder by the minute. It would be the lead story on the morning news in Omaha.

The sun sat an inch above the mountains to the east of Reno when Roper left the office.

Driving his own car at normal speed, it took an hour in rush hour traffic to get back to Sparks.

They'd moved Sam to a private room and Roper met Lemon and Dourcet outside the door.

"She's sleeping." Lemon warned.

"What's the latest on her condition?"

"Concussion and hairline fracture above her left ear."

"Did she get to spend some time with Dourcet?"

"Yeah. We had fifteen minutes with her, once they moved her up here. Then she fell asleep."

Lemon's leathery, tired face looked closer to seventy than sixty this morning.

"Can I get you a lift back to your place?"

"I won't leave her alone."

"She won't be. I'll be here. I'm staying at least part of the day. You can go home and get some rest, get the dog some food, and come back later today to relieve me."

Lemon hesitated. He glanced down at Dourcet curled up on the floor and nodded. "All right. You'll call me before you leave, so I can get back here?"

"Will do. What about her sister? You want to give her a ring and let her know Sam's okay? In case the press gets her name?"

"Yeah. I can do that."

"You have the number?"

"I've got it." Nothing more.

"Tell her to call the hospital for updates."

Lemon nodded and turned to Dourcet, but Roper caught hold of his arm. "You knew about her past?"

Another pause. "Suspected. Anna never said much. Just suspected something." Lemon gave Roper a narrow frown. "Sam's never done anything illegal in the twelve years I've known her. She's a good woman."

The last sentence was a challenge, and Roper sighed. "I know. You don't have to convince me. I might be a bastard from time to time, but I'm not stupid. I know the real thing when I see it."

"I don't see a bastard, Roper."

He looked closer at the man. "Thanks."

Lemon flashed him a full smile. "But I'll be watching you." He took up Dourcet's leash and headed for the door.

"Sure you don't need a lift?" Roper called out.

"Nope."

****

Roper sat in the brightly lit room, watching her chest rise and fall. The white bandage covered her forehead and in repose, she reminded him of a nun. He smiled and crossed over to the bed, staring down. She was alive. It was some sort of damned miracle. What the hell had gotten them to this point, and where were they going next? The silence in the room settled over him like a blanket of gratitude. He breathed it in, just happy to be here.

They were checking her vitals and changing her bandage when Roper slipped down to the empty waiting room to call home.

"Mom?"

"Joe! Are you all right? I called your office this morning, and they said you'd been there all night but had gone for the day. Why didn't you call me?"

"I'm sorry, mom. I was in the middle of wrapping up my case."

A long pause hung between them. "I saw the story on the news this morning."

"Saw what?"

"About your friend, Sam Neally. She's the woman you've been working with, isn't she? They said she was attacked in the desert. How is she?"

"She's doing well, now, Mom. She's got a concussion and some other injuries, but she's going to be okay." He didn't want to go talk about Sam's night yet. The feelings were too fragile. "How's Joey?"

"He's getting ready for nursery school right now. Hold on a minute, I'll put him on."

A conversation with a three year old was the simplest and sanest thing in the world. Roper wanted to keep talking and stay in that safe place his son inhabited where the hero always wins. His mother came back on the line.

"I'm thinking about bringing Sam down to Las Vegas for a week or so, if things work out. She's going to be in the hospital a couple of days, and then she needs some place quiet to recuperate. How would you feel about that?"

"Bring her down, Joe. If you like her, we will."

"I like her. She's had a hard time, and she needs some safety around her. You, Hector, and Joey are exactly what she needs." He hesitated, "She has a dog." He paused again. "He saved her life."

"Well then bring the dog along, too. Joey will be thrilled. He's always begging for a puppy."

"Thanks, mom. I'll ring you up before we leave."

Roper wandered to the window, watched as a young mother led a little boy in a red jacket toward a parked car. He thought about his son and smiled.

It was easier to breathe now, easier to walk slowly back to her room, inhaling the antiseptic smells mingling with the day. Roper stopped short at her door, struck by the sight of Sam propped up against pillows, a single tube connecting one arm with a bleeping machine. She gave him a small, tight smile.

"Roper. I thought you dumped me here and took off."

"Hell, no. You can't get rid of me that easily. We've got some talking to do." He checked his watch and held out his cell phone. "Want to put a call in to St. Joseph's in Reno? Keddie's there, and she's eager to talk to you. Too bad you didn't end up in the same hospital. You could have shared a room."

She reached for his phone with a bandaged hand, her face looking flushed with a rush of relief. "Good idea. Thanks, Joe."

"I'll give you some time to talk. Feel free to call your sister also. She's waiting for a call. I'll be back in fifteen minutes. He turned and left.

There were no sounds coming from her room when he returned. He pushed open the door and stepped inside. She reclined against the pillow, her smile broader.

"How're things with Keddie?"

"Good. Great."

"And your sister? She must be relieved to hear from you."

Sam nodded, still smiling. She exhaled, raising the bangs hanging over her bandaged forehead looking almost confident. It was an expression he'd never seen on her face before.

"I need to get a statement from you, Sam, but let's postpone it for a few hours. I'll field your questions, for now, as best as I can." He pulled up a chair beside her bed. "Shoot."

"Roper, you look exhausted. You haven't been to bed, right?"

He shook his head. "That's your first question? No, I haven't, but it's not the first all-nighter I've put in. If I can't do it for you, something's wrong with me."

She took a deep breath. "What about Evan Parry? Is he dead?"

"Yes." The one word held a lot of weight.

"I killed him, didn't I?"

"He's dead. If you were the one driving, you killed him, but it was a clear case of self-defense since you did it to save yourself."

She shut her eyes.

"Sam, Evan Parry was involved in your mother's death twenty years ago, and the evidence points to him being the killer of Robert Mathias. You didn't go along with him willingly, did you?"

"I met him willingly enough when he called me. He said he had Keddie, and if I didn't come, she'd die. I agreed to meet him."

He smiled. "We found her yesterday. You and she have matching concussions. Who was copying who here? At any rate, we got a positive ID from her on Evan Parry an hour ago." He leaned forward close enough to touch. "So leave off with the guilt for Evan Parry, okay?"

She nodded slowly. "All right, Joe. Sit back and let me tell you my story, though. Then you can fill me in on your side of it. I need to talk about this."

Roper took her hand and leaned back, resigned.

"He called not long after I spoke with you last night, around midnight maybe earlier. He told me he was writing a book on Homeland Security and wanted to interview me."

"But you refused a meeting in the middle of the night?"

"When I refused to meet him, he said he had Keddie." She let out a sigh. "I know it was stupid, but I was desperate. I didn't have a choice, Roper."

"I know. Let's leave that and switch to my answering your questions right now so you don't have to repeat it for a statement."

"Let me just tell you this part, okay, Joe? I've got to tell it to someone."

He nodded and sank back, tightening his grip on her fingers. "Go for it."

"I drove down to 447 and met him there. I got in his truck. He pulled a gun on me, bound my wrists, and told me we were going some place quieter. We drove about four or five miles. He was acting strange." She frowned, forcing out the words. "He kept driving. I begged him to let me go. Then I tried to jump out, but he had my door locked. Eventually, he pulled onto a road I recognized. It was Pipeline. At that point, I knew where I was, and I thought all I had to do was to figure out a way to escape from him." She stopped.

"Go on, Sam."

"This is the bad part. He started telling me about my mother, about how she died." She freed her hand and rubbed at her eyes. "He said he was only eighteen at the time." Another pause. "And that it was my mother who was into the dangerous sex."

"The autoerotic asphyxiation thing?"

"Yeah. He said it was an accident. He thought she was dead, and he panicked and shoved the car into the river,"

Roper sighed. "Sam, we may never know what really happened. He was a kid, and it could have been an accident. Robert Mathias is another story entirely. He was strangled; we've got Evan Parry's prints on the car and at the motel room where Mathias was staying. We're looking for witnesses who can place Parry at the scene. We've got a call from his teenaged daughter to his cell phone we've tracked to a tower near the parking lot where Mathias died."

"Oh God! He had a teenaged daughter?"

"Yeah, I'm sorry, Sam. Whatever the circumstances of his life, a family, a good reputation, he panicked and killed someone. He attacked Keddie, and he had serious plans to get rid of you." Roper shoved restless fingers through his hair. "If it's anyone's fault, it's mine. I let you down. I should have followed up on the guy, but I was too caught up in us to see there was a real threat to you from elsewhere."

She leaned toward him.

"Whoa, Neally, you'll pull your tube out. Just take my apology, okay? Can you do that? I went through hell trying to find you. Let me suck up a little guilt to make me feel better. A little grovel time, okay?"

She grinned this time. "Okay, Roper. Payback for your sending me to jail."

They both smiled, and it felt like coming home. "I've got my mom expecting us in Vegas soon, once they let you out of this place."

"She agreed to that?"

"Oh yeah. My mom's ready for me to settle down. She's prepared to like you."

Sam stared at him. "So she's willing to make do with a former fugitive?"

"Yeah, crazy, isn't it?" He couldn't suppress a grin. "She'd as unpredictable as you are." He crossed his eyes at her.

"So, Roper, you're taking me home to meet your mother. So far you've sent me to jail and kept me hostage in my own house. If this is the start of a relationship, I prefer something more romantic. I'm afraid to think what you have in store next."

"We'll see. Anyway, my mother has her heart set on a different sort of woman for me. Once you're released from here, we'll head down to Las Vegas, okay? Charlie can watch your place for a week or so."

"What about Dourcet?"

"He's invited. Joey's going to be jumping out of his skin when he hears we're bringing a dog."

"I'm meeting your son?"

"Sure. We all live together, by the way, so I hope you don't mind close quarters."

"Roper, you're a brave man, bringing me to meet both your mother and your son."

"Well, hell. You're going to have to meet them at some point, since we're exploring a future. Might as well get it over with while you're too weak to protest."

She smiled and sank back. "Okay."

"Okay? No more fight?"

"I'm too weak to fight."

He bent over and kissed her. "Get some rest, Sam. I'm heading back to the office to round up a recorder and a witness. Try and sleep."

She frowned up at him. "So is this how it's going to be, Roper? You issue orders to me like I'm one of your agents?" She shook her head. "I'll let it go this time, but don't think you're going to get away with that stuff after this." They both grinned and he bent down and kissed her again.

"I'll see you around five. We'll work on the orders thing then."

Epilogue

Four days later they fled Sparks, heading down the highway for Las Vegas. Still wrapped up in bandages like a Christmas package, Sam reclined her seat, hungry for every new mile. Dourcet sat in the back, calmly studying the passing scene.

Roper reached over, caught her hand and held on. "Nervous?"

"Yup. You?"

"What, nervous? Me?" He laughed. "Yup."

"Should I be nervous?"

"No. My son's going to love you, especially since you brought a dog along, Hector's going to love you as long as you eat his donuts and respect his wife. And my mother's going to love you because you're the first woman I've brought home for inspection."

"The first? Now I'm really nervous. What about the mother of your son?"

"They never met. She was my partner. It was a fling, and there was no opportunity since my mom and Hector lived in Phoenix."

"Your mother didn't meet her when your son was born?"

"Angie had moved on by then. He was born in Los Angeles. She handed Joey over to me and that was that."

"I'm sorry, Joe."

"For?"

"For all the women who've given you a hard time in life, including me."

He shrugged. "We had a pact, remember? No

living in the past, no complaining about it. Just a wide open future." He unzipped his jacket and cracked the window. "I have an amazing son and a great family. And a new girlfriend. Life is good."

"Undeniably."

He lifted her hand to his lips.

****

Dinner was in a small café in Tonopah, Nevada. Two hours later, without a word to Sam, Roper pulled into a small motel outside Beatty, Nevada.

"Why are we stopping here? We're only a couple of hours from Las Vegas, aren't we?"

"Yeah, but you're beat. And I'm horny. There's no hurry, so let's call it a night. I'll phone my mom and let her know we're arriving in the morning."

"And you're going to tell her you stopped for the night because you're horny?"

"Nope. She'll assume that's the case."

Roper gave her three hours of recuperative sleep time before he lifted her nightshirt and carefully lowered himself into her body. Starting out gentle, they attacked each other with a savage desperation that surprised her.

Sweaty and spent, Sam lay sprawled out beside Roper who was out for the count. Both Roper and Dourcet snored softly in the dark.

She smiled, pleased with herself. It paid to be a runner. She'd have to get after Roper to get in better shape.

"What the heck are you so happy about?"

"I thought you were asleep. I was gloating over the fact that having sex with an injured woman took everything out of you. While I'm fresh as a daisy."

"Yeah. Well, laugh while you can, but as soon as I get my strength back, we'll see who's fresh as a daisy after the next round."

"Huh," she grunted, lightly skimming a hand over his damp chest hair, past his navel, to wrap her fingers around the prize. He immediately sprang to life.

"What'd I tell you? Now you're in big trouble, Neally."

He rolled over onto her and she spread her thighs to accommodate him, running a hand up and down the warm flesh of his back.

"I can handle it, if you can." She drew her legs up around him and shifted her hips up. There was no more laughing.

****

They began the morning with more mattress exercise, followed by a slow run with Dourcet, ending with a big breakfast. They took the last fifty miles between Beatty and Las Vegas leisurely and reached Las Vegas just after eleven.

Her stomach fluttering, Sam kept her eyes fixed on the bizarre scene that was Vegas. Midday Sunday, when most of America was busy shaking hands on church steps, eager gamblers fought for parking spots close to the Strip.

"What's it like living here, Joe? It seems so..." she paused, "cheery."

"You've gotta be kidding."

"It is colorful. And busy. Not like a place where they'd need an office full of FBI agents."

"This is the cradle of organized crime. Happy tourists or not, we've still got it all—drugs, prostitution, racketeering, the usual."

"Great. Well it'll be a change from desert life."

"Give it a try and see what you think. If the life up north still calls to you, I'm easy. And the Reno office is already used to me."

"One day at a time, okay? Two weeks ago I was just another nasty little fugitive to you." She grinned at him.

"Who'd have thought a stiff-necked guy like me would be taking a suspect home to meet his mother?"

They pulled into the driveway of an old fashioned carport. The house itself shone pastel in the midday Vegas sunlight, one story spread across a long narrow lot, backing up to a golf course. "You golf, Roper?"

"Not me, but my mother's threatening to take it up. The way she gets about things, I'm afraid poor Hector's going to become a golf widower."

He pulled to a stop, and a small, dark-haired boy ran out the side door. Roper leapt out and reached down to scoop up his son. He turned toward her, Joey in his arms, matching grins on their faces. Sam got out slowly, standing back.

"Joey, this is Sam, a good friend of mine." Joey mumbled something inaudible and buried his face in Roper's leather jacket.

Coming around, his son in his arms, Roper reached behind Sam and pulled the seat forward, releasing Dourcet.

"Look, Joey. This is Dourcet, Sam's dog."

The little boy's face lit up, and he squirmed to get down. "Can I touch him?"

Sam took hold of Dourcet. "You sure can, but let me show you how to introduce yourself, so he'll know you're a friend." She caught Joey's hand and held it out for the dog to sniff.

"What's his name?"

"Dourcet."

Joey repeated it twice, his face flushed.

"Want to take him inside?"

Sam took out a leash and hooked it on as Joey stood solidly in front of her, studying the leashing process. He took hold of the strap and smiling broadly, led Dourcet into the house.

A dark haired woman in yellow stood at the open door, smiling. Roper and she exchanged quick hugs and Roper drew Sam forward.

"Mom, this is Sam. Sam, this is my mother, Dorothy Hernandez."

"Call me Dottie." She reached out and smothered Sam in a perfumy hug. "Joe told me the ordeal you've had these past few weeks. Come in and sit down." Still holding Sam's hand, she pulled her gently toward a chair.

Sam turned and glanced back at Roper. He was smiling broadly. The look on his face said it was going to be fine.

About the author...

Growing up in Detroit, Michigan, Lynn promised herself she'd live an adventurous life—and she did. At 23, she began her adventure, living first in Miami, then New York City, briefly in Europe, then on to San Francisco and Big Sur. She eventually returned to the Midwest, where she now lives. Settling down in Bloomington, Indiana, she rediscovered a hidden passion of her childhood—writing. Her first romantic environmental suspense book, *Leave No Trace*, was published in 2005, followed quickly by *Blind Spot*. *Long Run Home* is her third romantic ecosuspense novel, her first published with The Wild Rose Press. The context of Lynn's books and of her life is her commitment to a world fully expressed, every person with a voice.

Thank you for purchasing
this Wild Rose Press publication.
For other wonderful stories of romance,
please visit our on-line bookstore at
www.thewildrosepress.com.

For questions or more information,
contact us at info@thewildrosepress.com.

The Wild Rose Press
www.TheWildRosePress.com

Other suspense-filled Roses to enjoy from The Wild Rose Press

DON'T CALL ME DARLIN' by Fleeta Cunningham. Texas, 1957: Carole faces not only censorship but mysterious threats and a fire-setting assailant. Will the County Judge who's dating her protect or accuse her?
~from *Vintage Rose (historical 1900s)*

SECRETS IN THE SHADOWS by Sheridon Smythe. Lovely widow Lacy had taken in two young children—and the rambunctious little angels wasted no time getting her into trouble with Shadow City's new sheriff...
~from *Cactus Rose (historical Western)*

SOLDIER FOR LOVE by Brenda Gale—An award-winning novel set on a lush Caribbean island. As CO of the American peacekeeping force, Julie has her hands full dealing with voodoo signs and a handsome subordinate.
~from *Last Rose of Summer (older heroines)*

TASMANIAN RAINBOW by Pinkie Paranya. A concert violinist grapples with remote ranch life, intrigue and the mystery of a missing diary, the peril of a flood in which all could be lost, and the undeniable attraction of the man who would do anything to protect his son.
~from *Champagne Rose (contemporary)*

THAT MONTANA SUMMER by Sloan Seymour. Samantha has everything but love. Dalton has only one thing on his mind: land. Neither wants to be a summer fling or be stalked by a mysterious attacker.

A CHANGE OF HEART by Marianne Arkins. Jake Langley returns to Wyoming to find more than changes at the family ranch. Discovery of a well-kept secret sets duty against heart's desire, changing hearts and lives forever.
~from *Yellow Rose (contemporary Western)*

DRAKE'S RETREAT, by Wendy Davy. Maggie needs a place to hide. Drake's Retreat, deep in the Sierra Nevada Mountains, is the perfect solution. But she has to convince the intimidating resort owner to let her stay.
~from *White Rose (inspirational)*